"...Parshall delivers characters and a story line that are credible, honest, honorable, but above all real.

"[Lawyer Will Chambers] is a real character, one who is flawed, as most readers are. He is someone who most Christians can identify with. Simply put, Will Chambers is a man struggling to live by his faith while desperately pursuing liberty in an unforgiving world."

CBN.com

"Craig Parshall's Chambers of Justice series is made up of novels that feature not only the suspense and tense courtroom action expected in a legal thriller but also characters who regularly wrestle with questions of faith, ethics, and morality."

World magazine

"If you enjoy captivating legal suspense, Craig Parshall is definitely an author not to be missed."

Round Table Reviews

MISSING WITNESS

CRAIG PARSHALL

HARVEST HOUSE PUBLISHERS

EUGENE, OREGON

Cover by Left Coast Design, Portland, Oregon

Cover photo © Michael Aw/Photodisc Green/Getty Images

MISSING WITNESS
Copyright © 2004 by Craig L. Parshall
Published by Harvest House Publishers
Eugene, Oregon 97402
www.harvesthousepublishers.com

Library of Congress Cataloging-in-Publication Data

Parshall, Craig, 1950-
  Missing witness / Craig Parshall.
     p. cm. — (Chambers of justice ; bk. 4)
  ISBN 0-7369-1175-8 (pbk.)
  1. Chambers, Will (Fictitious character)—Fiction. 2. Inheritance and succession—Fiction. 3. Seaside resorts—Fiction. 4. North Carolina—Fiction. 5. Smuggling—Fiction. I. Title.
  PS3616.A77M57 2004
  813'.54—dc22

                                                          2003020632

       05   06   07   08   09   10   11   / BC-CF /   10   9   8   7   6   5   4   3   2

To the memory and heroism of my distant ancestor, Elias Parshall—
a ship's captain in the 1700s in the American colonies
who defeated an attack by pirates along the West Indies trade route
and saved both his ship and his grateful passengers.

And to my mother and my father,
who passed on to me an appreciation for the mysteries of the water—
whether the oceans, wild and untamed...
or the placid lakes of northern Wisconsin.

1

November 22, 1718

*Naval Battle near Ocracoke Island
off the Coast of North Carolina*

Isaac Joppa was not thinking about the criminal charges against him. Not now. Instead, it was a question of living—or dying.

Down in the belly of the ship—a large, triple-masted man-of-war called *Adventure*, bristling with heavy cannons—Isaac and the other men could hear the sounds of a ferocious battle being waged up on the deck above them. It would be the bloodiest fifteen minutes of naval warfare ever fought off continental American shores.

They could hear the explosion of pistols overhead, the mad clanging of swords, and the scuffling of feet, followed by the dull thuds of bodies as they fell. And there were the screams of men—hideous and tortured cries—that rose up from those who were wounded and dying.

Joppa was one of the few occupants of the pirate ship still remaining down in the hold. He was standing in the stairway—poised to run topside. But he hesitated.

Though he was only twenty-four years old, he looked older. During the past twelve months, he had lived with the treacherous gang of the most feared pirate in the British colonies. That had transformed him. His time at sea had creased his face, and the sun made his skin dark and leathery—and the terror of the company he had kept had given him a gaunt, harrowing look.

The young man knew that the captain of the *Adventure*, Edward Teach, was up on the top deck. From the Carolinas, across the Spanish Main, and all the way to England, Teach was known as the feared and ruthless

Blackbeard. Now he was ferociously exchanging blows, slashings, stab wounds, and pistol fire with sailors from Britain's Royal Navy.

Joppa had no way of knowing which way the battle above him was turning. But for him, time was running out.

He clutched at something hidden in his shirt. He quickly pulled out a small ceramic plate—only slightly bigger than a doubloon. He frantically studied the miniature portrait of the blond-haired beauty that was painted on the plate, memorizing her delicate ivory features. If Isaac Joppa was going to die, then he wanted her image to be the last thing that occupied his mind's eye.

"You run now, Mister Joppa!"

The command came from Caesar, a large, muscular African pirate who stood with a lighted torch in his hand. He was half hidden in the shadows.

Caesar glanced over at the barrels filled with gunpowder that were next to him. Three men—visitors who had stopped at the ship the night before for a drinking party and had stayed the night—now had Caesar surrounded, and they were slowly closing in, each brandishing a club.

"You run!" Caesar shouted again.

That is when the men rushed him.

Joppa stuffed the little plate inside his sailor's shirt, quickly tied the top laces tight, and fetched a small, short sword in his right hand for the fight above deck. And then he ran up the stairs. He was not moving like a man, but more like some jungle animal—sprinting, arms flailing—into the middle of the battle.

But as he launched out of the stairwell like a cannonball, he slipped on the blood that was pooled on the deck. Flipping up in the air and landing on his back, he narrowly missed the sword of a British sailor who was swinging for his neck.

Joppa kicked the legs out from under the sailor, who tumbled to the ground. Joppa scrambled to his feet.

On the port side of the ship Edward Teach, still standing tall in his long black coat, with his unkempt hair and wild beard flying, was swinging his sword around him like a crazy man—fending off the leader of the English attack, Lieutenant John Maynard, and several of his mates.

Maynard charged him, but Teach sliced his cutlass right through Maynard's sword, breaking it in two. Then the pirate grabbed one of his many pistols from the leather chest belt with his left hand. But before he could fire it point blank at the English officer, a burly sailor in a tartan coat swung his broadsword from behind and landed a powerful blow to the pirate's neck.

It would soon be over. Joppa could see that now. He looked frantically for an escape. Several pirates were leaping off the starboard side of the ship like rats off a burning boat. The young man threw down his sword and joined them, leaping into the water. As he did, he heard the English sailors firing pistols at them from the ship.

When he surfaced, Joppa saw one of the pirates, hit by a pistol ball, begin to sink—then another. He dove down as far as he could and swam through the murky waters of the Ocracoke Inlet as long as he could hold his breath—as the shots rained down into the water.

When he finally surfaced again, he was disoriented. He looked about quickly—but then he saw the *Adventure* drifting in his direction. Several English sailors were lined along the starboard side. Their pistols exploded, and shots hit the water—to Joppa's left and to his right.

Joppa swam wildly.

Then a third volley. Somewhere in his back there was a numbness and a burning and searing pain.

Still struggling to try to swim to shore, he saw planks and debris from Lieutenant Maynard's battered ship floating around him. And bodies of the pirate crew—several of them—floating face down.

But now he was dizzy...not sure whether his arms were still working... swallowing water and gagging and coughing.

More shots were fired. But they seemed distant—and Isaac Joppa knew it was the end.

The end of his sorrowful fall from grace—his journey of despair. He had plunged from the earlier promise of peace and happiness he once knew, to being counted among the world's worst villains. He gagged on the briny water. His mind flashed to the final, ugly picture—his graceless death in the Ocracoke Inlet from a pistol ball in the back.

He only had enough strength to utter a single word.

"Abigail."

And then the dark and cold of the ocean waters closed in all around him.

2

The Present

"RIGHT THERE—IF YOU LOOK CLOSELY—you'll see Ocracoke Inlet. That's what we're looking for—between the two islands."

A dozen heads turned and studied the end of the wooded island and the waterway that separated it from the stretch of island far across the inlet. On the right was Ocracoke Island. Off in the distance was the expanse of sand that ultimately led to Cape Lookout, the end of land along the Outer Banks, North Carolina—where the deep waters of the Atlantic Ocean run to the Gulf Stream and beyond.

"The fighting was fierce—and I've told you how the battle ended in gruesome death," the tour guide continued.

Twelve faces surveyed the dark blue waves of the Atlantic Ocean—tipped with a few whitecaps—and the coastline of both islands and the water inlet between them.

It was the bright blue of June, and there was a mild breeze that caused the women on the top deck of the tourist boat to keep one hand on their hats. In the back, the thirteenth passenger was not watching. Attorney Will Chambers had his head back in the sunlight and his eyes were closed behind his sunglasses. He was listening to the college-aged tour guide with only one ear. He was glad to be out of his law office for the summer.

His wife, Fiona, squinting through her sunglasses and holding her large sun hat to her head, was fixed on every word of the tale of a pirate's demise.

"Blackbeard, also known as Edward Teach—usually considered a cool and collected commander with nerves of steel—was simply not himself in that last battle with the English, who were being led by Lieutenant Maynard of the Royal Navy. In fact, you might even say, Blackbeard really lost his head…literally! His head was cut from his shoulders after his defeat, and it was hung from the bow of Lieutenant Maynard's ship as he sailed victoriously back to the little city of Bath, not far from here."

As Fiona was listening intently, she was unconsciously stroking her hands over her pregnant belly, which protruded beneath her sundress.

"Will," she said, elbowing her husband, whose face was turned up to the sun like a large, contented housecat. "You really ought to listen to this—it's fascinating!"

Will slowly turned to her, and lifted his sunglasses so he could study her face.

"You know," he said with a smile, "As a kid, I used to spend summers at the beach house of Uncle Bull and Aunt Georgia, down here on the Outer Banks. I read every pirate book ever written about Blackbeard—and I also heard all the stories that Uncle Bull would tell me."

"Oh—so you're an expert?" Fiona said, whispering with a chuckle.

With that, he nodded, and with a grin, set his sunglasses back on his nose and leaned back again.

"So—any questions?" the guide asked.

An elderly man in the front, who was wearing a baseball cap that said *I'd Rather Be Fishing*, asked, "Do we know where Blackbeard was born— where he came from?"

"Well, no one is sure about that one. Any other questions?"

Will's head was still leaning back on the deck chair, but his right hand shot up in the air.

"Yes, the gentleman who's been napping during my talk—do you have a question?"

Will slowly sat up straight in his chair. "Isn't it true that Blackbeard was generally considered to have been born in Bristol, England, but also spent some time in Jamaica in his younger years?"

"Well—yes—some people who have written about Blackbeard have guessed about it. But there's still no absolute answer to that."

Fiona gave Will another elbow and, trying not to smile, remarked, "Oh, you're such a showoff!"

"Now, sir," the guide asked with a grin, "may I ask you a question—as you appear to be the resident expert on Blackbeard here on the ship?"

Fiona smirked and turned to Will with her chin perched on her hand. "Good luck, Smarty-pants!"

Will sat a little straighter. "Sure—fire away."

"Well, Blackbeard—like any other pirate—even though he was manning a big ship, would occasionally need provisions to be brought to the ship from shore. I'm wondering if the gentleman who's the expert on Black-beard would know what they called the boat that would shuttle provisions from shore to ship?"

Will's smirk was slowly vanishing as Fiona, facing him with a broad smile, cleared her throat audibly. "Well, Admiral—I think you've got me there. What is the boat called?"

The guide, stretching his arms out for full comic effect, replied, "It was called a *bum boat*."

A ripple of chuckles broke out among the tourists.

And then the guide went in for the punch line.

"Which is now what we call a tourist boat full of experts who think they know more than the tour guide!"

Raucous laughter now broke out among all of the passengers.

Will bowed his head a little and chuckled. "Two points."

A young mother with a child on her lap raised her hand to ask a question.

"What about the treasure? We all hear about the pirates having buried treasure. Did Blackbeard have any? And have they found it?"

"Well, that's the question that everybody likes to ask. The truth is—they've looked in all kinds of different places from the coast, into Bath and the Pamlico Inlet, all the way up to Elizabeth City. As of yet, nobody's found it. And I suspect nobody ever will."

With that, the guide thanked his audience and then strolled to the metal stairs that led to the wheelhouse, where he joined the pilot.

Fiona snuggled up to Will and hooked her arm through his.

"Well, Mr. Chambers, do you agree with what he said about the buried treasure?"

"Well, he's certainly right about that. I don't suppose anybody's ever going to find it, even if it did exist. Then there are some experts who believe that a guy like Blackbeard was not exactly your cautious investor who would have set aside his treasure for a rainy day. So, he probably would have squandered it—spent it all."

Will helped his wife to her feet. They stretched and sauntered over to the railing of the ferry to watch the ocean waves roll past the ship below, and to watch the swirling seagulls that followed the ship like airborne scavengers.

"It does make an interesting mystery, though, doesn't it?" Will said, leaning over the railing and gazing out over the ocean.

"Speaking of great mysteries," Fiona said with a wry smile, "are you *really* going to spend a whole summer down here with me at the beach? Are you *really* going to try to run your law office remotely from Cape Hatteras?"

Will turned to face her and put his nose directly against hers. His face took on a serious expression. "Are you kidding? The doctor said you had a problem pregnancy—I take that very seriously. My number one job is to babysit you and make sure you relax, do as little work as possible—and protect yourself and our baby. Especially now that the trial against the government of the Sudan is over—I can really focus on my beautiful blushing bride and our ever-expanding family!"

Fiona took her sunglasses off and kissed Will passionately, then drew her face back slightly to study him.

"It's going to be wonderful."

Then Fiona thought about something that Will said.

"That case against the Sudan—were you surprised that they settled with you after the first day of trial?"

"Not really," Will said. "After jury selection and opening statements I think they saw the handwriting on the wall. They knew the evidence we had tying the government to the murder of those missionaries. And it did my heart good to know that the huge damages that we collected are going right back into the Missionary Alliance work to spread the gospel down there in the Sudan."

"Say," Fiona asked, "what did you think of your Uncle Bull when we saw him up in the convalescent home?"

"Yeah, that was sad," Will remarked. "I always saw him as this sturdy, almost indestructible force. After the stroke he just hasn't been the same. Anyway, I'm glad that Aunt Georgia is letting us stay in the beach cabin next to her house. I think it will be good to give her some company whenever she's not with him at the hospital."

Fiona remembered something else about Aunt Georgia and a remark she had made to Will and Fiona on the first day of their arrival down at the Outer Banks.

"What was it that Georgia said to you when we were bringing our bags in—something about a legal issue with a pastor down here?"

"I'm not sure. Some legal question she wanted me to answer for somebody she knows...Reverend Joppa, I think his name was."

"What was it about?"

"I think it was a question about an inheritance. Or a lawsuit about an estate issue. Real estate, I think. Something about a small private island. Actually, I wasn't really clear about it."

"Well, she said she would be home by dinner time, and I thought the three of us could eat together over at her place. Maybe you could get the details then."

Will nodded. But he was in no mood to talk about the law. He decided to change the subject.

"Isn't it great that our cabin has a piano in it? You said you were going to do some composing—now that you finally have the time to work on some new gospel songs for your next recording session. I'm looking forward to hearing them."

Fiona smiled and nodded, but her mind was still on Aunt Georgia and the legal case.

"So, are you going to talk to her tonight?"

Will laughed loudly and shook his head in partial disbelief.

"You're incredible! I want to talk about anything *except* the law, and you keep bringing me back to Aunt Georgia's legal issue!"

Laughing, they turned to watch a few of the seagulls hanging in the air in perfect formation, drifting stiffly in the wind just a few feet away from them. Then Fiona looked back at Will.

"So, my darling husband, you will talk to Aunt Georgia about that legal issue, and help her friend out—this Reverend Joppa?"

Will convulsed with laughter and nodded his head vigorously.

"Yes—I will—anything—I'll sign the papers—I confess—I'll do it!"

The two of them snuggled next to each other at the railing.

"Besides," Will added nonchalantly, "whatever this legal issue is, I'm sure it will be fairly simple."

3

AFTER TAKING THE FERRY AROUND THE ISLANDS, Will and Fiona had done some grocery shopping. Now they were putting the finishing touches on a full meal of salmon steaks, crab legs, boiled potatoes, and fresh vegetables.

Aunt Georgia pulled into her seaside house just as Will and Fiona were setting the table.

Georgia Chambers was a diminutive woman in her seventies, but with a wit that flashed like an ignited sparkplug. Her hair was black with streaks of gray and silver, cut short. She was dressed—as she always was—in a sweatshirt, blue jeans, and tennis shoes. A pair of bifocals was perched on her nose.

"Now, Fiona, you just sit at the end of the table and let me take over from here." She wrapped her arms around Fiona, kissed her, and then led her over to the chair—not satisfied until she had her seated comfortably at the table. "Now you two let me serve you—oh, for land's sake!" Georgia said as she surveyed the food that had been prepared. "Just look at this— king crab legs and salmon steaks—my favorite!"

The dining room table was situated in the corner of the front room, surrounded by a great number of small windows which, when cranked open, would let in the sound of the crashing ocean surf.

As they ate, they talked a little about Bull's recovery and slow rehabilitation. He was a tough, determined man, and he had kept his spirits up even though he had lost the use of his right arm and his speech had been affected. Georgia said that Bull would be in no shape to do anything for quite a while, and suggested that Will take out his big fishing boat, *Georgia Mine,* anytime he wanted.

They lingered over the dinner and talked until the sun was setting, casting a shimmering scarlet tinge on the surface of the ocean for a few minutes.

Will and Georgia reminisced together about the summers he had spent as a boy with Bull and Georgia.

The three were still talking when darkness fell. Will lit the candles on the table, and in the flickering light they talked on—about Will's long spiritual journey, the death of his first wife, and later, how a remarkable legal case involving Fiona's father had brought the couple together for the first time.

"Speaking of lawsuits," Fiona said with an impish smile, "Aunt Georgia, why don't you tell Will about this legal issue your friend needs help with."

"Well, I hate to impose on you while you're down here for the summer—I know it was a nice change for you to get away from the office and your law practice," Georgia said reluctantly.

"No, go ahead," Will said. "I'd love to help if I can. What's involved?"

"It has to do with someone I know—Jonathan Joppa. He's the pastor of the Safe Harbor Community Church."

"That's not your church, is it?"

"No, Bull and I always attended the Baptist church. But I got to know him because I worked with a number of the local churches when I ran the children's Vacation Bible Camp."

"So he's the one with the legal problem?"

"Yes. I was actually surprised when he called me and asked for my advice. Now, apart from knowing him through my youth ministry, I also taught his son in my high school biology class back in my school teaching days. Now there was a wild one for you!"

"So why does Reverend Joppa need Will's help?" Fiona asked.

"What is this, a land dispute?" Will added.

"Not exactly," Georgia replied. "Oh, it does involve some land. A little private island that's been in his family for nearly three hundred years. It's on the sound side of the island—on the way to Pamlico Inlet."

Will thought back to his fishing days with Bull, when they would cruise around all of the islands in the inlet, live-bait fishing for stripers and Spanish mackerel.

"Which island did you say it was?"

"It's that small one—Stony Island."

"I think I remember it. Looked like it was about forty acres. A lot of rocks around the shore. Just one house on it, I think—right?"

"Exactly. Actually, there's the main house—and I think there's a little cabin at the other end of the island, and maybe another little outbuilding."

"So, the case is about the island?" Fiona asked.

Georgia nodded her head but then paused.

"Well, about Stony Island, yes. But it's much more than that."

"What do you mean?" Will asked.

"First of all, I can't see into the man's heart, of course. But for as long as I've known Jonathan Joppa, there's been a real sadness there. His wife died back when he was the assistant pastor at that large church in Charlotte…oh, what was the name…oh, yes. First Evangelical Church of Charlotte. She had had health problems. Then, shortly after that, he left and accepted the pastorate of that small church in Manteo…Safe Harbor Community Church. Here in the Outer Banks. He never remarried."

"So, how is the island involved?" Fiona asked.

"Well, part of this is what Jonathan Joppa told me—and the rest is what I read in the newspaper some time ago in some articles when it talked about the case. In fact, I think Bull, before his stroke, had also shared something with me. You know, Hatteras Island is a small place. News travels fast."

"What news?" Will asked.

"Well—I told you that the island has remained in the Joppa family for—oh—just shy of three hundred years. And Randolph Willowby, one of the descendants of the man who originally owned the island, way back when in the 1700s—recently died. And there was a provision in his will that said Jonathan Joppa could take the island if he could clear the tarnished reputation of a distant Joppa relative."

"What do you mean by *tarnished?*" Fiona asked, riveted on the conversation and leaning her face into both hands.

"Three hundred years ago, a distant ancestor of Jonathan Joppa's was charged with a criminal offense—"

"What kind?" Will broke in.

"Piracy," Georgia replied.

"*Piracy!*" Fiona blurted out. "Are you serious?"

"Absolutely, but all of that was a long time ago—you know all the stories about the pirate Blackbeard, Willie, right?"

Will nodded and chuckled, thinking back to the tour guide.

"So, as I understand it," Georgia continued, "if this Pastor Joppa is able to *disprove* the criminal charges brought against this distant relative of his—then the island goes to him. I'm afraid that's as much as I know."

The three were quiet for a moment, as they listened to the surf roll and crash down below the house. The candles were flickering low. Will offered to do the dishes and, as he rose from the table, he asked one other question.

"It sounds like an unusual condition to put in a will—to clear the reputation of the family name. But I have a bigger question. Doesn't this guy already have a lawyer?"

"He did," Georgia said. "Boggs Beckford. But he was injured in a car accident. Almost died. So Reverend Joppa is looking for a new lawyer. I've recommended you."

"How valuable is the island?" Will asked nonchalantly as he was collecting the plates from the table.

"Well, I heard at the beauty shop that there is a real estate development company that's appraised it at two million dollars. They would like to develop some condominiums on it and would buy the island from Reverend Joppa if he wins."

"How long ago was all this?" Will called out from the kitchen.

"How long ago was what?" Georgia responded.

"This piracy charge."

"Well—you know your pirate history—it would have been the early 1700s, I think, right?"

"When you're talking about charges of piracy—what are you talking about?"

"Why—being part of Blackbeard's pirate crew," Georgia replied.

Fiona's eyes lit up.

"Oh, my goodness! *The* Blackbeard?" she exclaimed. "I was just learning about him today. That's incredible! Oh, but that's terrible! *He* was one of the pirates?"

"Oh, yes. The story of Isaac Joppa's dark past is well known down here on the Banks."

Will thought for a moment and then called out a question to Fiona and Georgia, who were cleaning off the dinner table in the next room.

"This case sounds like a tall order. Exactly how do you clear a name that's been defamed for nearly three hundred years?"

Georgia didn't answer, but Fiona was thoughtful. Then she spoke up. "Well, my dear," she noted with confidence, "you do it just like all your other cases. By pursuing the truth—and then proving it in court through your God-given legal brilliance."

Will returned her beaming smile with only a half smirk. He was now thinking about the long, languid summer days he wanted to spend on the beach alone with his beautiful wife. Maybe taking Bull's big fishing rig out and doing a little deep-sea fishing—all a welcome respite from the rigors of his law office and a legal career that had its share of courtroom mysteries...even brutal conflict. Most of his cases were David-and-Goliath contests—the other side being Goliath.

And that summer, Will Chambers was not in the mood for legal intrigue.

Yet, as he listened to the incessant, rolling roar of the ocean through the open windows, he was starting to get the suspicion he was being drawn into another convoluted legal case. Will just hoped that this one wouldn't be like the riptides that swirled around the Carolinas coast—the kind that draw swimmers out to sea and then pull them under.

4

I<small>N THE</small> U<small>NITED</small> S<small>TATES</small> D<small>ISTRICT</small> C<small>OURT</small> of North Carolina, Judge Turner glanced at his watch, then looked at the court clock on the wall. His patience had run out.

"Mr. MacPherson," the judge said, addressing the attorney standing at counsel table before him, "when we say nine o'clock A.M. here in federal court, we don't mean nine-oh-two. And we certainly don't mean nine-oh-seven. This maritime salvage case is not the only thing on the court's docket. So where is your client?"

MacPherson, a middle-aged man with horn-rimmed glasses, a loud, flowered tie, and an expensive pinstriped suit, was maintaining his poise. With a polite smile on his face, he nodded considerately and then addressed the court.

"Your Honor, I do give the court my heartfelt apologies. Mr. Morgan, my client, was supposed to be here half an hour ago. His testimony is, of course, crucial to our position."

At the opposing counsel table an attorney sat patiently next to his client, Dr. Steve Rosetti, an expert in ocean archaeology. Rosetti was in his thirties, with curly black hair and a well-trimmed beard.

The judge continued. "Well, having reviewed the pleadings, I would have to tell you, Mr. MacPherson, that your client, Mr. Morgan, is going to have to present some very powerful testimony to convince me that my original ruling was incorrect."

"Your Honor," MacPherson continued smoothly, "to reiterate our position here—as an intervenor, Mr. Morgan simply wanted to present this court with an alternative. This court, in its wisdom, originally granted salvor-in-possession status to the North Carolina Maritime Museum— with Dr. Steve Rosetti, its curator, as the principal in charge of the salvage attempt for the ship *Bold Venture*. However, with all due respect, we believe

Mr. Morgan's practical experience in salvaging ancient ships warrants this Court's consideration."

"All right, while we're waiting for the errant Mr. Morgan to arrive," the judge said, "perhaps somebody could fill me in a little. At the last court hearing we went into the background of this ship, *Bold Venture*—isn't this the one you believe may well have been scuttled by the pirate, Blackbeard?"

At the other counsel table, Dr. Rosetti's attorney rose to address the court.

"Your Honor, if the court please, I would ask that Dr. Rosetti explain to the court the background of this case."

Rosetti stood to his feet, taking the lofty stance of a college professor who was about to address his class.

"Yes, well—as we pointed out at the last hearing—most of the historical information had indicated nothing—at least originally—about the *Bold Venture*. But, recent scholarship has revealed that, in fact, Edward Teach had commandeered the *Bold Venture*, a Jamaican sloop. We believe now that, when the battle became imminent, Blackbeard may have given command to one of the pirate crew to scuttle and sink the *Bold Venture*. We're not sure why that order was given—but nevertheless, there's good historical data now that that is what happened. When we picked up the outline of the ship on our sonar, we made an initial investigative dive. Most of the ship is buried under the silt and sand. The court gave our institute the permission to continue in official status as salvor-in-possession so that the artifacts—whatever they might be—can be preserved and properly displayed in a museum setting, for the benefit of further scholarship and, most importantly, the enlightenment of the public."

"Yes, and all of that is fine," attorney MacPherson said in response, "but the fact is that my client, Mr. Morgan—not the marine institute—is the one that first discovered the coordinates of this vessel. And furthermore, in the ensuing months no work has even been commenced. There has not been *one* dive by Dr. Rosetti's group down to the site to begin the salvage process. With each day, the chances of successful recovery are diminishing."

"Look," Judge Turner replied with an edge of irritation in his voice, "I am not retrying this case. Let's remember what my role is here. The court is to give official permission to one qualified party to conduct an ocean archaeological expedition. You know, these laws were passed in order to avoid a bunch of maverick divers and modern-day pirates from looting these archaeological sites."

The judge was about to continue when something at the back of the courtroom distracted him.

A tall, athletically built man with bleach-blond hair down to his shoulders was holding open one of the two doors to the courtroom. An instant later, a second man, this one short and skinny, with thick glasses, opened the second door.

With both doors opened wide, a man in his late thirties, walking with a cane, appeared in the opened doorway and began to slowly enter the courtroom.

The man had long, jet-black hair, which was tied in a ponytail behind his head. He sported a black, drooping Fu Manchu mustache. He wore black boots with tall heels, white linen pants, a black silk shirt, and a shimmering red tie. His shirt was short-sleeved, and it revealed a large tattoo on his right forearm, consisting of a human skull with dollar signs in the eye sockets. Under the skull were written the words *IN GOLD WE TRUST*.

The man was walking slowly, limping slightly and leaning on his cane. His right leg was stiff and somewhat immobile.

The man used the cane in his right hand to steady himself and dragged his right foot behind him as he walked. The courtroom was hushed. The only sound was the echo of the tap of his cane, each time he placed it down hard on the marble floor, followed by the sliding of his right foot as he pulled it behind him.

"Is this your client, Mr. MacPherson?" the judge asked.

But before MacPherson could answer, his client, leaning on his cane, stiffening his back, and raising his head, answered for him.

"Your Honor, I am Blackjack Morgan," the man with the cane announced loudly.

"That's your name?" the judge asked somewhat incredulously. "I mean the Blackjack part—that's your name?"

"Your Honor, I filed the necessary papers and had a court hearing in an actual courtroom in North Carolina in order to legally change my name from Sylvester Morgan to Blackjack Morgan. So, yes—that is my name. You see, Your Honor," Morgan continued with a broad smile, "that name—Blackjack—is very important to me. That's why I went to court to get it added to my official name."

"Just out of curiosity, Mr. Morgan, this 'Blackjack' business—I know of only two proper uses of that word. One refers to a gambling game—a game of cards. And the other use of the word blackjack is to describe the instrument used by thugs and criminals to whack people on the head and knock them out. Which use of the word did you entertain when you got your court-ordered name change?"

MacPherson spread his arms out wide in front of him, hoping to block his client's answer and explain away the name himself. But his client was too quick.

"Your Honor," Morgan said, still smiling but narrowing his eyes ever so slightly, "the name 'Blackjack,' to me, is highly personal and *private*."

"Then that's where we will leave it…at least for now," the judge said, eyeing Morgan closely.

The judge returned to the papers on the bench in front of him, leafed through some of them, and then looked back at Mr. Morgan.

"Before I bring this hearing to the point, now that we have Mr. Morgan's presence, I was wondering what your reason was for showing up late to my courtroom."

"Your Honor, I can explain that," Morgan replied quickly. "You see, I have a handicap—as you may have noticed—a leg injury. It slows me down. Many years ago, I was diving in a deepwater salvage operation when a big mako shark came by and decided to take a bite out of my leg. Carlton Robideau, my chief diver, and Mr. Orville Putrie, my technical assistant—they're with me today—they got me to the hospital. So here I am today, Your Honor, with salt water in my veins and afraid of no creature, shark or otherwise. No dive's too dangerous—no treasure is too deep for my salvage operation."

Dr. Rosetti, at the other end of the counsel table, burst out with something between a laugh and a groan.

"Dr. Rosetti, do you have some comment about Mr. Morgan's statements to the court?"

Rosetti jumped to his feet and taking off his glasses and using them for emphasis, pointed them in the direction of Blackjack Morgan.

"Well, actually, I do, Your Honor. I happen to know, with absolute proof beyond question, that this supposed shark injury never took place. It's a fable. A myth that Mr. Morgan has concocted around the Cape Hatteras area to bolster his claim to be an expert in deep-sea salvage operations. Our investigation indicates that he was struck by a propeller on his own boat. If there were any sharks involved, they came sniffing around only when he started bleeding to death because of his own boating incompetence during one of his attempted dives."

Morgan turned to face Rosetti, and he was no longer smiling. He raised his cane in the air and then slowly lowered it until it pointed directly toward Rosetti's face.

"Do not attempt to embarrass me, little man," Morgan shouted. "Your Honor, just because this man here has himself a PhD degree and works at the Maritime Institute doesn't mean he has a right to put a stain on my reputation."

Rosetti was being restrained by his attorney, and the judge finally intervened.

"All right, everybody sit down and cool off. You, Mr. Morgan, put that cane down—and you, Dr. Rosetti, sit down."

Then the judge opened his file and located one of the pleadings filed by Morgan's attorney.

"I'm going to bring this thing to a head right now. Now, Mr. MacPherson, you make some allegations here as to why Mr. Morgan's salvage operation ought to be the one to be granted permission, by this court, to take over the salvage operation of the ship *Bold Venture*. Nevertheless, you're going to have to provide some very persuasive evidence as to why it was wrong for me to grant permission to Dr. Rosetti's team to run this operation."

MacPherson attempted to bend over toward Morgan and whisper something in his ear, but Morgan waved him off and stood to his feet.

"Permission to address the Court, please, Your Honor?" Morgan asked with carefully manufactured courtesy.

The judge nodded.

"Your Honor, I come before this court with new evidence—yes, sir, Your Honor, sir, I sure do."

"And what is that evidence? What's the additional proof that you have for this Court?"

"Guts."

"Guts?" the judge asked, his face revealing confusion.

"That's right, Your Honor," Morgan snapped back. "Guts. This Dr. Rosetti is afraid to go down when the weather gets a little nasty. When the waves are too high. That's why no salvage has begun yet. Now, me—and my crew here—we're maybe a little rough around the edges. We don't have the fancy degrees. But we got hair on our chests, salt water in our veins, and we go down and get those ships—and find that treasure and those artifacts. So guts, Judge, is what I got—and what this fancy PhD doesn't have."

Rosetti could no longer restrain himself. He jumped to his feet.

"Your Honor, we really need the chance to respond to the outrageous comments from this man. I happen to know—my attorney's got the proof—that in the last court-ordered salvage operation of Mr. Morgan— the *Queen of Boston*—most of the ship's artifacts ended up being sold on the black market. Now it doesn't take a genius to figure out that Mr. Morgan here was selling off the pieces improperly, without permission of the court—"

But before Morgan could respond—his cane raised again and pointing at Rosetti—the judge brought the courtroom back into control.

"Sit down, Dr. Rosetti. Mr. Morgan, I've heard enough from you, too. Sit down, please. Now here's my ruling. I don't hear anything very persuasive from Mr. Morgan—even accepting Mr. Morgan's overblown explanation of his adventures on the high seas. Motion of Mr. Morgan is denied. Now, Attorney Hathaway, will you draw up the order as a result of this ruling?" With that, the judge nodded to Dr. Rosetti's counsel, who agreed.

The judge, bailiff, and clerk rose quickly, and the judge disappeared into his chambers.

Dr. Rosetti wasted no time in quickly approaching Blackjack Morgan. MacPherson had to stand between the two men to prevent a confrontation.

"Just one thing, Morgan," Rosetti said with barely restrained rage. "You stay away from our diving site. This is a historical site, and I intend to preserve it for posterity. Not have it be sold off to the highest bidder like you would."

"You and your *history*," Morgan responded with a half smile. "All you want to do is make a name for yourself and get on television—to get your story on the Discovery Channel. But Blackjack Morgan here, I'm for free enterprise. I figure the best way to preserve history is to allow it to be sold on the open market. That is the American way, ain't it?"

Rosetti shook his head in disgust. "MacPherson, you tell your client not to come within a half mile of our diving site at the location of the *Bold Venture*. I see one of his boats near my dive site, and I'm going to call the court. I'll get federal marshals to arrest him."

"Dr. Rosetti, I wouldn't worry," MacPherson said in a honey-coated voice. "Mr. Morgan here knows the law. He's going to obey it. We may all be fighting about a ship belonging to Blackbeard, but that doesn't mean we have to act like pirates."

MacPherson smiled at his own clever quip. And his client was also smiling—but for a different reason.

Possessing no degrees higher than his GED, Morgan had read every historical account, research paper, and book having to do with the ships sailed or destroyed by Edward Teach. Morgan also knew that the scholars were wrong when they announced that the death of Edward Teach, the famed Blackbeard, marked the beginning of the end of the "golden age" of piracy.

With the new cravings and appetites of the twenty-first century, he knew for a fact that piracy was still alive and well. And Blackjack Morgan—without hesitation—considered himself to be its current dark hero.

5

THAT DAY BEGAN, FOR REVEREND JONATHAN JOPPA, the same as all the others. He had disciplined his life into a careful pattern of daily routines. Up at six A.M. He would open the shutters of his small, two-bedroom bungalow that was situated along the Croatan Sound on the outskirts of Manteo, North Carolina. The little town lay in the sheltered sound waters protected from the Atlantic Ocean by the Outer Banks, with their long, thin expanse of sand dunes, beach, and ocean homes that arced around the coast of North Carolina like a slightly bent arm for some hundred miles.

As usual, Joppa would take his black-and-white border collie, Hank, for a short walk and then feed him. After that, the minister would click on the radio for the morning news and quietly eat breakfast, alone, at the kitchen table that overlooked the quiet bay. After breakfast, he would shower, shave, and dress casually for his brisk walk to the church. And every other day he would put on his running clothes and jog the distance.

He usually took Hank with him. He had a dog bed and an open-air crate in the choir room—although Hank was well behaved enough to roam freely through the church building.

Joppa would usually arrive at the Safe Harbor Community Church half an hour to an hour before his loyal secretary, Sally, arrived.

Today he had to review the minutes of the church recreation committee, whose primary focus over the last three years had been a fundraising drive to build a softball stadium to be used as a youth outreach for the church. Then he had to do some work on his sermon for the upcoming Sunday—a message called "Maintaining Our Delicate Ecosystem—What Would Jesus Do?"

When he settled into his desk in the study, Joppa noticed that his new issue of *National Geographic* had come in. He leafed through it, noticing an article about the Australian Outback. He read the article from beginning to end. Putting down the magazine and staring blankly out into space for a moment, he resolved to start work.

Joppa wheeled around in his chair in his study, looking for a book to retrieve for his sermon. He noticed the familiar photos. One showing him in his baseball uniform when he played in a major-league farm team. Next to it was a picture of his son, Bobby, then fourteen years old, wearing his Peewee League uniform and shouldering a baseball bat, grinning radiantly.

Next to that, was a photograph of his late wife, Carol.

Joppa studied the pictures. Those two faces always forced him to take personal inventory. Yet that would quickly be followed by a flood of emotions—guilt, anger, and a feeling of frustration because he knew that he could not change the unchangeable.

His intercom buzzed. It was Sally.

"Minnie and Wes Metalsmith are here. I know that they don't have an appointment. But Minnie says it's very urgent."

Joppa grimaced. He had some idea of what they wanted.

"Okay, Sally," he replied hesitantly, "tell them I'll see them—but I have only a few minutes."

Before he had a chance to clear his desk, a tall, large-boned woman walked brusquely into the room, followed by her shorter, round husband, a balding man with a plain, pleasant face.

The two sat down in the chairs across from Joppa's desk. Immediately the woman commenced speaking.

"Reverend Joppa, I have some information and I felt that you should be one of the very first people to find out," she began in a loud voice, with her arms tightly crossed in front of her chest.

"Well, Minnie," the pastor responded diplomatically, "I'm sure whatever it is, it can be talked out and resolved."

"Well—I certainly hope so," she snapped. "Mr. Lawrence, our choir director—the one chosen by you and recommended by you to our board of overseers—just posted a music ministry schedule for Sunday services for the next month…"

Joppa nodded politely.

"I'm very concerned about the direction our music ministry is taking," Minnie said. She turned to her husband, who up to that point had been quietly enduring her monologue with his hands in his lap.

"Now, Wes, tell him…"

Wes Metalsmith looked at his wife blankly and shrugged.

"The other thing. Remember?" And with that she jabbed her shoulder into his.

"You mean the solo business?"

Minnie rolled her eyes and then nodded.

"Yes. Well, Reverend Joppa, this list for the music programs for the next month," Wes began, "the solos are all listed there. And Minnie has *not* been included in a single solo. And you know how her singing ministry is uplifting, and how it is enjoyed by the members of the church."

Joppa took a minute to think back to the last church solo sung by Minnie Metalsmith. *Yes…it was a singularly lackluster, off-key rendition of Cat Stevens' "Morning Has Broken."*

But then another thought struck Joppa. *Hadn't Cat Stevens converted to Islam? Maybe he'd heard Minnie Metalsmith try her hand at his song—maybe that's what pushed him out of the church.*

Minnie caught Joppa smiling and launched one of her surface-to-air missiles.

"Do you think this is funny? How dare you laugh at me when I come in here with a concern about the direction of the music in our worship services?"

"Please, Minnie, don't take this personally. I am concerned about whatever is concerning you. It's just that I try to keep a sense of humor as the shepherd of this flock. Sometimes it's all I've got."

Only half appeased, she unclasped her hands from the sides of her chair and crossed her arms over her chest again. After a moment she continued.

"I really see this as part of a bigger problem. Mr. Lawrence is leaving at the end of next month. We still haven't voted on a replacement. I have suggested that I would be a natural to fill in until such time as we select a permanent music director."

"Minnie," Joppa said cautiously, "I can appreciate your desire to volunteer your services to this church. But in all candor, I think we ought to wait on that suggestion. I know the board is going to be dealing with nominations to the position of church music director. I think we ought to leave it in their hands."

Wes Metalsmith was under the mistaken assumption that the meeting had been concluded, and he began to rise from his chair. But his wife gave him a withering glare, and he sat down quickly.

"Reverend Joppa, are you aware of my work with my husband in securing a commitment with Mr. Metalsmith's employer—Inland Sanitation

Services Corporation—to make a large gift to our church for purposes of the building of the sports complex?"

Jonathan Joppa was quickly losing his sense of humor.

"Yes, Minnie, I am aware. In fact, if you could give me the name of the gentleman I could write a thank-you letter to, I'd be glad to express thanks, on behalf of the church, for his generosity."

"Oh, no. The name will not be given to you—not yet," Minnie snapped. "Mr. Metalsmith and I would really like to hear how you're going to handle my role in the music ministry of this church first."

It all became very clear to Reverend Jonathan Joppa.

Joppa rose and walked quickly around the side of his desk and extended his hand to Wes Metalsmith.

"Wes, it's been good to see you. I'm afraid I must cut this short."

Then Joppa extended his hand to Minnie Metalsmith, but she rose instead and turned, walking quickly to the door. When she reached the door she turned abruptly.

"You must know," she added, "that there are rumors in the church. Some of the members of the board have just not been very satisfied with you over the last year or two. And also, I wonder what the board would think if they knew they were paying your salary so that you could read *National Geographic* on church time." And with that, after nodding toward the magazine on Joppa's desk, she swung the door open and disappeared.

Wes began following her, but then turned and gave a half smile to Joppa.

"Reverend Joppa, thank you for seeing us without an appointment."

After the two were gone, Joppa walked to the opening of his office and leaned against the doorframe. Sally, his middle-aged secretary, was seated at her desk in the lobby just outside his study.

"Reverend Joppa?" she asked. "Are you all right?"

Joppa was pensively gazing out into space.

He turned to look at Sally.

"I'm going to change into my jogging trunks and go running with Hank." His voice was flat and tired and his shoulders were slumped as he shuffled out of the church building toward his car.

6

WILL CHAMBERS PULLED INTO THE PARKING LOT of the restaurant. It had a large, bright sign with the words *Melvin's Café* in red painted letters against a yellow background. Along the bottom of the sign there were painted blue waves.

Will glanced at his watch. It was nine o'clock A.M. He figured that Reverend Jonathan Joppa was already there, with a table, waiting for him.

At Aunt Georgia's urging, Will had responded to Joppa's request for an initial meeting. "Melvin has the best French toast on the Outer Banks," Joppa had told him.

As Will walked to the front door, he noticed a friendly, tail-wagging border collie tied to a newspaper stand by the front door. The collie was stretched out on the warm pavement next to a bowl of water. Will stretched down and gave him a friendly scratch to the backs of his ears, and then entered the restaurant.

As he entered he looked around the room and saw a handful of folks eating breakfast. Over at a far table, a man reading the newspaper set the newspaper down, gave a look toward Will, and then waved him over.

"You must be Will Chambers," Jonathan Joppa said with a friendly smile, rising to shake hands.

The two sat down. Will, of course, decided to try the famous French toast—and so did Joppa.

After a few pleasantries about their common connection through Georgia Chambers, Will started going into the legal issues.

"I'm not sure I can help you, Reverend Joppa…" Will began.

"Just call me Jonathan. And I understand that. It's just that you came highly recommended. From what I heard from Georgia, and from Bull before his stroke, you have handled a number of high-profile and very unusual cases. This is not your average, run-of-the-mill lawsuit, I don't think."

"So this is a probate matter involving a will?"

"Yes, in a manner of speaking. I was mentioned in the will of a very wealthy businessman by the name of Randolph Willowby. He owned a fleet of fishing boats, and a fish cannery, as well as a shipping line. He died recently of cancer."

"Were you close?"

"Quite honestly, I can't say that we were. But he and I are remotely related. We have a common genealogy connecting three hundred years back."

"Well, what's the connection?"

"Thirteen generations back. A fellow by the name of Reverend Malachi Joppa. He was a preacher down here in the Bath, North Carolina, coastal area in the early 1700s. He had thirteen generations of male heirs who carried on the Joppa name. I trace my connection to the older of his two sons, Adam Joppa."

"How about Randolph Willowby?

"Well, it's this way," Joppa said, thinking back through the genealogy. "Randolph Willowby was the thirteenth-generation male heir on the Willowby side. Back in the early 1700s, there was a guy by the name of Elisha Willowby, who married Myrtle Joppa. Myrtle was Reverend Malachi Joppa's daughter, one of his three children."

Will was jotting down a few notes, but was already starting to find the genealogy a little confusing.

"All right, what you're saying is that this Reverend Malachi Joppa, back in…when did you say?"

"Well, let me give you some dates," Joppa said, noticing Will's confusion. "Reverend Malachi Joppa and his wife, Elizabeth, lived in Bath, North Carolina, in the early 1700s. Malachi Joppa died in 1719—the year after his wife, Elizabeth, died—1718."

Will jotted the dates down. "And how many children did Malachi Joppa have?"

"Three. His oldest was Adam. Next came his second child, Isaac. Isaac is the one who this whole probate contest is about. He was charged with piracy. And there was his youngest, his daughter Myrtle. Myrtle's the one who married Elisha Willowby. The line that led to Randolph Willowby."

Will had jotted a small chart on his notepad with Malachi Joppa at the top, connected to Elizabeth by marriage, and having three children, Adam, Isaac, and Myrtle. He then connected a line between Myrtle and her husband, Elisha Willowby, and then a long line from Elisha down to the bottom of the page, connecting that lineage to Randolph Willowby. On the other side of the paper he drew a long line connecting Adam Joppa down to the bottom of the page, where he had jotted Reverend Jonathan Joppa's name.

"You mentioned that this probate case is all about Isaac, the alleged pirate. But I didn't hear that Isaac had any descendants. What's the story there?"

"Well, as best as we can figure out, Isaac died at the battle of Ocracoke Inlet, without an heir. In fact, without ever marrying."

"You know," Will replied, "my Aunt Georgia told me a little bit about that. As much as she knew. The guy was apparently tied, in some way, to Edward Teach—Blackbeard—at the time of the battle that killed Teach and most of his pirate crew."

"Have you ever heard the stories about Isaac Joppa?"

Will shook his head. "Can't say that I have. Except what Aunt Georgia told me."

"Did you ever notice a tavern called 'Joppa's Folly' on the way to Hatteras?"

"Now that you mention it, I have. I guess I never thought about the connection between you and the tavern. What is it?"

"Well, there's a story behind why it got named that way, I guess," Joppa said, looking down somberly, "but that's a whole other story. The point is that the history about Isaac Joppa is the target of a lot of jokes down here. Apparently, Reverend Malachi Joppa was a real firebrand—hellfire and brimstone—Calvinist of the ninety-ninth degree. He felt that his son ought to help him convert all of the wild-eyed pagans down in Bath, North Carolina. And admittedly, from what I know, Bath, in the early 1700s, was a pretty wild, frontier kind of place. I mean, if Blackbeard the Pirate felt right at home in Bath, I guess that will tell you something."

Will chuckled and nodded. "Bath is at the end of the Pamlico Inlet, right?"

"Exactly. Past the barrier islands of the Outer Banks, into the waters of the Pamlico Sound. Upriver. Pretty well-hidden place. Which, I guess, is why Blackbeard decided to settle there before he met his demise."

"Well, tell me more about Isaac—you were in the process of describing Reverend Malachi Joppa…"

"Well, Isaac really wanted no part of his father's religious fervor, I guess. And so he took off, ran away from home in Bath, and set out for England. And the next thing you know, he returns a year later, on board Edward

Teach's pirate ship. Isaac Joppa had been in the English navy, but went AWOL from an English ship before joining Blackbeard's group."

"Interesting," Will replied. "Sounds like this Isaac Joppa made a series of bad decisions."

Joppa nodded.

"That's just the point. Around the Outer Banks Isaac Joppa is known as your fool's fool. He runs away from home—then runs away from the English navy—then he's shot while trying to escape from Blackbeard's ship during the Ocracoke Inlet battle. Some of the folks in my congregation, who have children who get schooled on local history, hear that kind of talk all the time."

"Well, that's all very interesting," Will said, trying to press in on the issue at hand, "but how does that concern the will of Randolph Willowby?"

"Randolph Willowby had a very large estate. Millions and millions of dollars. Most of it went to his present wife, Frances Willowby. But Randolph also included a specific provision granting some real estate to me."

"Is that the island that I heard about?"

"Yes. Stony Island. But there's a catch. To get the island, the last will and testament says I have to prove before the probate judge that Isaac Joppa was innocent of those piracy charges."

"Disproving criminal charges that are three hundred years old is a pretty tall order."

"That's what Boggs Beckford, my prior attorney, told me."

"He's the one who was seriously injured in the car accident?"

"Yes," Joppa answered solemnly. "And there were some disturbing, suspicious circumstances in that accident."

"I suppose I could talk to Mr. Beckford," Will remarked as he wrapped up the meeting. "See if he can shed some light on this case. Then I'll decide whether I can represent you."

Will was less than excited about this strange probate case. And the timing was not optimal. He wanted to spend the summer at Fiona's side, encouraging her to rest and awaiting the birth of their first child.

He figured he'd look up Boggs Beckford the next day and, barring anything unusual in that meeting, would get back to Jonathan Joppa, telling him that he didn't feel comfortable taking on this impossible case.

Whatever mysteries surrounded the life and death of Isaac Joppa, Will thought to himself as he drove away, *are probably lost forever at the bottom of the ocean. And who is going down there to get the answers?*

7

THERE WAS AN EERIE MYSTERY ABOUT the ocean at night. The moon was bright, but covered behind a layer of clouds, casting only an occasional glint of golden moonlight on the surface of the rolling ocean.

Blackjack Morgan knew the sensation well.

Morgan did his best illegal salvaging at night, under the cloak of darkness. But tonight he did not have his well-equipped ship, *Coastal Princess*, for his salvage operation at the site of the *Bold Venture*.

He knew that Dr. Rosetti would be on the lookout for his illicit attempts to get down to the bottom of the ocean, where the *Bold Venture* lay— ruined timbers and rusting iron and brass.

That's why Morgan and his crew were coming at night. And why, rather than using the sixty-five-foot salvage boat, Morgan had decided on a small skiff with an electric motor for minimal noise.

But the rolling ocean was pitching the small craft considerably.

Carlton Robideau was steering the skiff from the arm of the outboard motor.

Orville Putrie, operating a small pen flashlight, stared down into a geophysical positioning scope on his lap.

"Putrie," Morgan growled in a gruff whisper, "where are those coordinates? How close are we?"

"Just a minute…just a minute…" Putrie whispered. Then he pulled his baseball cap close down tighter on his head and wrapped the collar of his jacket closer around his neck against the ocean breeze.

Robideau was struggling at the motor, trying to keep the small boat cutting into the waves, rather than being tossed sideways. And with each wave the skiff lurched, jouncing Putrie's GPS system off of his lap. And each time, Putrie would give out a low curse.

"Putrie, get it on…get the coordinates and lock us in. I want to dump Robideau in there and start diving now," Morgan said.

"Hold on...almost..."

"Now, Putrie—now."

"Give me a break here..."

"I'll give you a break," Morgan growled. "How about I start breaking your fingers one by one until you get us to the site—how about that?"

"Got it," Putrie exclaimed in a hoarse whisper.

"You sure?"

"Oh yeah," Putrie said with a crooked little smile. "Oh yeah—oh yeah." Putrie caressed the GPS scope. "We're there. We are absolutely there."

"Cut the engine. Drop anchor, Robideau."

Robideau quickly rotated the grip on the handle and cut the engine. He flipped the handle back and slipped the anchor over the side.

Robideau was already in his wet suit, and he slipped into the harness of the air tank. He donned his mask after he wet it with some water. Then he attached the underwater magnetometer onto his diving belt.

Morgan handed him the underwater lantern.

Robideau slipped on his flippers, stuffed the mouthpiece of the air hose into his mouth, and gave the thumbs-up signal. Morgan handed him a large aluminum crate connected to a nylon tether line. The tether line was connected to a pulley anchored to the floor of the skiff. The line would serve the purpose of not only retrieving any artifacts found at the site, but also being Robideau's guideline to return.

Both Morgan and Putrie moved to the starboard side of the skiff as Robideau gracefully swung himself over the side of the boat and into the water.

Then the diver disappeared from sight as the nylon tether rapidly began rolling off the pulley.

The two sat quietly in the bobbing and rolling skiff, watching the coiled tether line on the pulley diminish in size, as it unwound in a high whine. The tether line started slowing down. Then, after a few more minutes, the pulley stopped.

Then, after almost an hour, Morgan saw a yank on the line, and then another pull. That was the signal.

Morgan told Putrie to start to attach the handle on the pulley and begin reeling in the line.

After a few minutes, Putrie began complaining that it was heavy. Morgan smiled and shoved him aside.

Morgan grabbed hold of the handle and began furiously winding in the line with the basket connected to it.

"There's something in this basket," Morgan whispered with a hushed sense of excitement. "It's heavier than when it went down. There's something in it."

Robideau surfaced before the basket. He placed one hand on the side of the boat, pulled out his breather, and spoke something indecipherable.

Then the basket surfaced. Morgan leaned over to gaze at the contents even before it was lifted in, moving so quickly that he almost capsized the small craft.

He yanked the basket out, and he could see immediately that there was a dark, square, corroded object in it. He set it down in the bottom of the boat, unlatched the top of the crate, and grabbed the small pen flashlight from Putrie's hand.

Robideau had both arms over the side of the boat and was calling for Morgan and Putrie to help him in.

But Morgan was ignoring him, reaching into the basket.

The object was rectangular, about a foot by eight inches. It was covered in barnacles and thick corrosion, giving it a blackish red color. There was a large blob of corroded metal on one side. Morgan grabbed his penknife, opened it, and began scraping the barnacles and corrosion off the heavy iron object on the front of the box.

He held the penlight in his teeth, casting the light beam onto the box as he scraped away the ancient collections of sediment, iron oxidation, and the deposits of hundreds of years of marine life that had attached itself.

He then moved his penlight closer to reveal the object under the barnacles and the corrosion.

It was an ancient-looking lock.

The keyhole, though misshapen, its edges lined with rust, could still be clearly seen.

"What have we here?" Morgan whispered in exquisite delight. "Oh yes, oh yes, oh yes. What have we here?"

8

"It's so quiet on the beach this morning. Hardly anybody's out walking."

"That's right. Look at the birds standing there in the sand. They're all looking in the same direction. Like they're hypnotized. Are those seagulls or terns?"

"I think they're terns. I think the smaller ones are terns."

"Oh, look at that one. That big, curlicue black seashell. Would you do your pregnant wife a favor and pick that one up too?"

Will was barefoot, carrying a plastic bucket along the seashore. He bent down, picked up the shell, and added it to the collection already covering the bottom of his bucket.

Fiona was barefoot too, carrying her sandals in her hand. She was walking just at the edge of the waves as they washed over the sand, enjoying the feeling of cold water and wet sand between her toes.

"So tell me again, why are we collecting these shells?" Will asked with a smile.

"Because I'm going to use them to decorate our garden."

"Back at home—back in Virginia?"

Fiona nodded.

Will reached his hand over and touched Fiona's belly, stretched tight with pregnancy.

"So how's Junior this morning? Is he enjoying our walk as much as we are?"

"What makes you think it's a he?"

"Well, then tell me—is *she* enjoying her morning at the beach?"

Fiona nodded vigorously and cupped her two hands around the underside of her belly.

"And the doctor did say there wasn't any problem with walking, right?" Will said with some concern on his face.

"Darling, you were there with me when we spoke to him. Remember? Back in Virginia? He said walking was fine. No strenuous lifting. Let him know if there's any more spotting. And Dr. Yager down here, she said the same thing. I just love her. I'm so glad she agreed to deliver the baby and take me as a patient for the summer."

"Well, I guess we're okay. When was the last time he kicked?"

Fiona laughed and then replied, "Well, the last time *she* said hello was early this morning. In fact, *she* was playing me like a snare drum."

With that, both of them laughed.

It was a mild day, no whitecaps, with only a moderate breeze. The ocean was turquoise along the shore, slowly fading into a deep, dark blue beyond the sandbars.

"So, are you worried at all about things with the pregnancy?" Fiona asked.

"No," Will answered firmly, "God's in control. This pregnancy is going to go through perfectly. We're going to have a healthy, perfect child."

"Really?" Fiona looked at Will as they walked, searching his face.

Will paused a minute.

"Well, I know that God is in control. And I really feel, down to my bones, that everything's going to be all right. But I do worry from time to time. I suppose that's natural."

"Me too. Exactly. You know I find myself constantly praying Hannah's prayer. You know, the one from First Samuel—'For this child I prayed, and the Lord has granted me my petition which I asked of Him.'"

"Which is why I thought it might be nice for you to take the time to do some music composition. I want you to do another recording session next year. You said that you had to work on some new songs. You've got a piano in our cottage that's actually in tune. But I haven't seen you sit down once to work on your music."

"There's a practical problem there. My belly's so big I can hardly bring myself up to the keyboard!"

Will chuckled and nodded.

"Who is it that you're supposed to interview this afternoon?" Fiona asked.

"Boggs Beckford. He's the attorney laid up in the hospital. He had been representing Jonathan Joppa until his car accident."

"So, tell me, how do you think the case is shaping up?"

"One thing I'm sure about," Will said with a slight degree of resignation. "This case could be a whole lot more complicated than I initially thought. In order for me to win this case for Reverend Joppa I would practically have to turn into an expert in eighteenth-century piracy, not to mention English maritime law. Plus, I'm down here on the Outer Banks without my legal staff."

"I have a wonderful suggestion for you," Fiona said with a beaming smile that revealed the dimples in both of her cheeks.

"And that would be…" Will said with a half-smile, eyeing Fiona suspiciously.

"Make me your paralegal," she blurted out enthusiastically. "I'm a quick learner. And I've studied your law practice since we've been married. And I helped you with Da's lawsuit when you represented him. It would be great fun. We could do it together. And I'm down here with you for the summer anyway. So how about it?"

"Whoa. Wait a minute. You're supposed to be taking it easy this summer. It's bad enough that I might end up handling a complex lawsuit rather than deep-sea fishing or lying on the beach with you every day. I don't want to drag you into this."

"Will, don't you see?" Fiona continued with excitement. "It wouldn't be work for me. And it wouldn't be physically strenuous. I could do some private detective work for you. Research. Talk to witnesses. Look over paperwork."

Will stopped walking, and so did Fiona. He looked into her beautiful, smiling face.

"You make a very persuasive argument, counselor," Will said, evoking a laugh from Fiona. "But the court is going to have to take your motion under advisement."

"You know, it's interesting how you use legal double-talk when you want to cover up a blatant act of evasion!" Fiona jabbed him in the side with her elbow.

"Seriously, honey, I promise to give it some thought."

Fiona continued staring at him as they walked. Her gaze was kind but unrelenting.

"So I'll think about it," Will said, noting her gaze.

As they continued walking, Fiona was silent but smiling, and her eyes were locked on Will.

"Promise? You'll seriously consider it?"

"Absolutely."

Fiona broke into spontaneous applause, and the noise startled some white terns that were standing on the beach a few yards ahead of them. The flock rose up with noisy squawking and flew off.

Fiona stopped on the beach, eyed her husband, and then looked out onto the ocean. And then she smiled mischievously.

"If you love your wife, you'll test the water for me. I was thinking about wading in. But I'm afraid it may be too cold."

"Take it from me, it's too cold." He flicked some water with his toes toward Fiona's bare leg.

"No, seriously. I want you to go in and test the water. Are you man enough?"

"Oh—ouch! A deadly blow to the male ego," Will said with a laugh. "But realistically, can't you feel how cold the water is? You've been wading up to your ankles."

"I repeat myself," she said, laughing. "Do you have what it takes to dive in this early in the morning?"

Will stopped dead in his tracks. His smile melted into a look of steely determination.

"Of course, you know I have to go in now. Of course, you know you've made the ultimate challenge. A challenge I cannot turn down. And what I want you to realize," he said with manufactured solemnity, "is when I dive into this water, into its near arctic temperature…that even though I be in excruciating and infinite pain, I shall do it for you, my beloved. And I will do it with such courage that you will hear no audible complaint from my lips."

With that, he stripped the terrycloth sunshirt off his back, dropped his sandals and ran headlong into the surf, taking one final, arching dive to immerse himself in the cold, crashing waves.

All was silent.

Then two seconds later, Will emitted a scream so loud that it sent another flock of birds from their stations on the sand…into the blue sky.

9

AFTER WILL AND FIONA RETURNED from their walk on the beach, Will climbed out of his wet shorts, showered, and put on some casual clothes. Fiona went out on the little deck that overlooked the ocean, taking her cell phone with her. Then she began a conference call with her concert manager. Meanwhile, Will used the landline inside the ocean cottage to call his office for an update. Hilda, his secretary, had little to report—which was good news to Will. His two associate attorneys, Jacki Johnson and Todd Furgeson, were keeping things well in hand.

Then Will was on his way to the meeting with Boggs Beckford at the local hospital.

It was warm and sunny, and Will enjoyed the ride in his '57 Corvette convertible. From Hatteras through the miles of national wildlife refuge, sand dunes, and open fields of waving sea grass, it was a good forty-five minutes before he reached the Oregon Inlet Bridge. The span took him high up over the ocean, which stretched out to his right. The sea was crystal blue and calm, and he could see through the clean waters to the sandbars that protected the shore of the Outer Banks on the Atlantic side. To his left was the darker blue of the Sound waters.

On the other side of the bridge he hit the usual heavy tourist traffic—the endless line of minivans crammed with rambunctious children, jeeps, old station wagons with surfboards strapped to the tops, and pickup trucks with multiple fishing rods housed in cylinders attached to their front grills.

A few minutes later Will was pulling into the Dunes Memorial Hospital.

He identified himself at the front desk and made his way to Boggs Beckford's hospital room.

Beckford was a man in his forties with sandy hair and glasses. Will found him in bed with his left arm outstretched in a cast tethered on a wire from an aluminum pole, and his right leg in a cast. At the tableside next to his bed there were files and papers stacked high, and the phone was placed on top of the papers.

Will introduced himself and shook hands with the only functional hand that Beckford had.

"Jonathan Joppa told me you were coming in and you'd be meeting with me," Beckford began. "I urged him to get new counsel. As you can see, I'm out of commission for a while. They promised they'd get me a walking cast and get me ambulatory by the end of the summer. So, what are you going to do…" Beckford said, his voice trailing off.

"I am sorry about your accident. It looks like you've had a nasty time."

"What you're looking at here is not the worst of it," Beckford commented. "I had a bunch of internal injuries. Injury to my spleen. Bruised kidney. I was a mess when they brought me in here."

"What happened?"

"You tell me," Beckford shot back. "I was crossing the Oregon Inlet Bridge. I was way up there. Minding my own business. Going about fifty miles an hour. And suddenly everything goes wrong. I lose my steering and the car flips off the top of the bridge. I go down in the water. It's just a good thing I had my windows rolled down. When I came to, my car was filling up with water, and I barely got out as the car was sinking. I barely managed to get myself to shore. I really don't know how I did it. I was like a half-dead seal with one flipper. I want to tell you, I was in a world of pain…"

"Why'd the steering go?" Will asked.

"That's the million dollar question. It was a new Acura. The dealership that does my regular maintenance had never worked on the steering, or anywhere near it. So then I thought, *Maybe I'll sue the manufacturer.* But then I did some checking. No recalls on steering problems. No history of steering problems. And no similar lawsuits against the manufacturer."

"So you really don't know?"

Beckford shook his head. "Well, let's just say I've had my suspicions. I had my car looked at by the best mechanic on the Outer Banks. And I brought the Sheriff's Department in, just in case there was some kind of vandalism. I thought maybe somebody tampered with my car."

"What did they conclude?"

"Well, 'ain't conclusive' is what they said. Plus they didn't have any suspects. No motive. As far as I know, their file is still open. But it's going nowhere. So here I am, laid up in bed. Trying to practice law out of a hospital room. I didn't mean to gripe at you, Mr. Chambers, but you just got me on a bad day."

"Don't worry about it. And call me Will."

"First off—let me say that I gave you a glowing recommendation to Reverend Joppa. I did a background check on you via the Web, and one of the attorney listings. Very impressive. I told Joppa he was lucky to get you. So how can I get you up to speed on this case?"

"Well, first of all, give me an idea of how far you've gotten in preparing Joppa's case."

"Actually," Beckford said, shifting himself painfully in a vain attempt to get a little more comfortable, "most of my time was taken up with the preliminary matters in the initial appeal. We challenged the contingency contained in Willowby's last will and testament. You know, the requirement that Joppa has to disprove the piracy charges against the ancestor— Isaac Joppa—in order to take the island under the will. I don't know how much you know about probate…"

"Not very much," Will replied. "The only time I've gotten involved in my career has been in contest matters. But the day-to-day, technical probate stuff, I'm not up on. So enlighten me."

"Well, the long and short of it is this. There's a difference in North Carolina law between conditions precedent and conditions subsequent. I'm not going to bore you with the details. The point is, we challenged the condition in the will on the grounds of impossibility, and a number of other grounds. We lost at trial. We took it to the Court of Appeals and then lost there too. The case got remanded back for trial on the merits—in other words, giving Joppa an opportunity to prove his ancestor's innocence in order to determine whether he takes that island. That's when my accident happened."

"Have you done any work on the factual issues—on the circumstances of Isaac Joppa's life? The piracy charges against him? The likelihood that you might be able to *disprove* any complicity between him and Edward Teach?"

"I had only gone so far as to contact the one guy that I believe knows more about local history around here than anybody else."

"And who is that?"

"A fella by the name of August Longfellow. He's a real piece of work, this guy. A little on the eccentric side. He used to teach regional history and a bunch of other stuff over at Duke University. He's semiretired. Now he's mostly writing books—I think he's working on one about the history of the Outer Banks. He's also published some poetry. I think he still teaches a class—some kind of philosophy class."

"What was your purpose in retaining him?"

"Actually, I had thoughts about his testifying as an expert witness. He's published two different books on piracy and regional historical events down here along the Banks. I figured he was the logical place to start. I mean, really, how do you put together three hundred years of history? Go back to the early 1700s. Put together the life of someone that the history books are silent about. We know there was a criminal indictment filed by the grand jury and an arrest warrant by the local magistrate there in the city of Bath. Then this Isaac Joppa character ends up getting killed in the big battle involving Blackbeard, where most of the pirates are either killed or captured. Really, where do you go from there?" Beckford let his voice trail off in a way that implied the absence of any logical answers.

"You've pretty well analyzed it the same way I did," Will said. "Did you tell Reverend Joppa how difficult this case was going to be for him to prove?"

Beckford nodded. "Told him that over and over again. I have to say, he's a nice fella. Easygoing. Always responded to my requests for information. Cooperative. And he's no slouch. You know the guy played triple-A baseball, don't you?"

"No, I can't say that I did," Will said with surprise.

"Yeah, from what he told me, I think he had aspirations of going into the majors. That was a long time ago, of course. You know the different kinds of clients. There are some that are really gung-ho. And you know that they're going to fight, bare knuckles and all, until the bitter end. Joppa isn't like that. He's a pretty easygoing guy. Which surprised me."

"What surprised you?" Will asked.

"That he wanted to persist in this case. Even after we lost the appeal. Even though it was apparent he'd have to perform a near-impossible historical feat in order to get that island. I really don't know what is driving him to continue this case. Maybe it's the money."

"I heard that there's some real estate development interest in that island. Possibly condos."

"Sure. I heard the same thing. In fact, Joppa confided that to me," Beckford said. "I know they're not paying him much over there at that church where he's the pastor. On the other hand, he doesn't strike me as one of these get-rich types."

Will was taking notes on his legal pad. Then he put his pen down and thought for a few seconds.

"Did this Longfellow guy give you any indication you'd be able to prove Isaac Joppa's innocence?"

"I had only had one conversation with him. But he sounded downright optimistic about that."

"Did he say what kind of evidence he was talking about?" Will asked with increased curiosity.

"Not really," Beckford replied. "I do remember him saying something about a woman, though. Or was it *women?* More than one woman in his life? I'm not sure."

"A woman, as in—a romantic interest?"

"I think so." Beckford tilted his head slightly in his attempt to recall. "I think he said there was some information that indicated that he had a woman he was in love with. Wait a minute. Now I remember. He said there was some kind of connection with a woman in England. And I think it was a love interest of Isaac Joppa's. That's it."

"A woman he had fallen in love with? Was he ever married?"

"Now you're going beyond what I remember. I do remember him saying that there was some information, historically, that indicated Joppa had a woman in England he had fallen in love with. And then there was something about a *second* woman. But I can't remember. You'll have to talk to him about that.

"Besides talking to this August Longfellow, is there anything else you think I ought to know?"

"Just this—the party on the other side of this lawsuit—Terrence Ludlow. See, if Reverend Joppa can't prove the innocence of Isaac Joppa, then the island goes to Ludlow—he's a shirttail relative of Randolph Willowby. Ludlow's got this lawyer—Virgil MacPherson from Raleigh. Comes off polite. But then he knifes you in the kidney. MacPherson's slipperier than the skin on a tiger shark. Keep your eye on him."

After another moment of reflection, Beckford spoke up again.

"And something else. Your real opponent in this lawsuit isn't Terry Ludlow. Or even MacPherson. Not by a far stretch."

"What do you mean?"

"Ludlow's a drunk. And probably a dope addict to boot. He's one of the low-life characters along the beach. He tends bar over at Joppa's Folly. There's no way in the world he could have come up with enough money to hire Virgil MacPherson. This much I know—there's a guy behind Terry Ludlow that's pulling all the strings. Somebody who's paying Virgil MacPherson. Somebody who's really running the show."

"Who are you talking about?" Will asked.

"A guy by the name of Blackjack Morgan."

"That his name?" Will asked with a chuckle.

"I'm not lying to you. The guy actually went into court and got a name change. I think he did it because of the way he won his first boat down here about ten years ago."

"Game of blackjack?"

"Exactly," Beckford said. "An ace and a king. Perfect twenty-one. The word down here is that Morgan has the luck of the devil. Came down here a little more than ten years ago. And in that period of time, he's set up a diving operation, a salvage company, and a tavern. And now he's working on a real estate development company. The guy's not educated. Not smart in that way. But he's street-smart, if you know what I mean."

Will nodded.

"And then there's the other stuff about Morgan…"

"What other kind of stuff?" Will asked.

"To my knowledge, he's never been convicted of a criminal offense down here on the Banks. But the word among the drug community is that he's buying and selling big-time. He's been clever enough to not get caught—yet. When he first came down here a grand jury almost indicted him for the suspicious disappearance of his girlfriend. Presumed dead. He managed to slip out of that too. That's the kind of guy you're dealing with."

"Well, what interest does he have in funding Ludlow? The island?"

"That I don't know. I just do know, based on our investigation, that Morgan's paying attorney MacPherson's legal bills."

Will jotted down a few more notes and then rose to leave.

"You've been very helpful. Anything else I should know?"

Beckford paused before volunteering the last piece of information. "The fact is," he said, reaching under the leg cast to scratch, "I have my suspicions. Not based on anything particular. But because of everything I know in general about Blackjack Morgan, it wouldn't surprise me if that guy was somehow behind my automobile accident. Morgan's done a great job of fooling a lot of folks on the Banks. He's even got a good rapport with some of the judges."

Will shook hands with the attorney, and then walked quickly through the hospital on his way to the parking lot. Beckford's last statement was not a welcome bit of information. The last thing Will wanted was a case involving another pathological opponent. He had had, over the years, too many of those kinds of cases.

On the other hand, Will's curiosity about August Longfellow—and the truth about Isaac Joppa—had been piqued. He decided there was one more conversation he needed to have. He needed to talk to Longfellow and find out something about the real odds of proving Isaac Joppa's innocence. And about the two mysterious women in Joppa's life.

10

BLACKJACK MORGAN, CARLTON ROBIDEAU, and Orville Putrie were in the back office of Ocean Search, Incorporated, Morgan's ocean salvage company. The two mechanics and the secretary had gone for the day. Now, the only light left on was in the grimy office, where a flickering, buzzing fluorescent fixture illuminated the room from the ceiling.

All three were staring at the corroded metal box on the desk.

"Give me the rubber mallet and the chisel," Morgan barked out to Robideau.

He took the chisel and laid it against the clasp of the lock. He swung the mallet back and then brought it down hard on the chisel. The box hopped across the desk from the blow. Then he tipped the box over on its side and began ferociously hammering down on the chisel, which lay against the clasp of the padlock.

Chips of old iron and corroded metal flew as he pounded.

After a few minutes, the lock gave way and broke into several pieces. Morgan grabbed the box and tried to pry the top open. But the top wouldn't open. He then took the box and slammed it down on the metal desk several times.

Then he took the chisel and mallet and began banging the chisel into the edge that separated the lid from the rest of the box.

When the lid still wouldn't open, Morgan turned to Robideau and said, "You take over. Smash it up. Split it open. I want this thing opened now!"

Robideau swung back the mallet—pulling his arm back so far he almost hit Putrie in the face—and then brought it down hard on the handle of the chisel—which split the corroded metal.

He grabbed the lid and box with his bare hands and began pulling the metal apart, bending and twisting it.

After a few minutes of effort, his muscles straining and rippling, he was able to twist the lid off and reveal the contents.

Morgan pushed Robideau away and put his face down close to the opening of the box and stared in.

Robideau was looking over his shoulder. "Hey. There's nothing but sand and a seashell in there," he said with a guffaw.

Putrie shouldered his way in between the two taller men, glancing in for himself.

Morgan took the twisted box and emptied the contents on the top of the desk. There was sand, some ocean water, and a single seashell.

"So you sent me down in a nighttime dive for this junk. A whole lot of nothing. Zero. I can't believe this," Robideau said in disgust.

Morgan lifted up the seashell. It was a light, bone-colored shell. But it was a unique-looking shell, tapered at one end and blunt at the other, about six inches long. And it was smooth and worn as if it had been polished in a machine shop. Morgan turned it over.

And then his eyes widened. He stared closer.

In the middle of the other side of the seashell, in what looked like an inscription with India ink, there were two almost hieroglyphic symbols. One looked like a "Y," but with a line intersecting up through the middle—perhaps it was a cross with the two arms bent up. And next to it was an upside-down "U."

Morgan held it close to his face and stared at the strange symbols.

Then his eyes moved to the tapered end. And there the shell had been inscribed with two letters, also in black ink. The ages—the centuries—had erased neither the symbols nor the initials that had been inscribed there.

The initials consisted of two letters. And when Morgan saw them, his mouth dropped open.

The letters were "E–T."

Robideau looked over Morgan's shoulder. "I get it—ET, phone home!" he said with a big grin, pretending to raise a telephone to his ear.

"You idiot!" Putrie said, shaking his head in disgust. "Don't you understand what that means? E–T?"

Robideau was still unenlightened.

"Edward Teach, you moron."

Morgan held the shell up in front of his face, gazing at the symbols, then over at the initials, then back to the symbols that had been inscribed in the shell in front of him. Then he noticed, in even smaller print at the other end of the seashell, a date: "Oct. 11, 1718."

"Well, well," he said with a smile. "We got ourselves something here."

Robideau reached out to touch the shell, but Morgan pulled it away, and pointed his finger directly in Robideau's face.

"No one touches this shell. That means you." Then he turned to Putrie and added, "And that means you. Nobody touches this shell except me."

When Morgan finished saying that, he had, unconsciously pulled the seashell to his chest, clasping it tightly over his heart.

"Nobody touches this—except me," he added with a guttural whisper. "Nobody."

11

JONATHAN JOPPA HAD BEEN THINKING about his son, Bobby, all day. His relationship with the twenty-year-old was never far from his mind. It was a constant source of frustration and despair.

Joppa had tried to call his son twice during the day, but had only gotten his voice mail at his small Kitty Hawk beach shack.

As soon as Joppa got home from the church that day he called his son again. This time he got through.

"Hey, Bobby, this is Dad," he said, trying to sound upbeat. "How are you?"

"Fine."

"Look, I checked the listings, and the Yankees are playing the Orioles tonight. I know you're a big Yankees fan—I never could talk some sense into you about the Yankees!" Joppa said, trying to turn the conversation into a joke.

But it didn't work. There was silence on the other end.

"So, how about it?" Joppa continued. "If you're not doing anything tonight, why don't you swing by and watch the game over at my place? I'll get a bunch of junk food. It'll be fun."

There was a long, pregnant pause on the other end. Then his son spoke up.

"I've got some stuff going on tonight. I'm busy."

"Well, you don't have to make it for the whole game. If you want to swing by anytime tonight…"

There was another pause, and finally Joppa decided to fill the silence.

"Look, Bobby, I'd just like to see you. Like to hang out together."

"I've got a lot going on," Bobby said unenthusiastically.

"It's just that we really haven't talked, not really. Not spent much time together since…" And with that, Joppa considered whether or not he wanted to broach the subject. *Why not*, he thought to himself. *I've got to break through somehow.*

"The last time we really had any kind of conversation was six months ago when you were in rehab. That didn't go very well. I know you think that I was strong-arming you. Getting you admitted for drug treatment…"

"The discussion on that is closed," Bobby said with a clipped voice. "You did what you had to do. I'm going to do what I got to do. I'm trying to live my life here…"

"I know that. And I respect the fact that you're a man, and you've got to make decisions on your own. I just want to be around with you. To help out. If I can," the father said, struggling for some words of encouragement for his son.

"Yeah, you tried to help. You stuck me in the hospital. I was going to kick the drug stuff myself anyway. I did not have an addiction problem. Anyway, it's my life. My choices, you don't understand that."

"Sure," Joppa said, now with some irritation in his voice, "it's your life. But you can't expect me to just sit in the dugout watching you self-destruct. I'm not going to do that. I love you too much for that. It feels like a no-win situation—"

"Look, Dad. It's okay. I'm fine. I don't think talking about this is going to solve anything. I'm okay. I've got a couple of part-time jobs. Enough money to pay the rent. And groceries. You've done your dad thing. You've checked in on me. So let's just call it a day."

"Bobby, just remember I love you. So just try and stop by sometime. Just call me once in a while. Anytime. Okay?" Joppa struggled to keep his composure.

"Sure. Right. Thanks for calling."

There was a click at the other end.

Joppa looked at the receiver and ran his hands through his hair. He shook his head and stretched his other hand out, making an empty gesture to the air, in helplessness.

He wanted to get down on his knees right there and pray to God for some insight on how to reach his son.

But then he had not been on speaking terms with God for some time. That, of course, reminded him of the hypocrisy—of being a Christian minister who, himself, did not commune with God.

Back in seminary, he had felt a mysterious, all-powerful tug to spiritual things. Once he let go of baseball, Jonathan thought that ministry would fill the inner abyss. And…for a while, it seemed so. But then, as he read the Bible and studied theology and the writing of the church fathers, there was a change. He felt hemmed in. Surrounded. It was all becoming much too personal. Though it felt like God was closing in, Jonathan managed to keep it out there.

After Carol's death, it had started with his leaving his pastorate at the vibrant First Evangelical Church of Charlotte to accept the position at the smaller, stodgy Safe Harbor Community Church in the Outer Banks. He would continue helping other people—and do it in the name of God. But whatever urge he once had to seek that place where God could truly be known—and be revealed—that was now past.

So now, with the telephone still in his hand—and the obnoxious tones of a disconnected line beeping on the other end—Jonathan Joppa had no spiritual mountain to climb, no burning bush to consult. He could only hang up the phone. And struggle against the rush of tears.

12

WILL AND FIONA ARRIVED AT THE SUNSET BISTRO long after the dinner rush had begun to wane. They were given a table by the window, overlooking the Pamlico Sound. The restaurant was an oak-paneled affair with mounted trophy fish on every wall.

Will's eye was captured by the last sliver of crimson light along the water. Fiona was lost in the seafood dinner before her. Her strange new affinity to seafood seemed to accompany her pregnancy.

Fiona stopped eating, remembering something. "Tell me how your conference went with Reverend Joppa's other attorney."

"Boggs Beckford. The poor guy really took a hit in this auto accident. He was wrapped up in casts."

"What was his feeling about the case? Do you think you're going to take it?"

"Something interesting happened today. Jonathan Joppa called me. The court contacted both parties to the probate trial. The local judge who's handling the case has scheduled a pretrial conference for tomorrow morning. The court wants to find out the status of Joppa's legal representation. They know about Beckford's auto accident and that he was out of commission for awhile. So I guess I'm down to the wire—and I have to make a decision now."

Fiona leaned forward intently. "Are you going to take the case?"

"Well, Beckford was very optimistic. He said he's got this local historical expert. A guy by the name of August Longfellow. Professor type who has a vast amount of knowledge about the Outer Banks region. Piracy. And even about Isaac Joppa's fate. Beckford told me that Longfellow felt pretty good about proving Joppa's innocence."

"*August Longfellow.* That's an interesting name."

"Apparently this guy's a real character. According to Beckford, he has some information that there may have been some women involved in Joppa's life. And that may be tied into proof of his innocence."

"Women? Connected in what way?"

"It sounded like there was one woman in particular that Isaac Joppa may have been involved with romantically. A woman in England. I stopped by Beckford's and they gave me what there was in his file. I was reading some of the background stuff. The historical information. We know that Isaac Joppa left Bath, North Carolina, and shipped out to England. Then he joined the Royal Navy. Apparently, he then deserted—and the next thing we know, he showed up on one of Edward Teach's pirate ships. One witness saw him assisting Teach and plundering a ship as part of his pirate crew. Then, Teach settled back in the Bath, North Carolina, area. That's only about an hour and a half down the coast from here. And then there was the Battle of Ocracoke Inlet. Teach—Blackbeard—is killed, along with a lot of his crew. Several pirates jump ship and try to swim to shore, but they're all killed. And supposedly, Isaac Joppa's one of them. A few of the pirates who survived were taken to trial in Virginia, and were all hung. A local English magistrate had signed a warrant for Joppa's arrest after a grand jury issued an indictment against him for piracy. But after it was learned that he had been killed, the indictment was withdrawn."

Fiona was riveted to Will's summary. Then her eyes widened.

"You said *women*. More than one woman. So first, there was this woman that he may have been in love with, in England. Right?"

Will nodded, and then smiled at the waitress who had just arrived with his salad and Fiona's clam chowder.

"Then who's the other woman?" Fiona asked.

"I'll have to find that out from this Professor Longfellow. I would have preferred to interview him before I made my decision. But I don't think I'm going to have the time. I've got to tell Jonathan Joppa by first thing tomorrow morning at the court hearing."

"Darling, you haven't told me what your decision is."

Will paused and jiggled the ice a little in his glass of ice water. Then he looked up and studied Fiona and gave her a smile.

"I think I'm going to represent Reverend Joppa."

Fiona laughed and then struck a pose—two hands up in the air, like a cheerleader celebrating the big touchdown.

"Yes!" she cried out.

Several couples in the dimly lit restaurant turned and smiled.

"Now you can tell me something," Will said, shaking his head and chuckling. "Why were you so adamant about my taking this case?"

"A couple of different reasons. First of all, I just have this feeling about this case. I know this sounds stupid. I don't know how to describe it. But the more I hear about it…I just think you're the right man to uncover the truth. There's a story here. Isaac Joppa lived a life that sounds like it ended tragically. Perhaps there is a woman who loved him. He runs away. Why? And I also think you were meant to help this pastor. Something's going wrong in Joppa's life. You heard Aunt Georgia say that he had been the pastor of that church for a number of years, but somehow his heart just doesn't seem to be in it. Something must be troubling that man. She also said that he lost his wife. So I think you're the right man—not only to win his case, but also to give him some good counsel too."

"All right. You've encouraged me…now tell me the rest of the reasons you wanted me to take this case."

"Well, I do intend to write some music this summer. But I sat down at the piano and nothing came. My mind is so fixed on this pregnancy. Some of the potential problems. And I want our child so very much to come into this world. And I want everything to be all right. This is a real faith-stretching experience for me. I know it is for you too," she added. "But frankly, I would love to get my mind on something else for the next two months. And working with you as your paralegal…that would be a wonderful change of pace. I'm really serious about that."

Will's brow wrinkled.

"Tell me what you're thinking," Fiona said.

"Just that I did have one assignment in this case…and you'd be perfect for it."

Fiona's face became animated. "Wonderful! What is it?"

"I need you to interview Frances Willowby. She is the widow of Randolph Willowby. Randolph's last will and testament is at the center of this lawsuit involving Jonathan Joppa."

"And why is Mrs. Willowby important?"

"One of the questions that's been plaguing me," Will continued, "is why Randolph Willowby put such a strange condition in his will—requiring Jonathan Joppa to prove the innocence of an ancestor regarding piracy charges hundreds of years old. This is not the kind of thing you put in a last will and testament frivolously. What motivated him to want to prove Isaac Joppa's innocence? Beyond that, why did he put the burden of proof on Jonathan Joppa to prove that as a prerequisite for getting the island?"

"So you want me to find that out?" Fiona asked eagerly.

"Exactly."

"That sounds exciting. I'll be glad to ask her those kinds of questions."

"Plus, I understand that the Willowby seacoast mansion is magnificent. Apparently Mrs. Willowby is quite the socialite and party organizer. I'm sure she'll serve you high tea in grand fashion, and let you in on all the gossip."

Fiona's expression grew solemn.

"Will, darling…you're not just sending me over to talk to Mrs. Willowby so that she can entertain me—serve me tea, and have polite ladies' chat—are you?"

Will laughed heartily and shook his head. "Of course not. I think she's an important component of this case. But, you be honest—when do you *not* like having high tea and lots of ladies' talk?"

Fiona blushed and tried not to laugh. "Okay," she said, giggling, "it's a chick thing, I know. But please take me seriously as your paralegal. I intend to pull my own weight."

"Well, actually, you're already pulling your own weight, and somebody else's as well!" Will said with a chuckle. "So the point is this—I'll have you help me on this case, I really will. But you're not going to exert yourself. You're going to take it easy. And you're going to remember that the most important thing is our healthy, happy baby."

"Sweetheart," Fiona said with a schoolteacherish look on her face, "do you remember who you're talking to here? Our baby is on my mind twenty-five hours a day. First thing in the morning. All through the day. The last thing at night. I even dream about this baby every night."

By now, the moon was already out, round and pale in the sky, and visible through the restaurant window.

Will glanced at it. It was so clear, its darker features could be distinguished with the naked eye.

"It's easy to see why people used to talk about the man in the moon," Will said, nodding his head toward the lunar features. Then he turned back and gazed intently at his wife's beautiful face. She was still busy dispatching her Seafood Extravaganza.

As Isaac Joppa sailed from England, apparently never to return, whose face did he carry with him in his heart, and in his memory? Will wondered. *Did some English beauty reject him? Or was there some other explanation beyond the mysteries of love—or the shattering heartbreak of rejection—that led him to his dismal fate? Perhaps love had nothing to do with it—maybe it was some baser motive, such as greed, or cowardice.*

Will refocused on his dinner. Looking at the case objectively, he couldn't help but think that his chances of solving the mystery were about as likely as his walking on the surface of the moon.

13

Local North Carolina Circuit Judge Hawsley Gadwell was already holding court, informally, in the front of the courtroom. His robes were on, but he was leaning against the bench with one elbow, giving off a rollicking laugh at something his bailiff had just told him. Attorney Virgil MacPherson was there also, joining in the mirth. At one of the counsel tables, Will, an outsider to the intrigues of the local court, was quietly opening his briefcase and pulling out his file for the pretrial conference that would soon begin. He felt a tap on his shoulder and turned to see Jonathan Joppa smiling by his side.

The two shook hands.

"I got your message on my voice mail last night. I appreciate your agreeing to take on my case."

"Is that Judge Gadwell?" Will asked quietly, motioning toward front.

Joppa nodded. Then something caught his attention, and he turned and saw a tall, skinny man entering the courtroom. He had a gaunt look and was wearing jeans and a T-shirt with a large colored logo of a skull and crossbones, with the words *Joppa's Folly* written on the top—and below the skull and crossbones, in smaller print, *Preachers will be lashed to the yardarm!*

"That's Terrence Ludlow, the other guy in this case."

As Ludlow sauntered past the counsel table where Joppa and Will Chambers were seated, the pastor stood up and reached out a hand, but Ludlow ignored it and gave a low, guttural guffaw.

Will bent over toward Joppa. "Did he wear that T-shirt as a message to you personally?"

Joppa clenched his jaw and tried to shrug it off.

When Virgil MacPherson caught sight of Ludlow, he quickly made a parting comment to the judge and scurried over to the counsel table.

Casting a quick look over at Will Chambers, he whispered something to Ludlow.

Then something caught the attention of everyone in the courtroom. Someone had just come through the swinging doors at the back of the courtroom.

It was Blackjack Morgan, with his cane in his right hand. He stood in the back, surveying the courtroom, then moved to the back row and began slowly settling down into one of the audience benches. Judge Gadwell noticed him from the front.

"Blackjack Morgan, is that you?" the judge bellowed.

Morgan straightened up again and raised his cane in a kind of salute.

"Did I hear right?" Gadwell continued in a booming voice. "I heard over at Mike's the other night that your charter just snagged the second-longest Atlantic blue marlin in the history of sport fishing in the Outer Banks. Is that right?"

"One-hundred-percent correct, Your Honor," Morgan said with a broad smile that revealed a silver tooth. "Eleven hundred pounds. We've got a big picture of it hanging right now down at Joppa's Folly. You ought to come by sometime and take a look at it. That thing's a monster."

"Seriously—what kind of bait did you use?" Gadwell asked as he made his way around to the steps leading up to the large, black judicial chair behind the bench.

"Well, sir—it's like this," Morgan crowed. "We took the biggest, heaviest-gauge hooks. We tied them off to the heaviest line we could find. And then we ran that hook through the belt buckle of one of those Virginia Beach city politicians on the other side of the state line. And threw him over the other side. Like I've always said—I figured those guys were eventually going to be good for something."

At that, Judge Gadwell exploded with laughter and slapped the top of his bench as he sat down. When the Judge's mirth had subsided, the court clerk called the court into session.

"In re: the estate of Randolph Willowby—a special proceeding relating to the devise of a certain island known as Stony Island. Counsel, please identify yourselves."

Virgil MacPherson jumped to his feet and announced his appearance on behalf of his client, Terrence Ludlow.

Will rose with Jonathan Joppa and explained his recent retainer in place of Boggs Beckford, who had been incapacitated due to his automobile injury.

"Now, Mr. Chambers," Judge Gadwell began, "you're going to need a local address here in the Outer Banks area for mailing purposes, for delivery of pleadings, for court notices to be sent to."

"Your Honor, Boggs Beckford has kindly made his office available to me. All notices can be sent to me in care of his office. Mr. Beckford's partner, Giles Norton, is to appear with me as local counsel, if necessary."

"Very well," the judge continued. "The court will recognize you as counsel of record for Reverend Jonathan Joppa. Now this case is on the docket today for a pretrial conference. The history of the case is known to everyone here. This is an ancillary proceeding to the last will and testament of Randolph Willowby. The devise of certain real estate, consisting of an island known as Stony Island, was contained in Mr. Willowby's will. The condition was that Reverend Joppa, the devisee of that land, would have to prove the existence of certain historical facts about the innocence of one Isaac Joppa as a prerequisite to taking the devise of that real estate."

With that, Gadwell smiled broadly. "So here we are. Reverend Joppa, you've indicated that you are willing to take that devise of property subject to the condition—in other words, that you are ready to proceed with counsel to try to prove the necessary condition—namely that Isaac Joppa was innocent of any piracy with which he was charged in an indictment that was filed in the year 1718. Is that correct?"

Jonathan Joppa nodded, and Will Chambers rose to his feet.

"Your Honor, we are willing to assume that burden and prove that condition."

"Very well. We're going to set this down for trial. This case has been going on for quite a while. I've been meaning to expedite it. I would think that, by the end of this summer, we ought to be able to try this case."

Judge Gadwell bent down to his clerk and they whispered something back and forth, then he addressed the courtroom.

"My clerk advises me that August twenty-fifth is available. We will clear an entire week for that trial. Is that acceptable to all counsel?"

Both Virgil MacPherson and Will Chambers voiced their agreement.

"Now, boys," the judge continued with a smile and a wink, "I don't want any unnecessary arguments here in court, or motions flying back and forth about discovery problems. Mr. Chambers, I'm going to tell you right now that Virgil MacPherson, down here from Raleigh, is an accomplished litigator. I'm sure he will be quite compliant with any reasonable requests for discovery. Do I make myself understood?"

"Perfectly," Will replied, musing to himself that Judge Gadwell was one of those jurists not likely to be misunderstood—primarily because he had all the subtlety of a flashing highway construction sign.

The judge adjourned for the morning and disappeared into his chambers with the clerk and the bailiff, laughing loudly over some indistinguishable amusement. Virgil MacPherson swept over to Will's position and shook hands with him.

"Mr. Chambers, it's a pleasure having you here down in the Outer Banks. I hope you have a pleasant stay and a wonderful vacation here in the splendor of North Carolina's ocean front. Now, if there's the least little thing you need, you give me a call. You're going to find me a most friendly and reasonable opponent."

With that, MacPherson returned to his client.

Will packed up his briefcase and walked down the main aisle of the courtroom with Jonathan Joppa at his side. As he approached the rear of the courtroom, Blackjack Morgan lowered his cane like a railroad-crossing gate across their path.

"Well, Reverend Joppa, congratulations on hiring your new lawyer here. Sad, though—I don't think it's going to do you much good."

"Move your cane, Morgan," Joppa snapped, "or you might just find yourself limping on both legs, rather than one."

Morgan threw his head back and roared with laughter.

Joppa stood firmly in front of him, and after a half a minute, his laughter subsided. Then his eyes locked with Joppa's.

"Tell me, Mr. Morgan," Will said, breaking the tension, "you're not a party to this lawsuit. Exactly what is your interest in this case?"

"Well, I'll tell you, counselor," Morgan said with a synthetic grin. "Terrence Ludlow here is one of my employees. He's my bartend at Joppa's Folly. And what concerns my staff, concerns me. I'm here, you might say, for moral support."

"I'm sure that's it," Will said. "Because if you aren't here for moral support—then that would raise some interesting questions, wouldn't it?"

Morgan glared at Will and then pulled his cane out of the path of Joppa and his lawyer.

Outside the courtroom Will asked his client a simple question.

"There is obviously some bad blood between you and Morgan. What's going on?"

But Joppa wasn't ready to talk about it. He simply answered, "Some other time." Then he extended his hand to Will, shook it, and walked off to his car.

As Will strolled to his Corvette, he thought about Joppa's reluctance to speak openly about Morgan.

But one thing was becoming clear. The mysteries Will had to solve in order to win his case might involve more than issues of piracy along the North Carolina coast. *The personal history between the current players in this legal drama,* Will thought, *may prove to be every bit as intriguing.*

14

AT THE JOPPA'S FOLLY TAVERN, Virgil MacPherson and Blackjack Morgan were seated at a corner table. MacPherson's suitcoat was hanging on the back of the chair and his tie was loosened.

The attorney glanced at his wristwatch. "It's getting late. The drive to Raleigh is a long one—I'd better get going. Do you have my check?"

Morgan pulled out an envelope and pushed it across the table to MacPherson, who opened it, glanced at the check inside, folded it, and stuffed it into his top pocket.

"Just so we understand each other," Morgan said in a low tone, "I want to know that you're going to outsmart this Will Chambers guy—and that I'm going to get that island."

"One little technical point, Blackjack," MacPherson said with an air of varnished politeness. "The island, if we win, goes to Terrence Ludlow. You keep talking about the assignment that he's going to execute, transferring his interest to you. But I still haven't seen it."

"You mean Ludlow hasn't given it to you yet?"

MacPherson shook his head.

Morgan turned and looked at the other end of the tavern, where, behind the bar, Terrence Ludlow was reading *Monster Truck* magazine.

"Ludlow," Morgan shouted, "I told you to sign that document and get it to Virgil. What's the matter with you?"

"I signed it already," Ludlow said nonchalantly.

"Where is it?" Morgan growled.

"I got it with me."

"Show it to me—right now."

Ludlow tossed the magazine on the bar counter, reached under the bar, pulled out a piece of paper, and held it high so Morgan could see it.

"Bring it over here," Morgan snapped.

Ludlow sauntered over to the table and laid the document in front of the two men.

"You can get back to the bar now," Morgan said.

Ludlow paused for a minute, standing next to the table with his hands thrust in his jeans.

"You need a hearing aid?" Morgan barked.

Ludlow slowly turned and sauntered back to the bar.

MacPherson grabbed the document and quickly read over it. Then he looked at Ludlow's notarized signature at the bottom.

"All right. You've read it. So this transfers any interest he has in that island to me, if he wins the lawsuit against Joppa, right?" Morgan asked.

"Yes, I think this does it. This is the standard assignment-of-interest language. But it only recites that the monetary value securing this agreement between you and Ludlow is 'valuable consideration'—and I'm really not sure what that is. Of course, any kind of money agreement—any kind of forgiveness of debt, or other monetary or financial consideration—would be sufficient to bind the agreement. Out of curiosity, what are you giving to Ludlow in exchange?"

Morgan's eyes narrowed, and he studied MacPherson carefully.

"Let's just say that Ludlow owes me some money. This assignment is a payoff of all those debts."

"All right. So I think that closes the loop on your potential interest in this case. There's still another issue."

"Like what?"

"Like the fact that I am still representing Ludlow as my client. Even though you're paying my bills and you have an interest in the island should we win the lawsuit—"

"*When* we win the lawsuit," Morgan countered.

"Right. *When* we win the lawsuit…the point is that even if you're paying the freight on this case, I still represent Ludlow. I could only represent you in this case as well—and follow your instructions in addition to Ludlow's— if there was no actual conflict—or even potential conflict—of interest between what you're asking me to do and what Ludlow asks me to do."

"Oh, there's no conflict there, Counselor MacPherson," Morgan said with a smile. Then he turned and shouted over to Ludlow, who was back reading his magazine behind the bar. "There's no conflict between the way you want things run in this lawsuit and the way I want things run in this lawsuit—right, Ludlow?"

The bartender put down his magazine, glared at Morgan for a few seconds, and then answered reluctantly, "No, there's no conflict."

Morgan turned to MacPherson. "See. No conflict. No problem. So you take your instructions from me. Ludlow and I have a complete agreement."

MacPherson rose to his feet, slipped on his imported silk suitcoat, and smiled back at Morgan. "I'll give you a call."

The lawyer walked past the trophy picture of the mammoth yellowfin tuna recently caught by one of Morgan's charter boats. "Nice catch. Keep reeling in the big ones."

"Don't worry about that," Morgan countered. "I always catch what I'm after."

After MacPherson had left, Morgan leaned back in his chair.

"You're making a run for me tonight, Ludlow. Two A.M. Same pickup point."

The other man cocked his head and chewed on the corner of his lip a little.

"You sure this is safe? I've been getting a bad feeling lately."

"So," Morgan mocked, "little boy's getting scared? You losing the cartilage in your spine? Maybe you've been snorting too much white poison."

"If the stuff I'm snorting is no good—I've only got you to blame."

"There's nothing wrong with the quality of the stuff I give you," Morgan said in a reassuring tone. "On the other hand, maybe the good doctor here's got to change your prescription. Maybe…if you're very, very good…I'll cut you a sample of the stuff you're picking up tonight. Free of charge. Just because I'm that kind of guy."

Ludlow set his magazine down and pulled a pack of cigarettes out of his top pocket. He tapped the pack until a cigarette fell into his fingers. But as he tried to light it, his hands shook…it took him several tries.

Morgan stopped at the door of the tavern and turned back to Ludlow, giving him one last comment.

"Just remember one thing," he said with finality. "About how good I treat you. Like you're one of my own children."

And then Morgan was gone. The heavy screen door with the broken spring slammed shut with a bang behind him.

But Ludlow was not watching him. He was still staring at the cigarette in his hand…and the way his fingers were shaking uncontrollably.

15

THE APPOINTMENT WITH FRANCES WILLOWBY was set for midafternoon. Fiona maneuvered her pregnant frame awkwardly into her Saab convertible, moving the seat back to get a little extra space. Then she began the one-hour drive along the Outer Banks down to the Willowby mansion.

She had heard about the great house—Aunt Georgia had described it to her that morning at breakfast. But when she approached the Willowby estate, having taken the long ocean road, then turning into the gated acreage, she was stunned.

It was a huge mansion, "Old Nag's Head" in style, with gray wooden siding, white trim, and a massive sloping roof that covered the top two of the three floors of the house. There was a winding wraparound porch with endless windows. The house was perched a mere one-hundred-and-fifty feet from the end of land, with a spectacular two-hundred-and-eighty-degree view of the crashing waves of the Atlantic Ocean.

Fiona parked and extracted herself from the front seat. She took her small steno pad, a pen, and her purse, and ambled up the slate stone walk.

Once on the porch, she rang the doorbell and then turned to take in the view of the ocean and blue sky. Off to her left, a quarter of a mile away, there was a lighthouse perched on the coast.

Shortly, the door opened, and a woman in a tidy black maid's uniform appeared and welcomed Fiona in.

"Mrs. Willowby will be with you shortly. She's asked that I take you into the conservatory. Follow me, please."

Fiona gazed around the great hall, where two tandem sets of spiral staircases led to the second floor. The foyer was black-and-white marble squares. Off to her right, at the far end of the house, she could see French doors leading to what appeared to be a library.

The maid was leading her to the other end of the house, and en route she took in the ocean view along its entire length.

Finally, Fiona was led to a large garden room with lots of glass and sky-lights, furnished with soft flowered sofas and overstuffed chairs. The room was filled with plants, flowers, and a handful of large potted trees that reached almost to the ceiling.

"We're serving high tea. Are you hungry? Would you like some tea and a light meal?"

"Oh, yes," Fiona said cheerfully, seating herself on a couch. "I'm famished. Of course I have an excuse—I'm eating for two!"

The maid smiled and went over to a large walnut rolling cart with a silver tea service on the top, and pastries, scones, and fruit on the bottom. She rolled it over to Fiona and handed her a china plate and a linen napkin. "May I serve you tea?"

Fiona nodded enthusiastically, and added, "With cream, sugar, and lemon, thanks."

"Mrs. Willowby will be with you momentarily," the maid said. "If there's anything else you need, just give a pull on the service rope over there." A heavy gold brocade rope draped from a hole in the ceiling down to eye level, situated just to the side of the entrance to the conservatory.

As Fiona was sipping her tea and indulging in the freshly baked scones, she was taking in all of the plant life in the conservatory.

"Oh my. So lovely. Just magnificent!" she was exclaiming out loud as she was studying the perfectly green, well-trimmed horticulture in the room.

"I'm glad you like it."

Fiona turned toward the voice, rising from her seat. She saw a thin, statuesque woman in her sixties, with a lovely face and soft eyes. Frances Willowby's hair, which was ivory white, was pulled back in a chignon style. She was wearing flared starched linen pants and a striped silk sailor's top, with a red silk scarf around her neck.

She extended her slender hand gracefully, and Fiona noticed she was wearing three diamond bracelets—each of a different yet exquisite design.

"Please sit down," she invited Fiona.

Mrs. Willowby sat on a large, fan-backed rattan chair across from the couch where Fiona was.

"The climate is so wonderful for growing things," she continued. "We have so much moisture. The sea air. Even the salt in the air, I think, as long as you're careful, gives some increased nourishment to the plant life.

Sometime, when you have a few extra minutes, you should come back and I will give you a walking tour of our gardens." She waved her hand dramatically toward the side yard that extended beyond the glass windows of the conservatory.

"We have four different garden settings. We have an English garden. That's one of my favorites. We also have a South African garden, with plants indigenous to that area. Very tropical. I call it my little slice of paradise. And we have the American garden, with plant life indigenous to the United States, mostly the southeastern coastal areas. And lastly, we have the Australian garden, with some of the more harsh, but interesting, landscape features from the Australian Outback."

Fiona's eyes lit up, her mouth opening in delight. Frances Willowby smiled. She was enjoying Fiona's naiveté and her appreciation for green things and flowering things that need tending and watering.

"Perhaps sometime I can also show you around this house. Give you the complete tour. But you're here on legal business. Concerning my late husband's last will and testament, correct?"

Fiona nodded, and picked up the pad sitting next to her.

"Yes. And I do thank you so much for letting me talk to you. I'm here on a case my husband is handling. He represents Jonathan Joppa. Regarding the condition in your late husband's will—the transfer of Stony Island from your husband's estate to Reverend Joppa, as you probably know, is conditioned on our being able to prove Isaac Joppa's innocence regarding criminal charges against him in the 1700s. I'm sure you're aware of all of that..."

"I most certainly am," Frances noted. "Almost all of the estate went to me, of course, as Randolph's wife. But I do know that he made a number of small, specific bequests. I really had no interest in Stony Island, of course. But do tell me one thing..."

Before she could continue, the maid entered the room and waited quietly for Frances to acknowledge her.

"Phyllis, do be a dear," Frances said, addressing the maid. "Please get me a gin and tonic."

Frances turned back to Fiona and then added, "I'm sure you won't be taking any alcohol—particularly in light of your present condition." She nodded and smiled in the direction of Fiona's pregnant belly. "How about some sweet tea?"

"That would be delightful."

The maid quickly disappeared from the room and Frances continued.

"What I was going to say…I was just wondering whether you are also a lawyer in your husband's office…"

"No. Not at all. I'm just helping him out this summer as his paralegal. Specifically on this case."

"So—you don't usually work as one of his staff?"

"No. Actually, I'm a singer. I have a very busy music ministry and recording career. But I offered to help Will—that's my husband—on this case."

Frances Willowby paused and eyed Fiona carefully. The corners of her mouth tightened ever so slightly.

"My, my. Not only do you bear your husband's children—you also help him with his legal cases. What a faithful, dutiful little wife."

Mrs. Willowby reached for her solid platinum cigarette case. She snapped it open, retrieving a long, imported cigarette. She reached for her crystal cigarette lighter on the table next to her—but paused, deciding not to light the cigarette.

"You'll have to forgive me," Frances said. "I've smoked all my life. I used to justify it—in my earlier days as a model—as the quickest way to keep my weight down. But now it's simply an ugly old addiction. But I shall refrain. I don't want you inhaling secondary smoke. For the sake of your baby."

As Frances was placing the cigarette back in the case, Fiona was struggling with her comment about Fiona as a "dutiful little wife." The slight sneer. The air of condescension.

She'd arrived at Frances Willowby's mansion with every desire of earnestly helping her husband discover the truth about Isaac Joppa and fulfill his representation of his client. She believed she could play an integral part in that case. But now, as she sat in the conservatory talking with Frances Willowby, she felt a little silly.

The maid entered the room, carrying the drinks, and she delivered the gin and tonic to the mistress of the house.

Despite her graceful air, Frances took a large, rather stiff gulp from the glass. Then she discreetly wiped the corner of her mouth with her manicured finger.

Fiona gazed at her. Elegantly dressed, wealthy beyond measure, a woman whose beauty, despite her advanced age, was still exquisitely preserved. And yet, in Mrs. Willowby's eyes, Fiona could see the frightened emptiness within.

"I'm sorry, my dear," Frances said. "You'll have to forgive my comment about you and your husband. I find myself saying the cruelest things lately. Unmeaningly. Unwittingly. Not having Randolph around anymore...I think when he was with me, he softened my edges. He did bring the best out in me. I hope I did the same for him..."

Frances Willowby's voice quivered a bit, and she lifted the glass to her lips, taking a second large gulp.

"I'm sure you loved him very much," Fiona said softly. "This must be so very hard for you. And I apologize if our conversation is bringing any of those difficult memories back."

"What a kind thing to say," Frances said, clearing her throat.

"And I love your hair," Fiona said enthusiastically. "I just love that look."

Frances smiled and reached back, delicately touching the contours of her hair.

"I try to change it every so often. I keep it long enough where I can do something with it. Did I tell you I had been a model?"

"Yes, I think you did. I'd love to hear about that..." Fiona said warmly.

"Oh, I don't want to get off on that. But I was one of the top models in the Arthur Williamson Agency in New York. I had been previously married. It was short-lived. Frankly, it was a disaster. So I threw myself into my modeling career after the divorce from my first husband. I was in New York. And that's how I met Randolph Willowby. He also had been previously married. Randolph was a college friend of Mr. Williamson, the founder and owner of the agency. Mr. Williamson and his wife, Gertrude, ran things. And they did a lot of wonderful things for me. At one point I was actually on the covers of nine different magazines in three years."

Then Frances balanced her liquor glass between the fingers of her two hands. "But I didn't miss modeling. When I met Randolph, it was the best thing that ever happened to me. He encouraged me to stay in modeling. But I didn't want to. We moved down here. He opened up a whole new world to me. He had a shipping line. And a fishing company. I fell in love with Willowby Manor—that's what we call it..."

"But you didn't come here to talk about me. You wanted to find out about my husband. And what he put in his will," Frances went on.

"Actually, I was fascinated with what you were telling me about your life. But I did want to find out one thing," Fiona said. "I'm wondering why your husband put such an unusual requirement in his will—as something that Reverend Joppa would have to prove in order to receive the transfer of Stony Island."

"I don't know that much about it," Frances explained. "Throughout our marriage he had a little bit of an interest in his own ancestry. Genealogy. That kind of thing. He was very busy with his business, of course, and highly successful. Then he was told he had cancer. About a year and a half before he died. And shortly after the diagnosis…something happened in his life. I'm not quite sure how to describe it…"

"Something happened?"

"Before then, Randolph was never very religious. And I wasn't either. It's just not something we talked about very much. But after they told him he had stage-three cancer, things changed. He started reading the Bible all the time. He said he had had some kind of spiritual rebirth. That's the phrase he used. Besides reading the Bible all the time, Randolph started pursuing an intense…how do I say this?…almost an obsession…tracing back to his ancestral roots. Back to Elisha Willowby. Who married into the Joppa family. Elisha Willowby was the thirteenth ancestor backward from Randolph. Elisha married Myrtle, Reverend Malachi Joppa's daughter. Randolph wanted to learn everything he could about Reverend Malachi Joppa. What his religious beliefs were. What he did in the city of Bath. How he tried to convert the local people. That kind of thing."

"Did your husband ever talk about his interest in Isaac Joppa?"

"The only thing I know is what he told me once. He said he wondered…and I remember when he asked me this. We were out in the garden. He was very weak at that point. Nearing the end. I had him in a wheelchair. It was a beautiful day. Bright sky. He asked me this question—he wondered what it was that had motivated Isaac Joppa to run away from his father. To run from everything that Reverend Malachi believed and preached. And he wondered if Isaac Joppa had ever found peace in his soul before he died. That's exactly the way he put it—'peace in his soul.'"

"That's very intriguing. Did Mr. Willowby ever talk to anyone else about this? Did he ever write any notes—or letters—or keep a journal or diary where he would have written down what he knew about Isaac Joppa? Or why he thought Isaac Joppa might have been innocent of the criminal charges of piracy?"

Frances Willowby looked closely at Fiona, then gazed off to the windows into the garden. Several long, quiet moments passed. She pursed her lips, and then glanced at the diamond-studded watch on her wrist.

"Oh, my—the time has flown. I am so sorry. I have to go. I have a nail appointment, and then I have a dinner scheduled with the charity league."

Frances extended her hand to Fiona, who shook it warmly and surrounded it with her other hand.

"I'll certainly pray for you, Mrs. Willowby," Fiona said. "That God grant you peace in the midst of this very difficult time."

Frances stopped and gave Fiona a somewhat startled look. Her eyes locked with Fiona's as they stood, holding hands.

Then she turned and began brusquely sweeping out of the room—but stopped and turned slightly to Fiona before exiting.

"You must come back again, darling, so that we can talk some more. I'll have my staff give you a call."

Fiona was led to the front door by the maid, whom she thanked for the hospitality. As she walked to her car, she saw the chauffeur-driven Rolls Royce, with Frances Willowby in the back, slowly making its way down the long driveway from Willowby Manor.

16

In the workshop of the Ocean Search salvage building, Orville Putrie was hunched over a panel of electronic equipment attached to a police scanner, a wireless receiver, and a keyboard. It was after eleven o'clock at night, and all of the other lights in the shop were out, except for a lamp over Putrie's workbench. He thought he was alone.

Putrie was startled and jumped a little when he heard a noise. He turned and spotted Blackjack Morgan in the doorway of the workshop.

Morgan was laughing, and he pulled out an extra-long Cuban cigar and began lighting it.

"You just about gave me a heart attack," Putrie exclaimed.

"You're too young for a heart attack," Morgan said, lighting the end of his cigar and taking a few puffs.

"You know that smoking really bothers me. Particularly when I'm concentrating here. Could you smoke outside?" Putrie whined.

Morgan took a few steps toward Putrie—until he was an arm's length away. Then he held the Cuban cigar out delicately between two fingers and showed it to the other man.

"Are you talking about this? Do you realize how hard these are to get—how much I have to pay for these?"

"They really make me gag." Putrie began to cough.

Morgan put his mouth to the end of the cigar. He took a deep drag and then blew the smoke in his employee's face.

"Get used to it," he sneered as the smoke sent Putrie into a coughing fit.

Morgan strolled over to the workbench and took a look at what Putrie was engineering.

"I've got a new job for you," he said nonchalantly.

"Great. Just keep piling it on. I'm still working on this project. I've got a ways to go. Why don't you let me get this one finished first?"

"The new project is urgent. This one's important—but it ain't urgent," Morgan said, pointing to the electronic equipment.

"That's not what you told me before," the smaller man snapped back. "You said we've got to figure out a way to monitor Coast Guard radio transmissions and radar from a several-mile distance. That's what you told me. So that's what I've been working on. I'm frying my brain here—working late—trying to jerry-rig this thing on a fast timetable."

"Yes. That's what I told you. But like I said, this new project is urgent. And seeing as I pay the bills—and I'm the one who picked you up and gave you work at a pretty good salary after you flunked out of MIT—I figure you owe me a lot."

"Not true," Putrie shot back, beginning to flush and shake ever so slightly. "I never flunked out of MIT. I was number three in my class. I had the highest entrance scores of any other engineering student. I was kicked out for conduct. And you know exactly why.

"Sure. Right," Morgan said with a chuckle. "Which makes me question exactly how smart you are. You threaten to kill one of your professors. So they boot you out. How smart is that? *Don't threaten somebody,* my motto is—you just do it. You do your payback. And then you make sure nobody finds out. You don't bother to make threats. Little girls make threats. A real man simply does it—quietly, in the night, when no one's looking."

Putrie was getting agitated. Both hands were clutching the stool he was on, to the point that his knuckles were turning white. Morgan laughed a little at his master technician and then continued.

"Let me give it to you short and sweet. I need some information. Historical. You need to retrieve this data for me pronto. I don't care how you get it. I want it put together ASAP. I need you to check every public record. Every piece of state information for North Carolina having to do with a date and a place."

"You're not making any sense," Putrie said, shaking his head.

"Okay. Let's do this again," Morgan said, becoming irritated. "Here's the date. October eleventh. Use the year 1718. And the geographical area would be from Bath, up the Pamlico Sound, and all through the Outer Banks coastal area. I want you to check every record and public document. Newspaper reports. Anything you can retrieve. I want to find out what happened on October 11, 1718, in the geographical area I just gave to you."

Putrie took off his thick glasses, wiped the lenses off on his T-shirt, and then put them back on. He continued staring with bewilderment at Morgan. And then the light broke.

"I get it. This has to do with the October eleventh date written on that shell we found at the dive site."

"There is no shell. You understand me?" Morgan demanded, walking up close—so close that Putrie could smell the cigar smoke on his breath.

"There is no shell. There never has been. You get my drift? And there was no shell with the date of October eleventh on it. Now, you input that date into your computer—you got that?"

Putrie smiled thinly, tilted his head a little as he studied Morgan, and then nodded.

"So—how do you think you're going to do this?"

Putrie was silent. After a few moments of near catatonia, staring off into space, he broke into a twisted little smile.

"I'm going to break into the database of the state of North Carolina. They got historical records for everything. Birth records. Death certificates. Real estate transactions and transfers. Judgments entered in civil cases. Criminal cases. Tax liens. I think some of this stuff goes back to the English colonies. I'm hoping most of it's been transferred from the old hardcopy records. I'm pretty sure a lot of it has. So I hack into it and do a selective search with a two-vector convergence. One by time, consisting of our date. The other intersecting line for the search consisting of every geographical place name within the area. The key here is to add some qualifiers. Modifiers so that I can narrow the search down to what you're really looking for."

With that, Putrie smiled and stared into Morgan's eyes. "So—tell me what the goal is," Putrie asked coyly. "What you're ultimately after. Then I can add some modifiers to my database search. That'll ensure accuracy. Exactly what are you looking for?"

Morgan had a small penknife in his hand that he was using to widen the hole at the end of his cigar. He looked up at Putrie, not smiling.

"What am I after?" Morgan asked with a tinge of disbelief in his voice. "You expect me to tell you that?"

"I need that information. Otherwise you got me doing a database search in the dark. I'll be retrieving this information—trying to pull it together like a blind man."

"Let me just tell you this," Morgan said, taking a step toward Putrie and raising the penknife until it was even with Putrie's right eye, only an inch away. "You ever ask me that question again, and you *will* be a blind man."

Putrie knew better than to push. He had heard the stories about Blackjack Morgan's background—in his younger years, in the merchant marine. How he had beaten a murder rap for the death of another sailor up in Nova Scotia. How one of his former girlfriends mysteriously went missing and was never found again. So Putrie did not respond. He merely waited for Blackjack Morgan to wheel on the heels of his black boots and limp out of the workshop.

It took a few minutes for Orville Putrie to refocus his attention on the electronics in front of him after his boss had left the workshop. By that time the only evidence remaining of his visit was the odor of his expensive Cuban cigar still lingering in the air.

17

WILL CHAMBERS CHECKED WITH Boggs Beckford's law office to get the address for August Longfellow.

Beckford's secretary made the call to Longfellow to explain that Will Chambers had taken over the case, and she set up the interview between the two of them.

Longfellow's beach house was a small, single-story cottage with a covered porch overlooking the ocean. It had once been painted yellow but was long overdue for repainting. The yellow had faded and was peeling down to the gray, weathered wood. The main entrance was in the back, facing the ocean, so Will made his way around to a porch that was surrounded by sand dunes and ocean grass.

As Will stepped up, he noticed two large flowerpots with plants that were limp, and in dire need of watering.

Over the front door there was a rusted metal plaque that read, *Know Thyself—You're the Only Self You Got!*

Will knocked on the peeling wood door, but as he did, he realized the door was unlatched. It glided open with a loud creaking noise.

In an instant, August Longfellow was standing in the open doorway. He was a man in his mid-sixties. His hair was iron gray and worn long, almost down to his shoulders, and parted in the middle. He had a gray beard that flowed down to the well of his neck. He was wearing a cardigan sweatshirt unbuttoned in the front, revealing a faded T-shirt that bore the message, *I Studied with a Tibetan Holy Man, But All I Got Was This Lousy T-Shirt.* Longfellow had a pair of bifocals perched on his nose, which he quickly snatched away so he could give Will a closer look. Longfellow had a handsome face, ruddy and rugged, with deep creases.

"You're the lawyer?" he asked, thrusting his right hand out toward Will.

Will introduced himself, and his host led him through the house, back to the kitchen.

The little cottage was awash with books. There were floor-to-ceiling bookcases everywhere. In the living room, there was a short stairway that led to a door. But each stair was stacked with books, like a bookshelf. On the coffee table, and on all of his end tables, there were books in various degrees of literary consumption, with torn pieces of paper as bookmarks.

The kitchen was small, with an old linoleum-top chrome kitchen set in the middle.

Longfellow reached into the refrigerator, pulled out a bottle of beer, and popped the top off. Then he held it out to Will.

"No, thanks," Will said with a smile.

"Teetotaler?"

"That's one way to describe it."

"If you don't mind my asking—why did you swear off alcohol?"

"I had a problem with it. Actually, it was my life. My problem with alcohol was simply the symptom. But I found it wrapping itself around me—like some big anaconda. It was dragging me down in this black pit. So…I managed to get away from that snake. I'd rather not have to wrestle it again."

"'Wrestling with an anaconda'…interesting turn of phrase, Mr. Chambers," Longfellow said, sitting down at the kitchen table and talking between slugs from the bottle.

"I spend a lot of time thinking about language," he went on. "I don't know how much you know about me. I dabble in poetry here and there. I write books. Teach some philosophy classes in comparative culture. Some people would say I've dedicated myself to the 'life of the mind.' But I don't prefer to look at it that way. It's really a life of language. Ideas come into the world like naked little babies. They need to be reared. And they need a good suit of clothes. That's where words and language come in."

Longfellow seemed particularly pleased with his last comment. He smiled broadly and took another large swig from his bottle.

"Professor Longfellow," Will said, trying to direct his host to the point of his visit, "I was told by Boggs Beckford you had agreed to be an expert witness for him in Reverend Jonathan Joppa's case. Beckford told me that you are quite knowledgeable about regional history down here in the Outer Banks. Going all the way back to the early 1700s. The age of piracy. Edward Teach and the Isaac Joppa story. Is that right?"

"Oh, I really don't like that word 'expert,'" Longfellow said, scratching his beard. "I've had two volumes of poetry published. But does that make me an expert? I teach classes in philosophy at Duke as adjunct professor.

Does that make me an expert? Actually, that's why I feel such an affinity to the eighteenth-century philosophers. Because generally speaking, they weren't *professionals*. They were always something else. They were monks, theologians, lawyers, merchants. Descartes was a soldier. Philosophy is what they did on the side. They did it because they believed it was a noble pursuit. But they had regular day jobs—that kept them honest."

"Yes," Will said in reply. "I've always figured the biggest problem with philosophy is that it is relegated to philosophers," Will remarked casually, grabbing for his legal pad and his pen.

His host burst into a roaring belly laugh at that. He slapped the kitchen table with his hand. "Well said! Direct hit to the broad side," Longfellow bellowed.

"I didn't mean any disrespect—"

"No, I know exactly what you're saying. Philosophy—literally—'the love of wisdom.' Isn't that what everybody needs? An appropriation of a maximum amount of wisdom."

"I certainly couldn't agree with you more," Will said. "Not just in the mundane, daily things. But also in the big cosmic questions too."

"Well, speaking of wisdom, perhaps I can shed some light on this Isaac Joppa business. Not exactly one of the mundane matters—and not belonging to the 'cosmic matters' you alluded to. But something in-between. Certainly an intriguing historical question. I'm in the process of writing a book right now. I'm attempting to reconstruct the ideological constructs, the belief systems, in play during the eighteenth century along the Carolina coastal areas. That really was a seminal point in American history. The years preceding the Revolution. The influence of the Enlightenment. Expanding transportation. Cross-cultural exchange. A collision between religious fervor and scientific progress. So the point is—I've been studying the Outer Banks for many, many years."

"Boggs Beckford told me you were fairly optimistic there was evidence indicating Isaac Joppa's innocence."

"You mean the piracy charges? The indictment that was filed against him down in Bath by the grand jury?"

Will nodded.

"Well, I'm not quite sure that I'd use the word *optimistic*," Longfellow said, hedging slightly.

"Well, what evidence do you have that he was innocent?" the lawyer said, probing.

"Let me see…I think I've got it around here somewhere…" Longfellow rose, put his bottle down, and began roaming around the house, looking through his bookshelves, muttering to himself.

After a few minutes, Will heard a victory cry from the other room.

"Here it is!" He had located a black book with the cover and spine crumbling from age.

"Very out-of-print book. I'm very proud of obtaining this. *The Shipping Trade, Piracy, and the Coastal Carolinas*. Nolan Kendricks. 1829. Way out of print. Very hard to find."

Will waited for Longfellow's punch line. And waited. Hoping against hope that it would arrive eventually.

18

Longfellow paged to the spot he wanted.

"So. Here it is. Page one hundred forty-five. Kendricks makes reference to the Ocracoke battle with Edward Teach and his pirate band. He makes mention of Isaac Joppa. And then...look here...he talks about the fact that Isaac Joppa was apparently engaged to be married to Abigail Merriwether. He found that of interest because, as you see in the footnote, Peter Merriwether, Abigail's father, was a prominent shipping magnate in Bristol, England."

Will was taking notes now, furiously.

"What else does the book mention about Isaac Joppa?"

"According to the footnote, Kendricks was citing a newspaper announcement in the *Bristol Recorder*. Now I checked into the *Bristol Recorder*, and it no longer exists. And it hasn't for more than a hundred years. So Kendricks, at the time he wrote his book, obviously had a hard copy of the actual newspaper article in his hands.

"In any event," Longfellow continued, "the footnote here says that Peter Merriwether was contacted for his good wishes about the engagement, but refused comment. Now that's an odd thing for a newspaper report in the 1700s to have said. There was a strong implication that Peter Merriwether was strongly opposed to this engagement."

"I'm not sure I understand," Will said, thinking through the information that Longfellow had shared. "What's your theory on why that is evidence of Isaac Joppa's innocence?"

"Just this," Longfellow explained. "Even if we assume that old papa wasn't crazy about his engagement to his daughter, nevertheless, it sounds like Isaac Joppa had a real leg up in terms of his future. All he had to do was please the father-in-law. That he had some ambition in life. Who knows? Isaac Joppa had every reason to believe that if he played his cards right, he might end up in his father-in-law's business. So the point is this—none of that fits with the profile of the typical social outcast who populated Blackbeard's crew."

Will jotted a few more notes down and then paused to reflect.

"What do we know about the period of time between Joppa's leaving Bath, North Carolina, and the point in time when he appears on one of Teach's pirate ships?"

"Some of that is fairly documented. There are admiralty records in England, quoted in a newspaper article in 1717, that indicate he was assigned, as an ensign, to the HMS *Intrepid*. That was a ship that had a captain by the name of Zebulun Boughton. Boughton was a real terror. He brutalized his sailors. That was widely known. Anyway, the *Intrepid* was part of the English Royal Navy. The admiralty records indicate that Joppa jumped ship in port at Ireland. It doesn't take too much imagination to figure out why he deserted, particularly with a violent, half-crazed captain like Boughton."

"And then what happened?" Will asked, riveted to Longfellow's story.

"Joppa boarded a ship out of Dublin called *Good Intent*. It was a merchant ship. And off the coast of the United States, in October 1717, it was boarded by Blackbeard and his crew."

"And Isaac Joppa?"

"Isaac Joppa, from the takeover of the *Good Intent* until the Battle of Ocracoke Inlet in 1718, made several appearances on board Blackbeard's pirate ship. He was spotted during at least one plundering of another ship."

"Everything you've said so far," Will said, ruminating on the information from Longfellow, "every bit of it could be consistent with the theory of his innocence. That he jumped ship from the Royal Navy because of a brutal, violent captain. He gets on the Irish ship, which is then taken over and plundered by Blackbeard. And then, if we assume he was kidnapped by Blackbeard and forced to remain on the pirate's ship during several other pirate attacks, that would certainly explain his presence there."

"It would," Longfellow said, finishing off his bottle of beer. "Except that there was testimony given to the magistrate in Bath, North Carolina, and to the grand jury, to the effect that passengers on that other ship plundered by Blackbeard swore that they saw Isaac Joppa partially in charge of the pirate attacks. He seemed to be free—roaming the deck and giving orders to assist Blackbeard."

"And that's what they based the indictment on?"

"Exactly. And that's pretty compelling stuff," Longfellow noted, scratching his beard.

Will glanced over his notes, which now filled several pages. He was missing something. But what?

"I can't believe I almost forgot to ask this one," Will said. "According to Beckford, you knew of Isaac Joppa's relationship with two different women. One was this Abigail in England. Who was the other one?"

"Oh, yes...the Indian princess..."

"What!"

"Yes. You'll have to get this from a better source than me. Now I'm just talking from anecdotal information I've heard. You know, oral history stuff from the Indian folks here in North Carolina. But according to legend, a white English sailor who was once associated with Blackbeard's crew married an Indian princess. To be precise, the daughter of one of the Tuscarora tribal chiefs—by the name of King Jim Blount."

"Now I'm confused. How does this work into the timeline of Isaac Joppa's life? Did he marry this Indian princess *before* going to England and becoming engaged to Abigail Merriwether? Or did this happen *after* his engagement in England? And did all of this happen *after* the battle at Okracoke Inlet? Which would mean that he survived the battle, right?"

"I'm not sure," Longfellow said. "To get the real dope on this, you need to talk to a woman by the name of Susan Red Deer Williams. She teaches Native American history at Carolina College. She spends her time down at this Indian center along the coast on the way to Pamlico Inlet."

"Why do they think that Isaac Joppa was the pirate that married this Indian princess?"

"Apparently, King Jim Blount and the Indian princess—a young woman later named Priceless Pearl—that was the Indian translation—were converted to Christianity shortly after meeting with this pirate. I suppose he proselytized them into the white man's religion. The only likely candidate for that would be Isaac Joppa, given the fact that his father was a well-known Calvinist preacher."

"And yet," Will said, thinking intensely on everything he had heard from Longfellow, "this marriage to the Indian princess undermines the theory of innocence I was suggesting before. If Isaac Joppa was truly in love with this Abigail Merriwether, then that would tend to indicate that he found himself on Blackbeard's pirate ship *not* of his own volition. On the other hand, if he ends up marrying this Indian woman—how much did he really love Abigail in the first place?"

"Ah, yes—the mystery of the ages..." Longfellow said, rising and stretching. "And therein I speak, of course, of *love*. Not that I'm an expert on that subject...but on the other hand, though I've never been married—frankly, I don't believe in monogamy—I've loved many a woman—perhaps loved them too well!"

Will rose to extend his hand to say goodbye.

"Or," he added in rebuttal, "perhaps it might be that you failed to love at least one of those women well enough to marry her."

"You *are* a philosopher!" Longfellow said, chuckling.

"Just a philosophy minor in my undergraduate days—and presently a happily married man," Will noted with a smile.

Longfellow escorted his guest to the front door.

"You know, Mr. Chambers, if you're not doing anything for dinner, I know a great crab house down the beach. We could carry on our conversation down there. I find you a stimulating conversationalist."

"Thanks anyway," Will said, "but I need to get back to my wife. But I do appreciate your help. Do you think you'll be able to continue working on this case with me as an expert witness for Reverend Joppa?"

"Most certainly," Longfellow replied. "I hope I was helpful. This business of digging up the untold lives of dead people is always an exhilarating—and frustrating—enterprise. And a sobering one at that. It reminds you that the grim reaper awaits everyone of us."

Despite his desire to extricate himself from Longfellow and get home to Fiona, Will felt he had to pursue that last comment. "It does bring into perspective your view of life, death, eternity, and an afterlife, doesn't it?"

"True. True," Longfellow said with an air of superiority. "You want to hear my philosophy on death? Here it is: 'No longer mourn for me when I am dead. Then you shall hear the surly, sullen bell give warning to the world that I am fled from this vile world, with vilest worms to dwell.' William Shakespeare. My sentiments exactly."

"Interesting," Will said. "But devoid of hope. You want to hear mine?"

Longfellow nodded eagerly.

"O death, where is thy sting? O grave, where is thy victory?"

Longfellow leaned against the doorway, smiled, and shook his head. "A true believer. One of God's elect. I should have known."

"Actually, I prefer to think of myself as simply a sheep that was lost. And now I'm found."

"Ah. Simplicity," Longfellow remarked. "Some philosophers argue that such is the characteristic of the most likely metaphysical truth. The simpler the postulate, the more likely it is to be true."

"That is the principle called Occam's razor, right?" Will asked with a smile.

"Exactly," Longfellow replied. "If you were one of my students, I'd give you an *A*. But we'll have to continue this conversation at a more convenient time," Longfellow gave a half wave to Will and closed the door.

The afternoon was waning and the tide was rolling in. The waves were crashing their way up the beach, toward the sand dunes that surrounded August Longfellow's beach house, which was perched on the sandy cliff. Will glanced at the darkening surface of the rolling ocean. Then he turned and walked to his car. The sound of the roaring surf was still ringing in his ears—just as it had three hundred years before, for another man—at another time. And at another place.

((((((

Isaac Joppa knew he was still alive. And he knew he was near the ocean because he could hear the crashing of the surf off in the distance. He was on his stomach, his face in the sand and pine needles. He did not know how long he had lain there. When his mind cleared, he looked around. He saw that he was in a hut with a curved roof, like a tiny barn covered with animal skins.

His back was in searing pain where the pistol ball had entered. Then he was aware of someone delicately tending to his wound. The person he could not see was gingerly putting something—something cold and mud-like—into it. Whatever it was, it was giving off an evil smell.

There was a movement at Isaac's side. Then a person was next to him, brushing the hair from his eyes with slender, nimble fingers.

Isaac looked and saw a pretty, young Indian girl looking back at him and smiling. She could not have been more than seventeen or eighteen years old. She had long, braided black hair decorated with seashells.

She got up and left the hut. Isaac could smell a fire burning somewhere. Then the girl returned with a crude wooden bowl. It contained cooked fish, a bed of large green leaves, and multicolored berries.

Isaac was suddenly aware that he was weak with hunger—he did not know how long he had been unconscious. He reached over and thrust his fingers into the food and began scooping it frantically into his mouth, which made the Indian girl laugh.

Isaac tried a question, hoping that she could speak some English.

"Where am I?"

"Camp," the girl replied. "Camp of Tuscaroras."

"How did I get here?"

The girl squinted her eyes and tilted her head. Isaac repeated the question again. Then she smiled a little in recognition and left the tent again. After a few minutes she returned with a large broken plank and showed it to Isaac.

Curious about it, he reached out and turned it over.

There was a large carving of a fish, and to the left of it, the letters of a portion of the name of the vessel—*LD VENTURE*—carved and painted. It was the name plaque off the ship *Bold Venture*.

Isaac was beginning to recall what had happened. There was a battle. He was down in the hold of Teach's ship. The Royal Navy brought its ship alongside. Teach's ship fired on it with its cannons. It looked as if the English sailors had been pulverized, so Teach ordered his ship, *Adventure*, to come up alongside the English naval vessel and board her.

But when he did, sailors who had been hiding in the English ship's hold poured up onto the deck, firing pistols and charging the pirates with drawn swords.

At some point in the melee, Teach screamed out an order to one of his crew members aboard *Bold Venture*, which was cruising alongside.

Teach called out for *Bold Venture* to be scuttled. It was the ship that Teach had looted, and then commandeered during his rampage along the Spanish Main.

A few minutes after Teach's order, the crewmen had lit the fuse leading to a barrel of gunpowder and a hole was blown in the hull of *Bold Venture*. The vessel quickly sank.

Caesar, the large, muscular African who was one of Teach's most trusted assistants, was given the same order—to scuttle and sink the ship *Adventure* if he determined that the English were likely to win.

But several local merchants who had been sleeping off a drunken orgy hosted for them aboard the *Adventure* by Teach, awoke and discovered the plan. As Caesar tried to light the gunpowder barrel in the hold of the ship with his torch, the three passengers jumped him. As Isaac mounted the steps to go on deck, Caesar was engaged in a ferocious struggle with the three visitors.

When Isaac had finally charged up the stairs and onto the deck, he had seen in an instant that the pirates were outnumbered and outmatched. He had known he could not surrender. Escape was the only option. He jumped off the ship, and into the ocean.

As he swam, he had been shot in the back. He had struggled to swim but began lapsing into unconsciousness and started sinking. That's when a piece of the *Bold Venture* floated up next to him.

Isaac had grabbed the plank and struggled to lay his torso onto it. As the waters of the Pamlico Sound washed over him in a strange baptism of survival, Isaac Joppa had blacked out.

He studied the wooden board and the pretty Indian girl's face. Now he understood what had happened. Somehow he had managed to cling to the wood plank. The Indians had found him and tended to his wounds. They had been his salvation.

But Isaac Joppa would soon learn that his miraculous rescue might be short-lived—that he had survived the ferocious battle at Ocracoke Inlet only to face, now, an even more daunting fate.

19

In the commercial tower in downtown Raleigh, North Carolina, the law firm of MacPherson, Trump, and Powers resided on the top floor. There, attorney Virgil MacPherson was ruminating on the Joppa case. His private investigators had done a background check on Will Chambers. They had also informed MacPherson about Fiona Chambers' pregnancy. Now MacPherson was laying out his attack.

Lying in front of him on the shiny walnut conference table was the first set of written discovery demands by attorney Chambers on behalf of Reverend Jonathan Joppa, addressed to Terrence Ludlow in care of his legal counsel.

MacPherson was flipping through the pages of the interrogatories and demand for documents that had been served.

Will Chambers' request for information centered around three categories of evidence:

First, he wanted to know any information possessed by MacPherson or his client relating to Isaac Joppa's guilt or innocence on piracy charges.

The second category related to any information that MacPherson or Ludlow had regarding "Stony Island, aka Joppa's Island," including its history of ownership, any of its physical features, or any buildings, structures, or artifacts located thereon.

Lastly, he demanded any information or documents that MacPherson and his client might possess "regarding Edward Teach, aka Blackbeard, including, but not limited to any information relating to his life, his conduct, or any contact between the said Edward Teach, aka Blackbeard, and Isaac Joppa."

The first category of information didn't pose a problem to MacPherson. He could easily enough play dodgeball with that one simply by responding, in writing, that they had no information or evidence tending to indicate that Isaac Joppa was innocent—to the contrary, the existence of an indictment issued by a grand jury in Bath, on or about the year of 1717, was strong evidence of Isaac Joppa's guilt.

However, when MacPherson studied the demand for discovery relating to evidence or information about "Stony Island, aka Joppa's Island," he balked. He knew, on a strictly technical level, that his formal and official client was Terrence Ludlow—not Blackjack Morgan. As such, Ludlow possessed no information about Stony Island or Joppa's Island.

In fact, MacPherson had concluded that his client possessed little or no knowledge of anything remotely resembling useful information, facts, or practical intelligence on any useful subject other than serving drinks at Joppa's Folly—and causing himself to be cited for a variety of misdemeanor criminal offenses.

On the other hand, MacPherson had met numerous times with Blackjack Morgan. He knew that Morgan was pulling all the strings on the case, paying the bills, and calling the shots.

He also knew, more to the point, that Morgan was engaged in a highly profitable drug-running operation on the coast of North Carolina, consisting of deliveries by boat at points from Cape Lookout all the way down to Wrightsville Beach. He knew that because Morgan had paid him well to represent him when he was the target of a grand jury investigation into drug operations in the Cape Hatteras area. Morgan, once again, had escaped unscathed. The local prosecutors had not had sufficient evidence to charge him.

In a strange twist of fate, in fact, it had been Judge Bull Chambers—Will Chambers' uncle—who had signed the search warrant that had authorized the police to ransack Morgan's home. They had found nothing—but the search had enraged Morgan. MacPherson wondered if Will Chambers knew that obscure bit of background. The Raleigh lawyer had gained enough information through his client conferences with Morgan to know that when it came to drug dealing, Morgan was as guilty as sin. Moreover, the lawyer had been able, himself, to piece together the reason why Morgan was so bent on winning legal title to Stony Island.

He had guessed that Stony Island was a strategic outpost. If Morgan was able to obtain possession of the island, he could use it as a dropoff and pickup point for his drug operations. Its location could enable Morgan to operate his drug ring relatively unnoticed and unhindered. If the island were entirely within Morgan's ownership, the local police would need a warrant to enter the island in order to search it. By the time they arrived with any warrant, Morgan would be able to hide or destroy any drugs.

Furthermore, the island was closed to the open Atlantic waters. Ironically, it provided the same shelter that made the Outer Banks, with their inner recesses of the Pamlico Sound, a favorite of Edward Teach, the pirate.

Without question, MacPherson had no intention of revealing that information to Will Chambers. Nor, considering the strict confines of the discovery demand, would he be required to.

His job was to win the case and permit Morgan to enforce his assignment of interest to the island. What Morgan did with the island after that, MacPherson had callously concluded, was none of the attorney's business.

But, as to the third category—the request by Will Chambers for any information dealing with "Edward Teach, aka Blackbeard," that was another matter.

A few days earlier, Morgan had sat in MacPherson's office and asked him a very cryptic question: "Supposing I came across something very old, an artifact, in the ocean, and it gave me some indication as to where Blackbeard's treasure was buried." As Morgan spoke his head was tilted backward, his eyes half closed. "Suppose that happened—is it possible for me to get a copyright on that information so that no one can use it except me?"

MacPherson had chuckled a little at the question—until he studied the stern, intent look on Morgan's face. Then he knew he was deadly serious.

MacPherson told his client there was no way he could copyright an artifact—at least he didn't think so, though he'd never researched the issue and had never encountered it in his practice before. After that, Morgan had stopped asking questions about Blackbeard, his buried treasure, and artifacts that might give a clue as to where it was hidden.

MacPherson suspected that Morgan had come across something—but he didn't know for sure. In any event, in responding to Will Chambers' discovery request, he would simply try to bury him in paperwork. He would send him a copy of every book, pamphlet, news article, and Internet story dealing with "Edward Teach, aka Blackbeard." He knew that there was almost no likelihood that Chambers would find anything useful in that information, at least regarding the innocence or guilt of Isaac Joppa.

Meanwhile, MacPherson would studiously avoid asking any further questions of either of his clients, Ludlow or Morgan, regarding Edward Teach or his treasure. That would insulate him from any duty to produce information to Chambers.

He pushed a button on his desktop and began dictating a letter:

Dear Mr. Chambers:

I'm in the process of giving you a full and complete response to your interrogatories and demand for documents in the case of *Joppa v. Ludlow,* as an ancillary proceeding in the matter of the estate of Randolph Willowby. I would appreciate you giving me a few extra days to complete our exhaustive response.

As promised, you will find me most accommodating and thorough in my responses to your requests for information.

Warmest professional regards,
Virgil MacPherson

After his dictation, MacPherson smiled and spoke to the empty room. "And, Mr. Chambers, I hope you and your pregnant wife enjoy your summer at the beach."

20

Jonathan Joppa had just finished baseball practice with his preteen church team. Now, a dozen of his boys were piling into Melvin Hooper's café for burgers and shakes, compliments of their coach.

The boys were collected in groups around the café. Jonathan had brought Hank, his dog, with him. And Hank was frolicking in between the tables. The boys were taking turns petting and tussling with the dog while they were waiting for their food.

Joppa sat down at one of the booths, alone, and eyed his team. Then he spotted one of the boys sitting alone.

"Hey, Ryan," Joppa called out. "Come here a minute."

The small, red-haired boy shrugged, slowly rose, and made his way over.

"Why are you sitting alone?" Joppa asked in a quiet voice.

"I dunno." He shrugged.

"Come on. Lay it out for me," Joppa said, prodding a little. "What's going on? Why are you sitting alone?"

"Coach, I don't know if I want to keep playing. I'm not doing good."

"Baloney," Joppa said with a smile. "You're doing much better. Your fielding has improved. You're starting to hit the ball. I'm proud of you. You keep it up, Ryan."

The boy's face brightened. "Okay. Does that mean I can start next game?"

Joppa laughed. "Let's take things one step at a time. You keep up the good work. I'll keep my eye on you. You know my philosophy—I try to play everybody—give everybody a chance. Now you go over and join the rest of the guys."

The red-haired boy smiled and skipped over to a table, then shoved his way in amid his friends.

Melvin Hooper came out of the kitchen, wiping his hands on his white chef's apron, and meandered over to Joppa's table. "It's going to be a couple more minutes for all the shakes and the burgers. The girls are getting the stuff ready for your team. They'll bring them out in a few minutes."

Joppa nodded.

"So—what's the team look like?"

"Honestly," he replied, lowering his head a little and talking in a low whisper, "we're going to have a tough time with the Baptists next weekend. They creamed us last season. They've got a great team again this year. So, we'll see…"

"Well, just for the record, I think you're doing a great job. It's too bad you don't have any help. Is that guy who brought some of the boys helping you out as assistant coach?"

Joppa shook his head. "No, he just picked the boys up after practice. I'm pretty much handling the coaching job myself. That's okay. I love it. I love being with the kids."

"Just the same, I think you need an assistant coach. Too bad your son can't help you out. He was a pretty good ballplayer in high school. I don't see him around much anymore…"

Jonathan couldn't manage anything more than a slight twitch on the side of his mouth. "He's busy. You know how it is when they start getting older…"

"Yeah. Sure. I know how it goes," Melvin patted Joppa on the shoulder.

"Hey, thanks for letting me bring Hank in here with the boys. I usually take him to the practices. I know it's probably a violation of the health code or something like that—to let a dog roam around a restaurant…"

"Don't worry about it," Melvin shot back with a wry smile. "At the rate things are going with my case against the city fathers, they're going to be closing down this restaurant just like they said. Pay me a little bit of money. And then shut me down. I don't think we're going to win our case. They're going to be laying that new highway just about where you're sitting now, in no time flat. It bothers me so much, I can't hardly even think about it…" Melvin's face flushed.

He turned to walk back to the kitchen and then remembered something. "Say—how's that new lawyer working out? How's your case coming?"

"Not bad. Attorney Chambers is just getting started on the case. It's a little too soon to know for sure."

Then Melvin called, "You want your shake to be chocolate, right?"

Joppa nodded and smiled.

"Keep the faith, Reverend Jonathan." Melvin gave him the thumbs-up as he disappeared behind the counter.

As Joppa leaned back against the plastic bench in the café booth and watched the rambunctious boys, he thought about Melvin's comment.

He interpreted it as a mere pleasantry—off-the-cuff. Because if Jonathan Joppa took it seriously, he knew he couldn't possibly "keep the faith." And that was exactly the sticking point. His position as the spiritual shepherd of the Safe Harbor Community Church required the very thing of him he knew he was incapable of.

21

Will SPENT THE DAY MOTORING DOWN the North Carolina coast along the waters of the Pamlico Sound. He was scheduled to meet with Susan Red Deer Williams at the Center for Indian Studies of the Carolinas, which was located at Bluff Point.

The center consisted of a one-story log cabin—a large, open room filled with displays of miniature Indian villages under glass, and two back offices. An older woman at the counter, with long black hair that reached down to the middle of her back, wearing blue jeans and a beautifully embroidered shirt, led Will back to Williams' office.

Susan Red Deer Williams was tall, almost Will's height, and had a square, thin face with high cheekbones. She had an athletic frame and wore her jet-black hair in braids. Her build was set off by long, dangling earrings made of multicolored beads, a plain blouse, and a spectacularly woven skirt with Indian designs.

As the lawyer entered the room with his briefcase, Williams rose slowly and extended a cautious hand. She did not smile.

Will thanked Williams for taking the time and indicated that he had been led to her by August Longfellow.

"Professor Longfellow and I, while we are cordial, do not always see eye-to-eye on Carolina coastal history—particularly when it concerns the Indian tribal groups and their treatment at the hands of the whites," Williams said bluntly.

"To be honest, I'm really not interested in starting up a new series of Indian wars down here."

Will smiled at his attempt at humor but Williams did not respond in kind. She glared at him and then said, "My time is limited, Mr. Chambers."

"Then let me cut right to the chase. I'm here because of an unusual probate lawsuit. There is a historical issue that has to be resolved in order to determine who gets a certain piece of property—"

But before Will could continue, Williams interrupted.

"After your initial phone call, Mr. Chambers, I did some research on the lawsuit you wanted to talk to me about. I'm well aware, because of all the newspaper accounts, of the litigation involving the last will and testament of Randolph Willowby. I'm also well acquainted with the background—apparently your client, this Christian minister, has hired you to prove that one of his ancestors, Isaac Joppa, was not guilty of piracy. You want us to prove that so he can get a piece of real estate and make a whole lot of money for himself…have I left anything out?"

Will smiled and tried to pour oil on troubled waters.

"I think you have the gist of it. But this isn't just about money. There's also a fascinating and very important historical mystery that needs to be resolved. For several hundred years Isaac Joppa's reputation, here in the Outer Banks, has been that of a fool, a coward, and a willing pirate on Blackbeard's ship. Reverend Joppa and I would like to find out the truth."

"Just so we're clear," Williams responded, "I'm not helping you because I want to see some rich white men get richer. So that lawyers can get paid huge amounts of money to represent their clients. Or so that the history books can be rewritten about what happened to Isaac Joppa at the Battle of Ocracoke Inlet. That's not why I'm talking to you."

"Well, perhaps you can explain it to me," Will said diplomatically. "Why are you meeting with me?"

"Because—for better or worse—I believe that the fate of Isaac Joppa was connected to the Tuscarora Indians."

"August Longfellow told me a little about that. There are some legends, among the Indians, that a white English pirate from Blackbeard's crew married an Indian princess."

Susan Red Deer Williams shook her head dramatically and sighed.

"I'm afraid Longfellow did not get it straight."

Will tapped his pen on his legal pad. He had traveled several hours for this meeting, entirely at August Longfellow's suggestion. Now, he was beginning to think he was on a wild goose chase.

"Well, perhaps you can straighten out the record for me." Will was trying to keep his demeanor professional.

"You have to understand," Williams said solemnly, "that what I'm going to tell you does not link Isaac Joppa to the Tuscarora Indians. Not precisely. And not by name."

Will leaned forward in his chair, eager to hear the rest of the story.

"First of all, you need to know something about the Tuscarora Indians. Are you familiar with us?"

"I can't say that I am. But I'd love to get some background."

"Well, the Tuscarora Indians helped the white English settlers here in the Pamlico Sound area in the early 1700s. Around 1710, things along the coastal area here were tough going. There were epidemics, wars, and a lot of mistrust between the English settlers and the indigenous Indian groups. Armed conflict broke out between the whites and the Indians in 1703, again in 1706, and yet again in 1707. The Tuscarora Indians began complaining, around 1710, that their Indian tribes were being subjected to kidnapping and that their lands were being stolen."

"I haven't heard of the Tuscaroras before," Will said. "Are they related to other Indian groups?"

"The Tuscaroras were the Sixth Nation of the Iroquois," Williams said, showing some pleasure in Will's interest in Indian history. "The fact is, they disappeared entirely from the Carolinas by somewhere around the early nineteenth century. By then they had relocated all the way up to upstate New York."

"Why the move?" Will asked.

"A lot of reasons. But what you need to know is that the Tuscarora Wars broke out between 1711 and around 1715. These were fierce battles. Bloodshed and atrocities on both sides. One of the Indian chiefs, King Bob Blount, was given a reward by the English when a treaty was finally worked out. Apparently he had been cooperative in resolving the wars, and so the English authorities in North Carolina appointed him as king over all the Tuscarora Indians, confining them to a reservation area near Lake Mattamuskeet. Not all the Indians were happy about that, of course."

"So how does this relate to Isaac Joppa?" Will said, trying to connect the dots.

"Remember, everything back then was oral history, transmitted from one generation to another by recitation. That's how the Indian history was passed down. Isaac Joppa's name never surfaced. But what we do know is, there was a lot of history recorded about an Indian chief named King *Bob* Blount. But you don't find his *brother* mentioned anywhere in the English history of the area. The brother's name was King *Jim* Blount. As the title *king* indicates, he considered himself a chief as well. But he was not given the favor of the English like Bob Blount was. And so, when the treaty was struck and his brother was made king, King Jim took his daughter, Priceless Pearl—that's the name she later used, and we're not sure what her original Indian name was—and took his warrior son, Great Hawk Blount, and headed off on his own, along with some other Tuscarora dissenters, away from the reservation area. King Jim Blount settled, for a while, with his son and daughter at Bluff Point."

"And so…" Will said, trying to probe further, "is that where they came in contact with someone you believe may have been Isaac Joppa?"

Williams nodded."Here is the story as it has been passed down from generation to generation. King Jim, Great Hawk, and Priceless Pearl had set up camp down at Bluff Point. Bluff Point extends out into the Pamlico Sound. It lies directly north by northwest, about fifteen miles or so, from the Ocracoke Inlet, where the battle between the English navy and Blackbeard's pirate crew took place."

Now Williams had Will's attention. "You think it's possible that Isaac Joppa met King Jim, his daughter, and his son there at Bluff Point?"

"All I know is that there was a white, English-speaking sailor. And he had been part of Blackbeard's pirate crew. And they met him there on the shore of Bluff Point. There was never an actual ceremony of marriage between Priceless Pearl and this sailor. But their encounter was…how do I describe this?" Williams' voice drifted off.

"Tell me about it," Will said eagerly.

22

"THIS IS THE STORY AS IT HAS BEEN PASSED DOWN," Susan Red Deer Williams began. "You have to realize how accurate the oral histories of the American Indians are. They were not, by and large, a people of written records. Rather, history was committed to memory. They relied on the ability to orally transmit accurate information about their exploits. Their battles. Their victories. Their defeats. The people that they encountered. And the events that mattered most to them."

"All right," Will said. "What you're telling me is that this story has a reasonable degree of credibility because of the fidelity with which the Indians would pass down their oral history...correct?"

"Exactly," Williams said with a half smile, recognizing Will's appreciation for her culture.

"So...what happened?"

"What I'm about to tell you is a story that has been communicated among the Tuscarora Indian tradition, and specifically those Indians down here along the Pamlico Sound."

Susan Red Deer Williams paused momentarily, leaned forward on her desk, and folded her hands in front of her. She was about to recite not only a small portion of the history of her people—but also the sketchy and woefully incomplete account of the remarkable occurrence between a Tuscarora Indian chief, his son, his daughter, and someone from Edward Teach's pirate ship.

❨ ❨ ❨

As Isaac Joppa lay in the sullen heat of the Indian hut, he recalled his knowledge of the Tuscarora Indians. Some of them had preferred to trade with the pirates—whose vessels carried goods from a variety of nations.

England had forbidden the import of foreign goods into the Carolinas, forcing them to accept English goods only. Some of the local merchants in Bath soon started buying stolen goods from pirates like Edward Teach. Soon, some of the Indians began following suit.

The Indians thought Isaac was a member of the pirate crew attacked by the English. Isaac concluded that was the reason they rescued him.

As Isaac pondered that, two more Indians entered the hut. One, a tall, barrel-chested man with a hook nose and a stern expression and who spoke a considerable amount of English, was identified as Chief King Jim Blount. He was accompanied by a young Indian man, who looked to be about the same age as the Indian girl.

At first, Isaac assumed the young warrior was the Indian girl's husband. But as he compared their faces, and observed their interaction, he concluded they were probably brother and sister.

Isaac had much he wanted to ask them, but he was so overcome by exhaustion that he fell asleep and slept soundly until the following day.

When Isaac awoke, he asked about the small porcelain plate he had been carrying in his shirt at the time he jumped off the ship—the one with the portrait of Abigail. The three shook their heads and shrugged. But finally they understood, when Isaac made the shape of a circle with fingers of both hands.

The big chief pulled out a deerskin pouch that hung from his neck, and produced the little plate, and displayed it to Isaac.

Isaac tried to reach out, but was stunned by a shooting pain in his back.

The chief stared at him and shook his head. Then he put the plate back in the pouch that hung around his neck and left the hut.

His young daughter, the Indian princess, smiled and lay down next to Isaac, caressing his face gently and speaking softly to him in her strange Tuscarora tongue.

For some mysterious reason, the Indian princess was claiming Isaac Joppa for herself. Isaac knew he owed his survival to these Indians. Yet, due to an inexplicably tangled set of circumstances—which were nearly incredible to Isaac himself—he knew he couldn't allow himself to be wooed into a relationship with the pretty Indian girl.

It would have been easy for Isaac to have compromised himself. He knew there were ways he could have rationalized it—reasons that included the great distance that separated where he was then from Bristol, England, which lay on the other side of the ocean.

But he could not permit this. Even though—as he studied the girl's smiling, inviting face—he knew what would happen if he rejected her. To spurn the invitations of an Indian princess would be considered an insult against her chieftain father—an outrage of the most unimaginable kind.

The consequences would be hideous. Death would likely be too quick and too lenient a punishment. He had heard of the exquisite tortures practiced by the Tuscaroras.

Joppa now had every reason to believe that, if he did not yield to the girl, he could soon face the worst they had to offer.

23

FOR THE LAST FEW DAYS, Will had noticed that his Corvette had an engine problem. Nothing major, but when it concerned his treasured vehicle, every problem was crucial. Particularly at higher speeds, the engine was stumbling—and there was hesitation in the combustion, particularly when he accelerated quickly from a stop.

Over the years, Will had done some of the mechanical work on his vehicle himself. And so, in the driveway of the oceanside cottage, he decided to replace the spark plugs. But that didn't solve the problem.

Then Will thought of Boggs Beckford at the hospital. Beckford had said something that had stuck in Will's mind. Beckford mentioned having contacted the best mechanic along the Outer Banks to evaluate his vehicle and why its steering assembly had failed. But he hadn't mentioned the name of the mechanic.

When Will called him, Beckford gave him the name immediately.

"Glen Watson. He's the guy for you. Particularly if you have a show-case vehicle like yours—a collector's item. What did you say—a '57?"

"That's right. And I don't want to hand it over to just anybody. This Watson guy sounds like just the ticket."

So Will drove over to Watson's Auto Specialists. The driveway of the garage was already crowded with a minivan—with steam cascading from under the hood—a truck with a dented vehicle in tow, and a local cab driver with a flat tire.

Will meandered through the confusion in the driveway and made his way to the office.

A mechanic who looked to be about thirty-five years old, in greasy overalls, was talking to someone on the telephone and, at the same time, responding to questions from the haggard tourist who owned the broken-down minivan.

Will was beginning to think he had picked the wrong day to try Watson's Auto Specialists. He mosied around the office, out onto the parking lot, and back into the office again. Five minutes went by. Then ten. Then fifteen.

When the young mechanic, who was the owner, Glen Watson, finally hung up the phone and finished with the distracted minivan driver, Will quickly stepped up.

"Mr. Watson, I'm sorry to bother you. I know you look like you're tremendously busy today. But Boggs Beckford—"

"Who?" Watson snapped.

"The attorney. Boggs Beckford. He referred me to you. You had evaluated his car—an accident involving the steering assembly."

"Oh, yeah, yeah, yeah," Watson said quickly. "Look, I'm really busy today…"

"I see that you are. It's just that I have this '57 Chevy Corvette…"

Watson's head snapped up, and he spied Will's red-and-white convertible in the corner of the parking lot. His jaw slacked slightly, and he began walking out of the office and onto the parking lot as if mesmerized.

"All original parts?" He ran his hand over the rear corner tail assembly.

"Absolutely," Will said.

"Oh man, oh man. '57. Great year. Is this the carbureted—or the fuel-injected?"

"Carbureted."

"Oh yeah. This is mint. This is really mint. Two hundred and eighty-three cubic inches. Two hundred and seventy horsepower. Optional Positraction rear axles."

The mechanic glided his hand along the thin, sculpted chrome that began on the driver's side door and ended at the front wheel well.

"Owoooo…" Watson cried out like a coyote in the prairie. "Yessir, this was a work of art. Oh—why'd you bring it in?"

Will explained the combustion problem.

"You changed the plugs already?"

Will nodded.

"If your plugs were oil-fouled, then the problem's probably a standard one. I think you may have an oil-pumping problem. Most likely you need to replace the piston rings. Not exactly cheap—but on the other hand, with a car like this, you don't want to go cheap."

Will quickly agreed and, with some hesitation, handed over the keys to Watson. The mechanic promised he'd get it done in forty-eight hours.

Will called Fiona on his cell phone and asked if she could come pick him.

Fifteen minutes later, she pulled up with the top down on her convertible, flashing her dimpled smile.

Will was walking over when he noticed someone pull into Watson's garage—someone in a gleaming black, double-axle truck with chrome detailing.

Fiona got out and walked over to the passenger seat and asked Will to drive. As he pulled away, he glanced back and saw Blackjack Morgan exit the truck, keys in hand, and begin walking toward the office, where Glen Watson was back on the telephone.

"Now, I wonder what's going on there," Will muttered, continuing to glance at Morgan in his rearview mirror.

24

AFTER LEAVING GLEN WATSON'S SHOP, Will and Fiona ran a few errands and then drove up to Elizabeth City for their rendezvous with Aunt Georgia at the rehabilitation center in order to visit Uncle Bull.

Bull's progress had been slow. There had been some complications from his stroke. He had aphasia on his left side, slurred speech—almost full loss of the use of his arm and left leg.

In the midst of it all, however, he was manifesting his characteristic inner strength and optimistic attitude.

He had struggled to articulate some comment. After a few moments of agonizingly failing speech, he took a pad of paper and a ballpoint pen, and slowly wrote, *Still have right side. God not left me.*

After the visit, Georgia was tearful. Will and Fiona comforted her and took her out to dinner. As Will talked a little about the Joppa case and Blackjack Morgan, Georgia's face was grim, and she grew strangely quiet.

They stopped by Georgia's house on their way home. She said she was quite tired and was going to turn in early. But while Fiona was occupied in the next room, Georgia quickly shared something with Will—about Bull and Blackjack Morgan.

Will listened intently. Though he said nothing in response, just kissed his aunt goodnight, he knew the complexion of the Joppa case had just changed.

As darkness fell, Will and Fiona went out on the small deck of the cottage, facing the rolling ocean tide. They lit candles and stretched out on their chairs, listening to the incessant surf and feeling the moist ocean air as it blew in with the tide.

The two of them caught up a little with each other. About Uncle Bull. How Fiona was feeling. Some of her goals in coming up with a few new songs for her next recording session. She said that the following day she was going to spend most of the day working on some music composition.

Will said he had been in touch with his office, but there were no real emergencies. He had asked Todd Furgeson, his associate, to do a public records search regarding Sylvester "Blackjack" Morgan, to determine whether or not he was involved in any other court cases. He had found only two.

The first was a very old docket entry, indicating criminal charges when Morgan was in the merchant marine. He was charged with assault with a deadly weapon and manslaughter in an incident in Nova Scotia. The records indicated that Morgan was acquitted of both charges.

Another record was a recent case in federal court in North Carolina. Will explained to Fiona how, according to their research, they had located a pending ship salvage case regarding a ship associated with Blackbeard— the *Bold Venture*—in which Blackjack Morgan had filed a petition against a Dr. Rosetti, asking the court for permission to take over the salvage operation—though his motion was denied.

"I put a call in to Dr. Rosetti's office when I found out about the case. I'm hoping, as an ocean archaeologist, he'll know some of the background of the battle at Ocracoke Inlet—maybe even some stuff about Morgan, his opponent."

Then Will remembered that he and Fiona had yet to discuss her recent visit with Frances Willowby.

Fiona described the meeting, the gorgeous mansion, and her impressions about Randolph Willowby's widow.

"With all her money and her beauty—even though she's well into her sixties—you should see how stunning she is," she remarked. "Still, there was this feeling of sadness when I was with her. Emptiness. I know she's certainly grieving over the loss of her husband. But it seemed to be something far beyond that."

"Did you learn anything about our case?"

"Well, it certainly sounds like Randolph had a conversion shortly before his death. She said he spent all his time reading the Bible. He probably got right with the Lord after he got the cancer diagnosis. But she also said he started developing an intense interest in his genealogy—particularly going back to Reverend Malachi Joppa. And she said he did make some comments, wondering whether Isaac Joppa was innocent of those charges. He also wondered whether Isaac had ever had a chance to be at peace with God after his decision to run away from things."

"Any indication why Randolph decided to give the island to Jonathan Joppa? Or why he wanted Jonathan to be the one to prove Isaac Joppa's innocence?"

Fiona shook her head. "I didn't get any answers to that. But there was something interesting. Something at the very end..."

"Like what?"

"I asked her whether Mr. Willowby had ever kept a diary. Or notes. Letters. I had the feeling she was uncomfortable with that. She cut the conversation short. Said she had things to do. And that was it."

"Where does that leave us?"

"Well, Mrs. Willowby did leave the door open for me to come back and talk to her again. And I definitely want to do that. Not only because of the case. But also on a personal level."

Will then shared his conversation with Susan Red Deer Williams in more depth than he had had a chance to previously. Then he thought of something that Williams had said at the end of their conversation.

"She told me there was *one piece* of tangible evidence that might be able to prove Isaac survived the Battle of Ocracoke Inlet, as the Indian legend had indicated. The Indians believe he was nursed back to health by the Indian princess and her family."

"What was the piece of evidence that she was talking about?"

"Apparently there was a small ceramic plate with a painted portrait of Abigail Merriwether. It ended up, somehow, in the possession of King Jim Blount."

Will studied the flickering candlelight within the hurricane lamp on the table. He listened to the surf and its rolling and surging.

"Apparently, years later, the descendants of King Jim Blount made a temporary return back to the Pamlico Sound area," he continued. "The plate supposedly was transferred from King Jim Blount to someone else— to a white man. That's when it left the custody of the Indians. Now the significance of the plate is this—Isaac Joppa apparently carried it on his person throughout his travels. If he was shot and killed, it would have gone down to the bottom of the ocean with him. On the other hand, if he survived, then he would have taken that plate with him. That's the most likely explanation of how the Indians got their hands on it—by coming into contact with Isaac Joppa. So, it does support the belief that Isaac survived the battle."

"Where's the plate now?"

"Williams gave me the name of this guy—she said he's a collector of oddities, so-called antiques, and quite a bit of ocean junk. He's inland, in the swamp areas. She gave me his name and directions on how to get there. She said the guy doesn't have a telephone—can you imagine that? He makes all his phone calls from a pay phone at a general store down the road."

"What's his name?"

"Oscar Kooter." Then Will smiled and added, "Apparently, his nickname is 'Possum.'"

"Why do I think that's your next visit?" Fiona asked with a cautious grin.

"Yes, I suppose you're right."

"You don't sound too excited about pursuing that lead."

"No, it's not that…" Will's eyes were now riveted on some unseen landscape. And, for the moment, Fiona was not in it. As Will talked, it was a soliloquy, not a dialogue. "It's just that all of this information I'm developing…all the evidence so far has indicated only a few things. First, that Isaac Joppa may have survived the battle that killed Edward Teach. He may have been taken in by Indians. He may at some point have been engaged to a woman in England, and may have had some sort of encounter with an Indian princess here in the Pamlico Sound area—though the Indians end up going one way and he goes another. But I keep wondering…how does any of this prove that Isaac Joppa was not a willing participant with Teach and his gang?"

Fiona reached out and took Will's hand and squeezed it.

But she didn't tell Will about the doubts she was now having about whether she should have encouraged him to take the Joppa case. Will had that look…she knew it too well. He was slowly becoming obsessed with winning…as he did in all of his cases. But now…with her first pregnancy, and their summer together…it was looking like this complicated case was becoming all-consuming for him.

Will broke out of his silence, noticed Fiona, and smiled back.

But he was holding something back as well. Georgia's conversation with him that night.

Georgia Chambers had confided in him that his Uncle Bull had been the presiding judge years before in the grand jury investigation of Morgan's drug enterprise. Bull had signed a search warrant for Morgan's homes and businesses. But the police search came up dry. Morgan retaliated—through attorney MacPherson—by filing a judicial ethics complaint against Bull

Chambers. Bull was being considered for a vacancy on the Court of Appeals at the time.

Morgan's frivolous but well-timed complaint was enough to bump Bull out of the running. And according to Georgia, he never quite got over the disappointment.

For Will, beating MacPherson and defeating Blackjack Morgan's obscure interests in the case had now become intensely personal.

25

FOR THE LAST FORTY-EIGHT HOURS Blackjack Morgan had been on the hunt for Orville Putrie. He wasn't in the shop. He was not over at Joppa's Folly. The secretary at Morgan's newly furnished real estate office had not seen him. And when Morgan called Putrie's house, he only got his answering machine.

So Morgan climbed in his black customized pickup truck and headed down the beach road.

At Putrie's handsome two-story beach house, he noticed, immediately, Putrie's car in the driveway. He yelled profanities at Putrie from inside the cab. Then he added, "I just pay these clowns way too much money." He grabbed his cane and quickly limped up the stairs to the front door. It was unlocked.

Somewhere, Putrie's stereo was blaring the frantic, industrial beat of techno-rock. Morgan made his way up to the second floor, where he found Putrie sprawled on the living room couch in his underwear. Junk food wrappers and empty soda cans were strewn all over the living room. Morgan looked at the coffee table and picked up a clear vial of a crystalline substance.

"Why, I do believe this would be crystal meth...or maybe angel dust..." Morgan held the test tube contents up to the light. "How much did you pay for this, genius boy? Whatever you paid for it, you could have got it cheaper through me. Hey, Putrie!"

But Putrie wasn't moving. Morgan bent down and grabbed him by his T-shirt, yanked him up off the couch, and then threw him down violently to the floor. Putrie opened two eyes...but separately, asymmetrically.

Morgan yelled his name again, but Putrie was still having a problem coming around. So Morgan bent down and yanked him up by the neck of his T-shirt, ripping it down the middle. Then he grabbed him, dragging him to the bathroom where he bent him over the bathtub and turned the cold water onto Putrie's head.

Putrie jerked his head up, gasping for air, but Morgan pressed it back down again under the water.

Putrie was spitting water and gagging, flailing his thin arms toward Morgan, who was amused at his reaction.

Then Morgan sauntered back into the living room, using his cane to knock empty cans off tables and look under the cushions on the sofa.

"You know, you've got a decent beach house, Putrie," Morgan said, casually hobbling around the living room. "But you live like some kind of zoo animal. I mean, look at this...you take absolutely no pride in your environment. Putrie...do you hear what I'm saying to you?"

After a few minutes, Putrie stumbled out of the bathroom, his hair, head, and torso soaked with water.

"What's the matter with you?" he whined. "Couldn't you see that I was sleeping?"

"No...you weren't sleeping. You were trashed."

"I was sleeping!"

"Putrie...you were brain-fried, spine-dried, garbage-dump trashed. And don't ever contradict me when I'm telling you something, you little creep..."

Putrie walked, wobbly-legged, to the living room where, he dropped like a dead weight into one of the chairs.

"You never got back to me," Morgan said, suddenly speaking in a soothing, reasonable voice. "You never got back to me about our interesting research project."

"Which research project are you talking about?" Putrie rubbed both of his eyes with his knuckles.

"The computer search for October 11, 1718, you moron!" Morgan screamed.

"I did your project. And I came up with exactly what I figured I'd come up with, considering the fact that you refused to give me the information I needed..."

"And exactly what's that remark mean?"

"The only things I found were a marriage certificate...having nothing to do with Edward Teach, or anybody involved with him. And one unimproved parcel of land way down the coast that was registered on that date. That was it."

"All right. Then you're going to do another computer search for me. The entire year 1718. The same geographical points I gave you before. But you're going to look for three letters. You're going to try to come up with what these letters stand for."

"Three letters?" Putrie ran his hands through his hair, scratching wildly.

"That's exactly what I just told you. Now listen carefully. The three letters are—I-Y-U."

Putrie dropped his hands to his knees and looked up at Morgan. After a few moments of concentration he laughed.

"I know what those three letters are…"

"You have no idea what those letters stand for," Morgan taunted him.

"I certainly do," Putrie said with a grin. "You must have figured that the two symbols on the shell are, in fact, three letters. The first symbol is the letter Y placed over the letter I. Therefore, you've concluded that the letters spell out…I-Y…and the third symbol is an upside down U. So it's I-Y-U."

"Sometimes," Morgan sneered, "you show these flashes of brilliance, Putrie. But, at other times…other times it's like I'm sitting on more brains than you've got in your entire head."

With that, Morgan burst into hysterical laughter.

"Oh, man, Blackjack…you've given me another incredibly complex and nearly impossible search." Putrie shook his head. "I've done some code breaking. The key to code breaking is to start with one part of the code—no matter how small—that you have the key to. You need a match on one small part of the undetermined code system. Once you have a determinant, then it's simply a matter of running through the variables. We need a key. We need to start with one of these letters."

Morgan was staring blankly at Putrie. He didn't much care how the eccentric genius figured it out. He just wanted the problem solved—and as soon as possible.

But Putrie's mind was beginning to work the problem like a Rubik's cube. "I know you don't want me to ask you…so I won't…but I know what you're after," he said with a twisted smile. "You want to know where Edward Teach put it. And if he put it anywhere…then it's land-based or sea-based. Either he hid it on a ship that went down or he put it on the land. And if it's on land, then somebody owns the land. And if Teach made a note to himself on that shell, using these symbols…then it may have something to do with land ownership—location on someone's land."

Morgan was still silent. Now he was bending forward, listening intently to Putrie's ruminations as he rambled on.

"So maybe I'll begin with the matrix of information and cross-index by land ownership that has a Y in it, or an I in it, or a U in it."

Putrie's eyes were fixed on the coffee table in the middle of his living room, staring at it as if he were looking right through the wood, right through the floor to something else.

"So I'll begin my search looking for land ownership under those three letters. But I'm going to start with one letter in particular. I'm going to start with the letter Y."

Now Morgan sat up straight, staring right at Putrie.

"Why are you going to start with the letter Y?"

"Because…in the last research you had me do I went through land records for the entire year of 1718. There aren't a lot of people whose last names start with I or with U. But there are a couple whose names begin with Y. In fact…"

"In fact what?" Morgan asked, his voice rising.

"I remember a guy who owned quite a lot of land. His last name started with a Y. He was doing land deals throughout 1718. Then he died. And after he died his wife sold that Stony Island to Malachi Joppa."

"What was his name?"

"Ebenezer Youngblood."

"This Youngblood guy owned the island."

Putrie nodded.

"Yeah…good thinking…"

Then Morgan rose, leaning on his cane, and walked over and patted Putrie on the shoulder.

"That sounds fine…good place to start…you do your computer geek stuff and get me some answers. I may even drop you a big bonus."

After Morgan had left, Putrie got up from the chair, searched until he found his thick-lensed glasses, and made his way to his computer room. He wasn't going to wait before starting on this project.

Putrie knew what Morgan was searching for, and he also knew that if he broke the I-Y-U code he would be the first man since Edward Teach who would know the location of Teach's treasure.

He smiled. When he broke the code, he would know where the treasure was before Morgan did. That would then present him with an interesting, even laughable, choice.

He could choose to tell Morgan immediately.

Or, on the other hand, maybe he wouldn't.

26

WILL DECIDED THAT HE WOULD SET OUT to locate and interview Oscar "Possum" Kooter.

That day was hot and humid. There was a haze in the sky that extended along the horizon, so that the line between the gray, iron-colored ocean and the sky was no longer discernible. The atmosphere above and the sea below seemed to be one unified expanse in the still, calm heat.

Will kissed Fiona goodbye and left the seaside cottage. It was already in the nineties, and it was only midmorning. In his island shirt and casual pants he was already sweating through to the leather of his bucket seats.

He was driving inland. Away from the refreshing sight of wide, deep water. Into the flatlands and the swampy regions of the coastal plains. Though not as plentiful as in the bayous of Louisiana or the tropical marshes of Florida, alligators could still occasionally be found there, Will had heard—within the black, odorous waters.

Will motored along an endless stretch of narrow country road. Tall grass and trees were mired in the canals on either side, and the air was overpowered with the stink of swamp gas. There was little sign of human existence for nearly an hour as he drove through the Alligator River basin. Occasionally a white crane would sweep overhead, and a possum or two would slowly edge along the dirt road.

Will slapped a baseball cap on his head to stop the sweat from stinging his eyes. Finally, he came to an intersection of dirt roads. The road he had been traveling intersected with another road—a clay-colored smaller one.

At the fork there was a gray, wood-sided general store—a square building with a tall false front to it and a lone gas pump outside. A large, rectangular sign simply said, *KOOTER'S*. The store could have been painted at one time, though Will was not sure in whose lifetime.

Then he noticed an elderly woman on the front step, sitting perfectly still. Her arms were slack, her shoulders slumped, and each hand was resting on a knee. She was wearing a dirty, loose-hanging dress. Her hair was disheveled and white as limestone.

"I'm looking for Oscar Kooter…" Will yelled out.

She gave him a funny look.

"*Possum* Kooter."

The woman nodded. Then she slowly, almost painfully, lifted an arm and pointed down the smaller dirt road. But she never spoke.

"Thanks," Will replied quietly. Then he began slowly driving down the rutted, clay-colored track.

After more than a mile of bouncing over the potholes and ruts, Will noticed something strange. Suddenly, the road had widened, and it was now paved with old, broken concrete. Weeds were sprouting in the cracks. An old highway sign on the side, entirely red with rust, had been blasted full of holes with buckshot. Whatever the name of the highway had once been, it was now long forgotten. Except by the local folks—like the old woman, perhaps. Or Possum Kooter. Wherever he was.

A half mile later Will saw a building up ahead. As he approached it, he saw that it was a house, of sorts. Out of the front, like a seagoing porch, the prow of an old, peeling fishing boat was jutting straight out.

The front yard was littered with corroded weather vanes, buoy markers, ancient metal signs advertising brands of talcum powder and molasses that had not been sold for decades, huge sea anchors standing upright, driftwood in all shapes, aged captain's wheels from sunken boats, crab pots, chipped and mildly grotesque lawn ornaments—chiefly of the deer and coachman-holding-lantern variety—and a bizarre collection, on the far side of the house, of old washing machines lined up in fairly regular columns.

Will pulled to a stop. Something, just a thought, warned him to keep the car running.

Dismissing the idea, though, he turned off the ignition and walked to the sagging front porch, which was directly adjacent to the ship that was sticking out of the house. Everywhere were piles of seashells, bird decoys, car license plates from several states, hubcaps, ropes, and fishing lures. There were piles of rubber boots and lamps, wooden crates with faded writing from foreign countries stamped on them. Some objects defied identification—like the large glass balls of various hues that were scattered around the porch.

Will stared. Like so many of the other oddities on the property, the balls looked to be part of an avalanche of flotsam and jetsam—as if the oceans of the world had deposited a part of their floating junk many miles inland. Here. At this strange house on the swamp flats.

Will looked closer at the large glass bulbs.

"Them's glass floats all the way from the Orient..."

Looking up, Will saw a man—short, stout, and with a full beard. On his head was a dirty captain's hat with a black patent leather brim that was cracked down the middle.

The man smiled, revealing a row of missing teeth on the bottom and a few missing on top. His eyes were ignited by some inner fire of information.

"From the Orient. Yessir. Singapore maybe. Or Hong Kong. The harbors of Hong Kong, I'd wager. The Chinamen, see, great fishermen them... see, them Chinamen would tie their fishnets with these glass floats at the corners. But sometimes they'd go loose. And the glass balls would float away. Sail away. Over the oceans. Hurricanes. Calm weather. Over they go. Weeks. Maybe years. Floating. Bobbing. On the waves. Down the coast. Around the horn. Past the Banks. And into the inlets. Can you imagine that, my boy? Down to where old Possum Kooter can get ahold of them. Treasures. All of them. Yessir. Treasures of the world. Come to rest. Here in my front yard."

"Mr. Kooter?" Will said, cautiously extending his hand.

"No mister. Just Possum. Possum to *you.* Possum to *everybody,"* the man shouted out and did not take his hand, but doffed his stained captain's hat.

"Okay," Will said, trying to break into Kooter's narrative. "Mr. Kooter—"

"Possum!"

"Sure. Right. Possum Kooter. I don't think we've ever met..."

"No, sir. I don't believe we have. Don't recollect. What's your last name?"

"Chambers. Will Chambers. I'm an attorney from Virginia. But I'm working down here in North Carolina on a case—"

"Chambers, you say?"

"Right. Will Chambers. As I was saying—"

"You got kin here in North Carolina?"

"Well, as a matter of fact I do. Anyway, I traveled down here—"

"Now let me see here...you kin to a judge by the name of Chambers?"

Will's eyes widened. He shook his head in disbelief and chuckled.

"Well, yes I am. I've got an uncle. Bull Chambers."

"Righto, yessir, just as I thought!"

With that, Kooter did a funny little sidestep, like a sailor doing a limping jig.

"You know him?" Will asked incredulously.

"No, sir. Can't say that I do. But I do know that there's a Bull Chambers…county judge, maybe? No…circuit judge. Circuit judge for a long time. Am I closing in?"

"Yes, you are," Will said. "He's been retired for a couple of years. But he was a circuit judge. He was pretty well known around the state…"

"Good judge?"

"Yes, he certainly was."

"Honest judge?"

"Tremendously honest," Will replied. "He's been sort of a hero of mine…"

"Good. That's real good. Because I got no truck with a dishonest judge. No offense intended…"

"No, sir. No offense taken."

"You interested in any of my treasures?"

"I'm afraid not. I'm actually here on a legal case. I had some questions for you."

"That's what I was afraid of. Lawyers. Always full of questions."

"I'll try to make this as simple as possible," Will began. "I'm trying to find out some facts about a man who lived several hundred years ago in the area of Bath, North Carolina. His name was Isaac Joppa. He was charged with piracy. At the time of the Battle of Ocracoke Inlet, when Edward Teach—Blackbeard—was killed, along with most of his pirates—Isaac Joppa was on board his ship. There was some question as to whether Joppa was one of Teach's pirates, or whether he just accidentally happened to be there at the time. Anyway, depending on what the facts are, my client, Reverend Jonathan Joppa of Manteo, North Carolina, may inherit an island under the last will and testament of Randolph Willowby."

"Willowby?"

"Yes," Will said, noting a flash of recognition on Kooter's face. "Do you know Mr. Willowby?"

"Know him? Why I manned his boats for twenty-two years. Before my injury. Before I went out on pension. First, I started handling his little flat boats, working the crab pots for his fishing and crabbing company. You know, the crab pots in and out of the inlets. Then he moved me up to captain of a couple of his fishing rigs. He was a right one, that Frederick Willowby. Full of gruff and bluff. Sure, he was an honest man. But he had a lot of vinegar. He had the sting of a Portuguese man-o-war."

"You said *Frederick* Willowby. Not *Randolph?*"

"No. Randolph was the kid. He picked up where the old man left off. And he was like his father—in some ways—but in some ways not. The old man was all business. Randolph…well…good at business too, I guess. But a little bit more friendly. He talked with the shop folks. To the fishermen. To the captains. He walked the aisles in the canneries and talked to the little people."

"You knew Randolph Willowby? You worked for him before your injury?"

"Sure. Last three years. Then I slipped from some rigging, fell fifteen feet to the deck of a ship. Broke my spine. That was it. The jig was up. I'm a pension man now."

"So…how well did you know Randolph Willowby?"

"Mr. Chambers…you got a whole lot of questions. And it's way too hot out here on the porch. You come on in where I got some fans set up. We'll talk."

Kooter wheeled and disappeared through the torn screen door, which slammed loudly behind him.

Will followed, still amazed at the revelation from Kooter. Amazed that this pilgrim from civilization, with his bizarre house of oddities tucked in the back swamps of North Carolina, had been personally acquainted with Randolph Willowby.

For Will, the task was now clear. He had to find out whether amid the labyrinth of Kooter's personal information there was at least a shred of evidence for Isaac Joppa's innocence.

27

"So, DID YOU EVER DISCUSS ANYTHING with Randolph Willowby about the history of the North Carolina coast, or Blackbeard the Pirate, or a man by the name of Isaac Joppa?"

Will and Kooter were seated in the stifling heat of the living room, surrounded by the incessant roar of floor fans and the flutter of newspapers flipping open and closed with the breeze from the fans. Kooter leaned back in a bent aluminum-frame beach chair.

"I did have myself a couple of conversations—just Randolph Willowby and me—when I worked for him. That's right. That's a fact."

"What did the two of you talk about?"

"Fishing, mostly. He grew up along the Banks like I did. We were both deepwater boys. Born and raised along the coast. We talked about them kind of things."

"Did you talk about anything else? About this Isaac Joppa person, who was a long lost relative of Randolph Willowby's?"

"Well, sir," Kooter said, taking off his stained pilot's hat and sweeping the sweat off his balding head, "there was one conversation…"

"And?"

"You see…even from when I was very young…I was always collecting stuff I found along the beach. Stuff that floated into the bays and the sound. Little treasures I bought and traded with other people who found things on the beach. So I'd tell folks about it once in a while. Randolph Willowby—I told him."

"Did you talk to him about something that you found?"

"Not exactly found…"

"Well, if it wasn't something you found, what was it?"

"There was this lighthouse keeper…back when lighthouses were not run automatically. They had lighthouse keepers, who stayed up in the lighthouses to make sure the lights were on and the ships were being warned.

Well, that lighthouse keeper had a son. Can't remember the father's name. But the son's name was Frank. Frank said he got this particular little piece… pretty little piece…from his dad. And his dad had gotten it from an uncle of his. Now that uncle had said that he got it from his dead father. Well… not exactly from his dead father…when you're dead you don't give anything to anybody. Fact is, that when this fellow's dad died, he found it in a trunk in his attic. Nobody really knows where it came from. Although, the uncle…he says that his dad had told him, before he died, that this little piece was kept by the Tuscarora Indians. And then was traded by the Indians to some white man. And the white man passed it down to his family. That was the family line I'm telling you about. And then, finally, it gets to the lighthouse keeper's son…and then it gets to me. Funny how things get passed down that way. I didn't pay that much for it. But at the time, this son of the lighthouse keeper acted like I was paying a lot of money for it. I figure it was worth a lot more than that."

"You talk about buying this *piece*…" Will said, running his hand down his shirt and pulling it away from his sweaty back. "What kind of piece are you talking about?"

Kooter looked at Will and laughed a little, as if he were enjoying his own private joke.

"You sure want to know all about that Isaac Joppa, don't you? Because if you find out about Isaac Joppa, then you're going to win your case. Is that about right?"

"Well…" Will considered his next statement carefully. "I'm trying to find out everything I can about Isaac Joppa, that's true. But I'm not sure whether the information you've got is going to help us win the case or not. First, I have to find out what you know…"

"Well, suppose I've got a piece…a pretty little piece…and it says something about Isaac Joppa. And it's the genuine, real-life article…"

"What kind of article?" Will was getting closer. He could feel it.

"Suppose I were to tell you that this lighthouse keeper's son sold me a little tiny plate. A plate with a picture of a pretty gal on it. A picture that had something to do with Isaac Joppa."

"You've got it? You've got the little plate?"

"And what if I tell you," Kooter went on, ignoring Will's last question, "that it has some information about Isaac Joppa and his being married. Would that be of interest to you?"

"You've got this plate? Where is it? May I see it?" Will asked emphatically.

"Well now…" Kooter spoke slowly and thoughtfully. "Did you know there's some talk about Isaac Joppa marrying this Indian princess? I heard about that story. A lot of people down here know about that."

"Is it true?"

"Well, there's another story, and I also heard that one. That Isaac Joppa didn't marry that Indian princess girl. That he couldn't have married her. Didn't want to marry her. I figure that little plate tells some of the story…"

"Where is it?"

"Mr. Chambers," Kooter said slowly, folding his hands in front of him with solemnity, "you see how many odds and ends and varieties of treasures I've got stacked here and there and everywhere around my place here? Do you see that?"

Will nodded, hoping that Kooter would finally get to the point.

"It would take me a whole long time to have to search high and low in this place to try to locate that little piece."

Will was starting to get impatient.

"Mr. Kooter," he said firmly, "why do I believe you know where every single item is in this place? It may look messy to the rest of the world, but I'm sure you've got things placed exactly where you want them, and you remember exactly where you put them. Isn't that right?"

Kooter threw his head back and began to laugh loudly. "I love you guys. You lawyers…you know all about my life, my business, my treasures…is that what you're saying? You know where I've hid things? You know where I put stuff? If I'm not mistaken, I thought you said this is the first time that you ever been down here and visited me."

Will leaned back, feeling the perspiration soaking his clothes, growing tired of listening to the roar of the fans.

"Mr. Kooter, let's talk frankly. Do you know where that plate is? And if you do, may I see it?"

Kooter swept the pilot's hat off his head again, this time very quickly, swiped his head with his hand, and placed it back on again just as quickly.

"Well, sir, here's how it is. I'm a busy man. I got responsibilities. If I were to take the time to look through this place, spending all kinds of time trying to locate that plate, well…the fact is, I think my time is worth something. Don't you?"

"What are you saying?"

"If I find this plate. And it shows that Joppa was married. And it has dates on it. Has information on it. It gives you some real good things about Isaac Joppa…and so you win your case. And your client gets his land. And he comes into all kinds of money. How's that going to help me? So, I figure we need some kind of little agreement here. Possum Kooter's got to come out ahead on this one..."

"Are you asking for money?"

"You got anything against money?"

"No," Will said. "Nothing against money. But I do have something against paying a witness under circumstances that might be improper. If I have to, Mr. Kooter, I could serve you with a subpoena and have you produce that plate..."

"*Possum.* Yes—sure you could. I know a little about the law. I know all about them subpoenas. But no subpoena...no piece of paper's going to make me find something that don't exist. Wouldn't you agree?"

Will now had a pretty good idea where Kooter was going. He was not going to be cooperative. And there was no way that Will was going to talk money with a man who was a potential witness. He had one final thought.

"If I were to serve a subpoena on you, I would be giving you a check for the standard witness fee according to the laws of North Carolina."

"And how much is them witness fees?"

"Not very much money. I'm afraid to say they are set by statute. Pretty nominal."

"Yeah. I was afraid of that too. See, I was looking to make some profit on this deal. This island's got to be worth a lot of money to your client. I sure would like to work out some kind of percentage—"

"Can't be done," Will snapped back.

Kooter jumped to his feet and extended his hand.

"Nice talking to you, Mr. Chambers." There was a hint of obligation in his voice. Then he motioned toward the screen door. His face had changed almost instantly. From that of an eccentric talkative neighbor to this—that of a landowner staring into the face of a trespasser.

As Will made his way to the front door, he wondered whether he would ever get to the truth about Isaac Joppa's supposed life of crime. Or his relationship with the mysterious Indian princess. Or his elusive love relationship with Abigail Merriwether back in England.

(((

That night Isaac Joppa turned away from the Indian girl, who lay next to him in the darkness of the animal-skin-covered hut. But at his back, he felt her—so close he could feel her breath on the back of his neck.

When he awoke, she was still there. That day she fed him and cared for his wounds. He was feeling stronger.

The routine of walking, eating, and gaining strength continued for several days. But by then, the Indian girl had become more persistent. At night she would run her hands over his chest, wrapping her limbs around him. As Isaac gained his strength, he was also finding it more and more difficult to resist the temptations.

The moment had come when he had to make his intentions clear. He would reject her in a very clear, physical way. Then, in the middle of the night when she was asleep, he would slip out of the hut, make his escape, and head south along the coast.

But that night when Isaac pushed the Indian girl away, saying "no" in a loud voice, the girl pushed back. Then she began yelling at him in her own language. She stood up and ran out of the hut.

Isaac immediately sprang to his feet and prepared to run. But before he could, the chief and the brother tackled him and dragged him into the clearing in the middle of the camp. The chief struck Isaac in the head with a club, knocking him into unconsciousness.

When Isaac awoke in the morning, he was lying on his back. One arm was tied to one tree, and the other arm tied to a tree in the opposite direction. One of his legs was also tied to yet a third tree. The bugs and mosquitoes had spent the night feasting on his naked torso, and now he was in agony, unable to scratch or move.

So, he thought to himself, *this is how it begins. And how it ends.*

When the chief arrived with the brother, Isaac braced himself. Then he noticed that the brother had a knife in his hand, which he displayed with great flourish. The Indian muttered something and then placed the blade against Isaac's throat. Isaac's heart was pounding so hard his naked chest was pulsating visibly.

Yet, to his relief, the young Indian man then took the knife and cut him loose from the ropes.

But any hope was to be short-lived. The brother dragged him to the center of the clearing. The Indian girl was sitting off to the side, rocking and weeping, and the chief was standing nearby with a spear in his hand.

The brother then tossed the knife to Isaac, taunting him and pointing to the knife on the ground. Now it had become clear. Isaac must fight the

Indian brother, who would defend the honor of his rejected sister and of his father.

For an instant, Isaac thought of running. But he looked at the chief with the spear in his hand. He had heard that the Tuscaroras could take a deer down at a hundred paces. And he certainly could not outrun the brother in any event. On the other hand, neither was he likely to win a knife fight with this young warrior.

Think. Think, he urged himself silently.

Then it came to him. A sermon he had once heard from his father, Malachi. It was an Old Testament story about David—how he had escaped from certain death by feigning madness.

Isaac suddenly dropped down on all fours, the knife on the ground just inches away from his face. He kicked his legs out from behind him like a mule. Then he started braying and snorting. Saliva began dripping down his chin. He shook and rolled on the ground, his eyes open wide with a wild look.

The young Indian man rushed up to Isaac, thrusting his knife at him menacingly. But Isaac ignored him, sometimes shouting, sometimes singing and rolling on the ground.

The Indian yelled. Then screamed. Then he moved to within an inch of Isaac, who was back on his hands and knees. The Indian continued to challenge Isaac to pick up the knife.

More yelling. The Indian was now half standing over Isaac, berating him and shaking with rage.

Then Isaac made his move.

He lunged for the Indian's legs, pulling him off his feet and violently throwing him to the ground. The Indian landed on his back hard, and his head whipped back, striking the ground with a spine-rattling smack.

Isaac grabbed his knife, jumped on top of the dazed Indian, and held it to his throat.

It was over. The chief's face, as he stood off to the side, was frozen. He expected to see his young warrior son killed. There would be no disgrace in that. After all, his son had protected the honor of his family.

But instead, Isaac stumbled to his feet, displaying the knife for all to see, and then threw it to the ground. Great Hawk, the son of the chief, couldn't believe it.

Isaac's legs buckled. His back, not fully healed, was wrenched with pain. And now he was feeling dizzy from the blow to his head. He made it back to the hut and dropped to the ground—and passed out.

28

WILL CHAMBERS WAS GETTING TIRED of pursuing a case that was going nowhere. So, perhaps out of desperation more than anything else, he thought that a visit to Stony Island might turn up some visual indication—a physical clue perhaps—about why Randolph Willowby had created the exceptionally unusual condition in his will.

Will and Fiona were to rendezvous with Jonathan Joppa over at the Safe Harbor Community Church in Manteo. They would meet mid-morning and boat over to Stony Island.

Joppa drove the three of them to a small boat landing on the sound. He rented a comfortable-sized outboard for the day and motored them across to Stony Island.

Joppa slowed the engine as the island's features came into view. Unlike most of the islands along the Outer Banks seacoast, which tended to be windswept, either bordered with sand dunes or consisting of marshy grounds, low to the ocean level, this one was rimmed, with large rocks and pine trees. There was a substantial rise to the top of the island. A person up there could gain a prominent view through the wide mouth of water separating Portsmouth Island and Ocracoke Island and could see beyond, out to the vast blue horizon of the Atlantic.

Joppa cut the motor and drifted up to a small wooden dock. A few of the planks jutted out of place. Jonathan tied up, and Will stepped out onto the dock. Then he and Jonathan both gingerly reached down and helped Fiona up and out.

The trio walked up the path that stretched from the dock to the top of the island. Will was walking with Fiona, urging her not to exert herself.

At the top, Jonathan pointed off to the south end of the island, where they could see a grove of trees and a gate of some sort.

"That's the family cemetery of the original owners of the island. They were given the charter by the English crown."

"Who was that?" Will asked.

"Youngblood. Ebenezer Youngblood was his name."

Will suggested they check it out.

They made their way to the rusted iron gate. There was an iron picket fence, equally corroded, that surrounded the small plot of ground. In the middle of the small cemetery there was a dark oak tree of immense size, with long, gnarled limbs that stretched out in all directions. The thick branches extended over and out of the graveyard.

There were five gravestones. One was tilted sideways, actually partly subsumed within the trunk of the tree.

"Someone must have planted the tree too close," Will remarked. "When the tree grew, it just sucked that grave marker right into it."

"Look," Fiona said, pointing to a smaller gravestone "It looks like an outline of a little lamb on this one."

"That's probably the Youngblood's infant son. He is buried here," Joppa noted.

"How old was he?" Fiona asked.

"Just a few months old, as I recall."

"Who are the others?" Will asked.

"One is Ebenezer," Joppa explained. "One is his wife—she sold the island to Malachi Joppa after Ebenezer died. But she got Malachi to promise that even though he owned the island from that point on, she could be buried with her husband and son when she died."

"And the other two?" Fiona asked.

"Those are Ebenezer's mother and father. They died before him."

"Can we tell who is buried where?" Will asked, squatting to try to read the indecipherable marks on the gravestones, which had been rubbed smooth over three hundred years.

"Except for the child's, not really. At least, I haven't been able to read them."

The group left the cemetery and tried to close the gate, but it was rusted open.

As they walked, Will wondered at his client's extensive knowledge of the island—and of its history. But he chose not to pursue it—at least not then.

"Let's go over to the remains of the Youngblood house," Joppa suggested.

Fiona spotted a roughhewn bench at the edge of the clearing, with a nice view of the ocean.

"I don't want to be a spoilsport," she said with a smile, "but I'm winded. I think I'll go sit down on that bench. You two go ahead."

Will and Jonathan picked up the pace, walking quickly across the clearing, and down a path until, in the midst of a group of overgrown trees and bushes, they saw the remains of an old house.

Two stone chimneys still stood upright. The stones of the foundation showed a rough outline of the perimeter of the house.

"This is the home built by Ebenezer Youngblood," Joppa said.

In front of the house—one to the left and one to the right—were two stone pots, each about two feet high, with onion-dome tops.

Will noted the name *YOUNGBLOOD* in block letters faintly appearing on both of them.

After walking amid the ruins of the house for a few moments, Joppa suggested they visit one more site—the existing log cabin at the north end.

En route, they traversed a wide, open area of sandy soil and pine needles—about the size of a football field. Then they arrived at the "cabin."

It had been built, Joppa explained, in the 1930s by Randolph Willowby's father. Will was surprised at its size. It was a large lodge built of whole logs fitted together, with a broad porch.

The two walked through it. The rooms were all vacant. The main room was a huge living room with an immense stone fireplace and a tall open-beam ceiling.

"This place reminds me a little of our home—Fiona's and mine—back in Virginia," Will said with a smile.

"Randolph Willowby stayed here when he was a boy," Joppa remarked. "After he died, they took all the furniture out."

After walking through the lodge, the two men walked outside. Will noticed an outhouse in the back.

"No indoor plumbing?" he said with a laugh.

"Guess not."

Will walked to the edge of the clearing that faced the open ocean. From there he could see the bright colors of several sailboats off in the distance. Even farther was the tiny outline of an ocean tanker slowly plowing the waters.

"Quite a view," he remarked.

Joppa nodded but said nothing.

After a minute or so, Will broke the silence.

"I'm impressed with your historical knowledge of this place. Did you do your own research?"

Joppa studied Will before he spoke.

"Some."

"You get any information from anyone else?"

Another pause.

"Yes. You might say that."

Will knew he had to start digging.

"Look, Jonathan. Don't think I'm prying. But I would like to know how you know so much about this place. The history. The characters involved. It may help me to win your case."

Joppa looked out toward the blue ocean.

Then Will thought back to something Fiona had told him about her interview with Frances Willowby.

"Jonathan," he said directly, "there is something I need to know."

Joppa eyed his lawyer closely.

"I need to find out...whether you ever discussed this island, personally, with Randolph Willowby. In that one contact you said you had with him."

After glancing off into the distance for a moment, Joppa answered his lawyer.

"Yes, I did. When we had our meeting."

"When?"

"Not long before he died."

"Where?"

"Here."

"On the island?"

"Yes."

"Randolph Willowby met with you right here on Stony Island? Why didn't you tell me that before?"

"Everything I thought was important—the history of this place as Randolph explained it to me—I just shared with you today."

"What else did the two of you discuss?"

"Other than the island—and the historical information?"

"Yes. What else did you talk about?"

Joppa was visibly uncomfortable. He put his hands in his pockets and studied the ocean. Finally he responded.

"Let's leave it this way...anything else we discussed doesn't really have anything to do with this case."

Then he turned and quickly started walking to the midpoint of the island, where Fiona was waiting on the bench.

Will followed, but walking slower.

As he strolled, he was pondering this last, strange interchange with his client. And he was thinking about Stony Island—with its vast view of the Atlantic, and its three centuries of birth and of life. And, of course, of death.

29

"I THOUGHT YOU SAID WE WERE EVEN UP. I thought everything was paid and I was in the clear."

Terrence Ludlow was standing behind the bar at Joppa's Folly. He was nervously drumming his fingers on the counter.

Blackjack Morgan was sitting on a barstool, tapping his cane on the floor.

"Yeah. Sure. And after this job, you will be all paid up."

"That's what you said the last time." Ludlow grimaced.

"Look, Ludlow," Morgan said casually, "let's do the numbers. Let's add it all up. First, you got all the gambling debts you owe me from our little casino. I can't help it that you're a consistent loser…And then there's the expensive little white party dust I provide to you—at a discount I might add—on a regular basis. Now anytime you want to stop using—all you have to do is say, 'I'm not using anymore.' But as it is, you keep asking, and I keep supplying. And you ran up a big tab."

Ludlow was shifting nervously.

"You said all I had to do was sign that piece of paper giving you the island if we win the lawsuit—and that was it."

"Sure. That was part of it."

"Then you want me to handle some incoming shipments for you. So I'm the bag man."

"Yeah, so? That was also part of it…"

"Now you want me to do something else. This stinks. I want to know this is the last of it. The end."

"Absolutely. You can count on it." Morgan smiled. "All you got to do is drop a small package of highly refined beautiful stuff at an address I'm going to give you. It's for a very special person."

"Am I supposed to pick up some dough at the drop-off, or what?"

"No. No money. I'm giving this as a free sample."

"So—who's the delivery to?"

Morgan asked Ludlow for a telephone directory. Ludlow bent under the bar and pulled it out.

Morgan flipped it open about halfway and turned it around, so that the residential telephone listings were facing the bartender. Then he took his index finger and pointed to a name and address.

Ludlow stared, then looked up at Morgan in disbelief.

"You got to be kidding," he said with an anguished look on his face.

"Do I look like a stand-up comedian?" Morgan sneered.

"Oh, I can't do this…this is way too close for comfort. How am I supposed to do this? What if somebody sees me?"

"You make sure nobody does. You slip into the place when no one's looking. You put it down on the kitchen table or some other obvious place. And then you get out."

Ludlow stared at the name and address in the phone book, swallowing hard and rubbing his forehead.

Morgan was studying him carefully. Looking beyond his furtive, twitching eyes. Beyond his pasty, yellow-gray complexion. Morgan spoke.

"I know what you're thinking. Maybe you'll drop a package off all right, but it'll be a package of sugar, not the real stuff. After all—how would I know? Or maybe you'll say that you did it—but you won't have because you're afraid that it could be tied back to you. That's the kind of stuff that's going through your mind. And you see, I know all that. And I know when it's all said and done, you're going to realize it isn't going to work. The only thing you can do is to follow my orders—exactly. Because if you don't, nothing else is going to matter. Because if you don't do exactly what I want you to do, someone's going to find you washed up on the beach. *There's Terrence Ludlow. Face-up on the beach. The birds picking at his eyes.* Now, that'd be a sad day for you, Ludlow, wouldn't it?"

The other man was going to respond, but they heard someone step into Joppa's Folly.

Orville Putrie was standing in the doorway, grinning. He had some papers in his hand.

Morgan stepped away from the bar and motioned to a table at the far end of the tavern. "C'mon over to my office."

Stretching his bad leg straight out, he nodded to Putrie, who had quickly sat down across from him.

"Let's go. What do you have?"

"Okay. About the I-Y-U business…"

"Keep your voice down," Morgan said in a hoarse whisper. "So what about it? You find something out?"

"First of all," Putrie said with a flourish of self-congratulation, "you have to understand how much data I had to go through. You have no appreciation. For me to run multiple vectors of information. And to look for a convergence. I mean, I'm good. I'm really good."

"So…lay it out for me. What do you got?"

"This is what I got." Putrie placed a few photocopied pages in front of him.

They were from an old magazine dated 1935. The article concerned excavation of the ruins of the house of Ebenezer Youngblood. By that time nothing had been left except for the two chimneys, part of the foundation, and a few other interesting architectural features.

Morgan stared at the photograph that figured prominently in the article. It showed several men digging around the foundation. After a few more moments, he threw it on the table and looked at Putrie.

"Don't waste my time. What's the point here?"

Putrie was giggling and shaking his head.

"Blackjack, look again. Look at the picture."

Morgan glanced again at the photograph, then at the words under it. Then he looked more closely at the photo. Now Morgan had a big grin on his face, and began humming, off-key, some unknown tune.

Grinning so broadly that he was revealing one of his gold teeth, he started laughing, took the photocopy, folded it carefully, and put it in his top pocket.

Putrie was grinning and laughing too. But for a different reason.

He had made his decision. He had chosen to reveal the latest information to Blackjack Morgan. But Putrie also had his own game plan—an intricate mental construct, a result of his research into Edward Teach, his missing treasure, Stony Island, and the history of that section of the Outer Banks. And he did not share that.

As Morgan and Putrie both laughed, looking at each other, the younger man was thinking about his private little joke.

And Orville Putrie had his own idea about who, sitting at that table, was going to have the last laugh.

30

"Aren't these flowers absolutely delightful? They really are my favorites. I even learned the technical name…Sarracenia flava. But we call them trumpet pitcher plants."

"They do…they really do look like long trumpets…or like a long, thin vase, looking up to the sky. Do they catch water?"

"Yes. They are indigenous to the North Carolina swampy areas. And isn't the yellow color just the most beautiful thing?"

Fiona agreed, as Frances Willowby finished giving her the little guided tour of the Willowby gardens.

The two of them entered the conservatory. The maid was already there setting the tea and dessert cart.

"As I recall, you like your tea with sugar and cream and a little lemon." Mrs. Willowby motioned for the maid to pour the tea.

"How thoughtful of you to remember," Fiona said brightly.

"And you enjoyed our freshly baked scones—so I had some brought with the tea today."

The maid pulled the sliding glass doors shut as she left.

"So how are you and your husband enjoying your summer here along the Outer Banks?"

"Oh, it's a lot of fun," Fiona said with a smile. "The change of pace has been fantastic."

"And your singing career. Your music. Are you taking a break from that this summer also?"

Fiona laughed. "Well, I'm supposed to work on composing a few new songs. The plan was for me to rough out a few of them this summer. Then to turn the roughs over to my musical director, who was going to do all of the instrumentation. Fill in the scoring. And then make some tentative plans for a recording session next year after I have my baby. Will and I have already been talking about building a recording studio on our property, next to our home in Virginia. That way I wouldn't have to leave the family every time I cut a new CD."

Frances Willowby was delicately sipping her tea from a china cup, but she was studying Fiona carefully. "It must be wonderful to have a musical ability like that."

"Oh, and I was just thinking what a remarkable, accomplished woman you were. A famous model when you were younger. Then you leave that career, get married to Randolph Willowby, and become one of his closest advisors in his business pursuits. And then you help design and build this beautiful estate. And what a green thumb! I know you have staff to help you, but I was so impressed that you designed the gardens yourself and did many of the plantings."

Mrs. Willowby's eyes brightened, and she smiled warmly. She wondered what it was that she liked so much about this young pregnant woman whose life was so very different from her own. "How is your pregnancy coming—if I may ask?"

"That's fine," Fiona said. "Thanks for asking. Very smoothly. We came down to the beach for the summer so I could take it easy because of some complications I had in the first trimester. But everything seems to be okay. I've had no further problems. The Lord's been very good to us."

The older woman narrowed her eyes and pursed her lips ever so slightly at Fiona's last comment. After a slight pause, she spoke.

"Did you have problems driving over here yourself? I would have been glad to send my chauffeur to pick you up."

"That's so kind. But I still drive myself around. I like the feeling of keeping active."

"How is the case coming for Reverend Joppa?" Immediately after she said it, she added, "Or perhaps I shouldn't ask that. I know when cases are in court you can't always talk about them."

"Thank you for asking. As you can imagine, it's a very difficult process. Trying to piece together what happened several hundred years ago." As she spoke, Fiona tried to ignore the feeling that Will was emotionally abandoning her because of his increasing commitment to the Joppa case.

But she looked at Frances and dutifully decided to delve a little deeper.

"That's the reason I asked you about your late husband the last time I was here. I was really wondering whether your husband had any specific information about the history of Isaac Joppa. Or the charges of piracy against him. Anything that may have led your husband to believe that Joppa was innocent of those charges."

"Is there something in particular that makes you believe my Randolph may have had some information?"

"Not really," Fiona said. "It's just that my husband, Will, thought there must have been a motivate for Mr. Willowby to put that in his will. He must have had some idea that Joppa's innocence could be proven."

Frances Willowby looked away, gazing out through the windows into the garden beyond. She seemed distracted.

"You like coming here, don't you?" she finally asked. "I can tell. You're a woman who lets her enthusiasms show. I like that."

Fiona smiled and looked down, blushing.

"Am I that easy to read?" she asked with a laugh.

"Oh, it's not all that bad," Mrs. Willowby said. "To be transparent. To be honest in what you feel. And what you show to other people. No, it's not that bad at all."

The older woman had a wistful look on her face as she glanced down momentarily. After a moment of reflection, she continued.

"Randolph and I...we had something very special...a wonderful marriage..."

Fiona watched her patiently and nodded.

"Yet..." Her voice trailed off.

"And yet...as he stood facing death...fighting cancer...he changed. Partly, I felt it was for the best...but part of me longed for the old Randolph. The man I had fallen in love with. Wild, yet ferociously disciplined. Brilliant mind, yet full of the mischief of a ten-year-old boy. Successful in his business endeavors far beyond what most men can ever imagine. But there was still a side of him that was ordinary, perhaps even humble. He loved people. And he loved me..."

Frances Willowby bent her head forward into her hands. "What is it..." she went on, her voice quivering, "about love...that is so...so impossible, and so painful?

"When you came here for the first visit," she continued, composing herself, "I thought perhaps it was my sense of embarrassment—"

"Embarrassment?" Fiona asked, slightly befuddled. "Embarrassment about what?"

"About the secrets...the little confidences...perhaps not important to anyone else except Randolph and me..."

Mrs. Willowby straightened up, putting her hands in her lap, and stared directly at Fiona.

"I imagine you love your husband very much."

"With all my heart. And all my soul…" Fiona said, trying to decipher the comments from the other woman.

"And if your husband were to die…and something that he wrote…" Frances continued, "some comment which might be embarrassing or questionable, even in the smallest little way…you would probably not want others to read it, would you?"

Fiona was beginning to understand. Frances knew something, but her loyalty to her husband and his memory, and the love they had shared, had kept her lips sealed till now.

"It must be so very hard for you," Fiona said with sympathy, "to have to share facts about your late husband with a stranger like me."

Frances smiled and raised a finger for emphasis. "I may not know you very well, Fiona…but I could not now call you a stranger. From the very first I felt some connection between the two of us. I can't explain it. But perhaps—when all is said and done—by the end of this summer, before you return to Virginia…perhaps we'll be friends."

Fiona leaned forward, her hands clasped in her lap. "I would like to be your friend, Frances. I would like that very much."

Frances didn't respond, but gazed away off into the distance. Then she turned—not as if she were rising to leave the room, though. She reached over to a drawer in the end table next to her and pulled it open slowly. There was a thin black leather book lying in it, which she carefully picked up.

Frances held the black leather book in both hands, clutching it to her chest.

"The last six months of his life my Randolph kept a diary. You must know how I struggled. There are no scandals here, no lurid secrets…simply Randolph's thoughts in the last months of his life. But there are some comments…some concerning me…that were difficult for me to read. Fiona, I would ask only that you remember how much he and I loved each other as you read this diary. And as you and your husband decide whether it may be of any use in your lawsuit."

She held the book out tentatively. As Fiona took it she also took Frances's hand in hers and squeezed it.

"I can only imagine how difficult this is for you…and how courageous it is for you to want the truth to come out, whatever it might be. You can rest assured that my husband, after reviewing this diary, will use only the information he feels is absolutely essential to his case."

Frances nodded, although some uncertainty still lingered on her face.

"And yet," Fiona continued, "as important as this diary might be, I'm not here just for those things. You have to know that."

The older woman studied Fiona and gave her a half smile.

"What do you mean by that?"

"I wanted to meet you again because I enjoy being with you. Because I find you to be a fascinating woman. Because I feel we could be friends. And also, I had the distinct impression there were some unresolved questions weighing on your heart."

Frances tilted her head ever so slightly. Then she placed her hands in her lap and looked straight at Fiona.

"Perhaps there are some things that need to be said. Some questions… things I need to get off my heart. I don't know about your schedule…do you have the time?"

Fiona placed her hands tenderly on the round contours of her belly and replied with a broad smile. She didn't know whether it was because of Will's preoccupation with the case…or her own fears about her pregnancy. But whatever it was, she was treasuring her talks with this lonely, cultured millionairess.

"Frances, I have all the time in the world."

31

F IONA DROVE HOME TO THE SEA COTTAGE and showed Randolph Willowby's diary to Will, who was buried in books on the history of piracy and paperwork from the Joppa case.

After glancing at the diary, he gave it back to Fiona and suggested she read every word, making notes of anything significant for their case.

"You're no fun," Fiona muttered quietly to herself.

"What?"

She repeated it, this time loudly.

"What does fun have to do with it? We've got a case to win," Will said firmly.

"What happened to the guy who was going to pamper his wife?"

"What about the wife who insisted that her husband take this case?"

Will was tempted to point out that they would not just be winning this case for Reverend Joppa—not even for Isaac Joppa's tarnished reputation. It would be a victory, of sorts, for Uncle Bull. Striking a blow for justice against Blackjack Morgan.

Instead, he refocused on the pile of information in front of him on the kitchen table.

There was a moment of silence. Then the combatants separated. Fiona, a little sullenly, took the diary out to the front porch, where she eased herself into the hammock to read.

Will had been searching for an expert witness with strong credentials in the area of early American history, particularly focused on the Carolinas. He had located Dr. Derek Hubbel at Yale University. He taught that exact subject—and had published several scholarly books on it. Will asked Jacki Johnson back at the firm to contact Hubbel.

Meanwhile, Will had to try to get hold of Dr. Rosetti to see if any of his background information about Blackjack Morgan, or about the battle with Edward Teach at Ocracoke Inlet, would help him prove Isaac Joppa's innocence.

Rosetti was loading gear onto his research ship when he got the call on his cell phone. He was not happy.

He snapped the phone open as he swung a waterproof briefcase and an armful of yellow rain slickers over the side of the ship.

"What?" he yelled. "Who is this?"

"My name is Will Chambers. I'm a lawyer. I need to talk to you—"

"Lawyer? I've got no time for lawyers..." Rosetti snapped, then yelled out to the crew on board, who could not hear him clearly anyway, "Like I have time for lawyers! We're finally getting this project underway and I get a call from another lawyer..."

"Let me explain—" Will countered.

"No. I'm going to explain to you. You're going to listen, whoever you are..."

"Chambers...Will Chambers..."

"Sure. Mr. Chambers. Great. I've got a crew of twenty-five on two ships—I've got a salvage trawler and my research vessel. We're fueled up. Ready to ship out. The clock is ticking and I don't want you to ever call me on my cell phone again..."

"Edward Teach..." Will said quietly.

Rosetti paused.

"What did you say?"

"Teach. As in Edward Teach. Blackbeard. I'm handling a legal case dealing—at least indirectly—with Teach. It actually involves a presumed member of Teach's crew. Isaac Joppa was his name. He was aboard Teach's ship. I thought maybe you and I could help each other—"

"I know this case. What's the name?"

"Joppa. Isaac Joppa."

"I know this. Is this the case involving some guy's will? The North Carolina Court of Appeals ruled on this, right?" But he did not let Will respond.

"Look, Chambers. I've checked every piece of documented evidence on the life of Edward Teach—specifically the ships he sailed. Where he sailed. Their routes...where they moored...where they weighed anchor...and even more specifically, any bit of information on the *Bold Venture* that he scuttled—"

"What I'd really like to do is talk to you."

"Okay. Listen, Mr. Chambers. I read your case. This Joppa lawsuit. I thought it might shed some light on our work with the *Bold Venture*. But it didn't. Your lawsuit has nothing to do with our salvage project."

"Blackjack Morgan," Will blurted out quickly before Rosetti could hang up.

"What did you say?" the other man asked, holding the cell phone closer to his ear. "Say again?"

"Blackjack Morgan. He was an intervenor against your court petition for salvor-in-possession status in the *Bold Venture* project."

"So?"

"He's involved…in a manner of speaking…in our probate case."

"Define 'in a manner of speaking.'"

"He's paying all the bills of the opposing attorney. He wants possession of Stony Island. To do that, he's going to try to prove that Isaac Joppa was guilty of piracy in 1718."

Rosetti paused to think.

"What do you know about Blackjack Morgan?" Will asked, probing.

"What do I know? Well, I know he's a slug…" After a moment's reflection, he added, "No—change that—Blackjack Morgan is the slime that the slug leaves behind."

"Did you know he's a drug dealer?"

"Doesn't surprise me. It wouldn't surprise me if you told me he killed his grandmother with a butcher knife, had her stuffed by a taxidermist, and then hung her on his living room wall. Nothing would surprise me about that guy…

"Look, I've probably said too much already…I really don't know you."

"I read some of the transcript in the last motion that Morgan brought," Will countered. "I know he's going to be a thorn in your side throughout the project. I really think we ought to spend a few minutes talking about some of our common interests, and do a mutual exchange of information…"

Rosetti was now on the deck of his ship. He ran his hands hurriedly through his hair and scratched vigorously. The crew were all on deck, ready to ship out.

"Fine. All right. I'll tell you what I'm going to do. You follow me. I'm not taking time out of my schedule. Talk to the harbormaster here at the marina. He knows where we are. You can tag along with me for part of the day. But stay out of my way. Don't slow me down. You and I can talk for a few minutes out on the open water."

Will had a momentary sense of accomplishment. Clearly, the ocean archaeologist would have a wealth of information that might be able to give some background on the Battle of Ocracoke Inlet, on Edward Teach, on his ships, and perhaps, even though indirectly, on Isaac Joppa.

Unfortunately, Will was scrambling to figure out what he had to give to Rosetti in return.

I guess I'll just have to come up with something while I'm driving, Will mused as he rushed around the cabin looking for his keys and then yelled to Fiona that he was going to be late for dinner.

He didn't stop to check with his wife out on the hammock. If he had, he would surely have noticed her withering glare.

32

IT WAS MIDAFTERNOON. Jonathan Joppa had collapsed in bed, uncharacteristically, and had taken a nap. He was fast asleep.

The night before he had gotten almost no sleep. He couldn't put his finger on it...but he felt a constant sense of dread and anxiety over his son, Bobby, and his drug problem. And he worried about his ministry as pastor of Safe Harbor Community Church. He couldn't shake the feeling, increasing every day, that he was playing a charade as its spiritual shepherd.

And so he was having more and more trouble sleeping at night. The evening before, perhaps only an hour of sleep. He went to the church that morning, dazed with fatigue, not taking his characteristic five-mile jog. He muddled through some business in the study, excused himself to Sally, and made his way home. Then he went to bed.

And now, there was the sound of ringing. A phone. He wasn't sure if it was a dream or real. But something told him to wake up and reach for the phone next to his bed.

"Jonathan, I'm sorry to disturb you at home. You didn't look well at the church this morning...I thought maybe you went home because you felt sick. But this is very important..."

It was Sally's voice, tense and pleading.

"What is it? What's up?" Jonathan scooted the edge of the bed.

"It's about Bobby—"

"What about him?" Suddenly, his mental fog was instantly lifted.

"I have some bad news..."

"What happened?" Jonathan asked in a strangely hushed voice, as if he were afraid to wake someone who was sleeping. "What happened? Is he all right?"

"I have this friend of mine, Gloria…she works at Dunes Memorial Hospital. She told me she wasn't supposed to be telling me this…it was confidential medical information."

Joppa squinted his eyes and thought hard, trying to understand what Sally was saying.

"What are you talking about? What does that have to do with—"

"Gloria told me Bobby was just checked into the ER. They think he overdosed on drugs. He's being treated right now. It's very serious."

"Dear God…" Joppa muttered.

After only a second, he snapped out, "I have to go see him. I have to go to the hospital…"

"Jonathan, I'm really sorry about this."

Jonathan said a quick thank-you and dropped the receiver down on the phone. He threw his clothes on, knocking over a chair in the kitchen, grabbed his keys, and ran to the car.

On the drive to the hospital, Jonathan had only one thought. Over and over again, he told himself this should be no surprise. Bobby had been admitted for rehab before. He had a drug problem. He'd tried to help him. But there was another question, one he didn't want to face—*wasn't there something more he could have done?*

And as he roared up to the hospital and raced out at a full run, he was still asking himself that question.

33

THE SMALL SKIFF, WITH WILL CHAMBERS as its only passenger, was approaching Dr. Rosetti's research ship out on the open sound. The dock hand guiding the skiff grabbed his CB and announced Will's arrival. There was a pause at the other end. Then a voice replied.

"We'll throw a ladder over the side. Tell him he doesn't have much time."

As the skiff reached the side of the ship, one of the crew members reached down and helped to pull Will up onto the deck.

Dr. Rosetti was in a huddle with several of the crew members. In one hand he had a cell phone, and in his other, a walkie-talkie.

Will stood off at a distance, taking in some of the gear and equipment that was laid out on the deck. One object in particular caught his attention.

There was a large device that looked like a hot air balloon attached to three nylon cords, which in turn were attached to a large square cage.

Rosetti quickstepped over to Will's position.

"I suppose you're wondering what we do with this," Rosetti said with a broad smile as he approached.

Will nodded. But before he had a chance to reply, Rosetti jumped in.

"It's exactly what it looks like—it's a balloon we use to raise heavy objects in the cage there."

Will glanced over at what looked like a Plexiglas phone booth resting next to the balloon.

"That's our communications booth," Rosetti said proudly. "We sink it at the dive site, and then our divers can swim in and out of it, close the door, and communicate to the other crew topside. We also have all our divers rigged up with umbilicals—you know, hoses that give them air— and communication cables."

Will wasn't surprised at Rosetti's warm reception. Will found it to be a trait of many scientists he had consulted as experts in other cases. Often they initially came across as cold and uninterested—but then he would meet them on their own turf, and they opened up like three-D birthday cards.

"Actually, your timing is fairly good…I was going to hop into the cabin and grab something to eat. Come on in and join me. I don't have that much time."

Rosetti scurried into the wheelhouse, and Will followed closely after.

Rosetti sat down, popped a soda can open, and began eating his peanut-butter-and-jelly sandwich.

"First of all, let me just say this. I'm not going to say anything more on the record about Blackjack Morgan. Zero. You know what I think about this guy…On the other hand, I'm not stupid. Any negative comments I make about Morgan pertaining to this project could find their way back to MacPherson—and that lawyer's a royal pain in the neck."

Will agreed.

"First of all, let me tell you something about my qualifications," Rosetti began. "I'm an ocean archaeologist. I'm not a maritime historian. That having been said, I do a heck of a lot of research into the historical context of the ships I investigate. Who sailed them. What they were carrying. Where they were bound. I've been reading about Teach's sailing exploits for a couple of years. So while you certainly can't call me a historical expert, I think I know a lot more than the average guy about the people and the ships involved in that battle."

"Well, I have done some background research with some experts," Will explained.

"Like who?" Rosetti asked with a tinge of skepticism in his voice.

"I'm hoping to retain Dr. Derek Hubbel, from Yale."

"I've heard of him. That sounds promising. Who else?"

"A professor by the name of August Longfellow, from Duke. He's kind of a self-created regional expert on the subject of Carolina coastal history. And also, there is someone who teaches Indian history of the Tuscaroras— her name is Susan Red Deer Williams…"

"With all due respect," Rosetti said, stuffing some more sandwich into his mouth, "I don't know these people. I really don't care. You'll find a lot of local yokels who say they know all kinds of stuff—some even claim to know where Teach's treasure is buried. It's all a lot of nonsense. It took us several years to get this fix on the location of the *Bold Venture*. I mean, for months all we've done is map out the wreckage by stereophotography. Based on that, we created a site plan. Thousands of photographs and measurements."

"Just as a matter of curiosity," Will said, "how much of the ship is down there?"

"Well," Rosetti said, wrapping up the rest of his sandwich in the plastic bag and throwing it back into a nylon cooler, "some of the stern, some of the bow—but the wood portions are all in pretty bad shape. No cannons—because this was a merchant ship—but because it was a commercial vessel we were hoping to find a whole lot of barrels down there."

"So, about Isaac Joppa…" Will said, trying to redirect the conversation.

"Oh yeah." Rosetti jumped to his feet. "Look, here's the bottom line in that. In my research, I checked the records from the trial in Williamsburg, Virginia—the trial of the surviving pirates of Blackbeard's crew. There was this former slave, this African crewman—a trusted member of Teach's group—his name was Caesar. Now Caesar gives a statement when he's arrested, because he survived the battle, that there's this Isaac Joppa guy who was on the ship with him."

"Caesar mentioned Isaac Joppa?"

"Absolutely."

"What did he say?" Will asked enthusiastically.

"Well, here's the deal," Rosetti said, walking out of the cabin with Will close behind. "Caesar was offered some kind of pardon if he cooperated with the authorities by ratting on the rest of the other pirate crew. He refused, except to say that this Isaac Joppa guy was some kind of indentured servant. That Teach had him in chains most of the time. Only let him out on deck when he wanted to show him off. He used him because he had some medical background, which he figured would come in handy when his crewmen would get shot or sliced up in some of their battles. Otherwise, he kept Joppa under lock and key."

Rosetti turned to approach a couple of the crewmen, but in his excitement, Will grabbed his arm and quickly whirled him around.

"You're telling me that the written proceedings up in Williamsburg, in the piracy trial, have this Caesar fellow saying that Joppa was an imprisoned slave on Blackbeard's ship?"

"Look, Counselor, don't get so excited. I gave you the good news. I haven't given you the bad news yet."

And with that, Rosetti removed Will's hand and then barked out some orders to a couple of his crew members.

"What's the bad news?" Will shouted.

Rosetti turned around and smiled. "The bad news is that it looks like it was all a lie. So what else would you expect from a pirate?"

"I don't understand..."

Rosetti took a few steps over and wagged his finger in Will's direction. "Because one of the passengers in the hold of Teach's ship—a local merchant who was nursing a hangover from a drinking party that Blackbeard had hosted the night before, was still there on the ship at the time of the battle. He was with Caesar. He was also with Isaac Joppa. He testified at the trial that Joppa was not in chains. That he didn't look like any kind of prisoner."

Rosetti, even from a distance, noted the disappointment that washed over Will's face.

"Sorry about that. I know it doesn't help your case."

Will was already deep in thought when Rosetti added one further comment.

"This Isaac Joppa was charged with piracy, right?"

"Right. A grand jury that was convened in Bath, North Carolina, heard some testimony, and issued an indictment. The local magistrate signed an arrest warrant for Joppa shortly afterwards."

"Well, for what it's worth, I find that a little unusual..."

"Why do you say that?"

"See, what they did with the pirate gang in Williamsburg back then is this—they didn't have grand juries convened. Instead, they had the charges issued by the Admiralty Court. Now I don't know how much you know about maritime law..."

"Before this case, less than zero," Will said with a smile. "But I'm trying to get up to speed."

"Well, you're the lawyer and I'm not. But at least the way they handled those cases back in the pre–Revolutionary War settlements was to issue charges by the Admiralty Court. It doesn't sound like your guy—this Isaac Joppa—was charged that way. That's a little strange. Anyway, all of Teach's gang were tried by the Admiralty Court in Williamsburg."

"Interesting," Will said, not knowing what to make of the fact.

"Look, I'm sorry I didn't have more useful information for you," Rosetti said. "I got to get back to work here. We'll call that skiff back to pick you up. Good luck."

As one of the crewmen used the radio, Will sauntered over to the railing and looked at the waves lapping against the side of the ship.

He never could tolerate losing a case, even if it was a difficult one. But his hope for winning the lawsuit for Reverend Jonathan Joppa—and indirectly righting Uncle Bull's mistreatment by Blackjack Morgan—was now in danger of sinking. Any optimism Will had about winning seemed to be completely scuttled just as surely as the remains of the *Bold Venture*, which lay in the shifting sand and silt at the bottom of the ocean.

34

Virgil MacPherson felt good about the direction of the case. He had just signed off on delivery of an avalanche of mostly useless information to Will Chambers in response to his discovery demand.

MacPherson's only regret was that he wasn't going to be there to see Will's expression when he received it.

The rest of MacPherson's day was spent in the conference room with Dr. Manfred Berkeley, a professor of marine history.

"Dr. Berkeley," MacPherson continued, wrapping up the meeting with his expert witness, "then you will rely on the grand jury testimony to disprove this possible theory that Isaac Joppa was a kidnapping victim, right?"

"Yes, and although the grand jury testimony amounted to evidence given by only one witness—namely, Henry Caulfeld—I think his testimony is very powerful."

"Because, he was an eyewitness?"

"Of course. He was aboard the sloop *Marguerite* at the time it was overtaken by Teach and his crew—at the height of Teach's piracy career. Caulfeld saw, with his own eyes, that Isaac Joppa was strutting around on the deck of Teach's ship, apparently giving orders to the crew—the same crew that forcibly boarded the *Marguerite*, manhandled the passengers, and stole all its merchandise."

After Berkeley was gone, MacPherson made a phone call to another expert witness.

A secretary answered, and after a moment's pause he was connected.

"Dr. Henrietta Clover," the female voice at the other end said.

"Dr. Clover, this is Virgil MacPherson. The attorney. I left a message for you the other day. I was following up on our conversation…"

"Oh yes, yes. I'm sorry I missed you."

"Were you able to put together that information? Arrive at some opinions?"

"You mean about the Joppa business?" Clover replied softly.

"Exactly. I'm wondering if you were able to piece that all together."

"Well, as a matter of fact, I'm almost nearly complete—"

"I know you like to be as thorough as possible," MacPherson responded smoothly.

"Oh, most certainly. I'll finish this business up in a few days. I've been delayed a little...my niece has been in town...and I visited with her...and I had to give a talk to the State Historical Society...and another little lecture to the Women's Auxiliary of the American Revolution..."

"So can we just say, the way it looks right now, that you'll be able to testify to the opinions you conveyed to me previously?"

"Oh, I believe so. Yes, I feel very comfortable saying that...of course, if there's anything I see to change my mind, I'll let you know."

Virgil MacPherson stopped drumming on the table. A smile came across his face. The world had just become very bright for him.

"And one other thing, Dr. Clover—just a warning..."

"Oh?" Dr. Clover said with a shade of concern in her voice.

"No, I didn't mean to startle you," MacPherson said in a reassuring voice. "Just a *reminder*. If you should get a call from anyone asking about your involvement in this case. You agreed that you were not going to be talking about this with *anyone*. *No one*, except me. Anyone calls, you simply decline comment—and then call me immediately. Is that agreed?"

"That should be fine," Dr. Clover said cautiously.

After hanging up MacPherson was exquisitely pleased. So pleased that he left his office a little early and headed for his favorite French restaurant, where he would enjoy spending a healthy chunk of the attorney's fees Blackjack Morgan had been paying him.

35

REVEREND JONATHAN JOPPA'S PRESENCE at the Dunes Memorial Hospital was a familiar sight. He would often visit the sick and elderly there. He was at the bedsides of some who were in their final, dying moments. He had a good relationship with the nursing staff and the doctors—though the on-duty unit nurse was unfamiliar to him.

"Which room is Bobby Joppa in—I forgot." he said casually.

The unit nurse studied him carefully and then looked down at her clipboard.

"I'm sorry, no visitors for that patient. Doctors' orders…"

"Are you new here?"

"Well…sort of…I'm swing shift…"

"I figured. Hi, I'm Reverend Jonathan." He smiled and reached out his right hand to shake hers. "I'm the pastor of Safe Harbor Community Church. You might say I'm Bobby's spiritual advisor and his dad. It's urgent that I get a chance to chat with him."

The unit supervisor tapped her pen on the clipboard and then shook her head.

"Sorry. Doctors' orders. Maybe some other time."

Joppa looked down the corridor frantically. Then he caught sight of a police officer sitting on a chair outside one of the rooms. He scurried down the hallway and approached him.

"I'm Bobby Joppa's dad. Is he being charged with anything?"

The officer's walkie-talkie was squawking something in the background, and the officer reached down and turned it off.

"I'm sorry, did you say you're his dad?"

Joppa nodded.

"He's not charged with anything. Yet. We just want to know where he got drugs. You wouldn't happen to know where your son came into several ounces of highly refined cocaine—would you?"

Joppa shook his head in disgust.

"Sure. I could give you some ideas," he said bitterly, "they're just suspicions…but I would be right…but then again, the last time I told you guys who supplied my son with drugs, you did absolutely nothing about it. And, as a matter of fact, things got worse…"

"I don't know anything about that." The officer put both hands up in the air.

Joppa was not in the mood for a dialogue. He turned from the officer and stepped quickly past into the hospital room.

In the room there was a single bed with a single patient.

Bobby had a saline drip attached to his arm, and a monitor. His lips were dry and cracked. His skin was pale, and his long hair was greasy and tangled. There were deep circles under his eyes.

Bobby moved his head slowly. When he recognized his father, he turned his face away toward the window.

"Bobby," Joppa said in a voice choked with emotion, and fighting back tears, "I love you. No matter what else, you have to know that."

Bobby slowly turned back.

"I didn't want you here. Who told you?" His voice was weak and almost indecipherable.

"This is a small town. News travels fast. You look rotten. Do you feel just as bad as you look?"

Bobby snorted weakly. He started to say something but did not finish.

"Who did you buy it from?"

After a moment, Bobby summoned his strength to answer his father. "You wouldn't believe me if I told you…"

Jonathan stepped closer to the bed, right next to Bobby's head. "Tell me who you got it from—you can trust me…"

"Really?" Bobby replied faintly.

"You need to trust someone. Let's start with me. Who sold it to you?"

"Nobody."

"What do you mean?"

"Just what I said…nobody sold it…it was just right there."

"Where?"

"On my kitchen table. In a wrapper. Sitting there when I got home from work."

"You have no idea who dropped it off?"

Bobby shook his head slowly. Then he took a deep breath and summoned the strength to say something else.

"Didn't want it…but I was afraid to tell the cops…I was going to flush it down the toilet…I just wasn't strong enough…not to use it."

Jonathan reached out, put his hand on Bobby's arm, and squeezed it. With his other hand, he stroked the pale, perspiring face of his son.

The pieces fell together.

"You were set up, Bobby…and so was I…"

A young doctor with a clipboard walked into the hospital room brusquely.

"I'm sorry, Reverend Joppa, but you have to go. We have restrictions on visiting this patient."

At first, Joppa didn't move. He studied the pleading, helpless look in his son's eyes.

"Can't beat this…can't beat this, Dad…"

"You can beat this. And we're going to beat this." Joppa squeezed his arm again, and then rose to his feet.

Joppa strode over to the young resident.

"You're going to have to change your restrictions on this patient," he said firmly. "Because I *am* going to be visiting him on a regular basis." And with that, he turned and walked out into the corridor.

As he walked, Jonathan's legs and ankles felt as if the joints had all been unstrung, like those of a marionette. He was barely able to keep his feet moving, one in front of the other.

In his despair, Jonathan could only wonder at the malignant and evil hand that was pulling the strings.

36

Will's cell phone was ringing. He had forgotten he had slipped it into the pocket of his shorts just before he and Fiona had gone for a beach walk.

As he grabbed it and took a few steps away from the crash of the surf, Fiona threw him a forlorn, slightly pouty look.

Will mouthed the words *I'm sorry* as he strained to hear who was speaking at the other end.

"I said," the female voice at the other end continued, "that this is Susan Red Deer Williams. I'm calling because I thought of something."

"What is it?"

"It's a follow-up to something we had talked about."

"About Isaac Joppa?"

"Not exactly. It's about the Indian family we think Joppa may have had contact with. Chief King Jim Blount and his son, and his daughter. The Tuscaroras."

"What do you have?"

"Just one item I forgot to tell you. I explained how Blount and his family had apparently been converted to Christianity by the time that they got to New York and joined the other Tuscarora tribes. But there's something about that I forgot to tell you. About a cross...a painted cross..."

"I hope this isn't another artifact that takes me on a wild goose chase," Will said bluntly.

"Don't worry, Counselor. This isn't an artifact. But it is a historical item that may be of interest."

"Fire away." Will watched Fiona slowly wade ankle-deep, into the small pools of water on the beach. She flashed him an impatient look.

"When Blount and his son and daughter showed up to join the rest of the Tuscaroras, he was reported to be wearing a cross around his neck. It was painted red and white."

"A painted cross? Who painted it?"

"I'm not sure. I don't know any of the details. But it was painted red on one side and white on the other. It was a wooden cross, apparently. And he had a leather strap through it and wore it around his neck."

"Anything else?"

"No," Williams said, "that's all. You can file that away in your 'for whatever it's worth' drawer."

After thanking Williams, Will hung up, turned off the phone, and dropped it back into his pocket.

As Will slowly walked over to Fiona, he wondered whether the little red-and-white cross mentioned by Williams had anything to do with Isaac Joppa. *Who painted it? And why?*

((((((

Isaac Joppa could have run away any number of times. After winning the match with Great Hawk, he was no longer bound and, as far as he could see, was no longer being observed. He was free to come and go as he wished. He was given his own tent. Great Hawk made another tent for his father—the chief—and himself. The Indian girl slept in the third tent.

The real question was, why wasn't he taking off down the Carolina coast? He knew there would be a danger, as he traveled, that he might be spotted by some of the English colonists. And that was a risk he was willing to take. But for some reason that he could not entirely explain, he felt compelled to stay with the Indians.

He found himself thinking often about his father. Malachi Joppa was not a jovial man. He was often stern. But he was also thoughtful and probing.

Reverend Malachi Joppa had felt called to Bath, North Carolina, even though he knew its reputation as a wild place—more hospitable to pirates, drinking, and thievery than to the establishment of churches or the enforcement of the standards of decency.

Isaac had dutifully gone with his father to some of his outdoor evangelistic meetings. His older brother, Adam, and his sister, Myrtle, were also required to be present.

But they were rather dismal affairs, with only a handful of locals showing up—most of them to jeer and mock. Isaac sometimes wondered, derisively, whether his father had required the three children to be present so the roughhewn pews in the outdoor church he tried to establish would not look so pitifully empty.

Rather than face his father and reveal his longing to leave the provincial, suffocating environment of his life on the Pamlico Sound, he chose to run away instead. He left no note behind. He realized now how heartbreaking...how terribly painful that must have been to his father.

Perhaps, in a small way, Isaac's continued stay with these three Tuscarora Indians had something to do with his father—the completion of a task that, somehow, his father was unable to complete.

Malachi Joppa was generally disliked by the locals. And Isaac learned, after joining the English navy out of Bristol, England, that his father had been stabbed to death on a side street of Bath. His murderer was never found.

Since that time, Isaac had struggled to rebuild the memories linking him to his father. But now, as he lay in his hut made of animal skins, resting from the heat of the day, he thought back to one particular encounter.

Symbols are powerful things, Malachi Joppa had told Isaac. They were sitting on the split-log benches after one of his poorly attended evangelistic meetings. Joppa asked whether Isaac had seen the skull-and-crossbones of the pirate flag. Isaac nodded. His father pointed out that it was the symbol of death, and crime, and sin. It was meant to strike fear into the hearts of all who saw it.

Then he pointed to a cross he had on a table at the front. *God's symbol of the Cross is more powerful than any pirate's flag,* he explained. *The blood shed there has the power to cleanse the most hellish of men and the most hideous of crimes. That is why I must do as the apostle Paul confessed. Woe to me if I do not preach the cross—and Christ crucified.*

Isaac thought about that. And about his new relationship with his Indian captors.

They had softened toward him. Lately, Great Hawk had invited Isaac to go clam and pearl hunting along the inlets of the coast. They collected oysters and crabs together. Great Hawk taught him how to fish with a sharpened spear. King Jim Blount had kept his distance, but allowed Isaac to sit around the fireside for meals with them.

Isaac felt the most troubled about the girl. Since his rejection and his match with her brother, she had seemed more pensive and forlorn. Isaac knew he had to be careful—not to inflame any passions nor imply any romantic commitment. And yet he felt genuinely sorry for her in what appeared to be a desperate loneliness—separated from the rest of the tribe and having few prospects of a husband.

One day he found her kneeling before a mound of sand, apparently in great emotional distress. As he walked closer, he saw that before the prostrate girl, on the top of the pile of sand, there were two carved figurines. One was painted white and was facing east. The other, facing west, was painted red. The Indian girl was speaking passionately, almost pleading, to the white figurine. Then, she would break her conversation with that figure and would plead with fear and trembling to the red figure.

After an attempt to calm her, Isaac was able to piece together the significance of this ritual.

The white figurine represented a good god—and the red figurine represented the bad god. Her soul seemed to have been caught in an inner turmoil—an irreconcilable conflict between these symbols of two, mutually exclusive deities.

Isaac sat and watched her weep and wail. As he studied her, he suddenly had a thought.

He gathered her into his arms and had her stand up. She was still sobbing and chanting in her Tuscarora tongue, pointing at the red figurine of the evil god.

Isaac told her in a strong, calm voice to walk some twenty or thirty feet away and be seated. Then he scurried across the clearing and into the forest, collecting a large pile of red berries. Then he gathered some small sticks, brought the red berries and sticks, and placed them before the sand mound. By then, the girl was wiping her tears and had regained her composure. She studied Isaac with curiosity.

Then he ran off to hunt some of the white chalk stone he had seen on the sandy edge of the forest. He quickly came back with it and gathered his materials in front of him.

After a few moments, the girl stood up and walked slowly toward Isaac's position. He jumped up, playfully waving her off so she wouldn't see what he was doing. She laughed a little at that but resumed her seat. After a while, though, she became impatient and again walked over closer. Isaac again jumped to his feet and playfully shooed her off so she could not see what he was doing.

Finally, after a considerable period of time and intense work, he invited the Indian girl to join him and see the result of his endeavors.

She walked slowly over to Isaac. Next to the sand mound where she had been worshiping stood a second mound of sand created by Isaac. He had set there a crude wooden cross. He pointed to the cross and nodded. Then he pointed over to the mound with the two figurines and shook his head with disapproval.

After a dramatic pause, he reached for something behind him, slowly pulled it out, and showed it to the Indian girl. At first, she gasped.

Isaac had shaped, out of sticks and reeds, a small stick man who was painted red with the juice of the berries. The crude cross he had carved was also painted red on the side facing out.

Isaac patted his chest and bowed his head in grief as he placed the red-stained human figurine on the cross.

The Indian girl's eyes widened as she wondered what would happen next.

Isaac took three sharp thorns and placed one in each of the arms of the figurines, and one in the legs—to the Indian girl's horror and amazement.

Then he took the red-stained figurine, carefully cradling it in the palms of his hands, and placed it in a hole he dug at the foot of the mound. He gently covered it with a large rock. Then he motioned toward the sky to indicate the lapse of time.

Then he took the stone and removed it from the hole in the ground, lifting up the figurine. But as he did, he flipped the figurine so that the other side faced the Indian girl. She cried out as she noticed the other side had been painted white. Isaac took the figurine with the white side showing and reached for the cross, which, as he turned it around, was shown to also have been painted white on the other side. He then placed the white-sided figurine next to the white side of the cross and bowed down before them.

He turned to the Indian girl, whose unblinking eyes and searching expression told Isaac that she was comprehending this new and powerful mystery. She sat down before the two sand mounds—the one with her pagan symbols of a battle between two equally powerful but morally opposite gods—and the other with a figure of a man who had been painted with evil, yet had conquered it through his own inexplicable goodness.

She sat for hours, glancing back and forth from one sand mound to the other. From one set of symbols to the other.

As darkness fell, she left. Isaac retreated to his own hut. Then he did something he had not done for many years—he fell on his face in the sand of his hut and cried out to God. He cried over his past transgressions. Over his wasted life. Over the betrayal of his father's confidence in him. And over the ignorance and darkness that covered the minds and souls of these Tuscarora Indians—who, after all, had saved his life.

Isaac was sleeping. The moon was full. Then he heard voices outside. He glanced out of the hut and saw the Indian girl talking quickly and passionately before the two sand hills, pointing to the symbols he had painted. Her brother, Great Hawk, was standing next to her and listening intently.

Farther off, perhaps ten or fifteen feet away, was her father, the chief. He was standing, motionless, with no expression. But his eyes were riveted on the figurine and the cross, both painted white.

The next morning when Isaac awoke, he scurried out of his hut. To his amazement, the other two huts were gone. All traces of the chief, his pretty daughter, and his son, Great Hawk, had vanished.

They had left silently, without any goodbye. Isaac's eyes scanned the clearing which had been home to him for the last few weeks. Then he noticed something.

He walked over to the mound he had made the Indian girl. The white-painted figurine was still planted in the top of the sand. But the cross— painted red on one side and white on the other—had been taken. It was gone.

Somehow, Isaac Joppa knew he would never see the three Indians again.

37

FIONA HAD GONE OVER TO GEORGIA'S cottage to visit—in large part, Will figured, because of the rising tension between them. He knew he had become single-focused on the case. In his more honest moments he admitted he had become just plain insufferable.

I'll make it up to her, he thought.

That morning he looked over her log of notes from Randolph Willowby's diary. When he saw her painstaking detail, that's when he really felt guilty.

The diary made clear that Willowby had become, in the last months of life, a convert to Christ. He apparently had always had a mild interest in family genealogy. But as the end got closer, it became a near-obsession. He tried to study everything he could about his link to the Joppa line—through Elisha Willowby's marriage to Myrtle Joppa almost three hundred years before.

And he wondered about Reverend Malachi Joppa...and what caused Isaac Joppa to run away from his home and family...and whether he had been wrongfully accused.

Toward the end, he talked about his contact with Jonathan Joppa. He attended one of his church services, but found it uninspiring. "Joppa's sermon had no passion, and little Bible in it."

Willowby noted that after the service he had introduced himself to Reverend Joppa and invited him to take a boat ride to Stony Island some time soon.

That was a month before Willowby's death. He had to be in pain and great discomfort. Why a boat ride to the island?

And why with Jonathan Joppa? Will could only speculate that Willowby, who was childless, had felt some inexplicable responsibility for Jonathan.

Fiona's review of the diary did seem to raise some possibilities about Willowby's motive in requiring Jonathan to prove Isaac Joppa's innocence. But beyond that, Will saw no relevance to the issue of Isaac's *actual* innocence.

So after that, Will spent the day sifting through the information produced by Virgil MacPherson in response to his discovery demand.

Will had received a phone call from Boggs Beckford's law office indicating that a delivery had arrived for him. He had been told that it was from MacPherson's law firm in Raleigh.

"You got a truck?" the secretary had asked Will.

He had thought she was kidding.

She hadn't been.

There were seven large banker's boxes full of information. Will had to use Fiona's Saab to pick it up, because he couldn't cram even one of the boxes into the tiny trunk space of his Corvette. After doing a cursory inventory of the boxes, he figured that MacPherson had produced around ten thousand documents.

But after his initial review, Will had also reached another conclusion. Nearly all the records appeared to be irrelevant—and worthless to his case.

Three full boxes contained the court papers, transcripts, pleadings, and correspondence from the *Bold Venture* salvage lawsuit in federal court where MacPherson had been representing Blackjack Morgan.

The other four boxes contained copies of every conceivable newspaper, Internet, and magazine article about ocean treasure-hunting, ship salvage, the history of piracy, the early American shipping industry, the patterns of coastal tides, ocean routes from the Carolina coast, the variations of sea shells, fishing regulations, intercoastal highways, tourist information for the Outer Banks, and even listings of ocean real estate properties for sale or rent.

But Will was finally able to appreciate the full extend of Virgil MacPherson's audacity when, amid the thousands of documents, he found fully photocopied versions of Robert Louis Stevenson's *Treasure Island* and *Kidnapped*!

MacPherson knew that Will was down in the Cape Hatteras area in a semivacation mode—miles away from his law office and the support systems that it provided. It was clear to Will that his opponent was trying to divert him—to bury him in a mass of irrelevant documentation he would have to spend countless hours personally reviewing.

So he found himself on the porch of their sea cottage, buried in documents.

Inside, Fiona, having returned, was plunking on the piano, finally gaining inspiration for some new music compositions.

As he listened to Fiona, who was working on note combinations in a slowly emerging melody line, he gazed longingly at the swimmers and sunbathers down along the hot, white beach just a few hundred feet away—just down from the sand dunes where their little house was perched. Down where they were jumping into the surf, laughing, walking dogs, sleeping in the rays of the summer sun, or reading under big colored umbrellas.

Will had the sinking feeling of an unlucky schoolboy who had to take summer school classes—while his friends were all down at the city swimming pool.

Then he had a thought. He needed to connect with his client. Will called Joppa at his house, but he got only his voice mail. Then he tried the church. His secretary, Sally, answered. She was a little evasive at first. Will pushed.

Then she opened up and said that Jonathan's son was in the hospital, and her boss was spending quite a bit of time at the hospital visiting him. She gave Will the hospital room number for Bobby.

"If Jonathan isn't in the room, then check in the little prayer chapel in the hospital. It's on the first floor, just off the main lobby." And then she added, "This has been a very tough time for him."

After Will finished with Sally, he stopped at the piano long enough to wrap his arms around his wife, give her a kiss, and explain where he was going.

Fiona looked up from the keyboard. "Is it serious? What happened?"

Will shook his head and said he would find out at the hospital.

At Dunes Memorial Hospital, Will peeked into Bobby's room, but the bed was empty.

"He's downstairs getting some tests done," a nurse said, walking by. "You family?"

"Not exactly. I'm the lawyer for part of the family…" Will replied. Then he made his way to the tiny chapel.

The door was made of imitation stained glass. There was only one person in the tiny room—in the front pew. It was Jonathan Joppa.

Will sat down next to him but didn't talk at first. He just studied him.

The lawyer could see it—the desperate, longing confusion of a soul in disarray. He had seen the look on the faces of other clients over the years. But this time it was different. In Joppa's discouraged posture, troubled brow, and searching eyes that seemed overwhelmed by an ocean of questions, Will recognized himself just a few years before.

After several minutes of silence, Will spoke up.

"I'm sorry your boy is having medical problems."

"Drugs."

"Oh?"

"He's had a drug problem for several years," Joppa said quietly. "Cocaine. Someone, and I'm sure it was Blackjack Morgan, gave him a free delivery of some highly refined, very potent stuff. He snorted it—he overdosed. He's lucky to be alive. I never told you...but I'm sure one of Morgan's dealers first got my boy into drugs. So, back then, I reported him to the police. They couldn't pin anything on him. But he retaliated against me...by mocking me. By changing the name of his tavern to *Joppa's Folly*. He says it was a reference to the history about Isaac Joppa. But I figured it was meant to insult me as well."

Will was quiet, then he spoke again.

"You say Bobby's lucky...but how about you? Do you consider yourself lucky?"

Joppa eyed his lawyer for a few seconds. It wasn't that he didn't understand the question. Rather, he did not want to talk about the answer.

"Maybe not...But I'm a minister. I'm not supposed to talk about luck. I'm supposed to talk about faith. And God's mysterious plan. I'm sure you know the whole routine..."

"Why do you say that?"

"Because I know about you. Your Aunt Georgia told me a little bit. But I've read about you too—some interviews you gave about some of your cases...and your Christian beliefs."

"You know, Jonathan, the job of a pastor is one of the most demanding professions in the world. My father-in-law was one. You've got to wear twenty-five hats—sometimes all at once. Counselor, advisor, preacher, administrator, teacher, corporate controller, project manager, building and grounds engineer, fund-raiser, and master theologian—all wrapped up in one. Tough job...but putting that aside for just a few minutes...when you are here, in the hospital...with a son who is trying to get the demons from hell off his back...this has got to be so very lonely for you."

Joppa nodded, staring at his hands, which were folded in his lap, and fighting back the emotion rising in his throat.

"You learn to get along...as best as you can..." Joppa said, his voice a little unsteady.

"So, how are you doing it—getting along?"

Joppa leaned back into the wooden pew. After a moment of thought, collecting himself, he spoke.

"In seminary, I had this New Testament professor. He used to laugh when he told us what he really believed about the Gospel stories. He said they were contradictory…couldn't be harmonized…and lacked basic historical credibility. Yet he said that when he went out to preach at various churches, he would always preach directly from the Gospel stories about the life of Christ…See, he never told the people in the pews what he really believed."

Will studied him closely. "Did you ever ask him why?"

"Sure. You know what his answer was?"

Will waited.

"He said that some guys were in the business of selling cars—he was in the business of selling hope. That life is pretty tough. People need hope…just to get through…"

After reflecting, Will responded.

"On the other hand, hope has to be anchored to something—to a transcendent reality. To a real spiritual power."

Something in what Will said caught Joppa by surprise.

"You know, you talk about power. I've got a twenty-one-year-old kid in a hospital room here…He's about to be discharged and transferred into a drug rehab program…*again*. He looks at me and says, 'Dad, I don't have the power to get this monkey off my back. It's killing me…but I don't have the power.'"

Joppa paused.

"I thought I knew what that word meant—power—way back when…Before seminary—when I was young—my real dream was to play major league ball. I had two pretty good seasons in the triple-A farm leagues. My first season I batted three-oh-one. I could hit the long ball too. But then I decided I needed something more than just power hitting. I really focused on *placing* the ball…*directing* the power when I connected with the fat of that bat. The next season—guess what my average was?"

Will shook his head.

"Three-forty-three," Joppa continued. "But my sprinting time was a little too slow for the majors…and my fielding was only very average, so that sort of ended my baseball career. I decided to go into the ministry. Maybe I figured I could focus my personal power on doing something good for people. Back then I felt that God was there in the middle of everything I was doing. But then some things happened—and the spiritual fire felt like it was going down. The power for living seemed to be missing. I know this is starting to sound like true confession..."

"What I know about that spiritual power," Will said, "is pretty simple. Really. In my own life I had a personal resurrection of sorts...from a life that was bordering on complete disaster...into a new kind of life. And what I do know is that the power certainly didn't come from me."

"Are you preaching to a preacher now?" Joppa asked wryly.

"I suppose I am," Will said, smiling. Then he had a thought. "You know, I was thinking about that cemetery back on Stony Island."

Joppa nodded.

"There was a gravestone there—really remarkable. Looked as if it was placed too close to an oak tree. The tree must have been just a seedling back when the grave was dug and the marker was set. Anyway, I keep thinking back to the stone gravemarker—tilted sideways, being sucked right into the growing trunk of that big oak tree over the course of the years. Almost entirely enveloped by the tree. What a picture..."

"Of what?"

"A picture of power," Will replied. "You know the Bible verse as well as I do—'Death is swallowed up in victory...'"

Just then a nurse appeared in the doorway of the chapel.

"Sorry to disturb you, Reverend Joppa, but we are getting ready to discharge Bobby. I understand you'll be driving him over to the rehab unit?"

Joppa nodded.

After the nurse disappeared, Will rose and put his hand on Jonathan Joppa's shoulder.

"Being a father," he noted, "you're the veteran...You'll have to give me some pointers. Fiona is carrying our first child. I'm getting into the fatherhood game a little late, compared to you."

Joppa stood and smiled at Will. "Thanks for talking."

Then he walked quickly out of the little chapel and toward the place where his son would be waiting for him.

38

IT WAS LATE, AND THE WATERS OF THE SOUND were calm. The skiff that was guided by Carlton Robideau also carried Blackjack Morgan and Orville Putrie. It made its way to the edge of Stony Island.

Morgan had placed the island under surveillance, and he knew that the Willowby property manager, Leonard Moore, checked the island every Wednesday, during the daylight hours, like clockwork.

Which is why Morgan decided to make his trip to the island during the night on Wednesday. It would be a full week before it would be visited again. By then, if all went well, Morgan would have what he was after.

The moon was drifting between clouds, but there was enough light to see without the benefit of any boat lights or flashlights. They spotted the dark outline in front of them. Robideau cut the outboard engine to a slow purr.

As the boat drifted up to the shadowy dock, Robideau grabbed it, hopped off, and tied up.

"You stay here with the boat," Morgan whispered to him.

Then Morgan signaled to Putrie to follow him up the path to the high ground—to the ruins of the old house. Putrie was carrying a duffel bag. Halfway up the winding, sandy walk, he tripped over a tree root and fell facedown.

"Blackjack...let's turn that flashlight on," Putrie said, rubbing his face as he got up from the ground.

"No flashlights. The only light we're going to use is the penlight I've got, and that's going to be used only when we get to where we're going," Morgan growled. "Besides, the human eye adjusts to the dark. So start adjusting."

"Tell that to my face," Putrie whined. "I think I just broke my nose."

Even with his limp, Morgan made it to the ruins of the Youngblood house before the other man. He stood before the overgrown foundation, the two standing chimneys, and the urns where the front of the house had once stood.

Morgan squatted down in front of the two urns and ran his fingers across the raised stone letters spelling out the name *YOUNGBLOOD*.

As he did, he thought of the newspaper article Putrie had retrieved in his research, and of the letters I-Y-U, from the hieroglyphics inscribed on the seashell. They had concluded that I-Y-U was short for *In Youngblood's Urn*.

"Be in there, baby," Morgan whispered as he caressed the urn on the right.

Putrie arrived at the site, puffing heavily.

"So—you think it's in there? Gold, silver, diamonds?"

Morgan half-turned toward Putrie and shook his head.

"Course not," he barked. "Give me the duffel bag. What I'm looking for is the big clue. The last clue. I figure this is where it is. The last piece in the puzzle. Then I know exactly where Teach stashed his loot."

Morgan grabbed the bag and took a hammer out.

"Don't break it. Just take the top off."

With that, Putrie reached out to the onion-domed top of the urn and tried to lift it off. But it wouldn't budge. Either because it was cemented down originally or because the accretions of the years had fixed it, it was immovable.

"You really think Blackbeard would have put the last clue to his buried treasure in an urn where the top could be taken off? Where anybody could just look right into it?" Morgan said with a sneer. "Shine the penlight right on the name." He pointed to the letter B among the stone letters.

With one swing, Morgan cracked a large hole in the urn. He carefully retrieved the shards and motioned for Putrie to give him the penlight.

He shined it inside. Then he thrust his hand in, impatiently feeling around the interior. He took the hammer and smashed the rest of the urn, with stone chips flying everywhere. With the penlight he eagerly eyed each shard to see if something had been written on the inside.

"Nothing. Nothing!" he complained bitterly.

Morgan leapfrogged over to the left urn, hammer in hand, and swung directly on the name *YOUNGBLOOD*.

Again he shined the penlight into the interior. Then he let out a string of profanities as he broke the second urn apart and carefully scrutinized the interior of the stone shards.

When he was satisfied that nothing—absolutely nothing—was contained in the urns, he slowly rose to his feet, cane in hand.

Putrie, foreseeing an eruption of violence from his boss, took a few steps back.

"I got a charley horse in my leg from squatting," Morgan said softly. "Putrie, come over here and give me a hand, will you?"

Putrie edged his way closer to his boss, who seemed to be limping more than usual.

When Putrie got within an arm's reach, Morgan grabbed him by the hair and yanked him closer. Then he swung the butt of his cane as hard as he could into his stomach.

Putrie doubled over, gasping for air, and fell to the ground.

"You see, it's like—it's like this is a big classroom…" Morgan said philosophically, waving his cane in the air, "and I'm the teacher—and you're the student. Now it's all pass–fail, see?"

Morgan waited for a few seconds until Putrie was able to regain his breath.

"And you flunked…"

With Putrie stumbling behind him, Morgan began walking back to try to find the path that led to the dock. But the moon was now entirely covered by clouds, and it was difficult to tell the features of the island or find the path that led down to the dock. Still concerned about flashing too much light, he ended up walking farther than he intended. Putrie was stumbling along behind him.

Finally, he grabbed the duffel bag from Putrie, and pulled out a full-sized flashlight. It was then that he realized they were only a foot away from the front gate of the cemetery. He flashed the beam in a sweeping motion across the cemetery, beyond the limbs of the large oak tree, and into a clearing beyond. Putrie suddenly noticed something and stared, transfixed.

"I think we've gone too far. I think we're at the other end of the island. I think the path is back behind us," Morgan said as he clicked off his flashlight.

He turned—and saw Putrie staring, as if in a trance. The younger man was now beholding the verification of his privately constructed theory.

Morgan took a step toward him. "Putrie, you moron, you look like you've just seen a ghost. What's your problem?"

Orville Putrie turned slowly, and when his eyes met Morgan's, he smiled a nervous little half-smile. But he said nothing.

In fact, he just kept smiling, and he said nothing for the rest of the walk across the island, nor even when they climbed into the skiff and motored back across the waters of the sound to the mainland.

39

In his research on the subject of piracy along the Carolina coast, Will was eventually led back to a study of the practice of maritime law in the 1700s in the American colonies.

In 1718, at the time of the Battle of Ocracoke Inlet, the American colonies were still possessions of the English crown. As such, they usually followed the same forms of law as in England. But one chief difference lay in piracy cases.

In 1696, the English Parliament had passed an act that created the first "admiralty courts" in America—then called the "Vice Admiralty Courts"—in Virginia and North Carolina—specifically to try cases of piracy and maritime and sea-trade matters in the colonies.

The crown then issued commissions to the governors of those American colonies to appoint "commissioners" who would act as judges in place of the common-law juries. The point was to do an end run around the colonial juries, who were, in the view of the crown, too quick to acquit their fellow colonists.

The absence of trial-by-jury in those cases, not surprisingly, caused an uproar among the American colonists.

So, in 1718 in the American colonies, a pirate could actually be charged criminally under one of two different procedures. The usual was to be charged, as Dr. Rosetti had first indicated, in the specially created admiralty courts. But as Will observed, admiralty courts, having no "jury of one's peers," gave a strategic advantage to the prosecution and a distinct disadvantage to the defense.

All of that made very intriguing history, but it didn't answer the question that had plagued Will since his conversation with Dr. Rosetti on his research ship—why was Isaac Joppa treated differently than the other defendants who were later tried in the Admiralty Court of Williamsburg,

Virginia? Why, instead, was Joppa's case referred to a grand jury, which then issued an indictment against him?

To Will, that meant that if Isaac Joppa had been arrested and brought into custody, he could have demanded a jury trial—unlike those tried before an admiralty court. The average jury of merchants and landowners might have been more likely to view Joppa's defense sympathetically, as opposed to the political figures, government officials, and naval officers who would have acted as the commissioners—the judges—in an admiralty court.

Those were the thoughts preoccupying Will as he sat at the kitchen table—with files scattered throughout the kitchen and living room. He had the sea cottage to himself. Fiona was out running some errands with Aunt Georgia.

He had spent the morning reading for himself the diary of Randolph Willowby. Fiona had done a fine job picking up most of the salient points.

There was one short entry, however, that she had missed. It caught Will's eye immediately.

A few months before he had lost his battle with cancer, Randolph Willowby, apparently then preoccupied with reconstructing the history of Isaac Joppa, had contacted the county clerk to check into the criminal charges that had originally been lodged against Joppa.

The clerk had referred Willowby to the county archivist, who had informed Willowby that in 1719 the criminal indictment against Isaac Joppa for piracy "was dismissed."

Will wondered why it would have taken until the following year for the local magistrate in Bath, North Carolina, to dismiss the indictment. The reason for the dismissal—Will assumed—was that Isaac Joppa was presumed to be dead.

But that information should have been available immediately after the Battle of Ocracoke Inlet—because witnesses came forward to verify that he had been shot as he tried to swim away from the ship.

All this supported the possibility that the locals in Bath were aware that Joppa had survived the battle after all. Perhaps reports of a white man bearing a description similar to that of Joppa, living with the Tuscarora Indians, had made their way back to the settlements.

Will decided to contact the archivist personally. After several calls, he had a short conversation with Mrs. Helen Atwater. She pulled up a microfilm of the court record from Bath, North Carolina, for 1718. She verified the issuance of the indictment against Joppa at that time. Then she fast-forwarded to 1719. She also verified, as Randolph Willowby had reported in his diary, that approximately one year after the indictment had been issued, it was "dismissed."

"Is there anything else written there in the court entries at the time of the dismissal in 1719?" Will asked.

"What type of information are you looking for, Mr...."

"Chambers. I'm an attorney. I'm staying in the Cape Hatteras area for the summer. Can you see anything, by way of an additional explanation, for the dismissal of that indictment at the time?"

"Well, there's a name."

"What kind of a name?"

"Douglas Littlewood. Apparently the court clerk at the time."

"Yes, that would be the standard procedure. But anything else? Anything other than the fact that the indictment was dismissed, and the name of the clerk?"

"Well, there's something here. I did take Latin, but it's been a number of years—"

"A Latin phrase of some kind?"

"Yes, I believe it's two Latin words..."

"Would you do me a favor?" Will asked with an urgency in his voice that the archivist was now able to detect.

"Certainly, Mr. Chambers."

"Would you spell out, very carefully, those two Latin words?"

"Certainly. Do you have a pen?"

"Absolutely. Go ahead..."

"The first word is R-E-S..."

By now, Will's heart was already beating faster. He had an inkling—an unsupported but strong suspicion—what the next word might be. And if it was so, Will could hardly believe the implications.

"And the next word? What's the next word?" he asked urgently.

"Okay, here it is. J-U-D-I-C-A-T-A."

There it was. He had been right. He was astounded.

"You're sure that's what it says?" he asked excitedly.

"Of course I am," Mrs. Atwater replied, slightly offended by the question. "It's right here in front of me."

"Is there anything else? Any other entries?"

"No. That's the last entry in the Isaac Joppa case. The next entry has to do with a Horace Clemens, who was charged with stealing a horse."

"Mrs. Atwater, was there ever a trial in the Isaac Joppa matter—that you can determine? Any reference to a court hearing or a trial after the grand jury—but before the dismissal?"

Mrs. Atwater paused on the other end for a few moments. Then she answered.

"No. No entries about a trial. There's the original grand jury indictment after the jury heard testimony. On the same day, the magistrate issued an arrest warrant for Isaac Joppa. Then, approximately one year later, the next—and last—entry is the dismissal of the charges, as I have just described it to you."

"Mrs. Atwater, I'm going to need a certified copy of those records for purposes of a case I'm handling."

"Well, we've never had a request like that before. But I'm sure it won't be a problem. What type of certification are you looking for?"

"I need you to sign an affidavit verifying that the copies of the documents you'll be producing to me are accurate and authentic copies of the originals on file in your office. And that you're the official custodian of those records for the county."

Will gave the archivist the address for Boggs Beckford's law office. She agreed to send certified copies of the clerk's entries.

Now Will was totally baffled. *Res judicata* was a familiar legal term. It was one of the first Latin terms he had learned in law school. The literal translation was, "The matter has been decided."

But it was a term that applied *only* to a legal issue that had ultimately been brought to conclusion on the merits in a court hearing or trial.

Such a term was definitely never applied to issues of guilt or innocence when the criminal charges were withdrawn on purely procedural grounds... such as the presumed death of the defendant.

Could an eighteenth-century court clerk have simply put in the res judicata entry in error?

While it was possible, Will didn't think it was likely. It was not a term that courts would use lightly, precisely because it carried such profound implications. Once a matter had been decided in a full and final way, it would bar any relitigation or retrial on the matter again.

There were some exceptions to that rule, but very few. And where a full and final determination resulted in the dismissal of the charges, res judicata would always be applied for the benefit of the defendant. A finding of innocence on the merits could never be appealed.

Will got up and began pacing around the sea cottage. Then he blew through the screen door and out onto the porch that overlooked the blue–gray of the Atlantic Ocean. There was a warm wind blowing. White seabirds were swirling overhead, calling loudly. The beach was crowded with the usual army of sunbathers, couples, families with small children, and surf fishermen.

Will stood and stared. After thirty minutes of intense concentration, he ran into the house, picked up the phone, and called information for the curator of records for Richmond, Virginia. After multiple phone calls, he was finally connected to the historian in charge of the records for the early 1700s, when the capital of the English colony was located in Williamsburg.

Will verified, as he had heard, that the records of the trial of Edward Teach's pirate crew had been destroyed by a fire at the courthouse which had occurred during the Civil War. The only thing that remained was the clerk's notes summarizing the proceedings. The actual transcript containing the questions, answers, testimony of witnesses, arguments of counsel, and decision of the judges of the admiralty court had been destroyed.

"Do you have any record of the collateral proceedings relating to the same incident—namely, the charges of piracy against Edward Teach's crew—any trials or hearings involving a defendant by the name of Isaac Joppa?" Will asked.

The clerk said he'd have to check the records and get back to him, although he doubted it. He had often revisited the piracy trial records at the request of historians, scholars, and other researchers who were attempting to recreate the events following the death of Blackbeard.

An hour later Will got a call back from the clerk.

He wasn't surprised that the clerk reported that there were no records of any proceedings, criminal or otherwise, involving a defendant by the name of Isaac Joppa, in the court in Williamsburg, Virginia.

The clerk noted, though, that Isaac Joppa's name did appear in a statement of one of the accused defendants—a pirate by the name of Caesar. And Joppa's name was also referenced by one Samuel O'Dell, one of the witnesses at the piracy trial. Will nodded at that—it confirmed what Dr. Rosetti has told him. The clerk reminded Will, of course, that he was gleaning this information only from the clerk's notes, not from the actual transcript.

While he had the clerk on the line, Will requested a certified copy of the clerk's notes in the Williamsburg trial and asked that it be forwarded to Boggs Beckford's office in care of Will Chambers.

Will strolled back out onto the porch again and looked at the thin line where the end of the Atlantic horizon met the sky.

And he wondered.

If no piracy trial of Isaac Joppa had ever been held in the English colonies in America, then how could his case be considered to have been ultimately decided—res judicata?

Will lost track of time as he stared at the thin line of the ocean horizon, posing the question over and over again—a question whose answer seemed to be as remote as the distant lands that lay far beyond, on the other side of the sea. As far away as the shores of England.

40

THE COURTROOM OF JUDGE HAWSLEY GADWELL had been in session for more than an hour. He had heard two criminal matters, and issued a divorce decree. Now he was reciting his decision on a motion for summary judgment in an automobile accident case.

The Jonathan Joppa case was next case on the docket. The purpose of the hearing was to conduct a "pretrial conference," where final matters relating to the trial would be discussed.

In folksy repartee with both lawyers in the preceding case, Judge Gadwell finally finished ruling on the automobile accident lawsuit. Then the clerk called the case of Jonathan Joppa as an ancillary proceeding in the probate matter of the estate of Randolph Willowby.

Will and Jonathan made their way to the counsel table and sat down. At the other counsel table Virgil MacPherson was smiling confidently. Terrence Ludlow, seated next to him, slouched with his face resting in his left hand.

After reviewing the court file for a few moments, Judge Gadwell leaned back in his chair, rocked back and forth, and then welcomed the attorneys and the parties to his courtroom.

"Good to see you all here again. Okay. We're here for a pretrial conference. First I'm going to address pending motions. I see only one...no, strike that, make that two motions. Both of these motions are from you, sir...Mister..." and Judge Gadwell searched the file in front of him. "Mr. Will Chambers. And I believe...yes, you're representing the interest of Reverend Jonathan Joppa, the claimant to the Stony Island property. Mr. Chambers, you've got a motion here for continuance of the trial date. Now, Mr. Chambers, one thing you've got to know about my courtroom—and as a matter of fact—most of the courtrooms down here in the fine state of North Carolina—we give plenty of time to people to prepare for trial. We give them all kinds of leeway—and when we get as close to trial as we are now…two weeks away…well, quite frankly, judges in this state are not very prone to entertain such a motion for continuance."

Will rose to his feet and smiled politely.

"Your Honor, I thoroughly understand the Court's position. And I also understand the general rule, which is admirable and certainly has logic to it."

But the judge cut Will off before he could continue.

"Mr. Chambers, aren't you the one whose uncle—you've got an uncle, Bull Chambers. He was the circuit judge for a number of years here in North Carolina. Isn't that correct?"

Will smiled and nodded.

"Well, Mr. Chambers, I'm going to tell you something I heard your uncle, Judge Bull Chambers, say at a judicial conference once. We were addressing the problem of lawyers always asking for continuations of trial dates…constant demands for adjournments of trials after they had already been set. It's a problem that plagues this court to no end. Your uncle said that the problem with lawyers nowadays is that they were all raised on television. And in particular, Saturday morning adventure serials…you know the ones where the hero was always in great danger at the end of the show, and then you see the words 'to be continued…' appear on the screen. Now, your uncle made the remark—it makes me laugh to think of it to this day because it's so true—that you lawyers come in here, and every time you get a trial date you say, 'Your Honor, to be continued…' Your motion is denied, Mr. Chambers. You'd be well advised to heed the advice of your good uncle."

"Your Honor, just for the record, I do want to make sure that the court has reviewed the motion I filed and the reasons stated in that motion for my need for a continuance—"

"Mr. Chambers, you can assume I have read, and will read, every pleading that you file in this case. Now, your motion is denied, so let's move along…"

Judge Gadwell then turned to the next issue in the case.

"Which brings us to this point. Now everyone agrees in this case that Reverend Joppa here has to shoulder the burden of proof—as the moving party—in order to claim his entitlement to the Stony Island property. It's his burden to prove the innocence of Isaac Joppa relative to those piracy charges. Now I asked both of you gentlemen to address, in written pretrial statements, how you anticipate the burden of proof being handled at trial. Mr. Chambers, you made this argument about reasonable doubt…"

"Exactly," Will replied. "My argument is simply this—in the criminal case, Isaac Joppa, if he would have ever gone to trial, would have been entitled to a presumption of innocence. He could have required the prosecution to prove their case beyond a reasonable doubt. Those were rights and privileges accorded to him under English common law. Now, under the last will and testament of Randolph Willowby, the burden of proof is clearly ours to prove his innocence. Nevertheless, I believe it should be to a standard of raising only a reasonable doubt as to his guilt, not affirmatively proving his innocence—which is a whole different matter."

Virgil MacPherson jumped to his feet and began arguing.

"Your Honor, this is a very clever argument. It's a little like one of those magic tricks that you see on TV. I saw this one the other night...really unbelievable. The guy's doing this 'street magic'—he gets a crowd around him and the next thing you know...this guy's absolutely levitating off the ground by about six inches. No strings. No cables. Here he is, live television—the guy is raising himself right off the ground. It was unbelievable..."

Judge Gadwell began chuckling. "Oh yeah. I saw the same thing. My eyes practically bugged right out of my head. So I was thinking to myself, *How in the heck did that guy do that?*"

"Well, that's right," MacPherson continued. "That's just like Mr. Chambers' argument here. At first it looks for all the world like it makes sense. Then, I realized—Mr. Chambers here is nothing but a street magician."

With that MacPherson began striding back and forth in front of the counsel table with his hands swept behind his suitcoat and firmly planted on his hips.

"You see, the trick to Mr. Chambers' argument is this—he almost tricked us into believing this is a criminal case. But it isn't. This is a probate case. We're deciding the transfer of property under the last will and testament of Randolph Willowby. And so the constitutional guarantees about having to prove guilt beyond a reasonable doubt simply have nothing to do with this case. Reverend Joppa here has to prove the innocence of Isaac Joppa to the civil law standard of a preponderance of the evidence. Plain and simple. That's it."

MacPherson sat down and Will Chambers stood again.

"Your Honor, I'm sorry that Mr. MacPherson views legitimate legal arguments as magic tricks. Here's the long and short of it. Randolph Willowby's last will and testament did not define what he meant by having to prove 'the innocence of Isaac Joppa under the criminal charges of piracy.'

That's the language there. Thus, we have to determine the intent of Mr. Willowby. I think we can presume the plain and ordinary meaning of the words used. The clear and plain meaning of the term 'innocence' would be the way most of us would use it—innocent under the law. And both American and English common law presumed that Isaac Joppa was innocent and required that he simply raise a reasonable doubt as to his guilt. We can therefore presume that was the meaning intended by Randolph Willowby—as the burden of proof applicable to Reverend Joppa."

MacPherson was beginning to stand up to give a reply argument, but Judge Gadwell waved him back down.

"Don't bother, Virgil. Mr. Chambers, your interpretation is denied. I accept the way Mr. MacPherson stated it in his pretrial statement: 'The Reverend Jonathan Joppa must prove, to the satisfaction of the court, as an affirmative proposition, by a preponderance of the evidence, that Isaac Joppa, in the year 1718, had not participated knowingly, and intentionally, as a member of the pirate crew of one Edward Teach; nor did he knowingly, or intentionally, commit acts of piracy at any time or any place.' Mr. Chambers, that's what you must prove. To my satisfaction. If you don't prove it, you and your client lose, and Terrence Ludlow and his attorney win."

It was only then—after mention of his name—that Ludlow tuned into the proceedings around him, sat up straight, and flashed a grin at the bench.

The court next turned to a listing of expert witnesses to be called by each side at trial.

"Now, Mr. Chambers, let's start with you. Who are the expert witnesses you anticipate calling at the time of trial?"

"Your Honor, we've listed three potential expert witnesses."

"Yes, I see that," the judge said. "In reviewing your pretrial statements, I noticed that both you and Mr. MacPherson listed three expert witnesses. That's a nice balance. Three and three. So tell me about your expert witnesses so that Mr. MacPherson here can know a little about them."

"My first potential expert witness is Dr. August Longfellow." Will was reviewing his notes while speaking, but he heard a chuckle coming from MacPherson's table.

Then he looked up and saw Judge Gadwell chuckling as well.

"Yes, the court does have some familiarity with Dr. Longfellow. And I'm not talking about his being an expert witness. As a matter of fact, wasn't he a defendant in this court not too long ago? DUI? For the uneducated in this courtroom, that means driving under the influence—of alcohol, that is."

Will grimaced.

"Okay, let's go to the next one," Judge Gadwell said, still chuckling. "This Susan Red Deer Williams. What's she all about?"

"She's an expert in early American Indian history—specifically, on the history of the Tuscarora Indians."

The judge had a perplexed look on his face.

"Mr. Chambers, what are we talking about Indians for? I mean, what does that have to do with the issues in this case?"

"Your Honor, there is evidence that Isaac Joppa survived the Battle of Ocracoke Inlet, where he was presumed to have been killed. The fact is, there's good evidence that he survived the battle, had contact with the Tuscarora Indians, and then moved on—"

"So?" the judge said, raising up his hands. "What in the world does that have to do with the issues of this case?"

"Because his conduct after the Battle of Ocracoke Inlet may have relevance to questions of guilt or innocence."

Will could see that Judge Gadwell was entirely unimpressed by the potential relevance of Susan Red Deer Williams' testimony. And frankly, Will had doubts himself as to whether or not he would actually call her. On the other hand, if he failed to list her, then he might be excluded from calling her at trial should facts develop that required her expertise.

"The third expert is Dr. Stephen Rosetti. He's an ocean archaeologist."

That caught Virgil MacPherson's attention, and he jumped to his feet to address the court.

"And here is where we have a real problem," MacPherson said. "Here's an expert who spends his time researching sunken vessels. We're not here about sunken vessels. We're here trying to determine whether Isaac Joppa was guilty of piracy in the year 1718."

"If the court please," Will countered gingerly, "Dr. Rosetti, as an ocean archaeologist and an expert in ancient sunken vessels of the early eighteenth century, has a wealth of information and expertise about shipping customs, the practices of pirates, and matters of admiralty law as they applied to those charges of piracy in the year 1718."

"Well, I'm not going to make an advance ruling on these witnesses right now," the judge said with a skeptical look on his face, "but you're going to have to convince me at trial that these folks have something worth saying about the issues in this case."

Then the judge turned his attention to Virgil MacPherson. He was loaded for bear.

"Your Honor, my first expert witness is Dr. Manfred Berkeley, a world-famous maritime historian, who will be able to address, directly and forcefully, the fact that there is overwhelming evidence of Isaac Joppa's guilt as a member of the pirate crew on board the ship belonging to, and in the control of, Edward Teach."

Judge Gadwell's eyes were riveted on MacPherson, and he was nodding.

"The second expert witness listed by us is Dr. Wilson Auger. He's an ocean archaeologist. But unlike Mr. Chambers' expert—Dr. Rosetti—Dr. Auger is going to be able to directly address the issues of Isaac Joppa's guilt. He's going to be able to address the fact that none of the artifacts extracted from the sea at the site of the Battle of Ocracoke Inlet support, in any way, a claim of innocence on the part of Isaac Joppa."

MacPherson was now ready to address his third listed potential expert witness. However, as he mentioned Dr. Henrietta Clover, the judge held up his hands and had the court reporter halt transcribing. He bent over to his clerk to answer a question on a matter that had just come to her on the telephone.

While the judge was talking with the court clerk, Will leaned toward Virgil MacPherson.

"Virgil, can you give me any idea why you're calling this Dr. Henrietta Clover—who's an expert, according to your list of witnesses, in matters of genealogy?"

MacPherson smiled and bent toward Will, lowering his voice.

"Sure, Will. I thought it would be helpful in this case to sort of get the genealogy lines straight. You know, there's a lot of room for confusion about who Isaac Joppa was and who he is related to, and this Reverend Malachi Joppa who was his father, and how Randolph Willowby is a distant relative of this fellow who married one of the daughters of Malachi Joppa. You know what I'm talking about...I just thought, to avoid confusion, we could get a genealogical expert in here to kind of set the stage straight on who the players were, so to speak. Just by way of background—and to set the stage...nothing too significant...you know what I mean?"

Will nodded, but something in both MacPherson's tone and in Will's recently obtained knowledge of MacPherson's tactics led him not to believe much of what the other attorney had just told him.

"Okay, we're back on the record," the judge said. "And the last one that you listed, Mr. MacPherson, is this Dr. Henrietta Clover. And apparently you've indicated in your pretrial statement that she's going to address issues of genealogy. All right, let's move on then."

Will gestured to the judge.

"If I may, Your Honor—could we just put on the record what the substance of Dr. Clover's testimony is going to be—"

"Mr. MacPherson said right on his pretrial statement," the judge said with irritation in his voice, "that she's an expert on genealogy. She's going to be talking about genealogy in this case. So I suppose that's why he's going to call her. So, let's move on."

Will could see that trying to gain further information about the anticipated testimony of Dr. Clover was a useless endeavor.

"Your Honor, in terms of exhibits, we intend to introduce a certified copy of the clerk's minutes of Her Majesty, the Queen's Court of Vice-Admiralty of the American Colonies, of Williamsburg, Virginia, dated March 12, 1719," Will explained. "In addition to other exhibits we also intend to introduce a certified copy of the entries of the clerk in the docket of Bath, North Carolina, for the years 1718 and 1719, relating to the grand jury testimony that led to the indictment of Isaac Joppa, the issuance of an arrest warrant by the magistrate shortly thereafter, and the eventual dismissal, a year later, by the court."

MacPherson then indicated that he would introduce into evidence the testimony of Henry Caulfeld, who testified at the grand jury hearing in Bath, North Carolina, positively identifying Isaac Joppa as a person who was actively engaged in the pirating, along with Edward Teach, of Caulfeld's ship, the *Marguerite*. Caulfeld's testimony had formed the basis for the grand jury's finding of reasonable grounds for the issuance of an indictment for piracy against Joppa.

With that, Judge Gadwell adjourned the proceedings and disappeared into his chambers. Jonathan Joppa walked out with Will Chambers but said very little. But Will could read Jonathan's expression. To borrow an adage from Joppa's prior years in baseball, he was probably thinking now that he should be looking for a relief pitcher…because the other side was hitting the ball out of the park.

41

"Jimmy—you're swinging late!"

Jonathan Joppa was on the sidelines of the makeshift ball field, calling to the twelve-year-old who had just struck out.

"I don't know where you're looking—but you're not looking at the ball. Just concentrate on the ball coming in—and swinging into the strike zone. Don't bother about trying it. Just make contact. Just watch the ball, swing into the strike zone, and focus on making contact, when it comes."

The young batter shrugged and nodded.

It was late afternoon, and Joppa was halfway through batting practice for his Safe Harbor Community Church youth baseball league. He had two in the outfield, two in the infield, and his pitcher. The rest of his team was rotating at bat.

Joppa took off his hat and swiped the sweat from his brow.

There was a crack as the batter swung and smacked a line drive that shot past the pitcher and landed at the feet of an outfielder.

"Nice job, Jimmy! Way to keep your eye on the ball."

Joppa was having a hard time focusing on baseball practice. He was ruminating on the rumors his secretary, Sally, had reported to him earlier that day.

"The natives are restless..." she had said, referring to Minnie Metalsmith and her group of malcontents.

He tried to shrug it off, but it hung over him like a cloud. He looked out onto the field and called to the team.

"Okay, rotate. You five go in for batting, and the rest of you take the field. Howie, you do the pitching for a while."

Then Jonathan caught something out of the corner of his eye.

Off in the distance, on a side street adjacent to the vacant lot turned baseball diamond, there was a long, black Rolls Royce. It looked familiar.

"Wow, take a look at that!" one of the boys exclaimed. "It must be somebody really famous!"

"I think I know that car," Jonathan said under his breath. "It looks like the same limo...Randolph Willowby's limo...the day I met with him. A couple months before his death. Definitely looks like it."

Frances Willowby was in the back seat of the sleek black Rolls. The chauffeur was sitting patiently and dutifully while she was watching the practice—and Jonathan Joppa—through her opera glasses.

When she noticed that her car had been observed, she motioned for the chauffeur to drive off.

She stared back through the rear window at the humble sandlot baseball diamond, with Jonathan Joppa now shouldering a canvas bag of baseball bats and gathering up his young players for a final huddle at home base.

"How come we get millionaires watching us?" Ryan shouted out.

"Dunno." Then Joppa smiled and added, "Maybe it's the owner of the Yankees—checking you guys out."

There was an explosion of laughter and catcalling.

But while the boys were letting off steam, Jonathan's gaze was fixed on the limo. He watched until it disappeared out of sight.

42

WILL WAS AT THE SMALL KITCHEN TABLE, working on the Joppa case. Files, papers, and books covered the entire table, as well as most of the flat surfaces of the living room. Despite intense effort, he was stymied. He had produced almost no concrete evidence proving Isaac Joppa's innocence.

In the living room, at the piano, Fiona had been working on a melody line for a new song. But at some point—Will wasn't sure when—she changed moods. Suddenly she was playing Beethoven's "Emperor" Concerto.

At almost any other time, Will would have appreciated it if Fiona played the classics. As a pianist, she was almost as accomplished as she was a vocal performer.

But today he had little appetite for Beethoven, particularly when it was banged out loudly less than twenty feet from his workspace, as he struggled to unravel the knotted historical facts surrounding an eighteenth-century criminal charge.

His focus was to find an answer to the old res judicata entry by the court clerk in Bath, North Carolina.

So he launched a full-scale research effort into similar piracy trials in the early 1700s. He came across an account of one particularly famous case—the trial of Captain William Kidd. He had picked up a book on the subject from the local island bookstore.

Kidd had been tried for murder and piracy in 1701, found guilty, and hanged. Originally, his career was legitimate enough. In fact, he received, in 1695, a royal commission to arrest pirates who had been attacking the ships of the East India Company. But lawful "privateering" soon turned to criminal piracy, with Kidd and his crew attacking and plundering a variety of ships. Faced with an increasingly difficult-to-control crew, in one outburst Kidd struck and killed his quartermaster.

But now, halfway through the arcane record of the 1701 trial, Ludwig van Beethoven was vying for Will's attention.

Will looked over at Fiona, who was hunched over the keyboard, with the concerto rolling out so loudly that the floor under his feet was vibrating.

Snatching the book, he retired to the porch outside. But it was not to be. A dozen teenagers were on the beach, screaming and cheering each time the volleyball was spiked across their net.

Will walked back into the cottage. He stood for a moment in the middle of the living room as Fiona kept playing. But after a few minutes, aware of his presence, she stopped playing and turned around.

"Is something the matter?" Then she added innocently, "I'm thinking about doing the *William Tell* overture next. What do you think?"

Will wasn't sure whether she was serious nor not. But he threw her a look that left no ambiguity about the fact that *he* was serious. And not pleased.

"So," Fiona said with an eyebrow raised, "my darling husband, are we ill-tempered this morning?"

Will was losing it.

"No—but *we're* highly frustrated—in fact, *we're* growing more and more discouraged—as *we* try to construct a theory of this case for *our* client, Reverend Jonathan Joppa…*We* are growing tired of questions that have no answers. Of trying to reconstruct a historical and legal event that is three hundred years old, buried in obscurity, and is proving nearly impossible to reconstruct."

"Well…isn't that what you do?" Fiona asked with a tinge of sarcasm in her voice.

"What do you mean, what I do?"

"Well, it seems to mean that you've always specialized in taking on impossible cases and winning them. Sometimes at the expense of *everything else in your life*. Isn't that what you do?"

Under other circumstances Will might have taken the first phrase as a compliment. But not today.

"Look, what I really need is some peace and quiet today to concentrate."

Fiona, with cumbersome effort, raised herself from the chair in front of the piano and walked over slowly, throwing Will a look that indicated that she was about to check some baggage, and it wasn't just carry-on.

"Tell me something," she said, her voice quivering. "Have I been good about my pregnancy?"

Slightly befuddled by the question, Will replied, "I don't get it—what do you mean?"

"Exactly what I said. How have I been about my pregnancy? Have you heard me complain a lot? Have you heard me talking about my backache? Or my knees hurting? Or my trouble sleeping at night? Or what it's like being this pregnant in the heat of the summer? Have you heard me grumbling about those kinds of things?"

Will was still unable to connect the dots. "Well…sure, you've been great about it. But I still don't see what that has to do with what we're talking about."

Fiona put her hand to her forehead in exasperation.

"The point is this…the wife here is extremely pregnant, extremely uncomfortable, and constantly dealing with raging hormones and roller-coaster emotions. On the other hand, the husband is apparently concerned only with creating a working environment as quiet as his legal-office law library. And winning his case.

"Now, I'm the pregnant one here. You're not. I help you with your case…and how do you say thank-you? By becoming even more obsessed with this Joppa lawsuit."

"I don't know how else to say this—but I really need to win this case."

"You need to win every case. That's the problem," Fiona countered. "You're always driven—but this time you seem totally consumed. This is a little ocean cottage. Not a law office. It was supposed to be our summer getaway—and you've got the Joppa case taking over every corner of it."

"But you were the one—"

"I know. I encouraged you to take the case. But that's no excuse to lose all sense of balance. I've done my part to help you on this, remember? I'm a team player. But you're running the team into the ground."

"Look, I can't help it. MacPherson, and especially Blackjack Morgan, want to run all over us. And I haven't come up with a single decent piece of evidence proving our case—"

"So is it about justice? Or is it really about sticking it to this Blackjack Morgan guy?" Fiona's face was flushed. "I'm the same one who tells you all the time how the Lord is using your legal talent to right some of the serious wrongs in the world. Remember? I was there when you defended my Da…and also that case wrongly accusing those parents of child abuse in Georgia, where I flew out to be with you … and do I have to remind you what I went through in Caleb Marlowe's war crimes case? Do I? Or waiting to see if you would come back safely from the Sudan trial after getting death threats…"

Fiona's eyes were tearing up.

"Hey, come on…don't get yourself upset …" Will fumbled.

"You made me upset. So now you're going to hear what I've been carrying inside…"

"What you're carrying inside is our baby. I want you to sit down—"

"Convenient. Now you get pro-family! You never answered my question."

"OK. Here's the answer," Will said fiercely. "It's not about revenge against Morgan. Not exactly. It's about Uncle Bull—"

"Uncle Bull? What are you talking about?"

There was an awkward silence.

"What's going on…there's something else, isn't there? Something you haven't told me," Fiona said with a hurt expression.

After another pause, Will explained. About Morgan's vendetta against Uncle Bull because of the search warrant he had signed…how Morgan's revenge probably cost Bull a seat on the Court of Appeals.

"So, you *do* have an axe to grind. My Da used to say something about that—'If you've got an axe to grind, be careful where you point the blade…'" She tried to turn away, but Will put his hand gently on her arm.

"Don't go…alright. I have been absorbed into this case. I admit it. And I haven't been taking enough time for you. And I probably haven't been prioritizing this pregnancy. I'm going to start zeroing in on you and the baby. Promise."

"So I'm sure you remembered," Fiona said, still slightly caustically, "we've got another checkup this afternoon with Dr. Yager. Right? You remember that? Let's start by zeroing in on that."

Fiona turned her head away slightly, but Will still saw tears forming.

"Fiona," he said softly, "I want you to know how great you've been during this pregnancy. This really is a *big deal*. The pregnancy…our baby. It's a really big deal. And I'm so very proud of you."

Fiona started weeping. She covered her eyes and shook her head.

"I don't know why I'm crying. I really don't…"

Will held her tightly, and kept holding her for a while.

Then she kissed him, and turned to the piano.

"All right, Counselor, I'll knock off the Beethoven. How about I play a little Bach instead. *Very* softly…I'll even use the damper pedal! Now go back to work…"

Will went back to the kitchen table and returned to the trial proceedings of Captain William Kidd.

Fiona was gently playing Bach's "Sleepers, Awake."

As Will was reading the trial testimony, a thought struck him—a random thought. Quiet. Like just a snatch of a voice...as if he'd been walking down the halls of some university and, for only a moment, heard a few words floating out from a lecture through a partially opened door.

He flipped back to the beginning of the record of Kidd's trial:

> *THE TRIAL of CAPTAIN WILLIAM KIDD, for murder and piracy, upon six several indictments...at the Admiralty Sessions held at the Old Bailey, London, on the eighth and ninth of May, 1701...*

An *indictment*. Suddenly, he understood. William Kidd was indicted by a grand jury. Then Will flipped the pages of the book to the beginning of the jury trial. He studied the jury's charge from the clerk:

> *You of the jury, look upon the prisoner, and hearken to his cause. He stands indicted by the name of William Kidd, late of the English colonies in America, in the state of New York, who upon this indictment has been arraigned, and thereunto has pleaded not guilty, and for his trial, put himself on God and his country, which country you are. Your charge is to inquire whether he be guilty of piracy and robbery whereof he stands indicted, or not guilty.*

A sailor. A captain—based in New York, but tried in the Old Bailey criminal court in London, England.

As the structured chords of Bach formed an aural background, a picture came to Will's mind. It was an ancient drawing, a replica of the maps of the sea, in one of the articles in Virgil MacPherson's avalanche of documents. It showed the Old World islands of Britain—then the waves of the ocean, with a sea serpent's head appearing behind one of the waves—and then the shores of the New World of the Americas.

Two worlds. The Old World and the New World. Separated, yet organically connected, by one common ocean.

And more than that.

Two worlds connected by a common legal system.

The English common law ruled in both England and in the English colonies in America.

Unknowingly, Will had dropped the book and risen to his feet. He found himself walking to the window overlooking the ocean as Fiona played softly in the background.

"Which is why," Will muttered out loud excitedly, "it was possible for Captain William Kidd to have been arrested in New York for crimes of piracy committed on the high seas, sent back to the Old Bailey court in London, and there tried. Under one common law system."

He rushed back to the kitchen table and grabbed the book he had been reading. He turned to the notes at the back to find out the source of the trial transcript.

Old Bailey. Old Bailey. Old Bailey. Will kept turning the words over and over again. It was possible…theoretically possible…procedurally possible… that Isaac Joppa could have been charged by a grand jury in the American colonies but subjected to a full jury trial on the charges of piracy in the Old Bailey criminal court in London.

Will looked at his watch. It was only mid-morning. He might still be able to contact someone in England. He had to test his hypothesis. He quickly dialed the international operator for information about the source he'd found in the book.

"Should I stop playing?" Fiona whispered softly.

"No. Absolutely not. Keep playing…softly…but keep playing!"

Eventually, Will was connected to a researcher at the University of Sheffield who was in charge of transcripts for the Old Bailey criminal court in London.

After more than ten rings, someone picked up.

"University of Sheffield," the voice at the other end said.

"Yes, ma'am," Will said excitedly, "I have a request for you. A *very unusual* request."

43

"WHAT KIND OF REQUEST DO YOU HAVE?" The woman spoke with a proper British accent.

"I understand," Will explained, "that the oldest records of Old Bailey criminal trials held in London are managed by a project there at the University of Sheffield."

"Yes, that's quite correct. We've been working on the project for several years."

"I'm trying to determine whether a certain criminal action resulted in a trial in the Old Bailey in the early 1700s..."

"I'm going to transfer you to our research director. He's much more up-to-date with the specifics of the project and the information that can be retrieved. If you would hold on for one very short moment, I'll see if I can get him for you."

Will was put on hold. Fiona was still playing softly, but her attention was divided between the keyboard and furtive glances at Will, trying to read his expression.

After several minutes, Will heard another crisply English voice.

"Yes, sir, calling from the States?"

"Yes, I am. My name is Will Chambers. I'm an attorney. I am doing some research as part of a case I'm handling. The research has to do with someone who was charged with piracy in the American colonies—in 1717. In 1719 an entry was made in court records in North Carolina indicating that the matter had been dismissed. But another entry indicated that it was dismissed res judicata..."

"Very interesting," the other man replied. "Exactly how can I be of assistance?"

"Well, the question is this. There was never any trial held in the American colonies. I am speculating...wondering whether, even though the indictment was issued by a grand jury in the American colonies, whether

189

the case could actually have been tried in the Old Bailey in London. And so I'm trying to get some information on the case."

"Yes—well, you've certainly come to the right place. The University of Sheffield has been in charge of this project for some time. We've been trying to retrieve the trial transcripts of proceedings before the Old Bailey. And we're very proud of our ability to reconstruct trials going back several hundred years."

"That's exactly why I'm calling. I'm trying to find out whether you have any record of a piracy trial involving a defendant by the name of Isaac Joppa—J-O-P-P-A."

"Well, that's fine, Mr. Chambers," the man countered, "but that's not entirely critical information at this point. You have to understand a little about how the system works. Not all trials have been captured."

"What do you mean? How far do you go back?"

"Well, let me explain. The first thing that was done is that the original transcripts were microfilmed. As you know, microfilm is a very slow and cumbersome process. Furthermore, viewing is limited to on-site evaluation. You have to be physically seated in front of the microfilm...for instance, here at the university...and scan it."

"And that's why I have a problem," Will explained. "I have a trial coming up very shortly. I don't have the time to fly to England and go page by page through transcripts."

"Well, Mr. Chambers, that's where you're in very good luck," the man said cheerfully.

"Oh? How so?"

"Because, understanding the limitation of microfilm, we decided to transfer the proceedings to a digitized process. That was done in cooperation with the University of Herefordshire—"

"Yes, and that's very interesting," Will said impatiently, "but let's get back to the part where you said I'm in luck..."

"Well, that's exactly what I'm explaining to you. The files were created specifically for the purpose of transmitting the trial transcripts over the Internet. That means if someone—well, where are you right now?"

"Down in the Cape Hatteras area of North Carolina. Along the seacoast of the United States."

"All right, there you are. If you have a computer handy...and I'm sure even there along the seacoast they have computer terminals. You may even have a laptop with you. You could access the Web site we've created. But what you have to understand is the limitations—"

"What kinds of limitations?"

"Well, there are chronological limitations," the Englishman replied. "We've been able to reconstruct more than twenty-two thousand trial proceedings from the Old Bailey. But that's just a small portion of them. There are large blocks of time…certain years we simply have not had the time to get to yet."

"Well, I'm dealing with a trial that would have taken place—if it took place at all—probably some time during the year 1719."

"Then you're most fortunate, Mr. Chambers. Because the trial proceedings from December 1714 through December 1759 have already been recovered and posted. But there are some other limitations—"

"You mean to say I can go to the Web site right now and access a trial from 1719—if it was tried in the Old Bailey in London?"

"Most certainly." But then he added with a note of caution in his voice, "What I was explaining to you is that there are other limitations—"

"Others?"

"Yes. Some of the transcripts—in terms of their original integrity—were not capable of being recovered. There was a certain amount of bleed-through. You have to recall that in the eighteenth-century they printed the proceedings on those old printing presses, with heavy ink…It would bleed through sometimes from one side of the page to the other, and the text would be either partially or totally obscured."

Will ended the call elated at the possibility that he might be able to locate a trial at the Old Bailey with Isaac Joppa as defendant. It was a long shot—but he knew he had to check immediately.

But when he plugged in his laptop and tried to access the Internet, he was unable to log on.

For an hour he tried in vain.

Then he felt Fiona's hand on his shoulder.

"I'm sorry to interrupt you," Fiona said, purse in one hand and car keys in the other, "but we've got to leave now for my exam. You promised you'd come with me."

"Absolutely. I'm going to be there. Just give me one second…" Will now heard the connection being made. "Honey, I think I'm getting connected. This may be the biggest break of all in this case."

"Okay. I am going out to the car. I am going to start the car. And then I am going to honk the horn. And I expect you to be with me in the car within ten seconds after I honk—or else we're going to be late. Please,

Will—when I honk, you come on out, and let's take off. This is important."

Will frantically typed in the Web site address. He waited.

The retrieval indicator at the bottom of his screen was slowly inching
from ten, to twenty, to forty percent. In a moment, Will scrolled down the
introductory page, speeding through the instructions as fast as he could.

Then he clicked onto the search and typed in the year 1719.

Outside a car honked.

Will then typed in the name Isaac Joppa.

Again the car honked—this time twice.

The retrieval indicator slowly edged from one, to five, to ten percent.

Will threw up his hands and got up. He walked backward, looking at
the blank screen, until he got to the door.

Then he darted through it and sprinted to the car.

Fiona was in the passenger seat, wearing an expression of almost
exhausted patience.

Will said, as he pulled away in the car, "All right. Let's focus on your
pregnancy. Let's focus on the baby…okay? I wonder what Dr. Joppa will
say."

Fiona was half-smiling. "Yes. It's good to see you have your mind off
the case…"

As Will made his way down the ocean road and onto the main highway,
back at the cottage, the screen of his laptop finally lit up.

The rough characters of old type, printed nearly three hundred years
before, appeared on the screen. They read,

*THE PROCEEDINGS ON THE KING'S
COMMISSION OF THE PEACE
AND
Oyer and Terminer, and Gaol–Delivery of Newgate held for
the CITY of London, and COUNTY of Middlesex, at
Justice Hall in the Old Bayly
ON
Monday, Tuesday, and Wednesday, being the 10th, 11th and 12th
of this Instant, May, 1719, in the fifth year of His Majesty's reign.*

And below that, after a listing of the names of the jurors:

*Isaac Joppa, late of Bath, North Carolina, of the English colonies in
the Americas, mariner; stands indicted, for that he, not having God*

before his eyes, but being moved and seduced by the Instigation of the Devil, on the fifth day of December in the third year of His Majesty's reign, the said Isaac Joppa, in a certain ship called Queen Anne's Revenge, of which the captain was one Edward Teach, a pirate by common knowledge, and within the jurisdiction of the admiralty of England, in parts beyond the seas, did engage in acts of piracy and robbery committed against a sloop, Marguerite, for which offense, if found guilty, he shall be hanged by the neck until dead. On this indict-ment said prisoner has been arraigned, and on his arraignment has pleaded not guilty; and for trial, and has placed himself upon God and his country, whose country, as jurors, you are. Your charge is to inquire of him if he be guilty, or be not guilty...

44

THE PARKING LOT OF MELVIN'S CAFÉ was empty except for Melvin Hooper's own vehicle. He had positioned himself in front of the door, still wearing his cook's hat, T-shirt, and white apron.

His arms were crossed over his chest. A few minutes later, a sheriff's deputy's vehicle pulled into the parking lot and two deputies exited.

There followed a Department of Transportation car and a truck from the Municipal Department of Public Works.

The driver of the public works truck pulled into the driveway and quickly scrambled around to the back of his pickup, where he retrieved several sawhorses and arranged them across the entrance to the driveway.

One of the deputies approached Hooper with a piece of paper in his hand.

"Come on, Melvin, don't make this any harder than it has to be."

"I'm not the one making this hard," he snapped back.

"Look…I've got a piece of paper that says we're shutting you down today. It's noon. That's what the court order says. Now a court of law says we've got to demolish this place and run a new highway through here. This same piece of paper also says you are going to receive a fair price from the county for the value of your property—"

"Fair price?" Melvin yelled, nearly in tears. "You want to know how long it took me to build up my restaurant so that tourists and locals knew where to come for the best food on Cape Hatteras? It's not just brick and wood and kitchen equipment—it's my life here you're talking about…my blood and my sweat that went into this place!"

"And I understand that," the deputy said. "But there's nothing I can do about this. I've got a court order. I've got a job to do. And you've got to obey this order. Now move out of the way…so we can board up this building. They've got to start breaking up the asphalt. They've got a job to do too."

"And what if I were to tell you that you're going to get to this restaurant and board it up only over my dead body—"

By now the two deputies were standing shoulder to shoulder. One had a hand on his pistol.

"Melvin...the last thing in the world I want to do is have to use force. But we've got a job to do, and we're going to do it. If we need to use force, we're going to use it. Now, for the last time, remove yourself from the front of this door!"

That was when Jonathan Joppa pulled up. He had planned on getting lunch from Melvin's on this, the last day of the restaurant's operation, not aware that Melvin had to shut down by noon. He swung his vehicle into the shopping center next door and sprinted over to the parking lot of the café.

"Melvin, what's going on?"

"Reverend Joppa, you stay out of this." the deputy said. "You stay away."

"They're taking my restaurant away!" Melvin's voice was now choked with sobs. "This is just the last straw for me...the last straw."

"That's where you're wrong!" Jonathan said as he walked slowly and carefully around the deputies and closer to Melvin.

"Reverend Joppa!" shouted the deputy with his hand still on his pistol. "I'm warning you—move back!"

"Easy, Deputy. Melvin and I are old friends. And I'm going to walk him away from this front door—and over to his car. He's going to get into his car, and he's going to drive away."

"Jonathan, you've got to stay out of this," Melvin said. "You have no idea...I know you mean well...but this is it. I've really been pushed too far. This is the last straw."

"That's where you're wrong," Jonathan said in a firm voice. "This is nowhere near the last straw—"

"How would you know?" Melvin yelled, his voice filled with rage and grief.

"Because I know...I know what it's like to lose something," Jonathan said, taking a few steps closer to Melvin. "To feel like there's nowhere to turn. And the things that mean the most to you are slipping right through your fingers. I know what it feels like—but I'm here to tell you it's not the last straw. Not by a long stretch. Now, why don't you come along...let me walk you over to your car. Let's go pick up your wife, and then head over to my place. You can fix dinner...one of your great meals...for the three of us. And then we'll talk about your future. Where you can go from here."

Melvin's large, broad face showed the signs of a great internal struggle.

"Do you have your car keys in your pocket?" Jonathan asked calmly.

Melvin nodded silently.

Jonathan took a few more steps. He was now within arm's reach of the older man. He put his hand on his shoulder and slowly guided him down the steps, past the deputies, and over to his car.

He told Melvin to follow him. They would drive to Melvin's house to pick up his wife.

The deputy with his hand on his pistol finally relaxed his grip.

"Look...I appreciate the help, Reverend. You have no idea how this started. First thing this morning Melvin called in a threat to the public works department. We didn't know what to expect..."

"Sure, I understand," Jonathan replied with a smile. "You fellows did a fine job. I don't think you're going to have any more trouble from Melvin. I'll stay with him tonight."

Melvin slowly moved his car out of the parking lot and pulled behind Jonathan's.

Jonathan walked around to Melvin, now behind the wheel.

"Hey, Melvin—in all of the excitement I forgot which road you live on. You're over on Sandy Point Lane, aren't you?"

Melvin nodded.

As Jonathan turned away from his car, he reached out and grabbed his arm.

"Look...I appreciate all you've done...and for being a friend in need..."

"So, let's pick up your wife, do some grocery shopping, and have a great dinner," Jonathan said with a smile.

Jonathan pulled away slowly and headed for Sandy Point Lane.

He took a deep breath, and then very slowly let it out.

Then he said, "Thanks, Lord, for being with me back there."

45

Both sides had filed motions before the trial, which was only a few days away. Judge Gadwell was in his courtroom hearing the motions.

During Will's more than twenty years of experience as a trial lawyer, he had become used to this last-minute flurry of activity before the first day of trial.

He likened it to the opening of battle during the Civil War. The North and South would both discharge their artillery to soften up the lines of the other army. Try to break a hole in the offensive structure of the enemy. Those were the pretrial motions. Then the fury of the full-scale charge would begin. For Will, that was the trial.

In his first motion, Will was requesting that the court take judicial notice of the proceedings before the Central Criminal Court in the Old Bailey, London, England, from 1719. This would have the court accept, and announce to the jury, that the Old Bailey transcript was to be received as proof of the official judicial action of the English court on the question of Isaac Joppa's innocence or guilt.

But there was one problem with that argument. The only portion of the transcript that had survived the ravages of time was the testimony of Isaac Joppa and Abigail Merriwether during the defense's case. No other part of the transcript had survived.

And even more important, the verdict rendered by the jury had not been recovered either. Their decision of guilt or innocence had been lost to the ages.

"How can this court take judicial notice," MacPherson argued to Judge Gadwell, "when we don't know how the jury or the court decided in the case? That's like watching an old videotape of the Superbowl that contains only the first half of the game and then saying, based on that, you can tell who won."

Gadwell chuckled loudly at that.

"Well, Virgil," he said with a smile, "I read ya loud and clear on that one. It reminds me of the story of the two guys who went into court to argue about who owned a certain horse. The judge decided he'd compromise a bit in his decision, and he awarded half the horse to the plaintiff and half the horse to the defendant. When the plaintiff complained, the judge couldn't figure out what his problem was. 'What's the matter with you? I've given you first choice of which end you want.' So the point is, Mr. Chambers, that with only the testimony of Isaac Joppa and his girlfriend, this Abigail Merriwether, you're asking me to take judicial notice of only half a trial. I think I'm going to have to reserve my ruling until trial so that I can think about that one."

"Our second motion," Will continued, "is to permit us to expand our list of exhibits, particularly regarding the entry of clerk's notes in the magistrate's court in Bath, North Carolina."

"Is that the old document you've filed," the court asked, "where the court says that Isaac's Joppa's case in 1719 is dismissed res judicata?"

"Exactly," Will replied. "We're asking that the court permit us to amend our exhibit list to include the Old Bailey transcript, obviously; but the other document to be added to the list is this clerk's note. Lastly, we want the court to take judicial notice of that note as an official act of the court in Bath as of 1719."

MacPherson began rising from counsel table to respond, but Judge Gadwell motioned for him to sit back down.

"You can save your breath, Virgil, because I've already thought this one through. Okay—I think both of you want to be able to add additional documents to your exhibit list. And I'm going to let you do that. But this is it. Don't come flying back into my courtroom twenty-four hours before the trial—and the trial's just a few days away now—and want to expand your list with new surprise exhibits and that kind of stuff, because I'm not going to tolerate that. But Mr. Chambers, as to the business of me taking judicial notice of the clerk's notes as part of an official court record, I'm going to have to think about that one. I'll rule on that during trial after I've heard some of the testimony."

"Then am I to understand," MacPherson asked with a smile, "that this court is also granting my motion to add to our exhibit list the transcript of the proceedings in admiralty court in London, England, where Isaac Joppa pled guilty to a charge of desertion from the Royal Navy, which occurred shortly before the criminal trial on the piracy charges in the Old Bailey?"

"You've read me correctly," Judge Gadwell said. "You can introduce that document as an exhibit at trial as well."

Will was troubled, of course, by the fact that MacPherson had researched the admiralty court desertion case against Joppa and had come up with a copy of the transcript.

It was clear to Will how MacPherson would use it at trial. He would hit hard on the fact that Joppa had admitted his criminal behavior in deserting from the ship *Intrepid*. Regardless of the well-established reputation of its captain for beating, abusing, and occasionally even killing his sailors, the fact remained that Isaac Joppa had jumped ship just prior to his first encounter with Edward Teach. MacPherson would undoubtedly argue to the jury that Joppa's life of crime began prior even to his first appearance on Teach's ship. That, in fact, it began when he illegally deserted his post as a seaman in His Majesty's Royal Navy.

Before concluding the proceedings, Judge Gadwell offered one final reminder.

"Okay—finally, both sides have asked for a jury trial, so a jury trial is what you're gonna get. I want your proposed jury instructions and verdict forms on the first day of trial so I have a chance to get to look at them. Have a good day, gentlemen."

He gaveled the proceedings to an end and disappeared into his chambers.

A tall man in a Hawaiian shirt and wearing a wide smile, carrying a pad of paper, strode up to Virgil MacPherson.

"Mr. MacPherson, I don't know if you remember me…I'm from the *Tide and Times Daily* here on the Banks. I covered that furnace explosion case you handled about two years ago down here. The one where several kids got injured. You won quite a big verdict in that case…"

"Yes, yes, great to see you." MacPherson began. "Listen, if you want a couple comments on the record on this case, let's go out in the hallway and talk."

"Sure, that'd be wonderful."

MacPherson and the reporter walked away from counsel table, leaving Terrence Ludlow alone to slowly stretch and then rise from his chair.

As the reporter followed behind MacPherson, he added, "Hey, did you hear the news? It was all over this morning. There's quite a bit of commotion going on down at Stony Island."

MacPherson stopped in his tracks at the doorway.

Blackjack Morgan was only a few feet away, sitting in the last row of the courtroom. His eyes were riveted on the reporter.

"Yeah, the rumor started late yesterday," the reporter explained. "I guess the word got out on the grapevine that Blackbeard's treasure might be located somewhere on Stony Island. I think every person with a boat within fifty miles is heading over there today."

Morgan had heard enough. He pushed his way through MacPherson and the reporter abruptly and quickly stepped, cane tapping on the floor, out into the parking lot to his rented truck—the one he had been driving since the fender bender at Glen Watson's auto repair shop.

Will and Jonathan both heard the reporter's comments and then stared at each other for a few seconds.

"What do you know about this?" Will whispered to Jonathan.

The other man shook his head. "Nothing. I don't know what to say… what do you think's going on?"

Will shook his head. He didn't have an answer to that.

But he now had a new question of his own.

Was this case really about the innocence or guilt of Isaac Joppa? he wondered. *Or was it about an island that had successfully kept a secret over the centuries— a secret perhaps more spectacular than any of them could have possibly understood?*

46

T HE WATERS WERE FILLED with a frenzy of boats—an armada of fishing rigs, rowboats, and sailboats.

By the time the two Sheriff's Department boats arrived, several dozen treasure hunters were already swarming over the surface of Stony Island.

One of the sheriff's boats slowed to a glide as the deputy stood up with bullhorn in hand.

"Attention, all boaters! Please clear the waters around the island immediately. This is an order from the Sheriff's Department. You are required to comply immediately. Please move your boats from the shallows of the island."

At the top of the island, some of the would-be looters heard the bullhorn. They were now scrambling pell-mell down the sandy path to the dock, where their launches were tied.

The later arrivals at the dock had already managed to jump in and motor madly away, and the remaining treasure hunters scrambled to the other end of the island, where they had their rowboats and canoes.

Leonard Moore, the property manager for the Willowby family, was in the other Sheriff's Department boat. After both boats coasted up to the dock, one of the deputies helped him onto the dock and walked with him up to the ruins of the old Youngblood house.

Moore immediately noticed the smashed urns. He inspected the shards of stone on both sides of the crumbling front step.

"Looks like some vandalism, right?" the deputy asked.

Moore nodded his head.

Then the deputy's radio crackled. One of the others had caught two of the trespassers.

"What do you want me to do with them?" he asked.

"Take 'em in. Book 'em for trespass. We're not quite sure what we're gonna do...I have to talk to Mr. Moore here, and he'll talk to the owner, Mrs. Willowby. And then we need to talk to the sheriff."

"How in the world did all of this craziness begin?" Moore asked, as the deputy helped him straighten up from the ground.

"We're running down the leads right now. But I've got a pretty good idea. I heard from someone who was hanging around one of the bars the night before last. A local diver by the name of Robideau was on a drinking binge with some buddies. He starts bragging about how Blackbeard's treasure is buried over here on Stony Island. I think that's where it started. The next thing you know, it's all over the Outer Banks."

"Well, we had *No Trespassing* signs posted in a number of spots..."

"Hey," the deputy replied, "when these Blackbeard stories surface, nobody cares about trespassing laws. I've heard about this kind of insanity... a number of years ago, before I joined the force here, they had the same thing happen. Another part of the Outer Banks...somebody's property got demolished by all the looters. You know, they're just never going to find anything—but once these stories get started, they're really hard to put a stop to."

"Now about Mrs. Willowby wanting to prosecute these people—I really don't know about that. I'm not sure if she's going to want to bother, but I will have to speak to her about it."

"I understand. Just let us know in a couple of days what she's decided to do."

Then the deputy took a few steps toward the shoreline and surveyed the melee of boats motoring and sailing away from the island. Several boaters were screaming at each other. Vulgarities were faintly echoing over the island.

"Human greed," the deputy muttered to himself. "It's a scary thing, isn't it?"

47

With only two days left before trial, Will Chambers was busy with his final preparations.

Fiona was at the kitchen table with a tall stack of documents in front of her. She was three-hole punching and collating them into a large tabbed notebook. The material consisted of examination questions for each of Will's witnesses, cross-examination questions he expected from MacPherson, and legal research notes with arguments he planned to make to anticipated evidentiary objections from his opponent. Those were followed by a set of cross-examination questions for each of Virgil MacPherson's witnesses. Then there was the bulk of Will's legal research, not to mention jury instructions, verdict forms that would be submitted to the jury, and an outline of his opening and closing arguments.

Will was on the phone with August Longfellow, going over his anticipated testimony.

"Dr. Longfellow, about that reference by Judge Gadwell to your driving under the influence—"

"It's ridiculous!" Longfellow bellowed. "He must have me mixed up with some other person. I can't imagine where the judge would get such a ludicrous idea!"

"So," Will said, still asking for some reassurance, "you were definitely not convicted of drunk driving?"

"Absolutely not."

"Any other criminal convictions, legal problems, or points of potential embarrassment I ought to know about?"

Longfellow paused and chuckled a bit.

"I may be a philosophy professor, an eccentric, and a part-time poet, but I'm not a sociopath!" With that he gave a hearty laugh.

"I'm not suggesting you are," Will said, not sharing Longfellow's amusement. "I just want to make sure I'm not stepping into any quicksand. It's important that you tell me anything in your background that might create a problem with your credibility."

"Will," Longfellow said with an air of lingering mirth, "I'm as clean as your grandma's tea set."

Moderately satisfied that his witness's background contained no booby traps, Will gave him a few reminders of the date and time of his testimony and then said goodbye.

Will ambled into the kitchen, retrieved a large pitcher of lemonade from the refrigerator, and poured two glasses. Then he sat down next to Fiona and gave one glass to her.

"Do you know what I was just thinking?" Fiona said as she was sliding documents into a three-ring binder.

"What?"

"I was thinking…after our baby grows up and is off to college and I start getting old—not that old, but somewhere around Aunt Georgia's age—you know what I would like to do?"

"No, what?"

"I'd like to go to law school. Then you and I could practice law together." Will was chuckling quietly.

"Alright, what's so funny? Don't you think I could do it?"

"No, I don't have any questions about that," Will said, still chuckling.

"What are you laughing about then?" Fiona said, pressing the point with a bit of mischief in her eye.

"I'm just picturing the two of us in our old age. Both of us with white hair. We're in a courtroom. You are at one counsel table and I'm at the other. We're on opposite sides of some case."

"Then what? What happens?"

"Well, then you beat the pants off me!" Will burst into laughter.

Fiona was trying to be serious, but failed—finally laughing so hard that she got the hiccups.

"Besides—" Will said.

"Okay…here it comes…"

"Now you don't know what I was going to say. I was just going to make the point that in order to go to law school, you would have to stop singing. No more concerts, no more records."

Then Will paused for another moment.

"And in my humble opinion, if you ever stopped singing it would probably mean the death of music."

Fiona smiled, and her eyes were soft.

"I remember the first time I heard you sing," Will said. "I was offstage at that pavilion in Baltimore. I don't think you knew I had arrived yet. You were singing 'Let the Children Come to Me.' That's when I knew I was beginning to fall in love with you, even though I barely knew you."

"Oh, I was aware that you were offstage." Fiona's were filling with tears. "You just did not see me keeping you in the corner of my eye through the concert!"

They both laughed again. Then Will looked at his wife.

"Sing something for me. Just a capella. That would be perfect. I would really love that."

Fiona was surprised by her husband's look—intense, emotional, enthralled. She thought for a moment, then began singing an old Celtic hymn based on a Psalm:

> *The hevins furth-tellin are*
> *The gudeliheid o' God*
> *The hail lift furth-schawin*
> *Is his ain han's doen.*

But then Fiona stopped singing. Will looked at her and saw a startled look on her face.

She turned slightly in her chair and lifted up the hem of her sundress. A trickle of blood was flowing slowly down her leg.

She could only say, "Will…"

"Fiona, darling, stay right there. Don't move." Will jumped from his chair toward the telephone.

"I need to get my feet up on a chair right now," Fiona's voice was cracking.

"Yes, absolutely, but don't move. Let me do it…" Will dashed back to Fiona, gingerly lifted her two feet off the floor, and pushed a chair underneath them.

On the phone, Dr. Yager's receptionist indicated that the doctor would see Fiona immediately. Will was to lay her supine in the backseat of the car and drive her directly to the office.

As he carried her to the car, Fiona buried her face in his neck. Will could feel the hot stream of tears from her eyes. She was quietly murmuring a prayer for the safety of her baby—and for fast and safe travel to the doctor's office.

As they reached the car, Will finished by adding, "And protect my wife, Fiona, soul of my soul."

Fiona looked up and gave him a hard kiss on the lips. Then he laid her gently in the back.

When they reached the medical clinic the physician's assistant was waiting at the front door with a rolling bed. Dr. Yager immediately attached a fetal heart monitor, then commenced an ultrasound.

After an examination, Dr. Yager looked at both of them—Will sitting in an uncomfortable plastic chair, Fiona lying on the table.

She began. "I think we are looking at one of two scenarios. Sometimes you get very mild spotting when a small sinus leaks. But in this case, Fiona, you had blood flow. The position of the placenta is now giving me a great deal more concern. It may be tearing away—this may be the beginning of separation of the placenta itself. A real risk to you, Fiona—and to your baby of course. You can lose a lot of blood very quickly. This could be life-threatening. Of course we knew there was an outside chance of this when you first saw me. But now we've got a very high-risk pregnancy. Here's the big question— do you want to be hospitalized right now? Or, Will can you make sure she has complete bed rest at your place? Is there someone to look after her…either you or someone else?"

"I want to do what is safest—" Will began.

"I want to be at the cottage," Fiona blurted out. "Or you could take me over to Aunt Georgia's cottage. She could take care of me through the day, and then—with the trial coming up—Will, you could be with me at night. I really do want to be close to you, and close to Aunt Georgia. I think that would be just as safe, and I really prefer it…"

Will turned to the doctor expectantly.

"I think that will be alright," Dr. Yager said. "But you have to remain lying on your back except for getting up and using the bathroom. Any change—any blood at all, spotting or flow—you call me immediately and we'll admit you."

Will and Fiona both nodded.

After the doctor was gone, Will walked over to the examining table and kneeled next to his wife.

He brushed her dark hair away from her eyes and cupped her delicate features in his two hands, wanting to say something strong and reassuring. But his voice cracked—there were no words.

He simply cleared his throat and bent down to kiss the woman he loved, then carefully moved his hand down over her belly, and gave a blessing to the tiny traveler.

Then a shoulder, a foot, perhaps an arm pressed out toward the world from the inside. A sign of life, at least for the time being, from behind the curtain of flesh.

48

With the trial date approaching, Will had set aside half a day to drive up to Elizabeth City to visit his uncle Bull. But as he motored north, his mind seemed to be filled with a cacophony of thoughts, as if he were listening to some abstract and discordant symphony. Most of them focused on Fiona.

Her pregnancy had been a problem from the beginning. But now the danger was real and imminent. Will was feeling guilty and stupid about the way he had been ignoring her lately.

As a trial lawyer, one of his greatest gifts—his ability to focus ferociously on the narrow and sometime abstruse categories of fact, law, and jury psychology—had now become his biggest impediment. The recent problems with her pregnancy had now sent him into a jarring change of gears. He had even toyed with the idea of delegating the lead counsel position at trial over to Boggs Beckford, whose recovery had enabled him to begin getting around on crutches. But how could Will do that? The recreation of Isaac Joppa's life and the proof of his innocence had become imbedded in the core of Will's thinking. He walked in and out of it, like a well-furnished room where he knew each object, each proof, each logical argument—carefully shelved and indexed. He felt confident he could locate and retrieve each item with rapidity and accuracy.

Even beyond that, Will felt the moral force of absolute conviction that Isaac Joppa was innocent. He believed it deep down in his guts and sinews. It went far beyond even vindicating Bull by beating Blackjack Morgan now. In a strange sense, Will felt as if he was *meant* to try this case...and to reveal something hidden—long a secret—about the life and times of Isaac Joppa.

Thus it would have to be Will's task—and Will's alone—to argue this case.

But given that, Will wondered why he felt the compulsion to visit Bull Chambers *now*. Why not wait until after the trial?

Perhaps, Will mused to himself, *it has nothing to do with anything except the most simple and profound sense of loyalty and love for my uncle—the man who was like a second father to me.*

For Will, that was enough.

He arrived at the convalescent center and checked in. Bull was out on the side porch, where Will found him in a large cane-backed wheelchair, lying in the sunshine.

Bull looked like he had lost a little weight since just a few weeks before. The right side of his face drooped, and his right hand was curled into itself. His right leg was turned inward, his foot at an awkward angle.

When Bull saw Will quickly approaching, his eyes brightened, and he lifted his left arm in an open embrace.

Will bent down and gave him a hug that lasted a long time.

Then Will pulled up a chair. He did most of the talking, filling him in on his summer on the beach living next to Aunt Georgia. And about Fiona's pregnancy. About their hopes for the future. About his law practice in general—and about the Jonathan Joppa case in particular.

Bull offered only a few comments. Will had to strain to understand his garbled speech. But he seemed alert as Will was painstakingly describing the complex factual background of the life of Isaac Joppa, and the question of his innocence upon which the current lawsuit depended. When Will pointed out how Blackjack Morgan fit into the case, Bull looked away, an expression of sadness sweeping over his face.

Will decided to change the focus, and he began explaining his general theory of the case and what proofs he would bring to bear in an effort to establish Joppa's innocence at trial.

When Will finished, Bull leaned a little toward him, raising his left arm and vigorously making an ambiguous gesture. Will finally determined that his uncle was asking him to elaborate more about the case…but Will could not begin to figure out what fact or argument he had omitted.

Then Bull pointed to himself, opening his eyes wide and giving an inquiring look to Will.

"So," Will said with a smile, finally deciphering Bull's body language, "can I ask *you* a question?"

Bull nodded and gave a struggling, crooked smile with the left side of his face.

"Still the country judge, aren't you?" Will said with a chuckle.

Bull nodded even more vigorously at that.

"Alright, here's my question. How am I gonna get through to this jury that Isaac Joppa was innocent? I've told you all my evidence. I've told you my arguments. I'm just trying to figure out if there's something I'm missing. I get the feeling there is, but I can't tell you what it might be. It's like driving on the freeway and you sense there's another car real close to you, close enough where you could reach out and almost touch it. But the car is traveling at the same speed—so close, and on your blind side, you don't see it…but somehow you sense it's there. So what am I missing?"

There was silence for several minutes. Then Bull Chambers gave another labored smile, and said something.

Will could not understand. Three words…but what were the words? He apologized, put his hand on Bull's shoulder, and quietly asked him to repeat it, carefully.

Now Will thought he understood.

They were familiar words. Words well-known to Bull, and particularly his wife, Georgia—whose lives had been steeped in the language of the Bible. The three words were from Paul's first epistle to the Corinthians, chapter thirteen.

Faith, hope, love.

When Will had absorbed those three words, Bull, overcoming the tortured disability of the flesh, spoke the end of the matter.

Greatest…love.

As he motored back to the oceanside cottage, Will was still contemplating the conversation.

He appreciated the reference to First Corinthians, but he wondered whether there was some relevance in it to the Jonathan Joppa case. He was hard-pressed to fit it in logically. He finally resigned himself to the fact that his uncle's comments had little, if anything, to do with the upcoming trial.

Will called Fiona on his cell phone and told her he loved her and would soon be home.

He decided he would put in only an hour or two more preparing for the Joppa trial and then spend the evening holding his wife in his arms, talking with her about their family and life together.

Whatever it was that was plaguing him—giving him the sense that something was missing in his case—would have to wait until later.

49

On the day of trial, Boggs Beckford had made it to Will's counsel table. He still had one arm in a sling. But it seemed to be intensely personal with him that he make it to the courtroom that day.

Beckford watched as Will set out his trial notebooks, exhibits, and multiple legal pads.

Jonathan Joppa, seated between Will and Beckford at counsel table, seemed peculiarly at ease. Will thought that perhaps it was because he knew the trial would not require his testimony. He would simply be a bystander to the recreation of the events surrounding Isaac Joppa.

Yet Jonathan knew there was a force now at work in his life. He was now able to view the unfolding of the long-awaited trial with calm and confidence.

At the other counsel table, Virgil MacPherson sat next to an associate lawyer and two law clerks. They were huddled together in intense conversation.

Their client, Terrence Ludlow, was relegated to a seat in the row of chairs behind the counsel table. He was reading the sports page of the morning newspaper.

Beckford leaned and whispered, "How do you feel about the case now?"

"Much better," Will said with a smile.

"Yeah, I'm the same way. Especially because you dug up that Old Bailey transcript...now we've got a real horse race."

Will nodded. "Boggs, you hit the nail on the head. Before I came across that transcript, we had a critical problem...my most important witness, Isaac Joppa, was missing in action."

As Will waited for Judge Gadwell to mount the bench, and as the jury panel assembled at the back of the courtroom, Will couldn't help but think about the irony of the case.

After all, what would Isaac Joppa have thought if he knew that, nearly three hundred years later, people would still be debating whether he was guilty or innocent?

Suddenly the judge's chambers door swung open, and Judge Hawsley Gadwell climbed up to the bench. He gave a big wave to the jury and a broad smile.

The clerk called each of the jurors who had been empanelled, one after another.

Both Will and MacPherson had stipulated, prior to the trial, to the North Carolina code procedure that permitted a six-person jury.

For Will that was not a difficult decision. The historical complexities involved in proving Isaac Joppa's innocence presented a formidable task. He was depending that with the smaller jury, he ultimately had to convince fewer people. In fact, if he was simply able to convince the potential foreperson on the jury, he felt he had a good chance of winning.

Virgil MacPherson had the same game plan. With six persons having to decide, a quicker verdict was possible. And with a potentially shorter span of time in the jury deliberation room, MacPherson would be placing his primary emphasis on one irrefutable fact: Will Chambers' case had to shoulder the burden of proof. Any indecision on the part of the jury—any ambiguity about the facts—would mean that Will Chambers and Reverend Jonathan Joppa would lose, and Terrence Ludlow and Virgil MacPherson would win. Which would mean that Blackjack Morgan would win...an indescribably grotesque thought for Will.

After the *voir dire* process of jury selection, the six jurors who remained were typical. That is to say, they presented a not-so-encouraging cross-section, though still not grossly biased either way. Will studied them as they raised their right hands and took the oath of fidelity to the rule of law and to the instructions of the court, and couldn't help but think of a few potential problems.

Juror number one, a stocky, balding, and affluent-looking gentleman who was the president of a small construction company, looked harmless enough. Yet both Will and MacPherson viewed him as a strong potential for foreman of the jury. He seemed forceful, expressive, and quick to form opinions.

Juror number two was a high school math teacher, a quiet middle-aged woman with short hair and a studious, almost librarian-like affect about her.

An unemployed janitor was juror number three. He looked tired and drawn. He had complained, in his conversation with the court, of unspecified liver problems. But he indicated that he would be able to finish the trial.

The fourth juror was a pleasant, diminutive widow in her late sixties.

The last two jurors were a twenty-year-old checkout clerk at the Coastal Foods grocery store who continued chewing her gum even while being questioned by the judge; and a thirty-year-old plumber's assistant, who gave every indication of being bored out of his mind and wanting to be anywhere but in that courtroom.

When jury selection was finished, the judge broke for lunch, telling counsel and the witnesses to be back by one o'clock.

Will pulled his cell phone out of his briefcase and began walking out of the courtroom to find a quiet place to call Fiona and Aunt Georgia.

But before he could exit, Virgil MacPherson and Terrence Ludlow caught up with him.

"Hey there, Chambers," MacPherson said, thrusting his hand. "May the best man win!"

Will shook his hand politely and then turned toward the door again.

But MacPherson interrupted.

"Say, how's your wife's pregnancy doing? She's going to have a baby pretty soon, isn't she? I thought I remember hearing that…No problems, I hope."

Will turned. MacPherson was struggling, ever so slightly, to look nonchalant. Ludlow was grinning grotesquely next to him.

"She's doing just fine. Thanks for asking," Will was trying to control the anger that was boiling just below the surface.

With MacPherson, Will knew that nothing was off the record and nothing was as it seemed. MacPherson was no doubt playing a sick mind game with him, trying to distract him before the commencement of his direct examination in the afternoon.

MacPherson kept talking.

"You tell that wife of yours I hope everything goes all right…You know, safe delivery. No problems. No complications. Tell her 'good luck' from us." Then the two men walked away.

As Will flipped open his cell phone, he saw MacPherson and Ludlow greeted by Blackjack Morgan, who was standing in the corridor. Morgan caught sight of Will and waved mockingly, giving Will a thin smile.

Aunt Georgia answered.

"How's my sweetheart doing?" Will asked.

"Oh, you know the two of us. This is like girls' night out all day long!" Georgia said with a cackle. Then she put Fiona on the line.

"Steady as she goes," Will reminded her. "You're taking it easy?"

"Oh yeah," Fiona said with a little hesitation in her voice. "I've got my feet up, and Aunt Georgia is spoiling me rotten. How's the case coming?"

"Much too early to tell. We picked the jury. Not good. Not bad. We'll see when the evidence starts coming in."

"Do me a favor, will you?"

"Anything, darling,"

"Pray for our little bambino here. That everything's going to be okay…"
Fiona's voice was trembling a bit.

Will reassured her. Told her he loved her more than he could possibly say or describe. And how sorry he was he couldn't be there with her.

Sauntering back into the empty courtroom, Will surveyed the two counsel tables piled with law books, notebooks, pads of paper, and stacks of exhibits and pleadings that represented the history of the Joppa case.

Will sat down in a chair and took in, just for a minute, the quiet around him.

It was very clear what his task really was. Will understood that, within the four walls of this small North Carolina courtroom, he must literally *make history*.

50

AFTER THE LUNCH BREAK, Will approached the podium, which was situated in front of the jury box. He would begin the opening statements.

Will emphasized the power of the actual transcript of the Isaac Joppa case—and in particular, Joppa's testimony in the Old Bailey criminal trial of 1719. Joppa had denied any complicity in the acts of piracy of Teach and his crew. Will summarized the transcripts—the testimony by Joppa himself that he was taken as a prisoner when Teach plundered the ship *Good Intent* while Joppa was a passenger on it. Thereafter, Joppa had testified he was Teach's slave. He was manacled with leg and wrist irons in the hold of one of Teach's ships for months.

Will further pointed out that the entire transcript of the 1719 trial did not survive the ravages of time. Thus it was unknown what the original jury in London, England, had decided about Isaac Joppa's guilt or innocence. There was no historical record to indicate whether he was acquitted—or found guilty and condemned to death by hanging—the usual punishment for acts of piracy.

Thus, it would be up to this twenty-first century jury to determine what had happened in the years 1717 through 1719.

Will then moved away from the podium and struck an informal pose, hands in pockets. He paused, then continued.

"In law school they still teach Latin terms. Let me give you a legal term that you're going to hear in the facts of this case. It is 'res judicata.' That means that a certain legal matter has gone to court in a trial or final hearing and has been finally and fully determined. That the legal issue is ultimately settled. You're going to hear testimony about that term in this case.

"You're also going to see an exhibit, an authentic photocopy of the note of the magistrate's clerk in Bath, North Carolina, made in 1719. The evidence will show that a year before that entry was made, in 1718, other entries were made by that clerk—to the effect that a grand jury had heard testimony of a single witness, an individual by the name of Henry Caulfeld, who said he witnessed Isaac Joppa engage in acts of piracy on the high seas. Based on that testimony alone, the grand jury issued an indictment. An arrest warrant was issued at the same time. Then, a year later, in 1719, a mysterious entry was also placed in the court's records. It said, regarding the case of Isaac Joppa, 'case dismissed.'"

Will took his hands out of his pockets and pointed straight up in the air with both index fingers. He paused, then continued.

"But there was one more entry. Following the note about the dismissal of Isaac Joppa's case, the clerk entered these words—'res judicata.' I believe the evidence will show that this phrase was entered as a reflection of what had happened in the Old Bailey criminal court in London a few months before. That word had gotten back to the colonies that Isaac Joppa had been acquitted. The evidence will show that there is no other logical explanation for the entry of res judicata. Such a phrase closes the chapter on the charges of piracy that had been falsely lodged against Isaac Joppa. Furthermore, I think it's going to close the chapter on the evidence of this case…evidence I believe will persuade you to find in our favor—that Isaac Joppa was not a willing or voluntary member of Teach's pirate band, nor did he willingly participate in any acts of piracy at any time in his life. That Isaac Joppa was, and still is to this day—nearly three hundred years later—innocent of those charges."

Will had been concise and to the point. He deliberately understated his case for strategic reasons.

Unlike Will, MacPherson charged to the podium and gave an expansive, almost overblown, opening statement.

But there was a problem. As Will watched the faces of the jurors, they seemed enthralled by MacPherson's colorful portrait of Isaac Joppa as a low-life criminal whose life of piracy would soon be established.

MacPherson hammered hard on the grand jury testimony of Henry Caulfeld, who had testified as the only witness for the grand jury in Bath, North Carolina, in 1718. That Caulfeld was a co-owner of the sloop *Marguerite*. That he was an eyewitness to the takeover of the sloop by Teach's gang, and that the *Marguerite* was plundered and several of its crew severely beaten by Teach's men.

The defense lawyer was flailing his arms, his voice rising as he described the evidence the jury would soon hear—that Henry Caulfeld was less than two hundred feet away from Teach's pirate ship. And, he asked rhetorically, whom should he see striding back and forth on the deck, giving orders to Teach's crew, apparently instructing them to board the *Marguerite*?

MacPherson paused dramatically and took a few steps toward the jury box.

"None other than Isaac Joppa...that is exactly what Henry Caulfeld said, under oath—swearing to God to tell the truth, the whole truth, and nothing but the truth—a successful merchant and shipowner, a man who had no reason to lie. He saw Isaac Joppa helping Edward Teach plunder his ship, then aid and abet the manhandling of his crew."

MacPherson looked at the ground, giving a dramatic appearance of collecting his thoughts. And then he continued.

"It's said that a picture is worth a thousand words...but ladies and gentlemen, in the case of the testimony of Henry Caulfeld, the words are worth a thousand pictures. He's recreated history for us, with the eloquence of his description. The evidence is going to leave no doubt in your minds that this eyewitness testimony places Isaac Joppa on the deck of a pirate ship, giving orders, participating with those thugs and criminals. If this were the only testimony we presented in this case on the issue of Mr. Joppa's guilt, I believe such evidence alone would compel you to find him to have been guilty, not only of the crimes with which he was charged, but also even of crimes with which he was never charged. But ladies and gentlemen, that's not the only evidence you're going to hear..."

MacPherson then ticked off a series of other potent facts: First, the comments of Samuel O'Dell who, according to the clerk's notes in the Williamsburg, Virginia, piracy trial of Teach's gang, clearly indicated to the court that he, O'Dell was in the hold of Teach's own ship shortly before the beginning of hostilities in the Battle of Ocracoke Inlet. That O'Dell saw, with his own eyes, that Joppa was there in the hold with him, along with an African pirate by the name of Caesar. That Joppa was not manacled, in chains, or in handcuffs—not constrained, restrained, or limited in any way. That he was free to come and go. "Does that sound like Isaac Joppa was a captive—a prisoner—that he had been kidnapped?" MacPherson argued, almost at a full bellow.

Next, MacPherson mentioned the evidence they would hear indicating that Isaac Joppa had fled, like a common criminal, from the scene of battle when the British navy attacked Teach's pirate ship.

Further, evidence would be presented proving that Joppa had entered a guilty plea to the charge of desertion from the Royal Navy while aboard the ship *Intrepid*. Shortly after that, MacPherson argued, Isaac began his life of piracy and crime on the high seas.

Lastly, the attorney pointed out that he would be calling, as an expert witness, a renowned law professor, who would explain that the entry of res judicata in the court records of Bath, North Carolina, did not mean that Joppa had been acquitted by the London jury. To the contrary, such a term was perfectly consistent with a finding of guilt against him.

MacPherson strolled back to the podium and concluded his remarks.

"Folks, I view this opening statement as kind of a handshake agreement…between me and you. And between Mr. Chambers and you. Now when I tell you you're going to see these facts…and this evidence…if I fulfill my part of the bargain and produce the evidence I've promised, then you hold that for me. And for my client. And you decide in our favor. And I'm willing to bet that between now and the end of this case you're going to be convinced beyond any question. That Isaac Joppa was a scoundrel, a criminal, and guilty of acts of piracy…" MacPherson gave a look toward counsel table as if he had concluded his comments. But Will could see him thinking. He was gauging whether to take a chance.

He whirled around for one last volley to the jury.

"And just remember…" MacPherson said, wagging his finger at the air, "that Will Chambers and his client, the good Reverend Jonathan Joppa, have a whole lot to gain by trying to persuade you to vote for them in this case…a whole lot. Now I can't go into the particulars—that wouldn't be appropriate. But rest assured they have a powerful motivation to make you believe this story they've cooked up about Isaac Joppa's innocence."

MacPherson snatched up his papers, gave one last, broad smile to the jury, and scurried to his seat.

Will shot to his feet.

"Your Honor, I object. I move to strike the last portion of Mr. MacPherson's improper and outrageous comment about my client and myself. May counsel approach the bench?"

The judge gave an exasperated look at the wall clock.

"Mr. Chambers, is this really necessary? I was hoping we could move along and get a couple more witnesses knocked off this afternoon."

"*May counsel approach the bench?*" Will said forcefully.

The judge nodded reluctantly, and the two attorneys scurried up to the bench, out of earshot of the jury.

"Your Honor, I want Mr. MacPherson admonished by the Court. And I want his comments about my client's motivation, and my motivation, to be stricken from the record. Virgil, you know full well that it's improper to advise the jury, in any respect, about the effect or impact of their factual finding in the verdict. And the fact is you lied—by deliberate omission. You made it sound like the only person to gain something out of winning this trial is Jonathan Joppa. The fact is, as you well know, your client stands to win the same piece of real estate that my client does, depending on how the jury should decide. Your comments were misleading and prejudicial."

Will then turned to the judge and looked him in the eye.

"Your Honor, I'm moving for this court to strike Mr. MacPherson's comments."

MacPherson interjected immediately.

"Now, Will, you're getting off to a really bad start here," MacPherson spoke smoothly, with an air of manufactured sympathy. "I know you've got a lot going on...a lot of stress...you've got a pregnant wife who's ready to have a baby any time now. And you're new to this neck of the woods, being a Virginia lawyer and all...But I just can't have you making those kinds of nasty comments about me. I just can't have that. Judge, I think we need to get this case moving along, and I think Mr. Chambers needs to be told to sit back down at his counsel table."

Judge Gadwell was shifting uncomfortably in his chair, scratching his neck vigorously. Finally, he spoke.

"Mr. Chambers, I think I hear where you're coming from here...But the fact is, well, even if Virgil here was a little out of line...it really is harmless error. And you know, at the end of this case, I'm going to give the standard instruction to the jury about disregarding comments by counsel and basing their verdict totally on the evidence. So I don't think this jury's going to be too much influenced by what Mr. MacPherson just said."

Will smiled at the judge, turned, and walked quickly back to his seat at counsel table, where Boggs Beckford threw him a look that needed no interpretation.

Virgil MacPherson had begun the slow process of walking Will and his client out on a gangplank. And the judge, whatever his motivation or intent, was choosing to look in the other direction.

51

"AUGUST WAVERLY LONGFELLOW, PHD. I'm a professor of cultural studies and an adjunct professor of philosophy at Duke University."

As Longfellow sat in the witness chair with his dark suit, ironed shirt, and a tie that actually matched, he was looking the part of an expert witness. And after Will led him through the questions setting out his educational qualifications—the books he had written, the lectures he had given, the papers and books he had published, some of which dealt specifically with regional history of coastal Carolina—he began to emerge as the historian Will had hoped for.

Particularly because Will had been unable to secure the services of Dr. Derek Hubbel of Yale, Longfellow now had the crucial task of nailing down the historicity of Isaac Joppa's innocence.

"Dr. Longfellow," Will continued, "based on your experience and training as an expert on the regional history of the Carolinas, including the history of piracy in the 1700s, and based on the information you have reviewed in this case—including the trial transcript from the Old Bailey criminal court in 1719, the notes of the clerk in the piracy trials at Williamsburg, Virginia, and all the other court records you have seen—do you have an opinion as to the historical probability that Isaac Joppa was a willing member of the piracy activities of Edward Teach and his crew, specifically relating to the plundering of a sloop named *Marguerite* in December of 1717?"

Longfellow stroked his iron-gray beard for a moment before answering. Then he began an extensive and persuasive response.

He first pointed out that Isaac Joppa's testimony at the Old Bailey—his contention that he was a prisoner of Teach for many months—was consistent with the general practice among pirates at that time. Pirates such as Teach would often kidnap those they felt could be useful to them.

"As an example," Longfellow continued, "there is an unimpeachable account from a Phillip Ashton, a decent, churchgoing type of person, who reported being kidnapped by pirates in the year 1725. He was held against his will for a period of time until his release. There are many accounts of hostage-taking similar to that one.

"Secondly," Longfellow explained, "Isaac Joppa does not fit the typical profile of the sailor-turned-pirate, particularly in the eighteenth century."

He pointed out the evidence indicating that Joppa, after his escape from Teach, had contact with the Tuscarora Indians, and may even have made an attempt to convert them to his Christian religion.

"As son of the Reverend Malachi Joppa, a fervent evangelistic preacher in Bath, it's not surprising that Isaac Joppa would try to convert the Indians. What would be surprising," Longfellow explained, "is a person with that background becoming a member of the most degenerate subgroup of humanity at that time, speaking both socially and morally."

To substantiate this, Longfellow pointed to some of the historical and sociological studies of religious life in England and the American colonies in the late 1600s and early 1700s. There had been a general decline of religious piety among the general population, but particularly among sailors—those in the merchant marine, in the Royal Navy, and especially among those practicing piracy. There was violent resistance, particularly by the pirates, to any semblance of organized religion. Longfellow pointed out one instance where a pastor aboard a ship (one not even manned by pirates) attempted to hand out Bibles to the sailors in the hold. For his efforts he was rewarded by being beaten by the crew within an inch of his life.

"The Bath, North Carolina, area, as of 1718, certainly was a wild frontier type of place," Longfellow continued. "It was a place where the likes of Edward Teach felt right at home. And it was an area particularly hostile to religion. Malachi Joppa, Isaac's father, must have been a rather stern sort of preacher to be able to put up with the kind of abuse he must have certainly received from the locals.

"And as a collateral matter of interest—it is fascinating that the famous English evangelist, George Whitefield—one of the leaders of the Great Awakening of the mid-1700s—visited Bath in 1739 and made it a sort of headquarters for himself during his American evangelistic campaign. One can only scratch one's head and wonder why Whitefield would have visited a place like Bath…but then that's another story."

Longfellow chuckled a little to himself.

He concluded his opinion by evaluating the grand jury testimony of Henry Caulfeld, who testified in Bath, that he had personally witnessed Isaac Joppa assisting the Teach crew and plundering his ship, the *Marguerite*.

"Now the testimony of Henry Caulfeld simply isn't persuasive as a matter of history. I'm not evaluating this as a legal matter...but only as an historian. Caulfeld's testimony is ambiguous at best. He didn't actually hear what Isaac Joppa was saying to Teach's pirate crew. And the fact that Joppa was roaming around on the deck for a few moments unshackled or unhandcuffed—that doesn't prove that he was not a prisoner, nor that he had not been kidnapped for several months. There are several explanations for that. But the best is that the African member of Teach's crew—this Caesar fellow—had befriended Joppa. There is historical support for that. And Isaac may well have been released for a short walk around on the deck at the time the *Marguerite* was being plundered."

"And so your opinion is," Will said, concluding his direct examination, "that Isaac Joppa's testimony before the Old Bailey criminal court—his protestations of innocence—is supported by credible historical evidence?"

Longfellow's eyes drifted away from Will for a moment, and he seemed to be staring out into space, considering some obscure, historical picture.

"Yes...that's my opinion...And just imagine this Isaac Joppa fellow—running away from home. Joining the Royal Navy. Encountering a brutal captain, deserting, then hopping aboard a ship, the *Good Intent* out of Dublin—only to be forcibly kidnapped by one of the most fearsome pirates in the history of the high seas. Manacled and chained in the bottom of a ship. And then, when he is within miles of his original home, to be shot at—to be a target of the fury of the English navy during their attack against Teach and his gang. And of course, all of the surviving pirates of Teach's crew were found guilty and hanged. Then to escape...and encounter the Tuscarora Indians. And then end up, somehow, in the streets of London. To be apprehended—arrested and placed on trial for his life. One can only wonder what would have been going through his mind..."

☾   ☾   ☾

Isaac Joppa, standing in the witness dock in the cavernous Justice Hall in the Old Bailey Courthouse of London's Central Criminal Court, was thinking about something else.

His mind was not on the scarlet-robed judge, Mr. Justice Dormer, who sat presiding on the looming, high bench. Nor was it on the dozens of black-robed clerks and wigged barristers milling in and out of the huge hall, nor on the six jurors in the box on one side of him, and the other six jurors on the other, eyeing him closely. Nor, in fact, was Joppa's attention focused on his own lawyer, Oliver Newhouse, Esquire, who had just posed a question to him and was patiently waiting for an answer.

Isaac was thinking back to his arrival in London after leaving the Tuscarora Indians—penniless, his physical appearance and clothing in shambles. He had managed to stow away on a sloop from Charleston, South Carolina. And he remembered his arrival in the great, bustling, ugly, noisy, confusing metropolis of London.

After sneaking off the ship, he made a wide berth around the customs house, where a large force of officers milled about in their war against illegal smugglers.

He cautiously walked along Leadenhall Street, past the offices of the great East India Company and, a few streets later, past the South Sea and Royal African Companies as well. He continued up along the Thames River, along the Billingsgate Dock, where seamen and boatmen were repairing ships in the noisy, blackened yards. Then among the dismal warehouses of the harbor area, he spotted the Boar's Head Tavern. There he hoped to find some work—enough, at least, to pay for a meal and a night's lodging. And he would figure out what else he would do later.

He knew he must eventually face up to the criminal charges lodged against him back in the American colonies. But beyond even that, he had, these many months, lived with a desperate longing to see the face of the woman he loved. He needed, first and foremost, to find his way back to Bristol. To show himself to his beloved Abigail Merriwether. What must she have thought in this past year? That he was dead? That he had fallen out of love with her?

He trudged into the Boar's Head after evening had fallen. He begged the proprietor for some form of work…if only he could have a meal and a bed for the night. The owner eyed him suspiciously. But to his surprise, he was shown to a room that he would share with three other sailors. At least he would have his own straw mat on the ground to lie upon.

What Isaac did not know then but would soon discover was that the proprietor had made a fine business of turning over wayward and deserting sailors to the British Crown. He was usually given a small bounty from the government per head. He was regularly supplied with a list of every

English sailor charged with desertion, abandonment of his post of duty, or other miscellaneous offenses. Isaac Joppa's name was on the list—charged with desertion from the *Intrepid*.

So, shortly after his arrest at the Boar's Head, it was learned that he had also been charged, by the grand jury back in Bath, with piracy...

"Sir, I put the question to you again," Barrister Newhouse said sympathetically to Isaac. "You do admit you have entered a plea of guilty here in London, in the admiralty court, to charges of desertion from the ship *Intrepid*, which was captained by Zebulun Boughton of His Majesty's Royal Navy, is that correct?"

Isaac, steadying himself on the rail, nodded and then answered. "I admit I deserted the ship. I do not deny those things of which I am guilty, sir. But the truth is...I was a young and impressionable sailor, much inexperienced, I regret to say. I was assigned to the *Intrepid* under Captain Boughton."

"And without belaboring the point, sir," Newhouse continued, "did any barbarous or inhuman acts take place on the *Intrepid* while you were serving as a nonconscripted sailor?"

"Yes," Isaac replied, his voice slightly unsteady. "I remember one instance—it was most shocking to me. One of the crew had stolen a potato from the store in the hold. Captain Boughton ordered him to be beaten with thirty lashes. Then he was stripped bare and lashed to the foresail. It was a calm day, no wind, and the sun was quite hot. He was left there for two days without food or water. No one tended to his injuries, sir. At the end of two days, the man died."

Then Isaac Joppa gazed up and turned to Justice Dormer. "Rockdale, Your Honor. James Rockdale. That was the name of the sailor who died."

Oliver Newhouse had led his client, delicately and expertly, through his life from leaving Bath, North Carolina, to his romantic encounter with Abigail Merriwether in England, to his joining the English navy, through his desertion from the *Intrepid*, then his voyage out of Dublin on the ship *Good Intent*, and ultimately to his capture by Edward Teach. But now Newhouse was going to conclude his examination with the key facts surrounding the alleged acts of piracy against the *Marguerite*.

"Mr. Newhouse," Justice Dormer intoned from the high judicial bench, "This court has been most lenient, and with extraordinary patience has allowed you to participate far beyond the usual and customary procedure of the Central Criminal Court. As you know, Mr. Newhouse, it is routine for this court to exclude all defense counsel in felony cases...It has long been felt that the presence of defense lawyers in such cases does nothing to expedite justice. And such cases involving serious criminal accusations are thought the most forthright in their defense when they have the least encumbrance with the finer points of the law. You have persuaded me, perhaps against my better judgment, to allow you to appear as counsel for the accused…"

Newhouse smiled and restored an errant hair to his painstakingly powdered wig.

"I am, Your Honor, most appreciative of the wisdom, not to mention the patience, of the court. But, of course, you shall remember I am thoroughly convinced of my point to the court—that a charge of piracy is tantamount, in all respects, to a charge of treason against the Crown itself. And in such cases, this court has permitted defense counsel to aid in the administration of the justice of the cause."

"Yes, yes, yes," Justice Dormer said with a sigh, waving his hand vaguely in Newhouse's direction. "Just…get on with it, sir. About your business now, and conclude your examination."

"Isaac Joppa, you stand accused of acts of piracy, specifically as to the sloop *Marguerite,* at a point some one hundred miles off the coast of Martinique. What do you say, sir? Did you participate knowingly and willfully in any acts of piracy by Captain Edward Teach and his piratical conspirators?"

"No, sir, I did not," Joppa said firmly.

"But you were seen, sir, roaming about the upper deck of Teach's ship, without chains or manacles. Free to come and go. Would you explain that to the jury, sir, so as to provide a truthful accounting of that?"

"I'd been permitted some fresh air by a man who had befriended me. Indeed he was a member of Teach's pirate crew…that I truthfully admit. He was called only Caesar. I do not know his full Christian name…if any Christian name he had. He was a former slave. But he had become a trusted member of Captain Teach's assembly of men. Yet he, I think, had much affection for me. And showed kindness to me."

"And why is that, sir?" Newhouse said, his voice rising in intensity. "What did you do to earn the respect of such a piratical character?"

"Master Teach, in his continued acts of villainy, had attacked a ship called the *Concorde.* I had been, for some time, manacled down in the hold of one of his ships. I had spent many months chained and manacled with irons to a barrel of china and silverplate within the hold of the ship. Such barrels Mr. Teach had obtained by acts of thievery against another ship.

Teach had captured me and taken me as prisoner because he learned I had taken some medical instruction during my time in His Majesty's Navy. On one occasion, Teach unmanacled me and asked that I attend to the injuries of a group of slaves from the coast of Africa. Several had been injured during the taking of the *Concorde*. I asked Teach if he intended to release them. He threw his head back and roared out a laugh that sounded like the devil himself. *No!* He wanted them to be in prime condition to gain him a price most advantageous. There were, in total, some one hundred and twenty-five of these unfortunate fellows. I begged Captain Teach to allow some to go free. Then he grabbed me by the throat with both hands, and told me he would break my neck like a chicken's and toss me overboard if I raised the matter in his presence again."

"What was the response from this Caesar fellow?"

"From then after, at almost all times when it was just Mr. Caesar and I, he was most gentle with me, practically as a brother. And would unshackle me and allow me to have fresh air from time to time. When the sloop *Marguerite* was being plundered by Captain Teach, that was one of those occasions."

"And as for the accusation that you were on deck, waving your hands so as to give orders to the pirate crew of Teach...so that they would hoist the jib and let fall the foresail of the *Marguerite* after boarding her—what say you, sir?"

"I was waving my arms and moving my hands—it is a truth," Joppa answered quietly. "But I was not giving instructions, nor orders...how could I? I was, in truth, moving my arms as I had been in much pain and stiffness, being chained to the barrel for weeks and weeks. And I was rubbing my wrists out of the pain inflicted on them by the manacles."

For a moment the great Justice Hall was quiet. Justice Dormer cleared his throat.

Then Isaac Joppa caught sight of a figure entering at the back of the tall chambers. When he caught sight of the person, his eyes filled with tears and his shoulders began shaking with grief. He could no longer control himself. He placed his face in his hands and wept. He wept bitterly, sobbing as he leaned against the mahogany rail of the witness dock.

As Isaac Joppa's sobs echoed throughout the great hall, Abigail Merriwether, in a bright yellow silken dress, stood in the doorway.

52

Virgil MacPherson strode casually to the podium while August Longfellow stretched slightly in the witness chair.

"Dr. Longfellow, I listened with great interest during your direct examination. As you described the trial of the surviving members of the Edward Teach pirate gang. The trial in Williamsburg, Virginia. In admiralty court. And I made careful notes. And here's what my notes indicate—that you said, 'All of the surviving pirates of Teach's crew were found guilty and hanged.' Now that is what you said, is it not, Dr. Longfellow?"

Longfellow nodded confidently. "Yes, sir. That's exactly what I testified to."

"And you're here as a so-called historical expert. You're not a professor of history, you're a professor of cultural affairs—whatever that is. But you claim to be a historian of Carolina coastal matters, is that correct?"

"I consider myself a regional historian, that's correct."

"And if you're a historian, you'd better get your historical facts right, isn't that correct?"

"If you're a historian, then you'd better be historically accurate."

"Exactly," MacPherson said enthusiastically. "I couldn't have said it better myself. Which is why I'm a little confused...because you recited some bad history here today."

"How so?" Longfellow asked, growing slightly uncomfortable.

"You said that all the pirates who survived and who were tried in Williamsburg were found guilty and hanged. That's not correct, is it?"

Longfellow took a minute to reflect. The fingers of both of his hands were beginning to drum on the railing in front of him.

"On further reflection, I would amend my statement slightly. It is correct that all of the pirates were found guilty. But now that I think about it, there was one who was not hanged..."

"And can you remember that pirate's name?" MacPherson asked, his voice rising with just a tinge of ridicule.

"No, I'm sorry, I can't..."

"Does the name 'Israel Hands' ring a bell?" MacPherson's voice rose even more.

"Yes. That's right. He was found guilty, but not hanged. I don't remember the details..."

"He was not hanged because he was given a pardon at the last moment. You didn't remember that? As a historian—a so-called historian—of local matters of piracy along the Carolina coast, you didn't recall that?"

Longfellow shrugged. Will could see that his expert witness's resolve was beginning to disintegrate.

"And Dr. Longfellow, in addition to being a so-called historical expert, and a professor of philosophy, and a professor in cultural affairs, you have also written some books of poetry?"

"Yes. Two rather slim volumes of poetry, that's correct."

"Dr. Longfellow, I'm very impressed. You are, truly, a man of many talents."

Longfellow smiled and nodded, and then added, "Thank you."

"No, truly," MacPherson continued, pressing the point, "You are more than that. You are a Renaissance man."

Longfellow was now grinning.

"And thank you again."

"And you have other titles. In addition to being a Renaissance man," MacPherson paused dramatically "you are a criminal. You are, sir, a criminal, are you not? A convicted criminal?"

MacPherson's question had stilled the courtroom. All six of the jurors sat with stunned expressions.

Longfellow couldn't answer. He tried to talk but nothing came out. He lowered his head and thought intensely on how to answer.

"No response?" MacPherson said with ridicule. "Then let's make this easy. Is it correct, Dr. Longfellow, that you have been convicted of a criminal offense under the laws of the state of North Carolina?"

Now Will was on his feet, objecting and asking for a sidebar conference.

MacPherson and Will scurried to the judge's bench.

"Your Honor, Mr. MacPherson has to make an offer of proof to show the admissibility of this kind of evidence. And I don't know what he's talking about. I want to see some proof..."

MacPherson jumped in.

"Oh, I have the proof. Conviction, less than a year ago, of driving a motor vehicle after having a driver's license suspended. Under North Carolina law, that carries a potential sentence in excess of sixty days in jail. Under North Carolina Rule 609, that evidence comes in to attack the credibility of this witness."

MacPherson shoved a certified copy of the judgment of conviction in front of Will's face.

Will scanned it quickly, then turned to the judge.

"I withdraw my objection, Your Honor. I'm afraid this evidence is going to come in."

Now MacPherson asked the question again. Longfellow gazed sheepishly at Will, then looked back at MacPherson and answered.

"I'm afraid, Mr. MacPherson, you're right. I was convicted of a criminal offense."

"Now then," MacPherson said with obvious satisfaction, "let me finish my questions by turning to the Old Bailey criminal court transcript and the self-interested testimony of Isaac Joppa…"

(((

The Crown's prosecutor, Mr. Alexander Saxton, Esquire, strode to the witness dock where Isaac Joppa stood waiting for cross-examination.

Saxton placed his arms behind his back and clasped his hands together, bouncing on the balls of his feet.

"Mr. Joppa, we have all noticed your obvious expression of sorrow. Your tears have, undoubtedly, moved all of us. I put to you, sir, that your tears are tears of grief, are they not?"

Joppa nodded, wiping his eyes with his hands. "They are, sir. True enough."

"And they are tears of grief because, I would put to you, you have come to realize that your life of crime—your piratical offenses—your conspiracy with the likes of Mr. Edward Teach and his murderous band has caught up with you. You are now regretting that you ever assisted Mr. Teach in his devilish designs to rob and plunder the sloop *Marguerite* and assault her crew. Is that correct, sir?"

"No. Never. That is not true—"

"You deny it? You deny that your tears of grief are because you collaborated with the criminal acts of Pirate Edward Teach?"

"I deny that my tears are for anyone, or anything, except one person… the woman I love…whom, I regret, I have caused great pain and anguish because of my absence for these long months. Better that my hand be severed from my arm than I cause any more anguish, because of separation, to Miss Abigail Merriwether."

"Then we shall inquire as to this Miss Abigail Merriwether," Saxton said with bravado. "You became engaged to her even against the wishes of her father, Mr. Peter Merriwether, an outstanding and most industrious merchant of Bristol. Is that correct?"

"Yes, it is," Isaac said softly.

"And you joined the Royal Navy in an effort to gain the monetary circumstances necessary to fully, and satisfactorily, impress Mr. Merriwether with your worthiness as a suitor for his daughter?"

"I do not deny it. That is true."

"But you deserted, willfully, the ship *Intrepid,* despite the wages that you undoubtedly could have earned as a sailor in His Majesty's Royal Navy?"

"As I have said, I deserted because I had a formidable choice between two equally dismal possibilities. I could have stayed aboard the *Intrepid* and been forced to join in the mutiny, or I could have stayed on the *Intrepid* and supported a captain whose brutality and inhumanity was apparent for all to see."

"And so, after deserting, you found your way aboard the ship *Good Intent,* leaving Ireland and bound for the Americas?"

"That is correct. But, I overheard that the ship was to sail to England before going on to America. That did not prove to be correct."

"So—having boarded the *Good Intent,* you then found an answer to your need. You found a solution to the necessity that you become, as quickly as possible, a man of financial means. You discovered, in essence, that you could make more money with less effort, and with greater expedience of time, by becoming a pirate, than by working as a lawful member of His Majesty's Navy. Is that not correct, sir?"

Saxton's voice boomed to the four corners of the great Justice Hall.

"I would do nothing to imperil my chances of marriage to my beloved Abigail Merriwether," Joppa said firmly.

"Nothing?" Saxton bellowed.

"Nothing."

"And what proof do you have, sir, that you had any intention of marrying this unfortunate woman who became betrothed to a person of your character?"

"Upon our engagement, she had fashioned for me a small plate. It had a beautiful likeness of her on the front. And on the back, it had the dates of both our engagement and our intended marriage. It was a gift before I set sail with the Royal Navy."

"Oh, I see," Saxton said with a sneer. "And I presume that such a token of her love and affection, and such a memorial of your intended marriage, must have been of great value to you?"

"Of great value, yes, sir."

"And do you have the plate with you, sir? Can you show it to me? Or can you show it to His Honor, the good Justice Dormer? Or can you show it, perhaps, to the twelve good men of the jury who try this cause? We await your answer, Mr. Joppa. Where is the plate?"

Joppa lowered his head.

"I do not have it…"

"He does not have it!" Saxton said with his arms outstretched, his rich baritone voice taking on dramatic force.

And then, after a moment of pregnant silence—"And where, pray tell, is this valued and coveted token of your intended marriage?"

"It was taken by Indians."

"Indians?" Saxton bellowed. "Why not taken by flood, or hurricane? Or perhaps lifted up to the heavens by a fantastical and magical moonbeam?"

By now, laughter had broken out among the spectators. Saxton was smelling blood, and now he was circling his prey like a shark.

"You have admitted guilt in your act of desertion. You have admitted so before the Court of Admiralty of the Crown of England. And is it not correct that the admiralty court has suspended sentencing you pending the outcome of this trial for piracy?"

"That is correct—yes, sir."

"Undoubtedly," Saxton said with confidence, "the admiralty court did not wish to bother itself with any sentence—because when, upon the finding of your guilt in this case, you are hanged on the gallows at Newgate, there will be no further need for that court to worry itself—"

Oliver Newhouse was now on his feet, pacing quickly up to Saxton, who was standing before Justice Dormer.

"Your Honor, I do beg your indulgence…but I do believe Mr. Saxton exceeds himself. It is for this jury to find, and solely for this jury to determine, the guilt or innocence of Mr. Joppa. Such talk of hanging, particularly before all of the evidence is heard, and before Your Honor's eloquent and well-reasoned instructions to the jury are given, is precipitous at the very least."

Justice Dormer sighed impatiently, and then addressed the king's prosecutor.

"Mr. Saxton, do restrain yourself to the facts of the case."

Saxton nodded politely and continued his examination.

"Let us conclude the matter by focusing, sir, on the battle between His Majesty's Royal Navy and the dastardly pirate, Edward Teach, and his crew. Such a battle took place off the coast of the Carolina colonies, is that correct?"

"Yes, sir. We call it the area of the Ocracoke Inlet."

"And when you saw the Royal Navy approach…when you saw—as a confessed captor and kidnapped prisoner—that your rescuers were at hand, did you rush to the sailors of the English navy and beg for them to accept you onto their ship?"

Isaac Joppa paused, and looked down at the marble floor. He stretched both hands out on the wooden railing in front of him, and then he answered.

"No, sir, I did not. I found it most necessary—in the melee and fury of that moment—to try to escape injury or death."

"Most strange, indeed! A mystery beyond any understanding…for a kidnapped man to *flee* his rescuers…unless it be true, sir, that, in point of fact, you had not been kidnapped. And I put to you that you attempted escape from the Royal Navy because you were, in all manner of speaking, as guilty of piracy as Captain Teach, who was killed and beheaded in that very battle."

"Untrue! Untrue!"

"But it is true, sir, is it not, that you did not run into the arms of the Royal Navy when they approached the ship?"

"It is true."

"And it is true, is it not, sir, that you attempted escape by jumping from the ship and swimming *away* from the very Royal Navy that had come to apprehend the pirates?"

Isaac Joppa was weary. Not only in body, but in very soul. He made one last attempt to stand straight and lift his head as he answered the final question of the prosecutor.

"I did escape. And if I had it in my power, sir, I would change much of my life…I would have stopped running away from things. My conduct has shamed my God and the woman I love. But regret, sir, cannot change the months of misery and despair. I shall not compound the misery of my wasted life by putting forth that I was a criminal and a pirate. For that, sir, I was not. I shall not sink my dismal lot further with the dark ballast of a lie. I am no pirate, sir. I am no criminal. And that, my soul knows full well."

With that, Joppa glanced at the jurymen in the two jury boxes. He hoped to see some hint of sympathy.

But all he saw there was their solemn, unmoved expressions.

53

WILL KNEW THE FORMIDABLE TASK he had ahead of him—he needed to rehabilitate August Longfellow's testimony and do it quickly. If he failed, judging by the faces of the jury, his case was already shipwrecked.

"Dr. Longfellow, I want to address a series of questions that opposing counsel raised. Do you recall the question about your having a criminal conviction on your record?"

"Yes, that one I certainly do remember," he answered sheepishly.

"Now, Dr. Longfellow, that conviction wasn't for the crime of murder, was it?"

Longfellow smiled and shook his head.

"No, certainly not, I'm happy to say."

Will eyed the jury and noticed that juror number three, the unemployed janitor, was chuckling a bit.

"It wasn't for perjury—for testifying falsely under oath, right?"

"No, it was not for that either."

"And let me just venture a final guess," said Will somewhat sardonically. "Your criminal conviction had nothing to do with piracy, did it?"

Now the plumber's assistant was smiling also.

"Fortunately not, Counselor."

"As a matter of fact, your criminal conviction was for a driving offense—because you were driving your motor vehicle at a point in time after your privileges had been suspended?"

"That's exactly right."

"Perhaps, Dr. Longfellow, you and I and the jury can agree on something. If any of the jurors need a ride home tonight after the trial, we can agree that you shouldn't drive any of them home...how about that?"

The president of the construction company was laughing now.

"On the other hand," Will continued, "if the jury wants to arrive at a just and fair verdict based on historical fact, then can this jury rely on your opinions as a credible historian?"

"There they certainly can." Longfellow was now sitting a little straighter in his chair.

"Lastly, let's talk about this issue of Isaac Joppa deserting from the ship *Intrepid* because of the brutality of Captain Zebulun Boughton. Would you address the jury as to how frequent, or infrequent, such desertion was among sailors in the early 1700s—both English and American?"

"Yes. Be happy to address that. If you read the literature of the times— mariners' and sailors' accounts, admiralty historians—it's often remarked that sailors during that period, despite unbearable and unbelievable hard-ships on board the vessels of the day, would rarely complain. The reason was that they had two very practical alternatives. The usual one was that they would desert at the first opportunity. The second—which fortu-nately was much more rare—was the choice to mutiny."

"And Isaac Joppa chose to desert rather than be implicated in the mutiny of the crew, is that correct?"

"Yes. That's exactly right."

MacPherson decided not to attempt re-cross with Longfellow, and he was excused.

Will's next witness was Susan Red Deer Williams. After pacing her through her qualifications, which were unchallenged by MacPherson, Will led her directly into her expert opinions.

"As an expert in Native American history primarily involving the Tus-caroras, my opinion, Mr. Chambers, is that, to a reasonable degree of his-torical probability, it was Isaac Joppa who had contact with Chief King Jim Blount, his Indian daughter, and his son, the warrior Great Hawk of the Tuscarora Tribe. My second opinion is that, during contact with them following the Battle of Ocracoke Inlet, he attempted to proselytize those Indians into the Christian religion. My last opinion is that, at the time of his contact, Isaac Joppa was carrying a small ceramic plate that bore infor-mation relating to his engagement and intended marriage to an English-woman."

With that, Will felt he had accomplished everything he could through that witness. She had been called, after all, for a very limited purpose—to establish the religious piety of Isaac Joppa and his fidelity to his fiancée. That corroborated Longfellow's opinions that such religious beliefs on the part of Isaac Joppa would never have been countenanced by the pirate crew aboard Teach's ship—had Joppa actually been active in their schemes of piracy. And his engagement to Abigail Merriwether was a strong motive against roaming the seas as a pirate.

Will sat down at counsel table, and MacPherson charged quickly to the podium with a look of relish on his face. Whatever his direction in cross-examination, Will was fairly confident of one thing. It was going to be a bumpy ride.

54

"Ms. Williams, you referred in your opinions to the likelihood that Isaac Joppa had attempted to—in your own words—'proselytize' the Tuscarora Indians. Do you recall that testimony?"

"I do remember that. That was my testimony."

"Do you have any historical evidence that Isaac Joppa attempted to—as you say—religiously proselytize the *pirates* when he was with them those many months?"

"No. There's no evidence of that at all."

"So then, the only evidence of this religious zeal is after he has escaped from the Royal Navy by the skin his teeth, so to speak, and is temporarily staying with the Indians?"

"As far as I know, yes."

"Is it possible that Isaac Joppa, during the time he was with the pirates aboard their ship, was just as much of a heathen and bloodthirsty pirate as they were—but after escaping death in the Ocracoke Inlet, he repented of his wicked ways and suddenly 'got religion'—just in time for the Tuscarora Indians?"

"I'm not sure I follow your meaning..."

"The point is this—you don't know whether Mr. Joppa's religious zeal was gained *after* he left the pirates, or whether he had it *during* his time with Edward Teach and his crew?"

"I really can't answer that," Williams said.

"You refer to a token—a ceramic plate that your Indian lore describes as a gift from an Englishwoman to Isaac Joppa, is that correct?"

"Yes, it is relatively well-established by several different sources in the Indian histories I've studied. That there was a plate. That it was taken from Mr. Joppa by Chief King Jim Blount, and was still with him when he joined the rest of the Tuscaroras in upper New York state. He then gave it to his son, Great Hawk, who returned, at some point, to the North

Carolina area. It was then handed down from Indian son to Indian son—until it ended up being returned to the possession of white men at some point during the early twentieth century."

"Well, that's a whole lot of historical information. And it's certainly very fascinating. It's a great Indian story. But let me ask you this—have you ever seen the plate you're talking about?"

"No, unfortunately I haven't."

"Have you ever personally talked to anyone who has seen it?"

"No, I can't say that I have."

"Can you cite me a single scholarly historical journal, article, or book in which this ceramic plate has ever been referred to?"

"I'm afraid that there aren't any written records referring to it. This is all oral history—"

"Oral? In other words, a bunch of stories passed down around the campfire—that kind of thing?"

"I would dispute your characterization—"

"We'll strike the business about the campfire. The point is, it's a story that people have told other people who've told other people who've told other people…that's pretty much it, isn't it?"

"Bottom line—yes, it is."

Will was contemplating whether or not he was going to attempt redirect examination of Williams, but was inclined not to attempt it. In the words of his Uncle Bull Chambers, the former judge, *This stick of wood has been whittled down about as far as it can go.*

But then something caught Will's eye. He scanned the back of the courtroom and caught a glimpse of Blackjack Morgan sitting in the very last row. But that was not it.

Approximately five rows in front of Morgan was someone else. He was wearing a ship captain's hat, and he carried a large paper sack and was waving it furiously in Will's direction.

It was Possum Kooter.

Will rose to his feet and asked that Susan Red Deer Williams be excused.

"May I have just a minute before my next witness?" Will asked.

Judge Gadwell reluctantly nodded.

Will scurried across the courtroom to Possum Kooter, who was now standing in the aisle with his bag lifted shoulder-high.

"Mr. Chambers—got it right here—yes, sir. You and me. You put me on. One, two, three. I'll get right into this…"

"Mr. Kooter—"

"*Possum.* No *Mr. Kooter* stuff. Possum to you and everybody else. Just regular old Possum Kooter."

"Yeah, Possum. Right. What do you have for me?"

Kooter thrust his hand into the paper bag, rustling it loudly. Suddenly, there it was. Will was looking into a finely painted, only slightly chipped, and mostly unfaded portrait of a beautiful blond young woman. The plate was only an inch or two in diameter. He turned it over. On the other side it read:

> *Isaac Joppa and Abigail Merriwether.*
> *Betrothed May 1, 1717.*
> *To Be Wed—May 1, 1718.*

There was a smile, now, on Will's face. And a strange feeling of connection.

As Will gazed at the pretty painted face, he thought, *So this is what he was fighting for…you are who he survived for. How he must have loved you…*

"Mr. Chambers, are you done yet? Are you ready to proceed?" Judge Gadwell said abruptly.

"Yes, Your Honor, I'm ready to proceed."

"Sir," Judge Gadwell said, motioning toward Possum Kooter, "I don't know who you are, but in my courtroom, everybody takes off their hat. That includes you."

Kooter quickly snatched the captain's hat off his head. "No offense, Your Honor. No offense intended. Want to go by proper protocol here. Proper procedure."

Will asked for a sidebar conference with counsel and the judge.

"Your Honor," Will began, "there's been some testimony about an antique plate. It figures prominently in this case. And right now we have possession of it."

He pulled the ceramic plate out of the paper bag and displayed it to the court and to Virgil MacPherson, who was barely able to contain his amazement and rage.

"Your Honor, I want you to order him to put that thing back in that bag. I don't want the jury to see that thing. That's not evidence. That's not going to be evidence. Mr. Chambers, you cover that up right now."

"Your Honor, I know I didn't list this as a form of exhibit. And that's because this…well, we didn't have it before just now."

"Your Honor," MacPherson continued, his chin shaking with rage, "I am totally surprised by this new evidence…"

"You know what?" Will added. "So am I, Virgil. I'm surprised. The court's surprised. This Possum Kooter guy walks in with the plate right in the middle of trial. This is the first time I have seen this."

"I want a mistrial, Judge. Right now. Right here. I am asking for a mistrial because Mr. Chambers here flashed this plate in front of the jurors."

"Now just hold on, Virgil," the judge said, trying to keep a firm hand on a case that was quickly spiraling out of control. "Now, Mr. Chambers, you just put in this evidence in an orderly fashion. I'll make my rulings accordingly. And, Virgil, you just have to sit down. You're going to have to wait your turn."

MacPherson resumed his seat slowly, eyeing Will carefully all the time. Will strode to the podium and called Oscar "Possum" Kooter to the stand. After Kooter was sworn in, Will began.

"Do you prefer that people call you 'Possum' Kooter?"

"I sure do. You're finally getting it at last, young man."

"Okay. Possum, you brought a bag with you today?"

"Sure did. Here it is." And he held it up high for everyone to see.

"And in that bag you have a plate, is that correct?"

"Oh, yes, I do." And with that, Kooter thrust his hand back into the bag, pulling out the plate and displaying high so everyone could see it.

MacPherson jumped to his feet again, objected, and again moved for a mistrial.

"Now, Virgil, you sit down," the judge said. "I hear you. I know where you're coming from. And I've got some concerns like you do. But we're going to have to do this in an orderly fashion…"

"Possum, would you explain how you came into possession of this plate?" Will asked.

With that, Kooter gave the litany of personal contacts that had brought the plate down to him. But in his rambling narrative, he also added several side trips of information pertaining to his sailing days, his fishing life, his accumulation of injuries and various medical maladies, and the worst hurricanes on record…

After Kooter had gone on for some ten minutes nonstop and Will had caught sight of Gadwell rolling his eyes and rocking in his chair with visible agitation, Will decided to rein his witness in.

"Possum, is it correct to say that the Tuscarora Indians, according to the information you received, passed this item down to a white man, who then gave it to a man who inherited it from his dead father and passed it down to his nephew, a lighthouse keeper, who handed it down to his son, Frank, who sold it to you?"

MacPherson was on his feet, swinging his hands wildly. "Hearsay, hearsay, hearsay, and quadruple hearsay!"

"Well, I don't know exactly how many 'hearsays' that makes," the judge said, "but it makes enough for me to say it's hearsay. Mr. Chambers, I'm going to strike that question and that answer."

Will thought for a moment. Then he took a few quick steps over to counsel table, grabbed the evidence code, and turned quickly to a specific page.

"Your Honor, I'm going to invoke Section 803, subparagraph 13, which permits, despite the fact that they're technically hearsay, 'statements of fact concerning personal or family history contained in family Bibles, genealogies, charts, engravings on rings, inscriptions on family portraits, engravings on urns, crypts, or tombstones, *or the like.*'"

Judge Gadwell fumbled for his copy of the statutes.

MacPherson flipped through his copy rapidly and located the section. After a moment of consideration, he raised his hand and waved it at the judge.

"Your Honor, we've got a problem here. I can see that maybe the language could apply to something like this—except for one, big, insurmountable problem."

"And what is that," Judge Gadwell asked, still flipping through the code himself.

"We have absolutely no record, no evidence, no foundation, to believe that this little plate here—whatever this is—is actually an authentic family record of the Joppa family."

"It's got Joppa's name right on it," Will said emphatically. "And it's got all the information that's corroborated by the testimony in this case."

"Could be a forgery," MacPherson rebutted.

"Exactly," Judge Gadwell chimed in. "Mr. MacPherson's correct. Could be a forgery. How do we know it's authentic?"

"Oh, so you're talking about a certification…" Possum Kooter shouted from the witness stand, and already rising to his feet.

"You sit down, sir. You're a witness here. You will be quiet until you're spoken to."

"But, Your Honor," Kooter said, "that's just it. We're talking about certification—"

"Mr. Kooter—" the judge began.

"*Possum.* Even to a judge, I prefer Possum. I don't like this 'Mr. Kooter' stuff…"

Before the judge could instruct further silence, Kooter went on a rampage.

"And by the way, nobody's asked me why I don't like the *Mister* business. But I'm going to tell you right now. This is the right time and the right place…right here in this courtroom…the constitution of these United States forbids, in clear language, titles of nobility. It's right there in the constitution. And that would include *Mister*. As far as I'm concerned, that's a title of nobility. I ain't going to use it. And—no disrespect intended—but so is *esquire* after the name of an attorney. That's a title of nobility…and the constitution says it's *out of here*. And, Your Honor—no offense taken, no offense intended—but the use of the word *the Honorable*—even for a judge—it's a title of nobility. The constitution says it's *out*. Now, I haven't exactly figured out what I'm going to do with doctors…whether *Doctor* this or *Doctor* that is a title of nobility. I still have to figure that one out—"

"Quiet!" Judge Gadwell shouted.

Kooter's eyes widened. He took his paper bag and sat back down in the witness chair.

For a moment, at least, it was absolutely quiet in the courtroom. But then Kooter broke the silence with one quiet statement.

"I've got this here certification that you want, Judge…"

Kooter reached inside the paper bag and pulled out a piece of paper that appeared to have an embossed seal at the bottom.

"Your Honor!" MacPherson shouted. "You tell this witness to stash that piece of paper back in that bag. I don't want this jury tainted by it. And I move for a mistrial."

Before the judge could rule on Virgil MacPherson's objection, Will walked up to the witness stand, grabbed the bag from Kooter, and pulled out the piece of paper.

He studied it for a moment and almost burst out laughing. He looked at Kooter and whispered, "Where in the world did you get this?"

"Mr. Chambers, you will cease and desist from conversing with this witness until this court sorts out what is happening here." Judge Gadwell shouted. "This place is ceasing to function like a courtroom and is looking more and more like a session of the North Carolina legislature…"

After collecting himself, Gadwell continued.

"Mr. Chambers, do you have any evidence to substantiate that this plate is authentic, an actual family heirloom containing family inscriptions dating back to Isaac Joppa's lifetime?"

"We certainly do," Will said with an expanding grin.

Virgil MacPherson was halfway up from his chair, attempting to formulate another objection, but the judge beat him to the punch. He held a finger straight up, then aimed it in MacPherson's direction. The lawyer quietly sat down and maintained his silence.

"Your Honor, Mr. Kooter has brought with him—rather amazingly, I might add—what appears to be a certificate of authenticity for this plate. It's signed, under seal, by the director of the New England Museum of English and Early American Crafts and Guilds. The certificate verifies that the plate was created in or around the year 1717 in London, England."

"Your Honor," Will continued, "on the basis of that authentication, we move this plate into evidence."

Now MacPherson was back on his feet.

"Your Honor," MacPherson bulleted, "how do I know that this piece of paper itself is authentic?"

"Why you can call this director guy at the museum yourself," Kooter put in. "Real friendly...I bet you he'd be there right now..."

After thoroughly admonishing the witness to silence, the judge suggested that if Mr. MacPherson wanted to test the validity of the certificate, he could feel free to call the New England Museum of English and Early American Crafts and Guilds himself during the next break. But barring some report from MacPherson that the sealed and notarized certificate was itself not genuine, the court would treat it as such and would admit the plate into evidence.

MacPherson took pity on both the court and the jury and did not attempt cross-examination. After Possum Kooter bounded down from the witness stand with his bag in his hand and a triumphant look on his face, the court adjourned for ten minutes.

Halfway across the courtroom, Kooter suddenly whirled around and yelled to the judge, "Your Honor—I assume I'm going to get my plate back, right?"

The judge, not hiding his exasperation, yelled that he would certainly get it back after the trial.

During the break Virgil MacPherson wandered out into the corridor, talking intensely with Terrence Ludlow and Blackjack Morgan.

Although the lawyer had his cell phone with him—and despite his protestations about the plate being a forgery—it must have somehow slipped his mind to place a call to the New England Museum of English and Early American Crafts and Guilds.

55

Before resting his case, Will made a formal request that the court take judicial notice of the entry of the clerk at Bath, North Carolina, in 1719—that Isaac Joppa's case had been dismissed res judicata.

Judge Gadwell listened patiently to Virgil MacPherson's vague objections and then ruled.

"Mr. Chambers, what I'm going to do is this," he said. "I don't think anybody's objecting to the authenticity of the clerk's notes from that proceeding down in Bath. The real question here is what 'res judicata' means. I'm going to take judicial notice of the fact that that was what the clerk entered. But I will not...and I repeat, *not*...make a commitment that your interpretation of that 'res judicata' necessarily holds. This Court will take judicial notice of the fact that such a court entry was made at that time and at that place in the case of Isaac Joppa. Nothing more and nothing less."

Will rested his case, and Virgil MacPherson launched into a short but energetic motion for dismissal, arguing that his opponent's case had failed to meet the burden of proof with credible evidence to indicate that Isaac Joppa was innocent of the charges of piracy.

Judge Gadwell saw the whole argument as the perfunctory exercise that it was and took the issue under advisement pending the decision of the jury.

Then MacPherson commenced his case. His first witness was Dr. Arthur Hope, a stocky, bald man who dressed meticulously and carried himself with confidence, if not a measure of arrogance.

Hope was a civil procedure law professor at the University of North Carolina. In his background questioning on Hope's qualifications, MacPherson underscored Hope's interest in English common law and his widely published treatises and law review articles on that subject.

"Now, Dr. Hope, you understand the background of this case— regarding the trial of the pirate crew of Edward Teach in admiralty court, without benefit of jury, in Williamsburg, Virginia in 1719…and, by contrast, the issuance of a grand jury indictment against Isaac Joppa in Bath, North Carolina?"

Dr. Hope nodded vigorously and smiled.

"Yes…and I do understand the significance of the difference between admiralty court—which did not allow juries but had sitting commissioners acting as panels of judges—and the grand jury system, which allowed a jury of one's so-called peers. Which reminds me of a funny story. I'm a great believer in the jury system…but with limitations. There's a story about a jury in the backwoods that took a long time to arrive at a verdict in a personal injury case. The judge asked, 'Mr. Foreman, why in the world did it take your jury so long to decide?' 'Well, Your Honor,' said the foreman, 'half of us wanted to award the plaintiff four thousand dollars, and half of us wanted to award the plaintiff three thousand dollars. So we decided to compromise. We split the difference and gave the plaintiff five hundred dollars.'"

Several members of the jury laughed out loud.

Virgil MacPherson was beaming as he eyed the jury.

"Dr. Hope, I didn't attend UNC law school—but why do I think I would have enjoyed your civil procedure class?" MacPherson said, attempting to ingratiate himself. "I really do think I would have enjoyed your class."

Hope eyed him, and dropped his smile. "No, Mr. MacPherson, you wouldn't have."

Now the jury was laughing even louder—at Virgil MacPherson, who was slightly flushed.

After the attorney regained his composure, he continued. He led Dr. Hope through an explanation of the history of the term *res judicata*. How it was meant to signify the final judgment or last order in the case, which fully resolved the issues. That the purpose of *res judicata* was, among other reasons, to expedite judicial economy—to prevent relitigation of issues that had already been decided by a court of competent jurisdiction.

"Now, Dr. Hope," MacPherson went on, "you have seen the entry of 'res judicata' in the clerk's notes indicating dismissal of the Isaac Joppa indictment in 1719?"

"Yes, Mr. MacPherson. I've seen that record."

"Do you have an opinion, to a reasonable degree of legal certainty, as to whether or not the 'res judicata' can be viewed as consistent with the finding of *guilt* of Isaac Joppa on the charges in that same indictment—in the trial in Central Criminal Court of the Old Bailey in London, England?"

"Mr. MacPherson, not to put too fine a point on it...but you did not ask me whether I was familiar with the Old Bailey proceedings as a foundation for your question. So let me anticipate your failure to ask that question by answering it anyway. Yes, I have read the Old Bailey trial transcript in the Isaac Joppa case...such as it is. It contains the testimony of only two witnesses—the accused, Isaac Joppa, and his fiancée, a woman by the name of Abigail Merriwether. Apparently, the remaining portions of the transcript were destroyed or cannot be adequately deciphered."

Dr. Hope leaned back in his chair and finished his answer.

"So, in answer to your question—yes, I do believe that the entry of 'res judicata' in the clerk's notes in Bath, North Carolina, can be viewed as consistent—or alternatively, as not *in*consistent—with the assumption that Isaac Joppa was found guilty in the Old Bailey trial."

"And can you explain the basis for that opinion?"

"Yes, I'd be happy to. First of all, there was well-known historical hostility—politically, culturally, and legally—between the American colonies in 1719 and the British Crown regarding the nature of governmental proceedings. There was some resentment among the colonies relating to the creation of the admiralty courts with their deprivation of the right of trial by jury. Of course, the English Crown was well acquainted with the reluctance of any of the American colonists, through their common-law juries, to find defendants guilty...or at least to the extent the Crown would have liked to see...which, presumably, was around one-hundred percent. So the admiralty courts consisted of commissioners who would hear and try the cases and decide the verdicts...and, of course, the commissioners were persons of great political prestige and power, usually aligned with the Crown's cause. So, as a first possibility, we might presume that the entry of 'res judicata' was a form of protest by the local clerk or magistrate there in Bath. Although I view that as the least probable explanation."

"And what other explanations do you have?"

"Well, of course, the 'res judicata' entry could simply have been an error. Or a misapplication of law. Frankly, it's rather unusual for a phrase like that to appear in the clerk's notes. If you've ever seen notes from proceedings in the eighteenth century, you know they're pretty raw, pretty basic, pretty rough. They really got right down to business, and they're usually pretty sketchy. It is somewhat unusual that 'res judicata' would appear.

"It's also a little unusual that an indictment would be deemed to be dismissed after a finding of *guilt* in a collateral proceeding in a court, such as the one in London, which technically shared jurisdiction with the American colonies relating to charges of piracy on the high seas. I mean, taking the common parlance—when a defendant goes to trial on an indictment and is found guilty, the indictment, technically, is not *dismissed*. The indictment is only a pending charge—the charging document. Rather, it is *superseded* by the final judgment entered by the court as a result of the guilty verdict. All that's to say that, if there was an error at all, it wasn't in the 'res judicata' entry. It was in the entry that the indictment was 'dismissed' following a finding of guilt—if that's what the finding was— in the Old Bailey trial in England."

MacPherson saw that he was losing ground and wrapped up quickly.

"So, it would be correct to say, Dr. Hope, that the entry of 'res judicata' in the clerk's notes in Bath, North Carolina, is consistent with the hypothetical that the Old Bailey jury found Isaac Joppa guilty—is that correct?"

Dr. Hope smiled and threw a glance at Will.

"I thought perhaps there would be an objection from Mr. Chambers that your question was leading and suggestive. Perhaps he just figured it was leading in form, Mr. MacPherson—but it's hard to actually *suggest* an answer to an expert in his own area of expertise."

Then Hope paused a minute to recollect the question.

"In answer to your question, the answer is yes, as I had indicated previously."

MacPherson rested and quickly scurried back to his table.

"Dr. Hope, it's a pleasure meeting you," Will said politely.

"And it's good to meet you *in person*," Dr. Hope said with a smile.

"I want to limit my questions to one single point. Did you testify, on direct, that the reference to 'dismissal' of the indictment in 1719 before the words 'res judicata' was *inconsistent* with a finding of guilt in the Old Bailey trial?"

The witness paused for a moment. Virgil MacPherson was moving about uncomfortably at his table.

"What I said was—technically, when an indictment, as a charging document, is dismissed, it normally means something other than a finding of guilt. When a finding of guilt is made, the indictment as the mere charging document, in effect, merges with the judgment. It is superseded by the judgment, which reflects the final determination."

"So, in laymen's terms, would you agree that the reference to *dismissal* by the clerk in Bath—presuming the proceedings in the Old Bailey Court were communicated accurately to the magistrate in Bath—that the greater probability is that the reference to *dismissal* corresponded to an *acquittal* in the Old Bailey, rather than a conviction—would you agree?"

Now MacPherson was shifting in his chair and tapping his pen on the table.

A longer pause. And then Dr. Hope answered.

"On a scale of probabilities, I would agree with you—that the reference to the *dismissal* of the indictment is generally more consistent with a finding of acquittal rather than finding of guilt—all things being equal—and if those are the only choices I'm being confronted with."

Will smiled and sat down.

MacPherson scurried to the podium, frantically trying to think of a line of questions to rehabilitate his own witness. By the time he got there, he had thought of one—wasn't it possible, he would ask, that the word "dismissed" reflected the fact that the jury in the Old Bailey had found Joppa guilty of *other* offenses, and that the indictment on *piracy* was the one dismissed? But a moment later, he realized such a line of questioning would be totally fruitless. If the charges of piracy had been dismissed that would completely undermine his entire line of argument.

"Dr. Hope...I have no further questions," MacPherson said, trying to muster confidence.

MacPherson turned, not without some slight embarrassment, and returned to counsel table, having wasted his trip to the podium.

Dr. Hope scooted down from the witness chair, shook hands vigorously with MacPherson, and then walked over to Will and extended his hand.

"Good to meet you, Will," Dr. Hope whispered. "I just read the law review article by Dr. Len Redgrove, University of Virginia, about your successful trial before the International Criminal Court in the Hague... fascinating reading...can't say I agree with all your arguments on jurisdiction...but then that's a debate for another day."

And with that, Dr. Hope gave Will a smile, patted him on the shoulder, and quickly left the courtroom.

Will glanced over at MacPherson, who bore the expression of a man who wasn't sure just how many men he had lost in the last skirmish...but realized he had just yielded control of a small hill.

56

Dr. Manfred Berkeley's testimony would go to the heart of MacPherson's theory of the case. Berkeley was a professor of American marine history at the University of Connecticut. A tall, stately man with thick glasses and a scholarly air about him, his grasp of the early American shipping trade, admiralty law, and piracy were impressive.

He indicated he was familiar with the grand jury testimony of Henry Caulfeld, the co-owner of the sloop *Marguerite*, which had been attacked and plundered by Teach's pirates. As that of an experienced shipping merchant, Caulfeld's testimony, according to Berkeley, was particularly credible and believable. He witnessed Isaac Joppa's actions on the top deck as purely indicating someone who was acting in a concerted effort of piracy. Furthermore, Berkeley pointed out, Caulfeld understood what it looks like when a ship's crew is taking orders from a higher-ranking crew member.

According to Berkeley, Caulfeld's clear impressions, based on his eyewitness observations, were that Isaac Joppa was in charge of the activity of Teach's ship and was giving orders to a crew that was responding by arresting the *Marguerite*, and then boarding it with the intent to plunder.

Regarding the Williamsburg trial of the remaining pirates of Teach's crew, Berkeley addressed that as well.

"Here the testimony of Samuel O'Dell—although not in pure transcript form, but according to the clerk's notes—indicates some of the important background. An African pirate by the name of Caesar, a right-hand man of Teach, was in the hold of the ship *Adventure*, ready to torch several barrels of dynamite when it looked like the English navy was winning the battle. The order was clearly sent from Teach, who had also ordered, just minutes before, that the *Bold Venture* be scuttled. But Caesar was never able to accomplish this, because Samuel O'Dell and some of the others who were present on Teach's ship jumped him and prevented that. Now this same Samuel O'Dell, who was an innocent passenger on Teach's ship—

having attended a drinking party the night before—clearly indicated that he saw Isaac Joppa in the hold of the ship with Caesar, and that Joppa was not manacled or handcuffed. He was not restrained in any way, and had all the appearance of a free man."

"Dr. Berkeley, now is it consistent with Teach's usual practice for him to have taken Isaac Joppa prisoner…to have kidnapped him?"

"The interesting thing about Teach—and you have to admire his leadership abilities and his organizational skill, even if he was a notorious criminal—is that he thought through his strategy. He knew how to maximize his attacks on other ships. And he also knew that taking captives was a sloppy way of running business. So his modus operandi was not to kidnap or take hostages. In one instance, he took as a *temporary guest* a fellow by the name of Stede Bonnet, who had himself a pirating background…yet he freed Bonnet shortly thereafter and allowed him to go back to his own ship. That's the way Teach operated. So the argument by Joppa that he was a manacled captive, runs cross-current to everything we know about Teach's pirating methods."

MacPherson sat down, now satisfied that his case was back on track.

57

WILL STRODE TO THE PODIUM. He had five points he wanted to make, and he would do them rapid-fire.

"Dr. Berkeley," Will began, "In the grand jury testimony of Henry Caulfeld, true or not true—Caulfeld never testified that Isaac Joppa had any weapon whatsoever, but Caulfeld *did* describe all the other pirates as having either pistols, cutlasses, or other weapons?"

Dr. Berkeley took a moment to look through his notes.

"You are correct. There is no *overt* reference to a weapon by Isaac Joppa. That doesn't mean he wasn't carrying a weapon. It just means that Henry Caulfeld didn't testify he saw Joppa in possession of a weapon."

"Next point. In the early 1700's there was a 'pecking order' among sailors—even those engaged in piracy—there was an organization aboard the pirate ships much like on other maritime vessels. For instance, Teach had a quartermaster, a ship's carpenter, a bosun, a first mate, and so forth—the men in those positions were generally picked based on their experience and proven ability. True or false?"

Berkeley didn't need time to answer that one.

"Yes, that's certainly true. We know that's true on Teach's ship. As I indicated, he was a well-organized and highly efficient captain."

"Next point. The sloop *Marguerite* was plundered by Teach on December 5, 1717—that's when Henry Caulfeld testified he saw Isaac Joppa on the top deck. But that was only two months after Joppa began his journeys with Teach—because just two months earlier, in October 1717, was when the *Good Intent*, with Isaac Joppa as passenger, was captured by Captain Teach?"

"I'm not sure I understand your point..."

"The point is, that as of the date of the plundering of the *Marguerite*, Isaac Joppa had only been with Teach's gang for two months. Is that correct?"

"Yes, taking those dates…that's correct."

"Would you agree that it's highly unlikely that the experienced group of seamen on Teach's ship, let alone Edward Teach himself, would have taken a novice sailor like Isaac Joppa—with whom they had only sailed for two months—and put him in a position of authority at the time of the plundering of the *Marguerite*?"

Berkeley took a second to think about that one.

"Somewhat unlikely…but certainly not impossible. Joppa may have done his best to impress Teach with his sailing ability. Perhaps that's the explanation."

"But Isaac Joppa's sailing experience was limited. He had only been on the *Intrepid* a short time before he deserted. Is that correct?"

"Yes, that is correct. But Joppa may have lied to Teach and bragged about his sailing experience and tried to impress him so he could get a position of authority…to gain a bigger portion of the plunder."

"That's speculation on your part—isn't it, Dr. Berkeley?"

"That is somewhat speculative, that's correct."

"Next point. You referenced this Stede Bonnett as being taken as a 'temporary guest' of Teach, but then Teach, as a friendly gesture, simply released him back to his own ship. That incident occurred during the blockade of Charleston, South Carolina?"

"Yes, that's absolutely correct."

"During that blockade," Will continued, now speaking more rapidly, "at the zenith of Blackbeard's power, he manned several ships with hundreds of pirates, and they were able to literally blockade the entire port of Charleston until the local community finally gave them their requested medical supplies, correct?"

"You have your history accurate, Mr. Chambers. Which again goes to my point about Edward Teach's audacity, as well as his military skill in closing down an entire port city."

"But your point in your testimony today is that Teach generally did not take hostages, correct?"

"I said he didn't kidnap people and keep them captive…"

"But isn't that exactly what he did at the blockade of Charleston? He took a group of people hostage until the community acceded to his demand for medical supplies?"

"Temporary hostages only, Mr. Chambers. *Temporary* hostages."

"Dr. Berkeley, you have indicated your respect for Teach's leadership and organizational abilities, and his ability to win over his men and engender great loyalty in them. Is that correct?"

Berkeley nodded and smiled.

"Yes, he was a notorious criminal, but I have indicated that he was a talented man, certainly."

"And this same talented man, Edward Teach, according to at least one historical account, married a local plantation owner's daughter in the Bath area—and then on his wedding night, invited half of his pirate crew into the bridal room so they could take turns raping her?"

There was a hush in the courtroom. Berkeley shifted in his chair, glanced at his papers, and then looked up.

"I didn't say Edward Teach was a picture of virtue. He was a violent man, certainly. Although that information is only anecdotal…and is somewhat disputed…"

"My point is—if Teach was willing to do that, do you think he would have had any moral qualms about keeping Isaac Joppa in chains in the hold of his ship for months on end?"

Dr. Berkeley adjusted his glasses and smiled.

"It was not my testimony that Edward Teach had moral qualms about anything. But yes, your point is true to some extent…I doubt if Edward Teach would have had any twinge of conscience about keeping anybody in chains under any circumstances. I just don't think that was his particular mode of operation in his practice of piracy."

As Dr. Berkeley gathered his papers, and then slowly and carefully made his way from the witness stand, Will was beginning to get a picture of the scales of justice in the Joppa case. And, at best, they were dead even. And that wasn't a good thing.

With the burden of proof being his to satisfy perfectly, dead-even scales meant that he had failed to make his case.

Now, MacPherson had two more expert witnesses left.

Will's job was simple enough—he needed to tip the scales, ever so slightly, in his direction. And in order to accomplish that, he could not afford one stumble—one single trip—one faulty step.

58

"MY NAME IS DR. WILSON AUGER. I am a PhD in ocean archaeology, currently employed at Woods Hole Oceanographic Institute. I also work as a consultant to the National Geographic Society."

Virgil MacPherson walked Dr. Auger through his considerable credentials, including his participation in five deepwater salvage operations involving ancient ships. They ranged from sixteenth-century Spanish galleons to nineteenth-century ships sunk during the Civil War.

"Were you also involved," MacPherson continued, "on a more recent, perhaps even more spectacular, salvage operation on a sunken vessel?"

Dr. Auger smiled. He was a man of medium height with a ruddy complexion and an athletic build.

"Yes. I was one of the consultants on the locating and video archiving of the *Titanic*."

The jury was sitting stock-still, riveted on Dr. Auger's testimony, seeming amply impressed.

"And are you familiar, Dr. Auger, with the variety of salvage operations that have been conducted regarding the sailing vessels of the pirate Edward Teach, also known as Blackbeard?"

"Yes, I certainly am. I'm familiar with the salvage operations regarding the remains of two of Teach's ships, presumed to be *Adventure* and *Queen Anne's Revenge*. As well as some of the artifacts found in those searches."

"Would you share with the jury some of the items that were recovered from the sites of those ships?"

"Yes, I'd be glad to. There was the recovery of a bronze ship bell. Perhaps your jury is not familiar with the fact that bronze oxidizes differently than iron, more slowly, and therefore is preserved much better in salt water than iron. In addition, they found a syringe, which is presumed to have been used for injecting mercury—the treatment of the day for syphilis—something we can presume probably was rampant among Teach's crew. Also, the remains of a weapon called a *blunderbuss*—sort of a sawed-off shotgun of that time. A weapon that would have been used by pirates in the early 1700s."

"Thank you, Doctor. Now, have you read, by the way, the background materials my office provided to you, including the trial transcript of Isaac Joppa's statement before the Old Bailey Court in London, as well as the statements of an African who was a member of Edward Teach's crew, a fellow by the name of Caesar? In those instances, both Caesar the pirate and Isaac Joppa claimed that Joppa had been kept as a prisoner in the hold of one or more of Teach's ships, his hands manacled with irons. Did you read that?"

Auger smiled and chuckled a bit.

"I did read that information. I understand that was Isaac Joppa's defense at his trial. And his friend Caesar apparently tried to stand up for him in the trial at Williamsburg by claiming the same thing...mainly that Joppa had been kidnapped and kept under restraint by the use of irons."

"Now, can you tell the jury—among any of the artifacts that are known to have been retrieved from the sites presumed to be of the ships *Adventure* and *Queen Anne's Revenge*—did any of them include manacles, shackles, or any similar device used to restrain human beings?"

Dr. Auger paused a minute, turned so that he could face the jury almost directly, and then answered.

"There have been *no* objects retrieved from those two sites that would in any way correspond to what we understand to have been eighteenth-century shackles, manacles, or the like. None."

"Now lastly," MacPherson said, wrapping up his direct examination, "you are familiar, are you not, Doctor, with the current salvage operations regarding another ship presumed to belong to Edward Teach?"

"Yes, that's correct. You're referring, I presume, to the salvage site of the *Bold Venture*. It's being headed up by Dr. Steve Rosetti. Actually, I've been following their progress. And I can say that some of us who are not formally involved in that project have been concerned about its progress...it's been rather slow in getting down to the actual site. But we know that operations have finally been commenced. And as of my last review, no artifacts—at least, none relevant to this case—have been located."

MacPherson concluded his direct examination and strode confidently back to the counsel table.

Dr. Auger's testimony had clearly shown one thing in particular—that twenty-first century science had failed to corroborate, through any physical evidence, the story that Isaac Joppa had been a manacled prisoner in the hold of Edward Teach's pirate ship.

For Will Chambers, the task was now simple. He needed to take Dr. Auger and the jury back down into the hold of an eighteenth-century pirate ship.

And then convince them that what they would find there would conclusively prove Isaac Joppa's innocence.

59

"DR. AUGER," WILL BEGAN, "you did indicate that there is a substantially greater propensity for bronze to endure salt water, as opposed to iron. Is that correct?"

"Yes, that is correct,"

"I was wondering," Will continued, "whether you'd be able to explain exactly why it is, in laymen's terms, that iron disintegrates a lot more quickly at the bottom of the ocean than, let's say…well, as an example, that bronze bell you talked about."

"Certainly." Auger leaned back in his chair confidently. "First of all, you have to understand I'm not a PhD in chemistry…my field is ocean archaeology. But in that field we have to be aware of the chemical properties and the natural forces at play in the preservation of ocean antiquities. Now take iron as an example. Iron is the most abundant transition metal on the face of the earth. Most of us are familiar with products made out of unprotected iron. When it's exposed to the elements, rusting takes place. That's why an old automobile, one with iron parts, will begin rusting. Rusting is actually an electrochemical process. It needs three things to occur. It needs water, oxygen and, lastly, an electrolyte. In terms of the electrolyte, when you're talking about ocean water, particles of salt can be the electrolyte. The bottom line here is that unprotected iron corrodes very rapidly at the bottom of the ocean because of the presence of those elements. Now, there are exceptions to that…"

"Well, let's talk about that for a minute," Will said, beginning to probe. "One of the exceptions is—as I understand it—if a piece of iron has been buried under the sand or silt at the bottom of the ocean, that can protect it from the oxidation process. Is that correct?"

"Well, that's a very rudimentary way of describing it. But that is correct. That's why, when we find iron pieces buried deep in the sand, many times we can get lucky and find something that's pretty well preserved. But that's the exception."

"Well then," Will said, continuing on the same line of questioning, "let me pose a hypothetical to you, Doctor. Let's assume there was a pair of old-fashioned iron manacles in the hold of the ship *Adventure* or the ship *Queen Anne's Revenge*...or even in the hold of the *Bold Venture*, which is currently being explored by Dr. Rosetti and his team. Let's assume that, when the ship was sunk, those manacles were attached to something that left them exposed to the salt water above the surface of the sand—totally submerged. Would that be a condition likely causing, over the course of three hundred years, the total disintegration of those iron manacles?"

Auger took a few seconds to evaluate the question, smiled, then shot back.

"Unfortunately, there are a lot of factors involved that you have not included in your hypothetical. The facts you stated made it rather simplistic. It's really difficult for me to predict, with any kind of certainty, the level of disintegration or corrosion. For instance...I'd want to know where the iron came from...what its composition was...what the ocean temperatures were. What is the depth? What are the currents like in that part of the ocean? You see, Mr. Chambers, it's a much more complicated process than you've presented..."

"And I do appreciate that," Will said with a smile. "After all, that's what makes you the scientist and me only the, well, only the trial lawyer. But take a shot at it...what would your opinion be about the likelihood that those iron manacles would be preserved over nearly three hundred years, submerged in salt water and unprotected by sand or silt?"

After a few more moments of reflection, Dr. Auger asked Will a question.

"In order for me to answer that, I need to ask you a question, Counselor—is it proper for me to guess at the answer? I mean...can I speculate in answering this..."

MacPherson jumped to his feet.

"Your Honor, I'd ask that the Court admonish the witness not to speculate under any circumstances. That, if Dr. Auger is unable to form an opinion to a reasonable degree of scientific probability, then it is guesswork and inadmissible."

Judge Gadwell smiled and leaned forward, nodding his head toward Will Chambers.

"Mr. Chambers, you understand the rule on speculation by experts. We cannot let this expert witness simply engage in guesswork."

"All right, let's try it this way," Will countered. "Dr. Auger, I'm not a betting man myself. And I don't know whether you are or not. But— would you be willing to gamble your next month's paycheck from the Woods Hole Oceanographic Institute that those manacles I described in my hypothetical would have survived almost three hundred years of corrosion, if submerged in the salt water of the Atlantic Ocean because they were unprotected, not buried in the sand?"

MacPherson was on his feet again, shaking his head violently.

"No, sir. No, sir…Mr. Chambers is simply trying to evade the court's ruling…This really is a kind of contempt, Your Honor. The Court's already ruled that this expert not engage in guesswork…"

"Your Honor," Will said calmly, "I never asked Dr. Auger to guess at the answer to my most recent question. I just put it in terms that I thought he and I, as well as the jury, might be able to be clear on."

Judge Gadwell grimaced as he struggled with the objection and Will's rebuttal, and then turned to the witness.

"Dr. Auger…do you have an opinion that you can give us on this, or not? Because if you don't…"

"Your Honor," Auger said with a reluctant smile, "I think I can probably give an answer to that question."

The judge nodded.

"Let's put it this way…I don't get paid very much by the Woods Hole Oceanographic Institute…and that's no criticism. Most of us in my field labor in the vineyards of scientific inquiry more for the intellectual curiosity and thrill of the research than we do to become independently wealthy. And let me say—about that Spanish galleon I consulted on—the gold didn't go to me. It went to a private exploration corporation that has been engaged in litigation with the state of Florida, and the nation of Spain, and a couple other independent entities ever since they discovered it. So…maybe it's a blessing that we don't get rich. But that having been said, to answer your question, Mr. Chambers, no, I wouldn't want to bet my next month's wages on the preservation of those iron shackles. The chances are that they'd be pretty well disintegrated."

"So," Will said, concluding that line of questioning, "the fact is that the *absence* of evidence of iron manacles in the circumstances I described is not necessarily evidence that they were not there *originally*. Would you agree with that?"

"Yes, I think that's a reasonable statement. It has to be qualified, but it's reasonable."

"Now to conclude," Will said, "I just wanted to return to something you said on direct examination. You indicated that you were generally familiar with the *Bold Venture* exploration by Dr. Rosetti and his team. Is that correct?"

"Yes, I am familiar with that project."

"You are not actively participating in it, correct?"

"No. But we have access to weekly reports. Dr. Rosetti, like most of us, will post general information on the status of his investigation on some of the scientific Web sites."

"And you testified that Dr. Rosetti had discovered nothing of any particular relevance to this case—I presume, meaning dealing with the innocence or guilt of Isaac Joppa on charges of piracy, or dealing with the credibility of his claim to be innocent. Correct?"

"Yes, I did state that. And I stand by that."

"Well, I did have the opportunity to visit that site on one occasion. And I was informed that Dr. Rosetti had discovered the presence of some storage barrels. Barrels that had been submerged and buried under the sand. Are you aware of that?"

"Yes. I was aware of that. And I took that into consideration when I gave my answer."

"So you don't consider the presence of barrels at the *Bold Venture* site to be of any significance to the issues in this case?"

"No, I don't."

"But you have read the testimony of Isaac Joppa?"

Now Dr. Auger was leaning slightly to the side, with his head against his hand. There was an air of impatience about him when he answered.

"Yes. I have read the testimony of Isaac Joppa. And I anticipate where you're going…"

"Oh?" Will asked. "You know where I'm heading in my questioning?"

"Exactly. You're going to direct my attention," Auger said with a confident smile, "to the testimony of Isaac Joppa. Where he indicates he was manacled to a barrel…or barrels…in the hold of a ship under the control of Edward Teach. I read that. And it still doesn't change my mind."

"And yet you admit that Dr. Rosetti has found barrels matching the description given by Isaac Joppa. Barrels from the site of the sunken remains of the *Bold Venture,* one of Teach's ships."

"That is exactly correct. And that doesn't change my testimony. I do not believe the presence of such barrels adds or subtracts anything from what I said. That Isaac Joppa, in his testimony in the Old Bailey, mentions barrels in the hold where he was allegedly imprisoned, and that barrels were found in the vicinity of one of Edward Teach's pirate ships—all that is ultimately quite meaningless."

Will knew he had gone as far as he could go with this witness. The only question now was whether MacPherson was sharp enough to come back with the rebuttal that Will knew was available to him.

Will wouldn't wait long to find out. He had not even reached the counsel table when MacPherson had already rushed to the podium and launched into his questioning.

"Would you please tell the jury," MacPherson said with dramatic resonance, "exactly *why* Dr. Rosetti's discovery of the presence of cargo barrels at the site of the *Bold Venture* is irrelevant to the question of Isaac Joppa's fabricated story of innocence."

"It is irrelevant," Auger said, leaning toward the jury, "because almost every vessel on the ocean, as of 1717 through 1719, would have had barrels of some type in its hold. They kept foodstuffs there. They had commercial goods there, if it was a merchant ship. You might keep gunpowder there if you were a pirate or a military vessel. The point is, that's the purpose of a hold of a ship. Every one of them had barrels. The fact that Dr. Rosetti may have discovered some barrels at the site of the *Bold Venture* tells us absolutely nothing about whether or not Isaac Joppa was telling the truth."

MacPherson thanked the doctor for his testimony.

Will watched him stride back to counsel table. He had the gait of a man who had the wind fully at his back.

60

D<small>R</small>. H<small>ENRIETTA</small> C<small>LOVER</small>, <small>EXPERT</small> in early American genealogy, was on the witness stand.

Will recalled his pretrial discussion with Virgil MacPherson regarding Clover's anticipated testimony.

According to MacPherson, she was going to give only background information on the Joppa and Willowby family tree. Will thought it odd, however, that Clover's testimony—rather than coming at the beginning where it would logically fit—was coming at the end. With an opponent like Virgil MacPherson, that gave Will a sense of genuine unease.

After going through Dr. Clover's expert qualifications, MacPherson had her produce a large blow-up chart—an enlarged replica of a family tree contained in a family Bible.

"Is there something unusual about this?" MacPherson asked.

"There is," Clover said. "First, in that it was contained in the family Bible of Frederick Willowby—the father of Randolph Willowby, whose last will and testament is involved in this lawsuit. Although it was Frederick Willowby's family Bible, it is rather unusual. It includes not only the family tree of the Willowby side, but also the parallel Joppa family tree. It shows, all the way at the top, the conjoining point that relates the two families—the marriage of Reverend Malachi Joppa to Elizabeth Garfield. Their marriage produced Adam, the oldest, then Isaac, then Myrtle, the youngest, who married Elisha Willowby. That marriage between Elisha and Myrtle produced a line of thirteen generations of Willowbys, ending with Randolph.

"On the other side of the chart, as you can see, is the Joppa family line—descending from Adam, who married Deborah Henry. Their marriage produced, as the male heir, Jacob Joppa, and his marriage to Sally Lankin produced three children—Michael, Laura, and the oldest, Jonah. And then Jonah, of course, has a descending line—all of the other Joppas, ending with Jonathan Joppa. Who, I'm told, is sitting at counsel table over there."

MacPherson walked over to the chart with a laser pointer in his hand. He pointed the red beam at the spot of the family tree where Adam Joppa's marriage to Deborah Henry resulted in the birth of Jacob Joppa. Next to Jacob Joppa's name, where the date of birth should have been, was a blank line with a question mark. Then next to that was the date of death, 1781.

"Now Dr. Clover," MacPherson continued, "let's zero in on the child of Adam Joppa and his wife, Deborah. Adam was the oldest child of Malachi Joppa, and he was the brother of Isaac. He married Deborah— and according to this they had a child, Jacob. Correct?"

"That's certainly what the family Bible of the Willowby line indicates. By the way, this Willowby Bible was donated to the county historical society by Randolph Willowby shortly before his death."

"Is it unusual to have a question mark rather than a date of birth for a descendant on a family tree like this?"

"Well, somewhat unusual…but certainly not exceptional. We occasionally see it. Sometimes there is uncertainty about the date of birth. Sometimes you'll have two dates, two years separated by a slash mark, indicating that a person could have been born, for instance, in either 1719 or 1720. So, taking it merely as an artifact of a genealogy, we can't make any conclusions based solely on that."

"Fair enough."

MacPherson was at the podium with his arms crossed in front of him, and he had a smug look on his face. Will knew that whatever was about to surface in Clover's testimony was likely to come out of left field.

"Now, Dr. Clover, do you have reason to believe that one aspect of this handwritten genealogy, this family tree written in the inside of the Willowby Bible, is not accurate?"

"After my extensive research, I have come to a conclusion that there is one aspect of it that is not accurate."

Will rose to his feet.

"Your Honor," Will said in an even voice that disguised his concern, "may I have just one moment with opposing counsel before his examination continues?"

Judge Gadwell agreed, but reminded Will to make it short.

Will strode quickly up to the podium and addressed MacPherson in a controlled whisper.

"Virgil, what are you doing here? Where are you going with this witness? I recall distinctly your recitation in court about her anticipated testimony. You gave no proffer, no indication, that she was going to rewrite the genealogy of the Joppa line. This is coming as a complete surprise to us. And I think we're going to have a serious problem if you continue with this line of questioning."

MacPherson smiled but said nothing.

Will decided to press the point.

"You indicated in pretrial hearing that your *only* purpose in calling this witness was to give genealogical background information—not to reconstruct the genealogy of this family."

"And when did I say that, Will?" MacPherson said, still maintaining his grin.

"You said it at the pretrial conference as we were addressing the court."

"Correction—" he poked a finger in the middle of Will's tie—"whatever I might have said to you was not on the record. The judge was talking with his clerk and the court reporter was taking nothing down. Frankly, I don't even remember making such a comment. If it's not on the record, it doesn't exist."

Will stared him in the eye.

"You lied to me, Virgil!"

"Those are pretty strong words—"

But before he could say anything further, Will whirled around and strode back to his table. Something else was now clear to him.

Whatever storm was going to blow in from MacPherson's side of the case, he knew he had to batten down the hatches.

MacPherson collected his thoughts, smiled in the direction of the jury, and then addressed Dr. Clover again.

"And where, according to your expert judgment and opinion, does the error appear in this genealogy of the Joppa family?"

Clover raised the laser pointer, and a red laser dot appeared over the name *Jacob Joppa*.

"And what is it that is inaccurate?"

"Not that he was born, or that he died in 1781—that is not the inaccuracy."

"Well, perhaps you could elaborate..." MacPherson said, going in for the kill. "This chart shows that Jacob Joppa was the offspring of the marriage of Adam Joppa to his wife, Deborah. Is that correct?"

"No, it is not."

The jury was beginning to move forward in their chairs.

Will could sense Jonathan Joppa leaning forward at counsel table, his eyes riveted on Henrietta Clover.

"Well, if Jacob Joppa is not the son of Adam Joppa, then perhaps you can show where in this chart Jacob Joppa's real father is."

Clover turned again toward the enlarged chart on the easel, which showed Isaac Joppa with a "presumed dead" date of 1718. Having been presumed to have died in the Battle of Ocracoke Inlet, he was also presumed to have never married, and therefore to have no descendants.

"May I repeat myself?" MacPherson said dramatically. "Would you indicate with your laser pointer the identity of the real father of Jacob Joppa?"

Dr. Clover clicked the laser pointer on the name of Isaac Joppa. A few members of the jury muttered something almost audible.

Next to Will, Jonathan Joppa collapsed back in his chair, with a puzzled and stunned look on his face. He stared, now realizing the direct line of descent from Isaac Joppa to himself.

Jonathan knew that the lawsuit he had treated as an esoteric question on the life of Isaac Joppa and an ownership issue about an island, had now become something entirely different.

As he studied the family line, the blood relationship that linked him to his distant ancestor—a man who had tried to run from both family and God—he could not shake the notion that this lawsuit had suddenly become a case about himself.

"Would you explain to the jury," MacPherson continued with an air of confidence in his voice, "why you believe that Isaac Joppa was the father of Jacob Joppa?"

"As I explained," Clover replied, "the Willowby family Bible was the primary source of information regarding the two family lines, and specifically the identity of Jacob Joppa's father. I conducted an exhaustive search of the shipping documents from those vessels that called in the port cities of the Carolinas—documents following the year 1719, the date of Isaac Joppa's trial in London. For reasons I'll discuss in a minute, I assumed that Isaac Joppa was executed within a few months of his trial. That being the case, if you assume that Isaac was the father of Jacob, with Abigail Merriwether as the mother, Isaac only had a short window of time to have consummated a relationship with Abigail. That window of opportunity would have been the short time before he was arrested and tried. By that reckoning, Jacob Joppa would have been conceived shortly before May of 1719, and therefore, assuming a normal term of pregnancy, could have been born around January 1720."

"What types of documents did you search?"

"I looked at passenger lists and bills of lading for goods and personal belongings. I started in 1720, presuming that Jacob Joppa might have been brought back to the American colonies at that time. Actually, the first mention of his presence in the colonies turned out to be as an apprentice to the assistant of the harbormaster in Charleston, South Carolina, in 1738. Assuming my calculations regarding his probable date of birth, if Isaac was his father, that would have made him around eighteen years old. That would certainly fit for an apprentice's position like that."

"In your search of vessel records, did you find one year that was particularly significant?"

"I certainly did," Clover said with an edge of intensity in her voice. "In the year 1736, making Jacob Joppa around 16 years old, I found a passenger list from a vessel named the *Fair Haven*. That vessel shipped out of the West Indies and landed at the port of Charleston, South Carolina. Jacob Joppa was listed as a passenger on that vessel."

"Now tell the jury whether Jacob Joppa listed the identity of his parents on the passenger log at the beginning of the voyage, would you?"

"He did list himself as a passenger, and he filled in information on the identity of his parents. Occasionally, although not usually, a vessel would require next-of-kin information in case of accident."

"And who did he list as his parents at the *beginning* of this voyage?"

"Jacob Joppa listed Isaac Joppa as his father, and Abigail as his mother."

"But at the end of the voyage, after landing in Charleston, South Carolina, did Jacob Joppa list someone else as his parents?"

"He certainly did," Clover said with assurance. "A bill of lading for the delivery of some of his personal goods required his signature at dockside in Charleston."

"And who did he list as his parents on that document?"

"He listed Adam Joppa, and his wife, Deborah, as his parents."

MacPherson took a dramatic pause before addressing his final questions to Dr. Clover.

"Now, can you give the jury, based on your training and experience in matters of genealogy, as well as your review of the pertinent records in this case, a reason why Jacob Joppa would have listed Isaac Joppa as his father at the beginning of the voyage, but changed and listed Adam as his father after landing at Charleston?"

"There is a likely explanation—if we proceed on the assumption that Isaac Joppa was found guilty in London, England, of piracy, and was sentenced to hang. The explanation is this—Jacob's conception would have been extramarital. That is to say, he was deemed to be a bastard. I found no records of any registered wedding of Isaac Joppa to Abigail Merriwether in the records in either Bristol or London. So, I'm presuming that they didn't marry in the short span of time before he was hanged.

"Now, particularly in those days, it was a badge of infamy to be born out of wedlock. But couple that with the further besmirching of Isaac Joppa's name because of his conviction on charges of piracy. The news certainly would have traveled back to Charleston, South Carolina, regarding that. And Edward Teach's notorious escapades as a pirate had already become legend up and down the Carolina coast and throughout the colonies by then. It would not have taken young Jacob Joppa long to discover, after his arrival in Charleston, that it was far better to claim Adam Joppa as his father—particularly because Adam had been a relatively well-respected merchant in Bath, North Carolina, before being drowned at sea along with his wife."

"So would it be your opinion," MacPherson concluded, "that Jacob's actions in falsely representing Adam Joppa to be his father were likely a result of the obvious humiliation and shame that had been attached to Isaac Joppa at that time—humiliation and shame as a direct result of his conviction and hanging in London on piracy charges, and the out-of-wedlock birth that haunted Jacob himself?"

"Yes," Henrietta Clover said with finality, "those are my opinions."

"And with that, I have no further questions of this witness." MacPherson collected his papers from the podium, threw a smug smile toward the jury, and then walked slowly to his table with an air of satisfaction.

61

WILL WAS FACED WITH A NEARLY INTRACTABLE DILEMMA. Virgil MacPherson had misrepresented the nature of the testimony he would present from Dr. Henrietta Clover. He had described it merely as background genealogical information, rather than the blockbuster revelation that Jacob Joppa was actually the son of Isaac Joppa—but apparently was so embarrassed by the stigma of his father's conviction for piracy that he falsely claimed to be the son of Adam Joppa, Isaac's brother.

The problem was that Will's pretrial talk with MacPherson was all off the record. And MacPherson was the kind of opponent who would misrepresent that conversation to Judge Gadwell if challenged.

Rather than move for a mistrial, Will decided to conduct a short and highly focused cross-examination. He only had one weapon at his disposal. His two decades of cross-examining witnesses would now have to carry him. Coupled, of course, with a display of on-the-spot logical deduction.

Will took his time going to the podium, constructing his cross-examination as walked.

He took a moment at the podium to reflect. He had no notes in front of him.

"Dr. Clover," he began. "You indicated that Jacob Joppa sailed from the West Indies to Charleston, South Carolina, on or about the year of 1736. Is that correct?"

Dr. Clover nodded enthusiastically. "Yes, that's absolutely correct."

"Why the West Indies?"

"I'm not sure I get your meaning..."

"I'm simply asking why Jacob Joppa had made his way to the West Indies. You testified that you were basing your opinions on the assumption—the hypothetical—that Isaac Joppa had been convicted and hanged

267

in London following his piracy trial. That was your explanation as to why Jacob Joppa claimed Adam Joppa to be his father, correct?"

"That is correct."

"So if, as you speculate, Jacob Joppa was conceived in the short interval of time between Isaac Joppa's arrival in England and before his arrest and trial, then how did Jacob end up in the West Indies?"

"I have no idea. I was unable to locate any research that would explain that."

"But you do agree with me, Dr. Clover, that people change their names for a variety of reasons."

"Oh, I suppose that that's correct."

"And people may falsify information about their lineage for a wide variety of reasons?"

"Yes. There are a lot of reasons people may incorrectly or even falsely list a line of descent."

"Now you mentioned the embarrassment and potential shame that Jacob Joppa may have felt regarding his father's supposed conviction on piracy charges back in England. Correct?"

"That was certainly the most logical explanation as to why he would have falsely listed Adam Joppa as his father when he signed off on the bill of lading."

"Now, shame and humiliation—those are emotions that can certainly be expected by a young man whose father was in fact found guilty of piracy and hanged publicly?"

Dr. Clover nodded quickly. "Most certainly, and that was my opinion in this case."

"On the other hand," Will continued, his voice rising slightly, "humiliation and shame can also come from a public perception that is *in*accurate...a public perception within a community that a certain person is guilty—say, of piracy—even if that was not the fact. Do you follow me?"

Henrietta Clover paused for a minute, wrinkling her brow. Then she answered simply, "Yes, I see...Yes, I would agree with that."

"Are you aware that in the year 1719—a few months after Isaac Joppa's public trial in London, England—a clerk entered a note in the Bath, North Carolina, magistrate's court records indicating that the piracy charges had been dismissed on the merits? Are you aware of that?"

"I don't believe...no...I don't think I've heard that before."

"You mean, attorney Virgil MacPherson," and with that Will pointed over to MacPherson, who shot a glare in his direction, "Mr. MacPherson did not tell you what the clerk's notes in the Bath, North Carolina, magistrate's records showed?"

"No, I have never heard that before."

"I want you to assume a certain set of facts," Will said, building up speed toward his most important question. "I want you to assume, as a hypothetical, that Isaac Joppa was not convicted of piracy, nor was he hanged at Newgate. Rather, I want you to assume he was acquitted, found innocent by the jury, and that as a result the Central Criminal Court at the Old Bailey sent a message by boat to the Bath, North Carolina, magistrate's court—reporting the acquittal. I want you to further assume that the clerk at Bath entered the note indicating that the indictment was dismissed, and that it was dismissed on the merits—implying that the case had been resolved in Isaac Joppa's favor.

"Now…I want you to assume the clerk never communicated that information to another living soul. That the clerk kept the information of Isaac Joppa's acquittal entirely to himself. I want you to assume further that there were no newspaper reports of Isaac Joppa's acquittal by the Central Criminal Court in London—for whatever reason, the newspaper didn't cover it.

"In sum, I want you to assume that, for all practical purposes, the fact that Isaac was found innocent was never publicly known. That it was as if his innocence were a buried artifact, buried under layers of earth and stone, undetected and undiscovered by any archaeologist. I want you to also assume that the community in Bath, North Carolina, was well acquainted with Isaac Joppa's indictment for piracy charges, and that the community assumed his guilt as a result of that. Having never learned of his acquittal, the local community hostility against Isaac Joppa—because of his reputation as a member of Teach's murderous gang—was maintained in the popular thinking of North Carolina—and all the way down to South Carolina, including Charleston.

"Now, assuming those facts, wouldn't it have been logical—even understandable—for Jacob Joppa not to claim Isaac Joppa as his father…but rather to claim the more respectable Adam Joppa as his father?"

MacPherson leaped to his feet, waving his hands energetically.

"Objection! Objection. The hypothetical contains multiple items not contained in this record…he's asking this witness to speculate based on a hypothetical that assumes facts not in evidence. I move to strike. And I move to have Mr. Chambers admonished not to try that same hypothetical again."

Judge Gadwell was trying to recollect all of the components of Will's complicated hypothetical, and, at the same time, trying to decipher MacPherson's objection.

Will didn't want to wait for the light bulb to come on in the wrong compartment of the judge's brain, so he intervened.

"Your Honor," Will said confidently, "I challenge Mr. MacPherson here to point out one fact in my hypothetical that is outside the record in this case. Every one of the facts that I loaded into my hypothetical is either established clearly in this case or can be reasonably implied from the facts that have been proven. It just depends on which version of the facts—and which implications—the jury wants to believe. But the hypothetical I just put to the witness is simply a summary of the entire case we have put on."

Judge Gadwell was getting tired, and his state of confusion did not seem to be lessened.

"Oh, I'll answer Mr. Chambers," MacPherson said loudly, "I'll answer him all right. Here's the fact you've asked the witness to assume that has not been established—the fact that people would have known about Isaac Joppa's piracy exploits and his association with Edward Teach all the way down to South Carolina. You haven't established that."

"Your honor," Will said with a tinge of amusement in his voice, "Mr. MacPherson is trying to tell this court that such a fact has not been established. I find that bewildering. No—I find that astounding. Just a few minutes ago Mr. MacPherson himself elicited an opinion from his own witness that presupposed that the word had gotten down all the way to Charleston, South Carolina, about Isaac Joppa's tainted reputation. If the folks down there didn't know anything about Isaac Joppa, then what concern would Jacob Joppa have had about his father's reputation?"

Henrietta Clover, caught up in the argument of counsel and having listened to it carefully, began nodding noticeably in agreement with Will's argument.

MacPherson jumped in.

"No, Your Honor, Dr. Clover never gave any such opinion."

Now Henrietta Clover was shaking her head, disagreeing with the comment by MacPherson.

The judge was still trying to sort out the tangled web of facts and arguments that lay on his judicial desk crying out for a decision.

Suddenly, Henrietta Clover, unprompted, began speaking.

"Your Honor, it is my opinion that Jacob Joppa changed the name of his father because of the community reaction he received when he arrived in Charleston, South Carolina. So they must have known down in Charleston of Isaac Joppa's reputation for piracy—"

Virgil MacPherson was beginning to walk quickly toward Dr. Clover.

"Your Honor, I need time to consult with my witness," he said nervously, "I ask that the jury be excused so that we can continue this argument in its exclusion, and I do ask the court to permit me to consult with my witness—"

"What consultation is necessary?" Will asked sardonically. "Is Mr. MacPherson going to try to talk his own expert witness into a new opinion that contradicts what she just said? It's clear, Your Honor, that the facts from my hypothetical have been established by the record and that the form of my question was proper. And it's furthermore clear, we need an answer from this witness."

Judge Gadwell rubbed his head, and then waved MacPherson back to his seat. Massaging his scalp and scratching his chin, he took a glance at the wall clock.

"Dr. Clover…do you have an answer to the rather convoluted hypothetical that Mr. Chambers put to you?"

"Actually, I listened very carefully. I'm pretty sure I still have the facts in my memory. He basically wants me to assume a finding of acquittal for Isaac Joppa, but with that information never being disseminated among the people in Bath, North Carolina, nor the folks in Charleston, South Carolina, which would account for Jacob Joppa's reluctance to claim Isaac Joppa as his father. And the answer is very clear—"

Virgil MacPherson jumped to his feet again.

"Your Honor, I never received a ruling from the court. I want an opportunity to consult with my client, my witness—"

"Please, Virgil. Can we please try to bring this case to a close? Your request is denied. Dr. Clover…just give us your opinion."

"My opinion," Dr. Clover said, pausing for just a split second and then continuing, "my opinion is that your hypothetical, Mr. Chambers, would be a reasonable explanation as to why Jacob Joppa would have lied about Isaac Joppa as his father. If folks down in Charleston did not know the truth about Isaac Joppa's acquittal in England…then it would create a motivation for Jacob not to align himself with Isaac. So you're correct in that."

But MacPherson was not finished. He was on his feet again.

"I remember another one…I remember another one, Your Honor."

"Another what?" Judge Gadwell said with fatigue.

"Another fact that Mr. Chambers put in his hypothetical that has *not* been established in any of the evidence of this case. Thus rendering his hypothetical defective and subject to being stricken."

"And what fact would that be?"

"That the clerk in the magistrate's court in Bath, North Carolina, who made the entry that supposedly reflects the acquittal of Isaac Joppa—the 'res judicata'—never told anybody about the acquittal. There's absolutely no evidence as to whether or not the clerk did nor did not tell other people about his supposed knowledge that Isaac Joppa had been acquitted."

Judge Gadwell threw a look to Will, inviting him to respond.

"The answer to that is simple," Will said with a smile. "The answer is— if Mr. MacPherson is correct that the magistrate's clerk spread the news around Bath, North Carolina, that Isaac Joppa had been acquitted, then what are we doing here in this lawsuit? But the clerk could not have publicized that fact because the historical documents, records, and opinions of the community would have reflected it. And to this day...to this day there is a tavern on the coast called *Joppa's Folly*, apparently alluding to Joppa's ill-fated attempt at piracy. Schoolchildren learn in their regional history classes that a local man by the name of Isaac Joppa was one of Blackbeard's gang members and was killed at the Battle of Ocracoke Inlet, shot in the back as he tried to flee with his pirate cronies. No, Your Honor, that clerk, for whatever reason—and we'll probably never know why—chose to keep that information to himself."

Judge Gadwell sighed and drummed the fingers of both hands on his bench.

Then he cleared his voice.

"Mr. MacPherson...if I gather it correctly, you're asking that I strike the entire exchange between Mr. Chambers and Dr. Clover that we just heard. Is that correct? Do you want me to instruct the jury that they are to totally disregard it, and that the answer to the question is to be stricken from the record—correct?"

MacPherson, sensing an approaching victory, rose to his feet and smiled. "Your Honor, you've captured my objection perfectly."

Gadwell paused, but only for an instant. Then he rendered his decision.

"In that case, your objection is noted but overruled. The question and the answer will stand. The court is adjourned for the day!"

Judge Gadwell, exhausted, slammed the gavel on his desk so hard that it bounced before coming to rest.

62

Aᴛ ᴛʜᴇ ʙᴇɢɪɴɴɪɴɢ ᴏꜰ ᴛʜᴇ ꜰᴏʟʟᴏᴡɪɴɢ ᴅᴀʏ of trial, Virgil MacPherson announced he was resting his case. In the same breath, he moved to dismiss Jonathan Joppa's claim to Stony Island on the grounds that no reasonable jury could believe Isaac Joppa to be innocent of charges of piracy.

As had been his practice throughout the trial, Judge Gadwell reserved his ruling on that motion.

The judge then eyed Will Chambers.

"Mr. Chambers, do you intend to put on a rebuttal case?"

It was Will's intent to do exactly that—except for one problem. His entire rebuttal case would consist of the testimony of Dr. Steve Rosetti— who was to have shown up thirty minutes earlier. But there was still no sign of him.

"Your Honor, we're still waiting for our witness to arrive," Will explained calmly as he turned to search the courtroom. "But I thought we might want to take a few minutes while we're waiting to resolve some issues that the court has yet to decide with regard to jury instructions."

Judge Gadwell usually did not take kindly to counsel's suggestions as to how he should handle time made available because of late-appearing witnesses. On the other hand, he knew the issue of jury instructions still needed to be decided.

He reluctantly waved MacPherson and Will to sidebar, and he also motioned for the court reporter to position herself between the two attorneys so they could talk outside the hearing of the jury.

"All right. I'm going to make this short and sweet," he explained. "I've looked at both of your sets of instructions. They are virtually identical on the substantive issues. So I'll put together something that uses both of your proposals. But, on the burden of proof...well, here's the way it lies..."

He pulled his notes out.

"Here's what I'm going to do. Virgil, your jury instructions explain that the burden of proof is on Jonathan Joppa. And Mr. Chambers, you agree with that in your proposal as well. But here's the difference. Virgil, your jury instructions explain that what that means is that Jonathan Joppa must prove, by a preponderance of the evidence, that Isaac Joppa was actually and factually innocent of the charges of piracy. Mr. Chambers, your jury instructions say that the burden of proof can be satisfied by your simply proving, by a preponderance of the evidence, that there is a *reasonable doubt* about Isaac Joppa's guilt regarding charges of piracy. Mr. Chambers, I reject your proposal. In order for Reverend Joppa to get Stony Island, I am ruling—and I will so instruct the jury—that you must affirmatively prove the innocence of Isaac Joppa. I know that's a heck of a tough burden... extremely hard to prove. But that's what I'm making you do. I think that's what is reasonable and what is called for under the law. Now, I think that's all..."

But something at the back of the courtroom distracted the judge, and he looked up with bewilderment.

The court reporter stopped typing. Virgil MacPherson jerked his head around to look, so quickly that he risked whiplash.

At the open doors of the courtroom two men with hooded yellow rain slickers, dripping wet, were awkwardly making their way into the courtroom, each carrying one end of a large aluminum box.

A murmur broke out among the jurors and some of the audience.

"What in the world..." Judge Gadwell gasped.

"Your Honor," Will said reassuringly, "this is my witness. If I can have a few minutes with him in the back of courtroom, we will be ready, I think, to proceed with my rebuttal case."

Will hastened to the back of the room.

Dr. Steve Rosetti and one of his research assistants carefully placed the large aluminum box on the floor. Rosetti pulled back the hood of his rain slicker and shook the water out of his hair.

"Sorry I'm late," he said with a big grin. "Some bad weather just blew in."

"So what can you tell me?" Will said with a grin, "Other than the fact that you look like you're doing a TV ad for frozen fish filets."

Rosetti flashed a wide, smart-aleck grin. "Oh, yeah," he said, hardly containing his enthusiasm, "I've got a special delivery for you. And it ain't chicken-of-the-sea." He started laughing, and he slapped his assistant on the back.

"Dr. Rosetti," Will said, "you're going to have to explain...what's in here?"

Rosetti swung the lids of the metal box open so that Will could look in. Will stared. Finally, his eyes widened, and he broke into a wide smile.

"I want to take a look inside there." Virgil MacPherson had made his way across the courtroom and was now standing behind Will. "If you're going to pull some monkey business in this courtroom, I'm going to see what it is you're planning on introducing."

Rosetti quickly snapped the metal covers of the box shut.

"This is a private party, MacPherson. And you're not invited."

"Rosetti, this has nothing to do with you," MacPherson snapped. "This is a court of law, and I'm going to see this evidence before you start parading it in front of the jury!"

Will swung around quickly.

"Go back to your counsel table, MacPherson. I'll be advising you and the court what we're going to do with Dr. Rosetti's testimony and our new evidence."

But MacPherson stood his ground, alternately glaring at Will and Dr. Rosetti.

"Sit down, Virgil," Will said even more firmly.

Judge Gadwell, observing the interaction at the back of the courtroom, had had enough.

"Will someone please tell me what's going on?" Then he ordered the clerk to excuse the jury. The six jurors stood up, transfixed by the large silver aluminum box on the floor, and the argument of the three men at the back of the courtroom.

The jurors were taken to the jury room, and the door was closed.

Will asked Dr. Rosetti to strip off his slicker and move the large aluminum box to Will's table.

Then Will approached the podium to address the court.

"Your Honor, this is Dr. Steve Rosetti. He is the expert in our rebuttal case. He's here to address, specifically, Dr. Wilson Auger's testimony regarding which ocean archaeological artifacts may or may not have a bearing on this case."

"And I want to know what's in that metal box..." MacPherson said, charging up and positioning himself next to Will.

"What's in the box?" Judge Gadwell asked, his face that of a tired jurist whose desire now was merely to control the lawsuit in this courtroom at almost any cost.

Will began to explain. "Dr. Rosetti, less than twenty-four hours ago, recovered an artifact that directly relates to the contents in the hold of the *Bold Venture* ship. We intend to have Dr. Rosetti describe this artifact and display it to the jury…and then we intend to introduce it into evidence as an exhibit."

"Your Honor, I want to know what that is." MacPherson bulleted.

"And I, Mr. MacPherson, first want to know whether you have any preliminary objections to my introducing this into evidence," Will countered. "Because it's newly discovered evidence and has taken us by surprise as much as you, I'm assuming you will be willing to waive any objections to the fact that this artifact was not described on our list of exhibits at the time of the pretrial conference."

MacPherson looked over Will's shoulder at the metal box, which now rested on top of the counsel table where Jonathan Joppa sat next to Boggs Beckford.

"My position is this," MacPherson said with a sneer as he turned to the judge. "I don't think *any* evidence discovered recently at the *Bold Venture* site ought to be admissible. Your Honor, I'm simply remembering your words at the pretrial conference. You warned both counsel that you didn't want any last-minute revelation of new evidence…or either side trying to slip in some miraculous discovery at the last moment. That's what you said—that was your ruling. So based on that, I vehemently object to any 'newly discovered antiquities' being introduced into this case. I've had no advance opportunity to investigate this or to get our own expert in to rebut it."

"Mr. Chambers," Judge Gadwell said, "what do you say to that? Virgil is correct. That's what I said at the pretrial conference. And I was adamant about it. Now I know that everybody's all excited because of this so-called discovery…and we don't even know what it is yet…but it seems awfully unfair to Mr. MacPherson here to pull this rabbit out of a hat at the last moment."

"Your Honor," Will began, straining to speak in a calm and reasoned tone, "this case is about the innocence or guilt of Isaac Joppa. History, and the artifacts of history, are the most important evidence we have. And now, Dr. Rosetti has just discovered what I believe to be the most important piece of evidence in this case. It bears directly on the question of whether Isaac Joppa was imprisoned by Blackbeard or not…whether he was lying or not…whether his contention of innocence was credible or not. We were just as surprised by this evidence as Mr. MacPherson here. And if the court wants to inquire of Dr. Rosetti to prove there's been no conspiracy or collaboration between him and me to keep this discovery hidden until the trial, the court is free to do so."

"It's your intention to introduce this object, whatever it is, into evidence?"

"It certainly is," Will answered.

Judge Gadwell's eyes narrowed. After a moment of reflection, he ruled.

"Mr. Chambers, here's my ruling. The object itself—this antiquity you referred to—is, according to you, intended to be introduced as an exhibit in this case. Yet I warned all counsel I didn't want any last-minute arguments, either just before the trial or during the trial itself, over newly discovered evidence. Both sides have had ample time for discovery. I understand that Dr. Rosetti's recovery of this object from the site of the *Bold Venture* was probably beyond anyone's control…in terms of when he discovered it. But nevertheless, my ruling is that you may not affirmatively introduce this object as a marked and received exhibit."

A noise came from behind Will's counsel table. It was Dr. Rosetti throwing his hands up in the air and muttering some indecipherable expression of frustration.

"And Dr. Rosetti," Judge Gadwell said, pointing a finger at the ocean archaeologist, "you will restrain yourself from any comments about the rulings of this court. Do you understand me? Any outburst from you will result in a finding of contempt of court. And believe me, sir, you don't want to challenge me. Because I will be more than happy to cite you with contempt…"

As Will walked slowly back to his table, he glanced back to the far corner of the courtroom. Blackjack Morgan was leaning back confidently, his arms stretched out on the back of the bench, smiling as he watched the proceedings.

Will sat down pensively.

Judge Gadwell then ordered the clerk to bring the jury back into the courtroom. Dr. Rosetti seated himself in the witness stand, throwing an annoyed look at the judge.

Jonathan Joppa leaned forward to Will.

"Will, what's the secret? What's in the metal box?" Joppa was staring at the container just inches away from his face.

"Jonathan," Will said calmly, "that's what I'd like you, the court, and the jury to find out in a matter of minutes."

Boggs Beckford leaned forward and joined in the hushed conference.

"Okay, Master Trial Lawyer…" he began with a wry smile, "exactly how are you planning on achieving that? The judge said you couldn't introduce whatever is in that box into evidence…"

Will paused and considered the dilemma. He always thought best when he considered complex litigation as a form of military combat. This was no exception.

"Let's just put it this way, Boggs," Will continued confidently. "I thought I had the high ground, but now the island is surrounded and the enemy is charging the hill…"

"And?" Jonathan Joppa chimed in expectantly.

"Let's just say I have one last bullet left in the chamber."

Beckford's acerbic sense of humor got the best of him.

"Oh…I get it. Suicide?" he said with a smirk.

"No, not even close. More like one final, precisely placed sniper shot."

And Will tapped the aluminum case with his index finger.

63

FROM THE WITNESS STAND Dr. Steve Rosetti was responding to Will's questions about his professional qualifications and background, with short, snappy answers. He began with his undergraduate degree from Stanford, followed by his dual master's degrees in history and biology from Harvard, and finally, his PhD in ocean archaeology.

Then Will focused his examination on Rosetti's current salvage project at the site of the *Bold Venture*. He described the preliminary information that had led him to believe that the sinking of the *Bold Venture* might have taken place at the current exploration site.

"Under federal law regarding the salvaging of ancient vessels in United States navigable waters, were you required to apply for court approval to commence salvage operations?"

"Absolutely. I filed a petition to be recognized by the federal court as having salvor-in-possession status. In technical language, the ship would be the salvage. And the person recovering the salvage would be the salvor. Thus, what I was asking the court to do was to give its approval for our oceanographic institute—and for myself, as its director—to have sole and exclusive rights to locate the sunken vessel, perform any feasible retrieval of its structure and any antiquities in or about the vessel, and then safely preserve as much of the vessel as possible together with those antiquities. The court granted my request."

"And were there other persons or groups vying for permission to engage in this exploration of the *Bold Venture* in addition to your institute?"

"Yes, there certainly were," Rosetti answered. As he did, he stared at Blackjack Morgan, who, with arms crossed, was glaring back at him.

After refocusing the examination on the progress of Rosetti's exploration at the site and some of the preliminary mapping, tentative measurements, and photographs that were done, Will then targeted his questions on the artifacts recovered.

"Dr. Rosetti, have you located artifacts that you believe were once associated with the *Bold Venture*?"

"Yes. We definitely have."

"Would you describe to the jury the nature of the artifacts that you have located as recently as of yesterday?"

Rosetti smiled and leaned closer to the microphone.

"Approximately two weeks ago we had initially located what we believed to be submerged artifacts once carried in the hold of the *Bold Venture*. Of course, we then mapped out the entire area, in quarter sections, by stereophotography. We created a detailed site plan for the excavation. The length and configuration of the outline…and you have to understand that there were barely any remnants left of what we thought to be the hull… corresponded with the dimensions of the *Bold Venture*."

"And did you subsequently discover some objects at the site, which were then actually retrieved?"

"That's exactly what happened. We went down there with our scuba-diving team, initially taking close-up photography. Then we did some very gentle brush-away cleaning of the site. That is when it was very obvious to us what we had."

"What did you find?"

"We found a collection of barrels in the area of the hold of the ship."

"Barrels?"

"Yes…the kind of barrels that were in use in the early eighteenth century."

"And how is it, Dr. Rosetti, that these barrels would have survived the ravages of time at the bottom of the ocean? Particularly in light of the fact that, as I'm presuming, the barrels were made of wood…"

"They were made of wood, and that's an excellent question." Rosetti was now becoming animated in his answers, and his eyes were visualizing something that was not apparent to the attorneys, jurors, or judge.

"You see," he continued excitedly, "okay…so you really had to be there… here's this sandy bottom, but we're down there with our scuba gear…and there's a mound of sand that shows it has some debris. The debris consisted of round-ended wooden objects. Now, obviously…if you know anything about old-fashioned barrels…they had two main components in addition to the round top and bottom. First were the wooden planks that run upright—up and down like a picket fence—those are the *staves*. Obviously, the staves have to be encircled by something. And what they used were metal hoops. Now before we did the dive, because I felt we had probably come across some barrels from the ship, I did a little research on eighteenth-century barrels."

"And what did your research indicate to you?"

"What I found was that the barrels at our site closely resemble other eighteenth-century barrels. Wooden staves encircled by three metal hoops—one at the top, one in the middle, and one about a fourth of the way from the bottom. And then you have a circular wooden bottom and top. I actually compared the configuration of our barrels with another ocean archaeological recovery."

"And which recovery are you referring to?"

"One of the ships from the Siege of Yorktown that occurred during the Revolutionary War, 1781. On September 5 of that year, a British fleet arrived off the coast of Virginia. But they ran smack into more than twenty French warships that had anchored there to assist the colonials. Both lines of war vessels kept blasting each other for five days, after which the British high-tailed it up to New York. That led to the final British surrender."

"And how is that event significant to your findings at the *Bold Venture*?"

"Because the barrels at the *Bold Venture* site are very much like those found at the Siege of Yorktown site when those sunken vessels were excavated. Ocean archaeologists also found barrels. In that case they found the barrels preserved because they had been buried in sand ballast. The barrels in the *Bold Venture* were also preserved because they happened to be surrounded by sand ballast, which kept them from water damage."

"Now, did you actually make a recovery of some of the barrels?"

"Well, the hoops had burst, and the staves spread out. But they had kept their configuration pretty well. And the hoops, though broken were pretty well intact, all things considered. So we had both hoops and staves that were recoverable."

"And is there any question in your mind, as a professional ocean archaeologist, that the barrels that you found at the presumed site of the *Bold Venture* were in fact part of the barrels that were in the hold of that ship at the time of its sinking?"

"No question. There's no doubt in my mind."

"And how did you verify that?"

"Two ways. First of all, their location was in the midst of what would have been the hull of the ship. But secondly, we found some distinctive markings on some of the barrels that indicated their ships of origin. Some of those ships were known to have been robbed and scuttled by Blackbeard.

He'd taken the barrels onto his ship. It all adds up that this was part of Blackbeard's booty from other ships."

"And did you find something else in or around those barrels that you believe may relate to the issues of this case?"

"You're talking about the Isaac Joppa involvement with Edward Teach?"

"Yes," Will said. "Did you find anything in or around those barrels that relates to the claim by Isaac Joppa that he was a prisoner during the months that he was on the ships of Edward Teach and his pirate band?"

"Yes," Rosetti answered with a broad smile. "Oh, we sure did."

"Now, Dr. Rosetti, do you see a markerboard over on the other side of the judge's bench?" Will pointed to a large markerboard.

Rosetti nodded.

"I'd like you to walk over to that board…and if you'd just roll it into the middle of the courtroom area here so that the jury can see it, and the judge as well. And if you could draw for us, please, in as detailed a fashion as you can, exactly what you found in the area of the barrels—whatever it is you believe relates to the claimed innocence of Isaac Joppa."

Rosetti eyed Will closely, then scratched the back of his head vigorously. He rose and walked over to the blackboard.

Virgil MacPherson was still seated, but only barely. His head was down low—he was staring at Rosetti and his hands were planted on the top of the table. He had the appearance of an animal waiting to make an ambush.

Rosetti picked up a marker. But something stopped him from proceeding. Something unspoken. A scientist's desire for precision, perhaps. For accuracy. For objective presentation.

It was a trait Will had counted on.

"Dr. Rosetti," Will reminded him, "I want your drawing to be as absolutely detailed and accurate a representation as possible."

Rosetti put his marker up again but, again, did not begin drawing.

Then he turned around and smiled.

"Mr. Chambers, in order for me to really give you an accurate drawing of what we found—of the antiquity I think may be very important to this case—I really…the problem is that I need…I need to review, again, the object we're talking about."

"Would it be accurate to say," Will replied with a smile, "that your recollection of the exact configuration and appearance of the object we're talking about needs to be refreshed in order for you to testify fully? And give a full and accurate description?"

"That's exactly right."

"Then by all means," Will said, "if you have that object with you today, please retrieve it and examine it for as long as it takes for you to refresh your recollection."

Rosetti walked quickly over to the aluminum case, slid back the bolt, and opened its doors. As he reached in, Virgil MacPherson pounced.

"Objection! Objection!"

His right hand and index finger were pointing at the aluminum box, waving frantically.

"That is out of bounds. The court ruled that this can't come into evidence. Whatever is in there has to remain in there—and I do not want the jury to see anything contained within that box. And if they do, then I want a mistrial, Your Honor!"

Will stepped back from the podium with his hands calmly clasped behind his back.

"Your Honor, I see no basis for an objection by Mr. MacPherson."

"To the contrary. Very much to the contrary," Judge Gadwell retorted gruffly. "I thought I ruled…and made it very clear…that whatever is in that box cannot be introduced into this case as newly discovered evidence."

"Well, Your Honor," Will replied firmly, "we're not asking that it be received into evidence as an exhibit. Rather, I'm relying on our ability, under Evidence Rule 612, to use it to refresh the memory of a witness while he is testifying. Dr. Rosetti indicated that he needed his recollection refreshed about the configuration of this object, that the object is here in court, and to review it would, in fact, aid his memory and his ability to describe it and testify about it."

MacPherson grabbed his evidence code and quickly flipped through the pages.

"Your Honor," MacPherson said after reviewing the rule, "this is nothing but a lawyer's trick—"

"Well, then the state of North Carolina," Will responded, "as well as every other state in the union and the federal court system, is engaging in lawyer's tricks. Because they all have a similar rule allowing a witness to have his recollection refreshed by anything that would so aid it—including an object he is seeking to describe that is central to the issues of the case."

MacPherson tried to begin a counterargument, but Gadwell raised his hand for quiet. Nearly a minute passed as he consulted the evidence code, rubbing his forehead as he did.

"All this is fine and good," the judge said, "and I'm reading Rule 612. And it certainly seems to apply. But it does not answer the question as to what happens when a judge, such as myself, has given a ruling that certain evidence will not be introduced. In effect, a motion *in limine* was granted here—or at least to the same effect...so that certain evidence—namely whatever is in that metal box—is not going to be received into evidence."

"Your Honor," Will said softly but emphasizing every word, "this is the time. It happens in almost every case. Where one ruling will determine the outcome—whether it will rest on the foundation of justice or on the uncertain ground of facts hidden or truth distorted. There is an old Chinese proverb—it goes something like this, 'Even the faintest ink on a document is clearer than the best memory.' Of course, we're not talking about a document here—we're talking about an object found in an eighteenth-century ship. In the exact place where Isaac Joppa said he had been imprisoned by Edward Teach. But it is an artifact that, like an ancient document, seeks to tell us the story of Isaac Joppa's life. This ancient object, just as surely as if it were a letter in the faintest ink, tells us a tale that is still legible, even after several centuries—the truth about Isaac Joppa. The truth about this case."

Will walked slowly to the podium and rested his hands there, looking at Judge Gadwell.

"The question is yours, Your Honor—whether we can really do justice here today without heeding this message, buried for centuries but now revealed, I believe, by the hand of Providence."

64

JUDGE GADWELL STARED AT THE METAL BOX on the counsel table. Then he glanced again down at Rule 612 in the evidence code that lay before him. He gave a heavy sigh, moving his head almost as if he were both shaking and nodding it...in perfect equipoise of indecision.

Will Chambers spoke simply.

"If it would help, Your Honor, both sides could file legal briefs on this issue for your further deliberation. I have a huge amount of legal research that backs my position. I believe that it may not only clarify your ruling, but also sharpen the issue and—in the event you rule adversely to our position—would assist us in presenting the issue on appeal."

"I would like to get this case submitted to the jury today..." Judge Gadwell said, his voice trailing off.

He glanced at the clock. Then he stared at the evidence code in front of him. Then he ruled.

"Dr. Rosetti..."

"Yes, Your Honor." Rosetti was poised over the box.

"If it would assist you in the testimony and in refreshing your recollection, you may examine the object...whatever it is..."

Will glanced at the jury. The construction company president was staring intently, his eyebrows lowered. The rest of the jurors were slack-jawed and wide-eyed—all except the elderly widow. She was smiling politely as she had throughout the trial.

In a few seconds Rosetti and his research assistant were pulling out a large, clear glass box—much like an aquarium. It was filled with liquid. They set it on the counsel table next to the aluminum case.

Everyone in the courtroom was straining forward to examine its contents. Blackjack Morgan was actually standing on one of the benches to get a better view.

The tank appeared to contain a corroded metal band, approximately fourteen inches long. Attached to it was a chain—and at the end of the chain was another object.

Rosetti studied it, then walked to the markerboard and drew a picture.

"What is the long, thin object you've drawn that appears to be a band?" Will asked.

"That is a portion of a metal hoop that encircled one of the barrels we recovered."

"Dr. Rosetti, do you recall which barrel in particular this hoop encircled?"

"Yes, distinctly,"

"Fine. We'll return to that issue in a minute. Now you've drawn a portion of a metal hoop from a barrel. What is the chainlike object attached to the hoop?"

"It is exactly as you have described…a chain. The links are metal, almost certainly iron."

"And lastly—" This time Will half-turned to the jury.

"What is the object you drew at the end of the chain?"

Dr. Rosetti took a step away from the board, smiling broadly at Will Chambers.

"Connected to the end of the chain?"

"Yes. Dr. Rosetti, what is that object?"

"That, Mr. Chambers, is a manacle. A wrist manacle to be precise. An eighteenth-century version of what we would call handcuffs today."

Will sensed movement, even hushed muttering in the jury box. But he kept his attention riveted on the witness.

"One last question, Dr. Rosetti," Will said. "And by the way…you may resume your seat in the witness stand.

"Final question—about the barrel to which this hoop, chain, and manacle were attached—you will recall I had asked whether you remembered that particular barrel?"

"Yes, I recall that," Rosetti said with a broad smile.

"Were you able to determine the contents of that barrel?"

"Yes, I was."

"Before I ask you the last question—did I provide you with a copy of the testimony of Isaac Joppa before the Central Criminal Court in the Old Bailey, London, England?"

"Yes, you did. And I read it all."

"And did you read the transcript of the comments of the pirate Caesar before the Williamsburg admiralty court at the trial of Teach's crew?"

"Yes. I read that as well."

"And you recall what Isaac Joppa said in his testimony about the contents of the barrel to which he was fettered during his imprisonment in the hold of Teach's ship?"

"Oh, yes—I remember it quite well,"

"Now, Dr. Rosetti, would you tell the jury—right now—what you recovered from the interior of the barrel to which the hoop, chain, and manacle were attached, when you found it within the sand ballast of the wreck of the *Bold Venture?*"

"Yes, I'd be glad to," Rosetti said.

He lowered his head a bit and then gave a funny little laugh. Then he looked up at Will Chambers.

"Fine china plates from the eighteenth century."

"Just as Isaac Joppa described in his testimony in the Old Bailey?"

"Mr. Chambers," Rosetti said with a thoughtful look, "it was all…all of it…*exactly* as Isaac Joppa described in his testimony."

"Thank you, Dr. Rosetti," Will said, concluding his direct examination.

As he walked back to the counsel table, he stopped momentarily in front of Virgil MacPherson's position. "Mr. MacPherson—you may examine the witness."

MacPherson charged up to the podium and immediately began dealing out some verbal body blows. He questioned Rosetti's objectivity, arguing that Rosetti's fight with Blackjack Morgan in the salvor-in-possession case involving the *Bold Venture* somehow tainted his opinions in this case—since Morgan had a third-party interest in its result.

MacPherson accused Rosetti of harboring a personal and professional "grudge" against Morgan and anyone else who would interfere with his salvaging of the *Bold Venture*.

And then he aimed his invective at the eighteenth-century artifacts that still rested on the counsel table of the opposing party.

"You have not even scientifically tested the material of which those objects is made…is that correct?"

"That's correct. No ocean archaeologist with a brain in his skull would attempt that at this early stage. We have to maintain a chemical equilibrium in the solution designed to preserve the objects. We still have to remove some encrustations. And that's a very delicate process as well."

"But if I had my own archaeologist here today," MacPherson said, his voice now rising to a level just below a shout, "you wouldn't even permit him to dip his hands into this tank and start scraping away—because of the high probability that the object might disintegrate?"

"There, Mr. MacPherson, you're absolutely correct."

"So, as a result—strictly speaking, as a scientist—you cannot really say what this object is...or what it's made out of."

"Wrong," Rosetti snapped. "These are manacles...wrist manacles in particular, from the eighteenth century. They're made out of a ferrous metal, probably iron. I already testified to that, if you were listening—"

But in his wild, erratic cross-examination, MacPherson had accomplished one thing. He had ignited Rosetti's temper, which placed the witness square within the judge's crosshairs.

"Dr. Rosetti," Judge Gadwell bellowed, "that will be the last of those kinds of comments. I want no more snide remarks—no off-the-cuff criticisms—no personal attacks. You try that again in my courtroom and you *will be* confined to our fine county jail on a charge of contempt."

Rosetti shrugged nonchalantly.

MacPherson was tempted to forge ahead—slugging, slapping, and punching. But the smart trial lawyer in him knew well enough to stop after he had landed the most critical blow of all—the judge's rebuke to the most important expert witness for the opponent. MacPherson rested his cross-examination wearing an unambiguous smirk.

Will Chambers asked no further questions, and Dr. Rosetti was dismissed.

Now, Will could only hope that MacPherson's Fourth-of-July antics had not diverted the jury's attention from the centuries-old wrist irons that lay in the clear glass tank...nor from the innocence of the desperate man who had been forced to wear them.

65

"HAVE YOU EVER BEEN IN AN OFFICE or the lobby of a building where you take a look at one of the abstract paintings on the wall? And you study it for a minute because your brain is not processing it. What you are looking at, is just random dots within a frame. The entire picture is merely a collection of such dots. And, for at least a few moments, you cannot visualize for the life of you what you are supposed to be seeing."

Will's tone was casual, as if he were having a conversation—although a very serious one—with friends.

"But then you step away, a few feet back, and look again. And then it strikes you," he continued in his closing argument to the jury. "The farther you step away, the more the portrait begins emerging. The phenomenon is this—the farther you step away, the more clearly you can see the true picture."

Will then strolled over to the podium and clicked the control button on a projector.

The screen to the left of the judge's bench lit up, and an enlarged image of handwritten notes from the 1718 Bath, North Carolina, grand jury proceeding appeared.

The final entry read,

> *Isaac Joppa, late of Bath, North Carolina, was indicted for piracy, the same being suspected of being a willing member of the crew of Captain Edward Teach, and having committed various piratical acts of robbery among vessels on the high seas.*

"Now this," Will said, pointing to the image on the screen, "is a frame with dots in it. The grand jury in Bath, North Carolina, was too close to the events of the day to be able to see the true picture of Isaac Joppa's innocence. After all, they had the testimony of only one witness, Henry Caulfeld. Caulfeld, you will recall, was aboard the ship *Marguerite* at the time it was attacked and plundered by Teach's crew. The sole evidence upon which the grand jury indicted Isaac Joppa as a willing participant in an act of piracy was Caulfeld's observation.

"However, Henry Caulfeld's observations and testimony were ambiguous at best. What he thought were the gestures of Isaac giving orders to the pirate crew were, instead, meant to relieve the stiffness that had set in from long months of being manacled in the hold of Teach's ship with heavy irons. Further, Caulfeld observed weapons in the hands of all the men except Isaac. Thus, it is clear that Isaac was still under the control of the pirate crew and the captain, all of whom were armed and dangerous. And further yet, would it be reasonable to conclude that in just a few months, a novice, a frightened young sailor such as Isaac, would be elevated by Teach to a position of authority—indeed, to a position where he was giving orders to cutthroat pirates who had been committing murder and robbery on the high seas for years?"

Will argued to the jury that Isaac Joppa had been kidnapped by Teach merely because the pirate knew that Isaac's medical knowledge, learned while with the British Navy, though limited, might prove helpful to his syphilis-ravaged, battle-torn crew. Further, Isaac had neither the profile, nor the motivation, to pursue a life of crime.

While, admittedly, Joppa was guilty of deserting a Royal Navy ship while under the tyrannical rule of Captain Boughton, he had been faced with a dilemma—had he stayed on board, he would have to choose between joining a mutiny of the crew or supporting the savagery and brutality of the captain. Regrettably, Will submitted, Isaac chose the route most common among sailors of his day—to simply desert at the first available opportunity.

Will concluded his initial arguments by reminding the jury that the clerk in Bath, North Carolina, following the Old Bailey trial at Central Criminal Court in London, not only indicated the indictment dismissed, but also entered the words "res judicata"—which made sense *only* if Isaac Joppa had been acquitted, but could face a potential retrial in America unless it were known that the issues in his piracy trial had been "finally decided" in an English Court across the Atlantic.

Lastly, Will suggested to the jury that Isaac Joppa did not flee from the English navy during the battle of Ocracoke Inlet because he was conscious of his criminal guilt. Rather, in the melee of swords, bullets, and cannon fire, Isaac was simply running for his life.

"After all," Will argued, "Samuel O'Dell—who was also in the hold of Teach's ship at the outbreak of the battle but was more or less an innocent bystander—himself received some seventy wounds in the battle, and was mistaken for a pirate until acquitted by the court in Williamsburg.

"In other words," Will concluded, "the evidence we've presented, that I have summarized for you here, presents only one clear and unmistakable image. It is the picture of an innocent man whose life is tragically waylaid by a gang of seafaring thugs and murderers. The picture you see, I am confident, is one of Isaac Joppa's innocence. He was wrongfully accused once— let's not make that mistake twice."

As Will sat down at counsel table, Virgil MacPherson strode up confidently, placing himself squarely in front of the jury box. His manner was folksy, entertaining, and energetic.

He reminded the jury of one indisputable fact—that the witnesses for Isaac Joppa's innocence were neither disinterested nor objective. Isaac Joppa himself had been on trial for his life, he reminded the jury, and of course he would invent a story to save himself from the hangman's noose. The only other witness for Isaac of any substance was the pirate Caesar, whose comments were not transcribed but merely noted by the clerk in the Williamsburg piracy trial, and indicated that Joppa had been a prisoner of Teach's. "Yet are we to believe," MacPherson urged the jury, "the comments of a man guilty of piracy himself?

"On the other hand," he continued, "who were the witnesses against Isaac Joppa? Henry Caulfeld, an established merchant and co-owner of the vessel *Marguerite*. He saw, with his own eyes, Isaac Joppa's freedom of movement and his position of authority among the pirates. Did Joppa look like a man imprisoned by Edward Teach? Further, there is the testimony of Samuel O'Dell at the Williamsburg piracy trial. O'Dell, according to the clerk's notes, clearly testified that, in the hold of Teach's ship—shortly before the outbreak of hostilities in the Battle of Ocracoke Inlet, Isaac Joppa was there...unmanacled, with full freedom of movement. Does that sound like a man imprisoned in the hold of a pirate's ship?

"And what of the iron manacles found at the salvage site of the sunken remains of the *Bold Venture*? What of the testimony of Dr. Steve Rosetti?" MacPherson asked—and then cleverly suggested to the jury that Isaac Joppa would have been fully familiar with all aspects of Teach's ship and would have noticed the manacles in the hold on one of the barrels. Thus, when he was ultimately captured and tried, he concocted the story that the manacles had been intended for him...and that he had been the pirates' prisoner. How convenient, MacPherson sneered, that Joppa should remember there were irons aboard Teach's ship and use them in his plea for innocence. But was there, MacPherson submitted, any proof that Joppa's wrists were ever bound by those manacles? Was there any evidence ever presented to the jury in this trial that the person of Isaac Joppa was restrained by those irons?

"None whatsoever," MacPherson concluded, his arms raised to the heavens.

Reminding the jury that Isaac Joppa was convicted of deserting the British navy, he pointed to Joppa's escape *from*—rather than his escape *to*—Lieutenant Maynard and the English sailors who attacked Teach's ship. This was proof that Joppa, better than anyone else, knew he was guilty of crimes on the high seas.

"You know, in this country we build monuments to great men and women," MacPherson intoned. "We award medals to heroes. We do those things lest we forget the courage and deeds of those who are great among us. But not all deeds deserve to be remembered. Not all men deserve to be pinned with medals. There are those miserable men, cowards, and criminals who shame themselves, dishonor their families, and violate the laws of humanity. They deserve to be forgotten.

"Isaac Joppa was one of those men. Let's let the dead bury the dead. The evidence of this case tells us that Isaac Joppa should lie in a pauper's grave along with other criminals who were hanged in eighteenth-century England. He deserves to be forgotten. Don't be fooled by the legal tricks of my opponent. His case is smoke and mirrors. Isaac Joppa was a dastardly sinner—let's not be fooled into making him a saint."

MacPherson gathered his papers from the podium, and then, with his hands clasped behind his back, looked each of the six jurors in the eye, one after another, making his last, and perhaps most potent argument of all. Will had expected it. In fact, he would have been surprised had his opponent not made the argument. But still, when it came, it was a devastating blow. Will felt it. He could sense Jonathan, sitting next to him, slumping in his seat. Perhaps part of it was the recognition that this case had never been winnable, that the truth had never been quite clear enough.

"As a final word," MacPherson said, eyeing the jury and smiling. "I want to emphasize how the court is about to instruct you. Judge Gadwell will instruct you, once all the arguments have been concluded, that you are prohibited—let me say that again—you are *prohibited* from *speculating* about the evidence in this case. The court will instruct you that if the evidence is not clear enough, on the question on Isaac Joppa's innocence of the charges of piracy—as the court will define them to you—then you *must* rule in favor of my client, Terrence Ludlow, and you *must* rule against Jonathan Joppa. It's as simple as that."

As Virgil MacPherson took his seat, Will scanned the faces of each of the jury members, trying to discern whether MacPherson's argument had rung true with them. They were all, except one, blank-faced and expressionless. The sole exception was the elderly widow, who was still maintaining her unassuming smile.

Will rose slowly, and walked to the podium. And for a moment, he was swept away, wondering who he really represented. He felt an overpowering sensation that his real client was nowhere in the courtroom. Not really. His final comments in rebuttal would now have little to do with real estate entitlements, or the last will and testament of Randolph Willowby. Or even with vindicating Uncle Bull. Instead, he would address the secrets of a life long buried…and a reputation scuttled by human ignorance, malice, or even something worse.

66

WILL'S FINAL REBUTTAL ARGUMENT would be simple. Almost simplistic.

"Ladies and gentlemen, I'm not going to take much of your time now. I only have one final thought. Mr. MacPherson says that the witnesses for Isaac Joppa, namely Isaac Joppa himself and the pirate Caesar, were biased and not trustworthy. He then argues that the witnesses against Isaac Joppa, Henry Caulfeld and Samuel O'Dell, were credible and are to be believed. He discounts the physical evidence in the case, such as the indisputable presence of manacles, discovered exactly where Isaac Joppa said they were.

"But there's something else. Something has been forgotten, and I'm here to remind us. There was a small plate introduced into evidence through the testimony of Oscar 'Possum' Kooter. He irrefutably identified it as an heirloom given to Isaac Joppa by his beloved Abigail Merriwether on the occasion of their engagement. It shows, beyond question, not only that they were engaged to be married, but they had a date set in their hearts and minds at which time they were to be wed. But that date came and went. Where was Isaac Joppa when their intended date arrived? He was in the dank, stinking hold of a pirate ship, bound by irons and under the cruel tyranny of one of the most feared and hated men of the eighteenth century.

"Now I've told you that something has been forgotten. It is the testimony of Abigail Merriwether. We have it in the transcript from the Old Bailey trial. Mr. MacPherson may want you to forget about it...but I don't. So I'm going to read it to you. You'll have the opportunity to review it in your deliberations. But as you do...I'd like you to remember something very important."

With that, Will retrieved the transcript copy from his table.

"We've heard it said that there is faith, and there is hope, and there is love. But the greatest of these is love. Here is why Isaac Joppa could never have willingly joined Teach's degenerate band of murderers, rapists, and

thieves. I believe that Isaac Joppa only had one intent behind his actions...
to return to the arms of Abigail Merriwether. True enough, he had run from
the grip of his father. And then he ran from the tyrannical brutality of Captain Zebulun Boughton. Finally he found himself fleeing from the bullets
and cannon fire of the Battle of Ocracoke Inlet. But would he really ever
have wanted to pursue a life of crime—and thereby run away from the
steadfast love of Abigail Merriwether?"

Will then looked down at the Old Bailey trial transcript and began to
read.

(((

Sir Alexander Saxton, the prosecutor for the Crown, was building
momentum in his cross-examination of Abigail Merriwether.

She had been standing in the dock for nearly an hour now, in her yellow
satin dress with white ruffles. Yet, her expression was undisturbed by the
mounting antagonism of her inquisitor.

"Miss Merriwether," Mr. Saxton thundered, "you do concede, do you
not, madam, that your engagement to the accused, Isaac Joppa, was against
the express wishes of your father, Peter Merriwether...a prominent merchant and man of great respectability?"

"I do admit that, sir," Abigail said softly. "It caused me indescribable
pain to decide between the desires of my father and my love for my fiancé."

"But choose you did!" Mr. Saxton continued, "in contemptuous and fla-
grant disregard for your father."

"He did protest, I do admit that."

"And yet you expect this jury of good men, honest men, to accept your
testimony as vouching for the moral character and truthfulness of the
accused—while you, Miss Merriwether, admit that you have shamed your
father's name and brought disgrace upon his good reputation."

"I have said that it has caused me great pain."

"What I put to you, Miss Merriwether, is that Isaac Joppa's life has been
one long trail of wrongdoing. Do you not agree, Miss Merriwether, that
Isaac Joppa was wrong in leaving his family—his mother and father—in
the town of Bath, without a word? Without any notice of his intentions?
Did you not tell him, yourself, that you believed it was wrong for him to
leave in such a manner?"

"I did, sir."

"Do you not agree, Miss Merriwether, that Isaac Joppa was wrong in his actions—wrong under the law of the Crown of England, and wrong in the sight of God—to desert his post on the ship *Intrepid* while under the authority of Captain Zebulun Boughton? Do you not agree that this conduct was wrong?"

"I told my dear Isaac, during our short conversation while he lay in prison awaiting his trial, that I do believe it was wrong for him to commit desertion. Yet, what I would do if I were in his untenable position—had I been on board that ship and had to make such a difficult decision, what choice I would have made I do not know..."

"Yet you contend, madam, that your love for him, and his for you, burned unabatedly during his entire one-year absence, and that he never would have willingly joined in the piratical designs of Captain Edward Teach, because his whole and only desire was to return to you?"

"I do believe that, sir. With all my heart and soul."

"Is your love not misplaced in a fellow with such a history of wrongs?"

Abigail's eyes were beginning to tear up, and she retrieved a small white handkerchief from her sleeve and dabbed her eyes. Then she looked at Sir Alexander Saxton, the great legal lion of the English Crown, and answered his question with a voice that, though quiet, was intensely and unmistakably clear.

"Love, sir, keeps no records of wrongs."

"Perhaps love does not," Saxton said, rebuffing her, "but I can assure you, madam, that the law of England does! The proceedings of this court keep a record of wrongs. Know ye that full well! Do you not realize that, Miss Merriwether?"

"What I know," Abigail said, her head lifted ever so slightly in the confidence of her position, "is that the law cuts roughly against the man I love, and whom I would marry. The hangman's noose at Newgate that you would propose for my beloved Isaac...such a hanging would be more criminal than all the acts of piracy that ever occurred on the high seas, sir. For I swear to you, on my oath, and before the sight of God, that my beloved Isaac is innocent of these charges."

"Innocent!" Sir Alexander bellowed. "And what other evidence do you have for that preposterous pronouncement? Give forth that evidence! Come, Miss Merriwether, show us what new proof you have that the accused, this despicable man, was not guilty of piracy."

Abigail paused. Her chin was trembling, but almost imperceptibly. She turned to the jury in the boxes at both sides of the great hall, and fixed her eyes first on the one box, and then the other, scanning from right to left, back to front so that the gaze of each man met hers.

And then she spoke.

"This is my proof!" she declared with a sternness that surprised even Saxton. "I offer to you now, good gentlemen of the jury, my life. If you can be so blind as to condemn my beloved Isaac to an unjust death for his innocence and for the misery he suffered at the hands of cruel and criminal men, then I must be just as guilty. For in truth, I am just as innocent as he. If he be convicted and condemned on such faulty proof, then convict and condemn me also. And place my neck in a noose next to his. So his death could then be seen to be, in truth, as unjust as mine."

A stunned silence swept the cavernous Justice Hall. After a full measure of time, that silence was broken only by Sir Alexander Saxton nervously clearing his throat, then making his way back to the long oak table that housed his papers, slightly adjusting his carefully curled wig as he did.

67

After closing arguments were concluded, Judge Gadwell painstakingly read the instructions aloud to the jury.

Just as Virgil MacPherson had promised, the judge had selected, for the most part, MacPherson's version—including his definition of burden of proof. If the jury was going to believe the case presented by Will Chambers, then it would be an uphill struggle during the deliberations.

Now the courtroom was empty, except for Will and Jonathan Joppa. Boggs Beckford had hobbled back to his office. The judge had left the courthouse early for dinner. The clerk and the bailiff were gone. And Virgil MacPherson, Terrence Ludlow, and Blackjack Morgan had disappeared quickly—as soon as the jury had retired to the jury room.

Will glanced at his watch, then up at the large clock in the courtroom. It was twenty to five in the afternoon. The jury had been out for forty minutes.

"I suppose you've done this a lot," Jonathan said. "I mean, doing this... sitting in an empty courtroom waiting for a jury to come back with a verdict."

Will smiled, glancing over to the closed door of the jury room.

"More times than I can remember."

"What happens if they have a question for the judge?"

"Sometimes that happens. If they have a question, they'll knock on that door, the bailiff will open it, and they'll hand a note to the bailiff. Then the bailiff calls up the judge, has the judge come back here in court. And the judge talks about it along with the attorneys. And then the judge has to make a decision on what response to give."

After a few seconds of quiet, Jonathan spoke up again.

"Does it get any easier? I mean the waiting...the more cases you handle?"

"It never gets easier," Will said flatly. "This is always the hardest part... when it's beyond your control. When you've done everything you can—all the research, all the fact investigation, shaping your theory, carefully crafting your questions. Handling all the unexpected surprises during trial. But— waiting like this for the jury to give you a verdict—it's tough. There are no two ways about it. And the more you care about the case…and the client… the tougher it is."

Will threw a glance at Jonathan, who had been listening intensely.

"Let me tell you something, Jonathan, I really do care a lot about this case. And you as a client. And, in a strange way, about Isaac Joppa too."

Will glanced at his watch, and then he excused himself, just as Sally arrived with two Styrofoam cups of coffee.

He strolled out into the hallway of the deserted courthouse and called Fiona on his cell phone at Aunt Georgia's.

"How are ya, darling? Are you lying down?"

"I certainly am. Georgia is spoiling me rotten. She's waiting on me hand and foot. So…how's the case? Have you finished closing arguments?"

"Yes, and the judge instructed the jury and sent them into deliberations a little while ago."

"Well, I miss you," Fiona said tenderly. "I've been praying for you."

"I can tell."

"Really?"

"Absolutely So, how's our little one doing?"

"Oh, kicking. Moving around. Which overjoys me, of course. I'll go an hour or so, and then suddenly things will be quiet and I won't feel any movement. I'll get a little panicked. And then I'll get a little kick or roll, and I'll say 'Thank you, Lord!'"

"No bleeding?"

"No. Nothing," Fiona's voice was now growing a little quieter. "This has been a real testing period for me, for my faith. It's one thing to sing about it and put it on my CD's—but now, flat on my back, I'm getting so many life lessons. About patience. Endurance. Trusting…"

"We're getting so close to the finish line," Will said. "Pretty soon I'll get this verdict. And then I'll get back to you as quickly as possible." He heard footsteps coming down the hall, turned, and saw the bailiff rounding the corner.

"The jury's got a question," he said. "I've put a call in to the judge, and he's on his way. So's Virgil MacPherson."

"Gotta go, honey. I love you like crazy. Take care of our baby." Will snapped off his phone and hurried into the courtroom.

Will explained to Jonathan what had transpired. It would be a few minutes before Judge Gadwell and Virgil MacPherson, along with Virgil's client, would arrive. As they waited, the bailiff and the court clerk strolled in. The clerk sat at her desk just below the judge's bench, and the bailiff took his position in front of the door to the jury room.

"Were you on duty the other day when they were calling up the extra deputies to go over to Stony Island?" The clerk asked.

The bailiff shook his head.

"I wasn't on duty, and they didn't call me up—but I know a couple of guys who ended up spending the day over there making sure that people stayed off the property."

The clerk stood up and walked over to the bailiff.

"Where in the world did all that start?" she asked in a hushed tone.

"I heard they tracked it down to a comment that was made by Carlton Robideau."

"Robideau? He's the guy who does the diving, right? Gives diving instructions? And works for Blackjack Morgan's operation?"

"Yeah, that's the guy," the bailiff said in a whisper, but loud enough for Will and Jonathan Joppa to hear. "He was on a drinking binge and made a comment to some of his buddies about buried treasure on Stony Island—and the next thing you know, the rumor's flying around all over Cape Hatteras and along the Banks."

"Anybody ask him why he thought the treasure was there?" the clerk asked in hoarse whisper.

"No. Problem is…nobody can seem to find him. He's probably somewhere sleeping off his drunk. He'll show up in a day or so, I suppose. Then they'll question him."

Jonathan turned to Will.

"What is going on here? I heard about all the treasure hunters showing up on Stony Island all of a sudden and tramping all over the property. But I figured it was just another of those rumors. But that…" Jonathan said, nodding toward the bailiff, who had now resumed his position, "that makes it sound like this may be connected to Morgan. What do you make of all of this?"

Will shrugged. But before he could respond, Virgil MacPherson, with Terrence Ludlow in tow, came breezing in, briefcase in hand.

"Jury's got a question?" MacPherson asked. "Anybody know what the question is?"

"No...I'm sure we're not gonna hear until the judge gets here," Will responded.

MacPherson sat down at the table with Ludlow. They whispered something back and forth, and then MacPherson laughed loudly, with Ludlow snickering too. Will turned. Blackjack Morgan was, as usual, sitting alone in the back. A few minutes later, the bailiff called out, "All rise," and Judge Gadwell entered from his chambers.

He had a small piece of paper in his hand.

"Gentlemen, the jury has a question for the court. The message was received by the bailiff at four-forty-eight P.M. I see that both counsel and their clients are present. So I will proceed to read the note to counsel and get comments before I respond to their question."

The judge began reading. "'Your Honor. The jury would like to know the following: If we find that Isaac Joppa was guilty of piracy, then is our job done? Or are there other issues that would have to be decided?'"

Jonathan could immediately see the disappointment in Will's expression.

This was bad news. The mere framing of the question showed that they entertained the possibility of a quick finding that Isaac had committed acts of piracy—and thus wanted to make sure that the scope of their duties was limited only to that narrow issue. Unless there was an additional note or comment clarifying or modifying the impact of the first question, Will's case might be lost.

"'On the other hand...'" the judge continued with the jury's message, "'if we find that Isaac Joppa was innocent, then are there further issues that we should decide?'"

Will leaned back and breathed a sigh of relief.

"There it is, Counsel. There are the questions. How should we proceed?"

Will Chambers started first. He indicated that, obviously, the jury needed to be reinstructed that the only issue to be decided was the fact question inserted in the written verdict—namely, whether Isaac Joppa, on or about December 5, 1717, was guilty of participating in acts of piracy against the sloop *Marguerite*. However, Will did indicate, that the jury may have been misled by Virgil MacPherson's improper arguments implying that a great deal was riding on their verdict...creating, perhaps, an impression that there were other issues for them to decide.

MacPherson lashed out at Will, suggesting somewhat obscurely, that Will was in contempt of court for continuing to argue a point that the court had already ruled on—namely, refusing to strike his, MacPherson's, opening statement, which had addressed the fact that Chambers and his client had a whole lot to gain by trying to persuade them to vote in their favor.

Will rose, but the judge waved him back into his seat and indicated he had decided what he would tell the jury. "I think this is an easy matter," he said. "I'm simply going to reinstruct the jury in the section of the instructions that indicate that their sole and solitary finding of fact concerns Isaac Joppa's innocence or lack of innocence regarding the piracy charges...and absolutely nothing else. That's their only function here. When they've decided that issue, they're done with their work."

The judge instructed the bailiff to bring the jury in, and the six members entered. Both Will and MacPherson studied their faces, hoping to gather some glimpse, some window into their deliberations or their current leanings but they were unable to do so. All were stone-faced and sober, except for the elderly widow, who again was smiling, apparently unaware of the tension in the courtroom about the case.

Judge Gadwell instructed them just as he had indicated and sent them back into the jury room.

MacPherson and Ludlow hung around the back, talking with Blackjack Morgan and laughing heartily. Then, they left the courtroom.

Will and Jonathan decided to have dinner at a café across from the courthouse.

As they walked across the street, Jonathan asked Will to size up what had happened with the jury deliberations.

"The question," Will surmised, "shows they were a little bit confused about the judge's instructions on the questions they were to decide. I don't think it's a good sign or a bad one. But it does show that this is a jury that is spending a lot of time trying to sort through what their job is. And that's interesting. It looks like they're going to continue working through dinner. My guess is that they're going to try to arrive at a verdict tonight, before it gets too late."

Will opened the door for his client and followed him into the café, thinking about the decision for the jury. He did feel it was interesting that they seemed to be taking this case every bit as seriously as the Old Bailey jury might have in 1719.

Of course, Will was well aware there was one monumental difference. If the jury in the courthouse, now deliberating together, found that Isaac had been guilty of piracy, no one was going to be sentenced to hang by the neck until dead. The outcome of this case was, fortunately, not going to involve any matters of life and death. Will felt confident of that.

68

Will had informed the bailiff that he and Jonathan Joppa would be having dinner across the street from the courthouse. If the jury arrived at a verdict, he knew he would be contacted immediately.

Over dinner, the two men talked about a variety of things—but none of them having to do with the lawsuit. Jonathan asked about Will's law practice, and his marriage. He wondered how Will and Fiona had met. He seemed enthralled by the story of the lawsuit in which Will had represented Fiona's father, the lawsuit that had brought Will and Fiona together.

In turn, Will inquired about Jonathan. About his work as pastor of Safe Harbor Community Church. Jonathan addressed his relationship with the church very generally, but a few of his comments made Will think that things were not going smoothly.

Jonathan also mentioned a change in his approach to several things... not the least of which was the series of sermons he was now giving on the book of Jonah.

"What kind of a change are you talking about?" Will asked.

"Oh, a little bit more emphasis on the biblical text, and a little less... cultural entertainment, I guess."

"What kind of reaction are you getting from your congregation?"

Jonathan stopped eating, then looked at Will with an expression that was revealing much. But he was choosing to say little.

"I think that still remains to be seen."

"And how is your son doing...he's in rehab, right?"

"Yes, he is. I appreciate your asking. Maybe I'm just being overoptimistic, but this time I sense a difference. He's really putting an effort in. He and I are starting to connect. Maybe this time he'll really be able to turn things around."

"That's great. That's really terrific."

There was something on Jonathan's mind—Will could see it. Finally, he opened up.

"If you don't mind me asking," he said cautiously. "I remember your Aunt Georgia saying that your first wife died."

Will nodded.

Jonathan paused and then continued.

"My wife, Carol, died from a congenital heart condition. Bobby was two then. I did the best I could to raise him myself. But I think I was carrying a lot of baggage as a result of what happened. For a long time I've been trying to carry this by myself. Doing the best I can with Bobby. Plugging away at the church. But not exactly living an abundant life. More like mere survival. But lately...well...I've tried to get back to a kind of starting point with God..."

Will was silent, listening intently. Jonathan kept talking.

"And then, as far as myself...for the future...well, let's just put it this way—spiritually speaking, because I know that life really can swallow up death, I've decided I need to go back to living that kind of life."

Something caught Will's eye, and he turned and noticed the bailiff, who strode over to their table.

"Gentlemen," he said with an air of formality, "the jury has reached a verdict. You need to come back to the courtroom."

He disappeared. Will and Jonathan paid their tab and hurried across the street to the courthouse.

"What do you think, Counselor?" Jonathan asked expectantly. Will glanced at his watch.

"Well, as far as jury deliberations, that wasn't short...but it wasn't long either. What I'm concerned about is who the jury foreman is."

"What do you mean?" Jonathan asked as they approached the front doors.

"First thing the jury does in that room is elect a foreman. Usually it's whoever wants to volunteer first. I had some feelings about juror number one—the head of the construction company. If he's the foreman, I'm not sure that bodes well for us."

Before Will and Jonathan entered the courtroom, Will checked the batteries in his cell phone to make sure Fiona could reach him. As he and Jonathan breezed in, they were surprised by a large figure standing in the audience section.

Melvin Hooper gave them both a broad smile and a firm handshake.

"Melvin," Jonathan said with pleasure, "what are you doing here?"

"Oh, the bailiff is a buddy of mine. I asked him to do me a favor and give me a call when the jury reached a verdict so I could get over here to the courthouse. You know, give you some moral support in return for your helping me out that day...I guess I just wasn't thinking straight..."

Jonathan talked with Melvin, as Will made his way to the counsel table.

Five minutes later, Virgil MacPherson entered the courtroom, followed closely by Terrence Ludlow, hands thrust in jeans, wearing a bored sneer. As usual, Blackjack Morgan slipped in and positioned himself at the back.

Will waved Jonathan up to the table as Boggs Beckford made his way forward awkwardly. With the aid of Jonathan, he seated himself.

The court personnel appeared and, less than a minute later, the door to the judge's chambers opened, and Judge Gadwell strode in, clad in his black judicial robe.

"All rise!" The clerk called out, and the courtroom rose to its feet.

Judge Gadwell seated himself.

"Be seated."

The clerk called out the name of the case and the case number.

"The court has been informed," Judge Gadwell began, "that the jury has reached a verdict. Bailiff, please call in the jury."

The bailiff nodded, opened the door, and motioned the jury to enter.

Juror number one, the owner of the construction company, entered first with a stern look on his face. He did not look at Jonathan Joppa or Will Chambers. Instead, his gaze went to Virgil MacPherson and his client.

Each of the jurors, in turn, entered and took their seats in the jury box. Juror number three, the unemployed janitor, seemed to have a quizzical look on his face. The elderly widow, who followed him into the courtroom, was smiling as always. She gave a quick glance to Joppa and Chambers, and then turned to look at the judge.

The checkout girl, juror number five, was still chewing gum. The last juror, the plumber's assistant, looked only slightly less bored than he had at the beginning of the trial.

"Ladies and gentlemen of the jury," Judge Gadwell said, "I've been informed that you have reached a verdict. I would ask that your foreperson please stand and give the verdict form to the bailiff for delivery to the court."

For one long, silent instant, no one stood up from the jury.

Then the elderly widow, still smiling, rose to her feet. She unfolded a single piece of paper, handed it to the bailiff, and resumed her seat.

The bailiff worked some of the creases out and handed it to the judge.

Judge Gadwell studied it. Then, for some reason, he squinted, holding it closer to his face.

After another long pause, the judge placed the paper in front of him and turned to the jury.

"Mrs. Foreperson, is this the verdict of the jury?"

The widow stood, nodded, and answered simply, "Yes, Your Honor, it is." Then she sat down.

"The court has received the verdict of the jury. I will now read it. The sole and single question put to the jury was whether Isaac Joppa, on or about December of 1717, was innocent regarding acts of piracy committed against the sloop *Marguerite*. That was the *only* question that was put to the jury for their deliberation and verdict."

The judge picked the piece of paper up and held it in front of him.

"As to that question—whether Isaac Joppa was innocent of piracy charges—the jury has answered that question."

In the momentary pause before Judge Gadwell announced the verdict, only one sound could be heard in the hushed courtroom. It was a tapping from the back of the courtroom, where Blackjack Morgan was knocking his cane nervously against the bench in front of him.

Judge Gadwell threw a quick glance toward him, and the tapping stopped.

"The jury answered this question—whether Isaac Joppa was innocent of piracy charges—by inserting the word *yes.*"

In the back of the courtroom, Morgan slammed his cane down onto the floor with a bang.

Jonathan Joppa's face lit up, and he shook Will's hand vigorously.

"But there is something else...something further written on this verdict form," the judge continued.

Suddenly, Will, who was accepting the congratulations of his client, was concerned.

"There is something here that does bother the court..."

Will heard a noise in the back. He turned and saw a news reporter sitting down a few rows behind them.

"I'm going to read the other comment that was added to this verdict."

The judge held the piece of paper closer and began reading.

"We, the members of the jury, would like to ask the court if it is possible to publicize this verdict regarding the innocence of Isaac Joppa to our public library and all public buildings where notices are posted. And perhaps the court could order that a copy of this verdict be sent to the public schools in this district—for inclusion in the curriculum dealing with local North Carolina history of the eighteenth century."

The high school teacher, who had sat expressionless during the entire trial, began smiling when Judge Gadwell read the last comment.

"And underneath that final message," he continued, "are the signatures of each of the six jurors."

The judge considered something, his forehead wrinkling and then spoke again.

"So it is clear to this court that the verdict here was unanimous."

Virgil MacPherson jumped to his feet.

"Your Honor, I want the jury to be polled immediately! I want each of the jurors to be asked individually whether or not this really was their verdict."

Judge Gadwell gave an exasperated look to MacPherson and said, "You really want to do that, Virgil? Didn't you hear me? I just said that every one of the jurors had personally signed the bottom of this verdict form."

MacPherson gave a halfhearted smile and then withdrew his request.

The judge thanked the jury for their service and then dismissed them. When the last juror was gone, MacPherson jumped to his feet again.

"Your Honor, I move for a mistrial—that last comment added on the verdict shows in itself that this was a perverse jury result. They were obviously swayed by prejudice, bias, ill-will, malice, or undue sympathy—"

"Motion denied," Judge Gadwell said with a sigh.

"Your Honor, I want a time and date set for motions after verdict so I can ask that this court overrule this perverse verdict." MacPherson said, pressing on. "I feel there was an entire lack of evidence supporting Isaac Joppa's innocence. Mr. Chambers failed utterly in presenting a case from which any reasonable jury could credibly have concluded that Isaac Joppa was innocent."

"Virgil, you can file any motions you want, but this court has a busy docket. Why don't you argue your motion right now? While the case is still fresh in your mind…"

"Well, Your Honor, you heard my arguments in closing. You heard my arguments during the trial. The evidence was overwhelmingly in favor of a finding of guilt against Isaac Joppa. And with all due respect, I believe that the court made an evidentiary error in permitting Dr. Rosetti to display that manacle in full view of the jury while he was testifying."

"Yes, and the court considered all that, Virgil. And you made some really good points. You made a truly fine argument to the jury. And I have to say that I just might have, if I had been sitting on that jury, voted a different way than they did. But that's not the point here, is it? The point is, could a reasonable jury have arrived at this verdict based on the evidence presented? I believe a reasonable jury could have decided the way they did, even if I may have personal opinions otherwise."

MacPherson was going to argue the point, but Judge Gadwell cut him off as he glanced at his watch.

"Virgil, you can make your case to the court of appeals if you want, but your motion for judgment notwithstanding the verdict is denied. Your motion for a new trial is denied. The extra comments of the jury—those about publicizing Isaac Joppa's innocence—well, I'll let them stand, for what they are worth. So I think that's it. We're closing up shop here. Court adjourned."

As Jonathan and Boggs Beckford exchanged congratulations, Will was suddenly aware of his cell phone vibrating in his pocket.

He snatched it out and put it to his ear. He could recognize Aunt Georgia's voice at the other end but was having a hard time hearing her through the noise and jubilation in the courtroom. He excused himself and walked quickly out to the hallway.

"I'm sorry, Aunt Georgia, I couldn't hear you…say that again?"

"Willy boy, it's about Fiona. There's a problem…"

"What kind of a problem?" Will asked anxiously.

"I'm afraid all of a sudden…she started gushing blood. We called 9-1-1. They're over here right now. Carrying her out. You'll have to meet us at the hospital immediately."

Will strained to hear what was going on in the background. He heard other voices…male voices, and Fiona's as well.

"Is she all right?"

"Fiona's a trooper," Georgia replied. "We just have to pray that she's going to be fine."

"How's the baby? Are they checking on the baby? Is anybody using a monitor to make sure the baby is okay?"

"We're doing everything we can here," she replied, trying to calm him down. "But you must get to the hospital as soon as you can. We'll meet you there."

Jonathan came out of the courtroom and saw the anxiousness on Will's face immediately.

"What happened?" he asked.

"My wife…Fiona…she's being rushed to the hospital. It's the baby… there are some serious problems."

"What can I do to help?"

"Just…just pray for us…"

Then Will turned and sprinted to his car and gunned it out onto the road toward the hospital. Darting in and out of traffic and passing every other vehicle on the road, unknowingly he was gripping the steering wheel so tight that his knuckles were white.

"Please…please…" he muttered out loud as he wheeled his car into the hospital parking lot.

69

THE OBSTETRICS NURSE MET WILL as he was heading down the hospital hallway at a dead run.

"How is she?" he blurted out.

"Stable now—Dr. Yager will have to fill you in on the rest."

She led him up to the scrub room next to the delivery room and gave him a seat in the hallway. He was told that Dr. Yager was scrubbing and gowning and would be with him immediately.

Less than a minute later, the door swung open. Dr. Yager came directly over. Will reached out his hand, but Yager stopped him, reminding him she had already scrubbed.

"I'm not going to beat around the bush. Fiona has lost a lot of blood... We had to stabilize her before we could do anything...A baby is always in jeopardy during that crucial time..."

"What...what..." Will began.

"Where we are is this," she continued. "We slowed the blood loss—but you know, Will, she really was losing a lot of blood...experienced LOC... lost consciousness, but only momentarily. I don't think that was a problem for the baby, but we have to get ready for an emergency transfusion. We've had the baby under constant monitoring, and I'm not too concerned about the baby's status. So we are going in now. This is going to be a caesarean... you'll recall that the amnio showed good lung development, so I think baby is going to be okay if we can do this immediately. So, any questions?"

"I want to be in there—with her during the procedure..."

"You lawyers, always so demanding," Dr. Yager said with a smile. But then her face took on a serious expression. "Will, I think you had better stay in the waiting room. I'm sorry."

"I've got to see my wife..." he said forcefully.

"Go ahead," Dr. Yager said warmly, "there she is."

Will turned and saw two nurses quickly rolling a surgical bed through the hall. Fiona was lying on it.

She had a blue surgical cap on her head, and underneath the sheet that had been tightly tucked around the circumference of her belly. As he ran up he noticed immediately that her face was pale, her lips were colorless and dry.

She was in mid-prayer.

"'For this child I prayed, and the Lord has granted my petition which I asked of Him'…" She noticed her husband by her side.

"Oh, Will, I feel weak…so glad you're here…please, God, help my baby…my baby…oh, please…'for this child I prayed and the Lord has granted me my petition which I…'"

And as Will strode alongside his wife all he could say was, "I love you… I love you…"

And then her voice faded as she was pushed into the delivery room and the swinging doors closed. A staff nurse walked Will down the hallway, around the corner, and into the waiting room.

There was an older couple sitting in the corner. They smiled politely. After a few minutes, they left, and Will was alone.

He sat down on a couch. He glanced at the big wall clock. Then looked at his wrist watch. Then back at the clock on the wall again.

His cell phone rang. It was Aunt Georgia. She said she was wrapping up at the house and would be coming over immediately.

Will hung up and called Angus MacCameron, Fiona's ailing father, who was now living in a residential care center. Delicately avoiding any mention of the danger, he simply shared the good news that Fiona was now delivering their baby…a little earlier than they had planned…but welcome nevertheless. He promised to call the minute he had the particulars.

"And did you ever decide on a boy's name…if that is what the Lord blesses you with?" the old Scottish pastor asked in a voice weakened by age and ill health.

"I think it's going to be Andrew," Will said. "We were thinking about that…"

There was a pause on the other end. Angus MacCameron could sense the strain in Will's voice.

"You know, Will, that the Good Shepherd knows His sheep and always looks after them," MacCameron said. "And that also includes the wee little lambs, too."

Will choked back the rush of emotions. There was little he could say to his spiritual mentor and father-in-law at that point. So Angus Mac-Cameron ended the conversation himself by offering up a short prayer.

After one hour and fifteen minutes, Will's waiting ended.

Then Dr. Yager came in with a gentle look on her face. Her mask was still hanging around her neck.

There was blood on her gown.

"When we cut in..." she began, "well, there was more blood lost during the operation...than we would have anticipated."

Time stopped.

Everything in Will—his powerful analytic ability, his ability to intellectually solve any problem, to understand and process any set of facts—all of it had ceased. None of it mattered now.

There was only the longing for his wife and for their child. The ache to know that he would be able to hold them both. He needed to know that—that they were all right.

Please tell me, right now...that they are both fine, Will was saying somewhere in his head.

"So, let me just say," Dr. Yager concluded, "that while we did have to do a transfusion, everything else was uneventful. And both mother and baby are doing fine."

Then she added, "Congratulations, Mr. Chambers—you have a son."

In a few minutes Will was allowed to see his wife, who was even paler than before. She smiled up at him. He gave her a long kiss, bending down and surrounding her with his arms.

A few minutes later a tiny wrapped-up baby was brought into the room...with closed eyes, wrinkled skin, and small little fingers aimlessly and awkwardly reaching for something near his face, but not quite able to find it.

Will held his son, and caressed the lamb-soft skin of his forehead, and blessed him with kisses.

Just then, Jonathan Joppa found Will in the hallway outside of Fiona's room. He grabbed Will's hand and warmly patted his shoulder.

Will Chambers, master trial lawyer and communicator extraordinaire, then expressed the age-old exultation of new fatherhood in the simplicity of the ages.

"It's a boy!"

He yelled it so loudly that a few dismayed nurses poked their heads out from the rooms that lined the long hospital hallway.

70

THE DAY AFTER VISITING WILL AND FIONA and their baby at the hospital, Jonathan Joppa sat at his desk in the pastor's study at Safe Harbor Community Church. On the right side of the desk were his notes for that Sunday's sermon, which would be delivered in just a few minutes. He looked out the window and saw the trees and bushes swaying, and the rain pelting down from the dark gray sky. The nor'easter that had buffeted the Outer Banks for a week, and then subsided, had returned again.

He had asked the organist to play "What a Friend We Have in Jesus" during the collection, while he remained in the study until the last minute. One of the deacons methodically reviewed the bulletin of the week's upcoming activities for the congregation.

Jonathan glanced over at the left side of the desk. There was a report from the soil engineer who had finished his testing on Stony Island for potential construction of septic systems and residential condominium units.

He turned his eyes back to his sermon notes, then back to the engineering report.

There was a strange correlation between the two. He could see that now.

He gathered up his notes and his Bible and entered the sanctuary.

Today, he announced, he would continue the series he had been preaching on the Old Testament book of Jonah.

As he flipped his Bible open, he gazed out at the congregation.

It was a jammed service, something unusual in the waning weeks of summer. Usually he would not get a "full house" until they were well into fall.

Then he looked at the third row from the front. Minnie and Wes Metalsmith were there. And next to them there were several of their sympathizers, as well as the full membership of the church board.

He realized why attendance was up.

There was to be a regularly scheduled meeting of the board immediately after the morning service. But any action taken against the pastor, according to the church bylaws, required a quorum of the members. Minnie and her cohorts had obviously been busy recruiting a sufficient number of like-minded members to show up.

They had come to pick a fight. And they were undoubtedly keeping their powder dry and their bayonets sharp.

For an imperceptible instant, Jonathan wavered. Did he really have to preach this message today? How about improvising—didn't the church body really need a healing message about reconciliation instead?

But just as quickly he dismissed that idea. To the point of shaking his head back and forth in the pulpit, amazed at his own willingness to indulge the whims of others.

So he began.

"Jonah, chapter 1, verse 3. If you have your Bibles today, go ahead and look it up. If you don't, then between now and the service tonight, maybe you should go up into the attic and pull out the family Bible...or look for that one that Aunt Tilly gave you years ago...or stop by the bookstore and buy one. Because as long as I am the pastor here—and from now on—God is going to do the talking. From His Word. I'm just here as the mailman. My job is to hand you the letter. To put His message into your hands. The mailman never writes the letters he gives you—he just makes sure they get to you—safe and sound—through wind, snow, and sleet."

Then, Bible in his hand, Joppa stepped away from the pulpit.

"And the letter we find in the mailbox today is Jonah chapter 1, verse 3."

The congregation, hands in their laps, just stared.

Jonathan read verse three.

"But Jonah ran away from the Lord..."

Then Jonathan said it again.

He repeated the verse a third time.

He reminded the blank, unmoved faces in the sanctuary how God had commanded Jonah to preach to the great, dreaded, pagan metropolis of Nineveh.

But Jonah would not.

So he ran away instead. To a port city. He paid the fare and boarded a sailing vessel, thinking to escape from the burden of God's command.

But God was there in the port city. Watching. And waiting.

Then Jonah buried himself in the hold of the ship as it slowly left the harbor waters; as wives and loved ones waved goodbye to the captain and his crew. As the vessel departed the safety of the shoreline, bound for far-away ports.

But God was there, Joppa told them, down in the hold of the ship. Watching. And waiting.

And a mighty, frightening wind rose up. So powerful that it rolled the ship, and rocked it violently, and crashed cold, raging waves as tall as buildings down over its deck, and shook the mainsail like a branch on a tree. And the sailors—tough, mean, and courageous though they were, were dumbstruck with fear.

But God was there, amid the storm, and the waves, and the wind.

And Joppa explained, his voice ringing like a bell, how Jonah confessed his sin to the crew—that his disobedience was the cause of the storm—and pleaded with them to throw him into the ocean.

And when all other measures had failed and the ship was about to sink, they tossed Jonah into the roiling, rolling chaos of the sea.

And the storm was stilled.

But Jonah went down, deep down. Sinking into the dark of the ocean depths, seaweed wrapping around him like a green funeral garment.

Joppa lowered his voice to soothe, like the lullaby of a mother.

"And God was in the midst of the sea with Jonah. Yes, He was there too. And He appointed a mammoth fish to swallow Jonah up. To save him. To protect him. And from inside the confines of that huge fish, its belly stinking with half-digested fish and ocean water, Jonah sang out a prayer, a song of praise. And he sang it to God."

Then Joppa closed his Bible. He walked away from the pulpit into the full view of the congregation.

"This verse, and this message from God's Word, has at least two things to tell us today. All of us. Both me and you. And if you miss this, you may miss your eternal destiny. It's that important."

There was a hush.

"First. There is no running from God. People try to run for a variety of reasons. Out of pain, perhaps, or guilt. Or fear. So we run. What do we use as the means to try to escape God's voice? Drugs. Relationships. Careers. Money. Sex. Recreation. Possessions. Maybe even a position of authority, pridefully pursued, in the church itself. Anything to try to drown out the quiet little voice—the polite knock on the door—the reminder that we have necessary business to take up with the great God of the universe. So we run. But never successfully. Always, and ultimately, destructively. But He is still there. Always there. Saying, through His Son, 'Come to me, all of you who are heavy-laden. And I will give you rest.'"

Jonathan paused. He heard no movement within the sanctuary.

"And here's the second thing," he continued. "There are runners from God right here in this place today. I was one of them. And so are some of you. Maybe most of you. Perhaps every one of you. Is it going to take some huge tragic event that swallows you up and spits you out onto dry land before you stop running—and begin walking back to the Lord?"

Jonathan knew what he had to do.

"Everyone close their eyes."

A few members of the congregation looked at each other suspiciously but then complied.

"With head bowed, I want to ask you a question. If there is a runner from God who wants to stop running, who wants to come to the Good Shepherd of their soul for forgiveness, and restoration, and salvation—if there is someone out there like that, then tell God. Tell Him by raising your hand."

A pause. An uncomfortable silence. There were no hands raised in the auditorium. Just members of the Safe Harbor Community Church squirming in their pews—whose only prayer now was that this embarrassing situation would end, and end quickly.

Jonathan surveyed the sea of bowed heads. Unmoving and unyielding.

There was a momentary flush of despair, of utter failure, that coursed through him. But he was not going to give into it. He had spoken the message, come what may.

And having done that, he reassured himself that it was enough.

He gave a somewhat clumsy benediction and closed the service.

The occupants of the third row quickly emptied the pew and, to a person, moved quickly up to the front of the church, where Reverend Jonathan Joppa was still standing.

Almost all of the other members of the congregation remained in the sanctuary, milling about.

"Reverend Joppa," Minnie Metalsmith declared, "it really is too bad it had to come to this. But it's not as if you weren't warned. Wes, give him the notice."

Her husband mumbled something, produced a single sheet of paper, and handed it to Joppa.

"Tell him what's in the notice, Wes," Minnie said sharply.

But before Wes Metalsmith could speak, Jonathan took the paper and began reading it.

"Don't bother, Wes," he said. "I have a pretty good idea what this is about."

He read the formal notification from the church board advising him that, in their regular meeting to be conducted momentarily, they would be seeking a vote of the congregation to remove him as pastor of Safe Harbor Community Church.

The charges were nebulous. *Causing disharmony in the church. Failing to meet the needs of the congregation. Neglect of duties.*

"You have a right to be heard," one of the board members said.

"Sure I do. But I won't be staying for this meeting. My life here…my ministry among you, that is my defense. If that doesn't satisfy you, I'm not sure any speech I could make would."

With that, Jonathan Joppa excused himself and walked through the muttering congregants.

He would make his way to the pastor's study and then to an adjoining room, where Hank was sleeping in his dog bed.

Then he and Hank would take a long walk together and try to sort things out.

71

AT LONG LAST WILL GOT A CALL from Glen Watson at the repair shop, indicating that his beloved Corvette was repaired. It was late Monday afternoon, and Will had just finished spending a day visiting with Fiona at the hospital, proudly holding their beautiful baby boy. Fiona was scheduled to be discharged the next day.

Will dropped off his rental car and called for a cab to take him to Glen Watson's shop.

The nor'easter that had blown in on Sunday was slowly beginning to wane. There were only mild gusts and fine mist. The driving rain and howling winds had gone.

As the taxi driver smiled and took Will's fare, she remarked, "Weatherman says it's finally going to start drying up. We're finally going to get some clear weather."

Will smiled. As he stepped out of the taxi, in one corner of the drab sky a ray of sunshine was breaking through.

He spotted his Corvette in a corner of the lot. It looked like Glen had washed and polished it after finishing the repairs.

Will strode into the office to settle up the bill. Glen Watson was sitting behind his cluttered metal desk.

"Sorry it took a little longer than I expected," he said, "But I consider your car a work of art...I wanted to make sure I did it right."

"I appreciate that," Will replied, "and thanks for babying my baby. And speaking of babies...my wife just had a baby boy! His name is Andrew."

Glen rose to congratulate him and shook his hand vigorously.

Then Watson glanced around the office as if he had a secret to share.

"Yeah, and congratulations on winning Reverend Joppa's case. I heard about that. Read it in the newspaper."

"Thanks." Will eyed Watson. The auto mechanic obviously had something on his mind. Some thought he was struggling with.

"I heard that Blackjack Morgan was in the courtroom every day of the trial," Watson was carefully studying Will's reaction.

"That's right. We found out he had an interest—a legal interest in the outcome."

"An interest in Stony Island?"

"That's right. Why do you ask?"

Glen Watson grabbed a grease rag and wiped his fingers, then reached into his right-hand pocket and pulled out a small, crumpled piece of paper.

He opened it up. Then he looked Will in the eye.

"I always had a feeling about Morgan—you know, after Boggs Beckford had that car accident. I looked at the steering components of his car. And to me, it looked like it had been tampered with. I mean, a pinch bolt in the rack and pinion just doesn't fall out like that. Somebody loosened it. And then Morgan kept coming, asking me about what I found. And what I told the sheriff's department. And that kind of stuff."

There was a pause. Will gave Watson a questioning look.

"The point is," he continued, "Morgan brought his truck in to me...he comes here regularly to get it serviced. And there was a little fender bender in my parking lot. I had to climb into the truck and drive it into one of the bays. So I look down on the seat. And there is this black velvet bag. Kind of strange-looking. I suppose I should have minded my own business...but knowing Morgan the way I do, I get curious. So I look inside. There is this piece of shell. And I'm thinking...why in the world would Morgan be keeping this piece of seashell next to him in his truck? So I flip it over and there's some writing on it. It looks like...like ink. Something that penetrates deep into a shell. It's a little faded but I can still see it. So I write down what I see. And here it is."

Watson presented a small scrap of paper to Will.

He stared at the markings Watson had made—

Ψⴼ   ET   Oct?   Nov? 11th 1717.

"I thought this might be important," Watson said, "especially when I heard the rumors flying around town. You know...Carlton Robideau... one of Blackjack Morgan's divers...spreading rumors around town that they had discovered some kind of treasure on Stony Island. I thought you were the right person to tell. I wasn't too sure about what month was written on that shell, though..."

"Can I keep this?" Will asked, pointing to the note.

Watson nodded and walked him out to his Corvette.

Will waved goodbye, drove a few blocks away, and then pulled onto a side street that led down to the ocean. He parked near a pier, where he could hear the searching, roaring tide.

Will stared at the inscription jotted down by Watson.

At first it made absolutely no sense.

He took the paper, took his shoes and socks off, and headed across the sand dunes to the beach.

The storms had driven most of the tourists away from the beach. There were only a few walkers and children digging for shells. Will walked along the firm, wet sand, staring at the inscription on the piece of paper—for a good half hour as it slowly grew dark. As he headed back to his car, he wondered, *What do these hieroglyphics mean? Anything? Nothing? No, they must mean something.*

E–T. That could stand for Edward Teach. But then, does it refer to something else?

But then there was the date of 1717, with the month of October or November before it. It would be no mere coincidence if the initials of Edward Teach were also inscribed on a seashell. The date corresponded with the zenith of Teach's power and exploits.

So what about the strange inscription that looked like a Y interposed over an I, with an upside down U next to it?

Then Will had a thought. He looked up Dr. Rosetti's number on his cell phone and rang it, but just got his voice mail. He decided to just leave a quick message that he needed some historical information about a date in 1718.

He snapped his phone shut and looked out over the rolling blue-gray ocean, in the last remnant of daylight, and thought of all the sea stories he had ever read. Powerful tales generated by the power of the ocean. Melville's *Moby Dick.* Stevenson's *Kidnapped.* Dana's *Two Years Before the Mast.*

And of course there was the Bible's account of Jonah, who had tried to flee from God and was swallowed by a great creature of the sea, then spit out onto dry land three days later.

Will glanced again at the scrap in his hands. The ocean breeze was stiff now, and the little piece of paper began flapping. The last ray of light was breaking here and there in the gray clouds. A picture was forming.

Will stopped dead in his tracks, his feet buried in the cold sand. Icy water washed over his feet.

He stared. Was it really a Y over an I? Was it really an upside down U?

Or was it something else? *Death is swallowed up in victory.* He remembered the Bible verse. The one he'd spoken to Jonathan Joppa in the hospital.

And then the mass of dots—disconnected, oblique—began to form into a picture in his mind. Something he had seen. He had been there.

Suddenly Will was beginning to grasp the meaning behind these strange symbols.

And with that realization, he felt something...something ominous. A penetrating cold raised the hair on the back of his neck and swept down his spine.

72

WILL CHAMBERS' VOICE REFLECTED stunned disbelief. So Jonathan Joppa, at the other end of the telephone line, repeated what he had just said.

"After yesterday's service, the board of overseers at Safe Harbor fired me as pastor."

"I'm so sorry…"

"I appreciate that, Will. I'm…trying to put things together in my own mind. Trying to decide where God is leading me in all of this. I've done some thinking. Maybe it's for the better. Although I also had some other bad news."

"What was that?"

"I received the soil engineering report on Stony Island. The soil tests and percolation tests indicate that the island probably cannot support any kind of major construction project, in terms of residential or condominium units. According to current zoning, we could continue using the big lodge, the existing outhouse, and the other outbuildings. But the idea of converting it into a development of condos doesn't look possible."

"Well, in light of all that," Will said, "maybe I've got some good news for you. Or maybe not. Maybe some strange news. It's hard to explain…"

"What is it?"

Will glanced out the window of his Corvette. The sky was still gray, but the wind was blowing only mildly, and there was very little rain coming down.

"Look, Jonathan," he continued. "How would you like to go for a boat ride?"

"Now?"

"I know it's getting dark. But the storm looks like it's waning. And this really is urgent. I may be totally off base on this. On the other hand…let me just explain it to you when we meet. Can you get down to the marina where we launched from last time?"

"Sure. Do you want me to call ahead and have them get a launch ready?"

"Yes, and if you can grab some rain slickers that might be good. It's still drizzling. I just want to take a quick trip to Stony Island and then come right back. Then I can still get over to the hospital to visit Fiona and Andrew."

"Will, I trust your judgment on this…If you think this is important…"

"I'm afraid it is. And if I'm right…well, we may have to get an immediate court order. A security detail…Just hurry—I'll meet you at the marina."

Will hung up and pulled over to the shoulder. He called up Dr. August Longfellow's home number and rang it immediately.

After ten rings, Longfellow picked up.

"Dr. Longfellow," Will began, "I have an urgent and rather unusual request for you."

"Sure. Anything." Longfellow said cheerfully. Then he added, a little sheepishly, "Listen, I never got a chance to apologize to you. I think I should have been a bit more candid about my driving suspension. You know, the way it came up in court during the trial—"

"Forget about it," Will said quickly. "We won. You were great. But here's the deal…I need you to check on some historical facts for me…like right now."

"Sure," Longfellow said, intrigued by the urgency in Will's voice. "I'll just turn the stove down under my jambalaya. What do you need?"

"You know the book you've been working on, dealing with regional North Carolina history, particularly along the Outer Banks?"

"Yeah. It keeps dragging on and on. My publisher is complaining because I keep asking for extensions. Maybe it's just me…we scholars have a notorious habit of getting bogged down in minutiae, and getting topheavy with the research…but then we don't get around—"

"Dr. Longfellow," Will interrupted, "do you have any data…any historical research about the original owners of Stony Island? All I recall is that Malachi Joppa bought the island from the widow of a guy by the name of Youngblood and let Mrs. Youngblood live out her days there. Which only amounted to about a year or so…."

Longfellow was silent as he stirred his dinner.

"I'm thinking…"

"Let me narrow this down even further," Will said, pulling his Corvette back into traffic. "I need to know everybody that lived on that island prior to Reverend Malachi Joppa getting it.

"All right—"

"And something else…"

"Yeah?"

"I need to know who died on the island."

"Oh my, this is beginning to sound rather gothic," Longfellow said with a chuckle.

"If you've got the information, I'll need it in the next forty minutes or so."

"Oh," the professor said, laughing, "that's good. I was afraid you might really be in a hurry."

"I'm sorry about the rush. I'll be able to explain it later. Call me on my cell phone. Do you have that number?"

"Sure. It's right here on my caller ID."

"Thanks, Dr. Longfellow. I really do appreciate this."

"By the way," Longfellow said, putting his spoon down on the stove and taking his phone into the cluttered living room, where he immediately started wading through stacks of papers, "exactly where are you going on this dismal night?"

"For a boat ride," Will said somberly, "I think I'm heading to a crime scene."

73

FOR ORVILLE PUTRIE, IT WAS NEVER a matter of physical courage. He was puny and outmatched when it came to violent crimes or physical confrontations. He always left that kind of thing up to Carlton Robideau or Blackjack Morgan. And between those two, Carlton was clearly the more powerful. But Morgan was more vicious—exceeding his scuba-diving assistant in the sheer audacity of his aggression.

That is why, even though nothing was said, Putrie knew exactly what had happened to Robideau. And he knew who it was who had taken care of him. If there was one thing that Blackjack Morgan wouldn't tolerate, it was people on his payroll, or in his life, who didn't keep their mouths shut. His old girlfriend had been like that—and then she disappeared. Now Carlton.

Because Reverend Jonathan Joppa had won ownership of Stony Island, Morgan's plans for a drug operation based there had evaporated.

And Carlton was gone. He was likely bobbing with the fishes somewhere at the end of a weighted line—clearly food for the sharks.

The way Putrie saw it, he was all alone in the task at hand. The clock was ticking. Morgan wanted to strike at the most likely location for Blackbeard's treasure before Joppa took full possession of the island. Morgan wanted answers from Putrie. But he had managed to dodge him for the last few days.

And now it was Orville Putrie's time to win—and for Blackjack Morgan to lose. Putrie didn't need brute animal muscle. He would triumph now because he had a one-fifty-three IQ. And he had used it to figure everything out.

But he did need a little muscle for this one last thing.

In the drizzle and windy dark of Stony Island Putrie found this final part repulsive...even for him.

He had rented a small skiff with an outboard. Put a hand truck in. And a flashlight. Together with a metal detector—and a shovel, of course.

He had had to hurry. Morgan was still looking for him.

Putrie had found the spot and positioned the light. At the start, he'd been a little queasy about it. But that was foolish, he'd thought. So he'd started digging.

The moist ground, in the drizzle of rain, was muddy. His first task was to dig through the tangle of weeds and vines that had overgrown the area. Years of neglect. Why hadn't anyone else figured it out before now?

Perhaps, Putrie thought to himself with a smile, *because there was never anyone quite as smart as me.*

He kept digging. The soft sandy ground was heavy. Down, deeper and deeper. Every so often he would stop, pull the metal detector into the hole, and turn it on. It would hum, but not give off the shrill sound he wanted to hear.

The tiny mosquitoes and night bugs had found him and were swarming around his head. He kept digging, occasionally waving off the flying invaders.

He was starting to feel exhausted. He hadn't counted on the sheer stamina needed to dig to this depth.

He stopped. He thought he heard something. He whirled around in the hole, nearly tripping over the shovel, and looked out into the gloom of the overgrowth. But there was nothing.

He continued to dig. Another six inches. He was having difficulty breathing.

He put the metal detector onto the bottom of the hole—and a high-pitched, warbling tone came out.

"Oh yeah, oh, oh yeah. This is it. Baby, oh baby, this is it," he said, giving an exhausted cackle.

Just a few more inches now. He tossed the metal detector out of the hole. With a second wind he furiously sped up his digging.

Then he stopped.

A sound. Was it a sound?

He strained to hear, but there was only the faint howl of the wind, the crash of the surf down at the shore, and the surging of his own pulse in his ears.

Then his shovel hit something. Suddenly he had a momentary sense of revulsion. But he had come too far to hesitate. He was nearly five feet down, now. It had taken him two hours of digging. And now he would know, at last. The sleeping were about to be disturbed.

But then he stopped short. Everything ceased as he froze in the hole.

And then, in slow motion, as if something else were moving him, he felt himself turning around. He looked up out of his hole.

Out of the hole he had dug at the foot of the ancient, blackened oak—the tree that had swallowed up the marker within its trunk, and that sheltered the Youngblood grave plot under its limbs.

He peered up into the darkness—and screamed. From his bowels.

Putrie threw his arms out in front of him like he had been electrocuted as he beheld the dark figure standing over him, now, at the edge of the grave.

74

Will HAD JUST ARRIVED AT THE MARINA when Longfellow called him back. He waved to Jonathan Joppa, who was already there throwing some rain slickers, a battery-operated lantern, and a flashlight into a skiff.

"Say again?" Will said.

"I said that I came across a survey that had been done by a researcher named Collier," Longfellow repeated. "He was doing a review of eighteenth-century cemeteries along the coast. What was then called Joppa's Island, now called Stony Island, was unusual because of the graves located there."

"Who is buried there?"

"Ebenezer Youngblood—"

"Right. The original owner."

"Oh. So you've done some of your own research on this."

"I went out to the island once before the trial. I saw the cemetery."

"Okay. Then you probably saw several markers. One for Ebenezer. One for his wife. Another for an infant child that died. And…let's see…also his mother and father. And that's it."

"Any way to tell which marker is which? They look like sandstone… and the writing is pretty much erased."

"You know, some of the better-preserved cemeteries have these little maps…but I don't think I've got anything like that. Frankly, I'm amazed I saved this survey."

"That's okay," Will motioned to Jonathan that he would be just one more minute.

"Dr. Longfellow, one more thing. What you told me pretty much verifies what my client said. But there's one bit of critical information missing."

"What's that?"

"I need to know if anyone died—or was buried—sometime in October or November of 1718," Will said, peering at Glen Watson's note.

"Give me a minute…Let me pull that Collier survey out again…"

Outside, Joppa was waving to Will and pointing to the sky. Will could hear the wind picking up, and off he saw, along the dark horizon, a muted flash of lightning within the black clouds.

"Okay, here it is," Longfellow exclaimed. "It's Ebenezer. He died on October 8, 1718."

"Tell me something—back then…how quickly did they bury after a death?"

"Real quick. Not to get too maudlin about it, but a corpse had to get taken care of immediately in the old days …"

"And so," Will was putting the pieces together in his mind, "if Ebenezer is buried the next day, the dirt would still appear disturbed for at least several days. If someone wanted to dig up that grave after Youngblood's burial and put some valuables, some treasure in there, then cover it back up, say during the night of the eleventh, by the following morning no one would have been able to tell that it had been disturbed."

Longfellow agreed, with one additional warning.

"I've heard the rumors about Teach's treasure being somewhere on Stony Island," Longfellow remarked.

"I'm heading out there right now by boat. We may need to consider getting a court order to exhume the grave of Ebenezer Youngblood."

"One additional historical factoid," Longfellow added. "Those pirates, being a superstitious bunch, besides stashing treasure in the grave of a recently buried person would also often kill someone and bury them at the spot. They figured the ghost of the departed would haunt the place and keep prying visitors away."

"Doctor," Will said, ending the phone call, "you always have such cheerful information."

Will locked up his car and sprinted over to Jonathan.

"That storm seems to be heading back at us," Joppa said. "We'd better do this quick."

Joppa fired up the outboard and, after turning on the fore and aft lights, headed them fully into the wind, which now was whitecapping the waves.

As the boat lurched over the choppy water, Will shouted to Jonathan, telling him everything. Halfway across the sound, the rain started pelting down, and both of them donned the slickers. As the skiff neared the island, Will turned the beam of the flashlight onto the dock. No boats were moored there. Then he scanned the beach, which was empty.

"So far so good."

After tying off the boat, they sprinted up the sandy path, with Jonathan's lantern lighting the way and the beam from Will's flashlight bouncing wildly up into the trees ahead of them.

Jonathan, running at a good pace, was ahead of Will.

He turned left to head toward the little cemetery.

"We're almost there," he cried to Will, increasing the distance between them.

Then suddenly, Will lost sight of Jonathan's lantern light. He was tempted to call out, but something warned him not to.

Instead, he focused his flashlight straight ahead. There was the gate to the cemetery. He flashed the beam left and right. Jonathan was not there.

He flashed the beam up a little, revealing, through the sheeting rain, the great oak tree with its immense spreading limbs.

Will had slowed to a cautious walk now, peering ahead. Searching for any sign of Jonathan. There was no sight of him.

And there was no sound except for the whining wind of the nor'easter, which, in its fickleness, had turned once more against the mainland and the islands—and the sound of rain pelting loudly on the hood of Will's slicker.

75

WILL HAD A STRONG FEELING OF FOREBODING. Undefined, but palpable.

But it wasn't until he walked through the gate to the cemetery and saw the hole that had been dug at the foot of the oak tree—at the grave of Ebenezer Youngblood—that he fully understood.

He knew he had made a terrible mistake coming to the island that night. But by then it was too late.

He stepped closer to the hole and gazed down into the grave as the rain poured down into it, the wind at his back now feeling more like a gale force.

Someone had dug down, and broken through to what occupied the grave, exposing it to the outside world.

There was a skull. As Will shined his flashlight down he could see the eye sockets. Below it, more scattered bones, surrounded by vines that had penetrated the coffin.

There was a crunch in the underbrush to his left.

He wheeled around, flashing his light.

A gun barrel was pointing at him, only a few feet from his face.

The bearer of the weapon stepped a little closer, through the sheeting rain, out of the shadows.

In a black raincoat and wide-brimmed hat, Blackjack Morgan was steadily pointing the revolver at Will's forehead as he stepped forward.

He tucked his cane under his arm and patted down Will's coat to make sure he was unarmed.

As he did, he was half-humming, half-singing some kind of off-key tune under his breath.

Will stood perfectly still, madly searching with his eyes for Jonathan Joppa. He was still missing.

Morgan was still muttering something in a sing-song voice, something vaguely familiar. Then Will recognized it. Only Blackjack Morgan would be sick enough to be singing that song, over an open grave, while threatening a man with a gun.

> *With a yo-heave-ho! and a fare-you-well*
> *And a sudden plunge in the sullen swell*
> *Ten fathoms deep on the road to hell*
> *Yo-ho-ho and a bottle of rum!*

"Putrie!" Morgan screamed over his shoulder, but with the gun still trained on Will. "Get out here!"

Orville Putrie stumbled from behind the oak tree. He was also holding a revolver and was wiping the water from his face.

"Get the good reverend up on his feet," Morgan yelled.

"He's still out cold," Putrie replied. "You really whacked him. You know, if you fractured his skull, he may be dead."

"What a wimp!" Morgan exclaimed, laughing. "I only bopped him once. Slap his face a couple times. He'll come to."

Several minutes later Putrie and Jonathan Joppa, who was still groggy and rubbing his head, appeared together.

Morgan was still laughing and singing his little song. Then he walked over to Putrie and whispered something in his ear.

"See—you can trust me, Putrie. I gave you one of my guns, didn't I? Does that look like somebody who doesn't trust you? I always take care of my people. And you'll get a cut of this. But not the share you would have. That's the penalty you get for trying to do this without me, see?"

Putrie eyed Morgan, but didn't answer.

Morgan turned to Will.

"I've got a special job for you, big-shot lawyer." Then he pointed to a blackened, ancient-looking metal box, about the size of a small suitcase, that was on the ground, and had been extracted from the Youngblood grave.

"Put this on the hand truck and wheel it down to your skiff. We'll take yours. Putrie and I both anchored ours over on the other side. Yours is closer."

But then he added, "If anything falls out of that box, I start shooting."

The four of them made their way down to the dock through the slant of wind and rain. By now, the waves were surging over the dock, and the lightning was flashing closer, up within the cloudy recesses of the sky.

Jonathan and Will went in first, barely able to stand up as the boat rocked and slammed against the pier. Then the box went in. And then

Putrie, finally followed by Morgan, who took his seat in the bow with his revolver pointed at Will, who was back at the outboard, given the task of motoring the boat through the swells.

As Morgan sat down his raincoat opened, and Will noticed two handguns stuffed under his belt.

Morgan shouted for Will to take them around the side of the island and pointed the way. As the small craft slammed down, then surged up again, the bow dropping and then lifting again wildly, Morgan sat unperturbed, smiling his Cheshire-cat grin.

Then Will caught sight of a large fishing boat anchored about a hundred yards off the shore. Morgan yelled for Will to steer over to the ladder on its side. As they closed in, Will noticed that Morgan had painted the bow with his name, BLACKJACK, and next to that, the image of two cards—one, the ace of spades, and the other, the king of clubs.

Morgan saw Will was looking around for some possible escape from the skiff.

"Don't waste your time thinking about jumping," Morgan yelled with a sneer. "I'll shoot you in a heartbeat. Face it, I always win. I never lose."

Then Morgan had Will tie off onto the side of the big rig that was bobbing wildly in the sea and told him to climb up.

With his handgun pointed at the lawyer, Morgan was following him up the ladder, just out of kicking range.

Then Jonathan Joppa made his way up. He was ordered to lift the heavy metal box up to Will.

When the box was safely on board and Joppa had climbed up, he and Will were told to go to the stern. Then, with his weapon still pointing at his two captives, Morgan barked out a command to Putrie, who was still in the skiff.

"Scuttle it!"

"How?" Putrie yelled up.

"Like this." Morgan fired a couple shots into the middle of the skiff, which quickly began taking on water. In an instant, it disappeared under the waves.

Putrie scampered up the ladder, still clutching his revolver, and moved toward the bow, pointing it toward Will and Jonathan at the other end.

Morgan entered the wheelhouse, walking like a drunken man across the rolling deck. He turned on the ignition and kicked in the big, dual inboard engines.

Will looked down on the deck. There were two ropes with heavy drag anchors attached.

But there was something else on the deck also. And when he saw it, he knew that their time to escape was quickly evaporating.

There were two nylon ropes coiled up. At the end, each had been knotted through the hole of a large cement construction block. Anything, or anyone, tied to those ropes and thrown over the side would head straight down to the bottom of the ocean.

Will looked at Putrie, who was nervously clutching his weapon with both hands. Then Will looked down at the black metal chest on the deck. Then he glanced over at Jonathan, who was sitting with his head down and resting his hands on his knees, trying to maintain his balance on the rolling ship. He was groaning in pain.

"How's your head?"

"Bad." He lowered his voice and said, "Tell me that you've got a plan to get us out of this."

"I'll figure something out," Will replied guardedly.

But he had already been considering their dilemma.

And had no idea how he was going to do that.

76

Blackjack Morgan was heading the big fishing boat out to the open sea, that was clear now.

The storm was increasing in ferocity. That was also indisputable. The boat was rising up with each wave, then pitching and slamming down. The terrible undulations of water were pouring torrents up to the bow, against the wheelhouse, and flooding the deck.

And the black metal box was slipping a little this way, then that way, with each roll of the boat.

Will was now facing the inevitable.

With their skiff scuttled, Will and Jonathan could easily be presumed drowned in the heavy seas. They would probably be shot first, then tied to the cement and sunk to the bottom. And the nylon cord would weather the currents and salt water well. They would dangle, lifeless, down in the frigid depths, until time or the creatures of the sea reduced them to mere polished bones, buried in the sands of the sea.

And when it was discovered that Ebenezer Youngblood's grave had been desecrated, speculation would run wild—but most of it would settle on the scenario that Jonathan, who had won the island, had dug the grave up with the help of his lawyer.

Whether they had found any treasure would be an unanswered question, but most folks would conclude that the pair had vanished in the storm while attempting to cross the sound in their skiff.

And Fiona would watch for Will. But he would not return to see her in her hospital bed. And then the next day, a police vehicle would drive up. Perhaps she would have little Andrew in her arms. And the officer would take off his hat and express his sympathies.

Will just hoped that Aunt Georgia would be visiting—in case Fiona collapsed after her world began to crumble.

He could play it all out, in an instant, in his mind.

And then, as the rolling ocean cascaded over the deck, causing Putrie to hang on for dear life, and as lightning flashed above them, something happened.

Anger, furnace-hot, was boiling over.

Deep inside Will, like a burning incandescence, there was a resolve. The kind that fires the soul, hot as lava, and lights up the mind.

Will would not let this happen. He *would* live to return to see his little family—his beautiful bride and his infant son. He would call upon the God of heaven to intervene.

Will silently petitioned the Ruler of the earth and all the seas, He who commands the waves and the great fish of the deep.

And now Will would act.

As the boat rocked wildly, he leaped forward, grabbing at the treasure chest.

But it was just beyond his grip, and as the boat rose up Will slipped backward to the stern, carried by gravity and the flood of seawater pouring down the deck.

Putrie screamed out a string of profanities and lunged at the box himself, waving the gun in Will's direction and yelling for him to get back.

Up in the wheelhouse Morgan jerked around and glanced back, then steadied the wheel to meet the next crashing wave that engulfed the front third of his boat. The boat rolled to the side and pitched wildly almost straight upward.

Then Morgan whipped around again, just in time to see the black metal chest slide toward Will, and Will make a lurching leap toward it. Now his hands made contact, and he gripped it with all of his strength.

Putrie was sliding across the deck on his back in the flood of water, still trying to point his pistol in Will's direction.

Jonathan jumped toward Putrie, landing on his legs.

Yanking him away from Will's position, Jonathan was now on his belly, skimming across the deck on a torrent of water. He had his arms wrapped around Putrie's legs.

But Putrie twisted so he could point his gun at Jonathan.

"Look out!" Will screamed.

But it was too late.

In the roaring wind and the crash of the sea, no one could hear when Putrie pulled the trigger.

But he had a stunned look on his face.

He pointed the revolver at Jonathan's face and pulled the trigger. And again. And again.

Nothing.

Then it became clear, not only to Jonathan and Will, but to Putrie as well, that he had been betrayed by Blackjack Morgan—with a weapon that was not loaded.

By now Morgan had seen enough. He saw Will leaning against the stern rail, holding onto the black metal chest. Morgan was going to put an end to it all.

He jumped out onto the deck, his bad leg pumping at high speed like an oil rig badly out of kilter.

As he grabbed at the railing for support, he began firing his revolver at Will, narrowly missing him.

Will held the chest on the railing, ready to drop it over into the raging sea.

"You move and this goes into the water!" he yelled out.

Morgan was sliding himself along the side, inching his way closer to Will, half-crawling, half-swimming in the flood smashing down onto the boat.

"No you won't," Morgan screamed. "You don't have the guts!"

"Watch me!" Will screamed back, and let the chest further down, out of Morgan's sight. "You kill me—I know where I'm going," he yelled, "but I drop this," he glanced down at the box he was barely holding onto, "I let this chest go…and your whole world goes with it."

But in the half-instant Morgan took to decide whether to shoot to negotiate, or lunge toward the dangling chest of treasure, he had forgotten one thing.

He had vacated the wheelhouse. And now, the wheel was whirling on its own, to the left and then to the right, with each wave that smashed against the bow.

The boat suddenly lurched to port side—at a perfect parallel to the oncoming waves.

The next wave crashed over the entire length of the boat, catching Will, the chest, and Morgan with its fury.

The box was carried up and out of Will's grasp, and it slammed down onto the deck. Will was thrown to the far side, and Morgan, who had lost his weapons in the deluge, swam, clawed, and rolled over to the chest.

He grabbed onto it at mid-deck, where the ropes from the drag anchors and the nylon ropes tied to the cement blocks had intertwined into a tangled net that stretched from wheelhouse to railing.

A second wave smashed down, tossing the boat sideways in what was almost a half-barrel roll.

Morgan still clutched the box to his chest, but his legs and torso had become wound up in the tangle of ropes. The only way that he could free himself was to release the treasure chest, reach down, and separate the ropes that bound him.

Blackjack Morgan would not—could not—do that.

He kicked like a wild beast at the lines that wound around his lower half and screamed a flood of curses.

But the ropes became more tangled.

Orville Putrie was scrambling to his feet in a full-blown panic. Staggering to the box that contained the inflatable life rafts, he pulled one out, clutched it to his chest, and pulled the string to inflate the limp rubber raft. He leaped over the side and disappeared into the darkness.

And then Will and Jonathan saw it. A wall of water the height of a small building, plowing over the half-submerged fishing boat, crashing down, and now flipping the boat in a complete roll—one that sent Will and Jonathan flying into the night, and slamming into the cold ocean, underneath the boat. Down into the frigid, watery turbulence.

There was darkness and swimming for the surface, wherever it was. Will pulled himself upward, breaststroking as hard as he could.

He finally broke the surface, gasping for air. He could see the boat upside-down, lying on the water with its hull facing the sky, but only for an instant.

A massive wave caught the boat and rolled it back up—revealing Blackjack Morgan.

Will doubted his eyes at first.

Morgan was still tangled in the web of ropes, held down fast against the deck. But his face was white—as white as limestone. And his eyes were empty and staring.

And he was clutching—still clutching—the treasure chest.

But the box opened, and a frenzy of sparkling diamonds and rubies and emeralds, and gold pieces and gold dust, began pouring out of it.

All of Edward Teach's loot captured from along the Spanish Main, around the capes, down to Cuba—gathered from his career of piracy and murder and mayhem—all of it, cascading out of the box in a twinkling, glittering shower, like a million fireflies. Out of the box still clasped to Blackjack Morgan's chest—within his cold, lifeless grip.

The boat did one more powerful, groaning roll, and then began to quickly go under.

Will found a flotation cushion and held it fast, trying to keep his head above water through the massive waves.

The last thing he saw was the insignia on the side of the boat as it upended and began sinking straight down to the bottom. He witnessed the ace of spades and the king of clubs slipping below the waves.

And then the boat was gone.

That was when Will also saw Jonathan, about two hundred feet away, holding onto a round life preserver.

But just behind Will, where at first he did not see it, there was a ship, churning its way slowly through the wild sea. It was large, notably seaworthy.

August Longfellow had alerted the Coast Guard to keep an eye out for Will and Jonathan as soon as he saw on TV that the nor'easter had blown back in with redoubled power.

The Coast Guard, in turn, radioed a rescue bulletin to all ships in the vicinity.

Only one ship was near the coordinates of the quadrant in which Stony Island lay.

It was Dr. Steve Rosetti's research vessel. And it had come to find, and to save, two souls, and to pluck them safely out of the bone-chilling waves of the sea.

77

Nine Months Later

THEY WERE PREPARED TO TAKE THEIR DEFEAT with honor. The group lined up, in order, to shake hands with their victors.

The team of boys had lost—but not badly. The Methodists had beaten them by a hair's-breadth—nine to eight. And the Methodists were looking strong that year, having beaten even the Baptists, the week before. So there was still hope for Jonathan Joppa's fledgling team. After all, the season had only just begun.

"This is so cool," the Methodists' pitcher said to Ryan, Joppa's starting right fielder, as the two headed over to the table of food that had been spread out for the post-game festivities. "Having a baseball field on an island like this, and with lights for night games, and a real dugout, and full bleachers, and an electronic scoreboard, and an electronic message board… just like the majors!"

Ryan was trying to play it cool, so he merely smiled back and slapped the opposing pitcher on the back. "Yeah, this island is really okay…"

Up in the bleachers, Fiona was cuddling little Andrew. She did secretly wonder if she would ever be able to convince her husband to steer clear of perilous lawsuits in the future. Admittedly, she had encouraged his involvement in this last one. Yet she still did occasionally yearn to join the ranks of other lawyer's wives—ones who could talk mundanely about whether their husbands won, or lost, this or that case…rather than wondering if they would ever make it home alive by the time it was all over.

But then again, she mused, that would not be like Will. Nor would it really be like her—to want to settle for that.

She smiled as she nuzzled Andrew's face and watched her husband stride over to Jonathan Joppa, who was shaking hands with the opposing coach.

She was glad they had come down that day from Monroeville, Virginia, to join in the celebration of the "rebirth" of Stony Island. Although the island could not support the hoped-for condominium development, it was now, they all agreed, being put to an even better use. It had already become affectionately known as "Baseball Island." Jonathan Joppa's termination as pastor of Safe Harbor Community Church had given him the opportunity for a work that now consumed his imagination and fired his soul—a spring and summer baseball camp for boys, especially those who were troubled, and who had drug problems or juvenile court backgrounds.

The boys had wanted to name their team the *Pirates*. But Jonathan had a strong aversion to that. So they settled on the *Islanders* instead.

During the morning they would receive baseball training. In the afternoon, on the days they didn't have games, they would get instruction from what coach Jonathan Joppa called "The Ultimate Handbook for the World Series of Life"—the Bible.

"Hey, Coach."

One of the Islanders pitchers was calling Jonathan's son, Bobby, who was picking up balls and bats. Bobby smiled back. Even though he was officially only an *assistant* coach, he like the sound of that title, *Coach*.

"Can you work with me tomorrow? I walked four guys today. I got to work on controlling my fastball."

"Yeah," Bobby said with a smile, "but just remember—you had ten strikeouts today. Not bad. Not bad at all…"

Will shook hands with Jonathan and told him his new ball team looked really good. And as the two walked over to the food tables, they reflected on the events that had occurred after the night they survived their final confrontation with Blackjack Morgan, and the sinking of his boat.

Dr. Rosetti had offered to contact a reputable commercial salvage operation out of Florida, and that outfit ended up paying a large fee to Jonathan for all of his rights to Blackbeard's treasure that had spilled into the waters of the Atlantic.

That was more than all right as far as Jonathan was concerned. He figured that Rosetti's calculation was right—that the salvage company would spend the next three years, if they were very lucky, recovering just a portion of the loot—and would then spend the next ten years in court, litigating against the competing claims of the State of North Carolina, the distant heirs and relatives of Ebenezer Youngblood, and the nation of

Spain—which was now claiming that most, if not all, of the booty had been stolen from its ships.

So, that money was a great financial boost to Jonathan—though it didn't begin to cover all the expenses of constructing a baseball stadium on the island. That money came from another source. A very unexpected one at that.

To some folks along the Outer Banks, it was an inexplicable mystery why Frances Willowby had become such a rabid baseball fan. But to Will, Fiona, and Jonathan, it was understandable. It wasn't really about baseball. It was really about her feelings for the island where, she would often remark, her late husband Randolph had spent so many happy days when he was a boy. And it also had to do with her perspective on life, as she was finally becoming able to pick up the pieces following his death. She was writing to Fiona regularly now. And she mentioned her new "spiritual pilgrimage," and how she longed for the day when she and Randolph would again meet—and then, without pain, or illness, or goodbyes.

The huge donation for the construction, and for a special ferry to take visitors back and forth to the island, was only the start. Frances also financed the equipment and the baseball uniforms, specially designed by her personal clothes designer. They were blue and yellow. Blue, for the ocean that could be seen sparkling in the background from the bleachers— and yellow, for the yellow trumpet pitcher plants that were her favorite. She now was often seen being chauffeured through the little coast towns in her Rolls Royce, sitting in the back and wearing an Islanders baseball cap.

Frances had also insisted on paying for special catering at the camp. The boys loved the food whipped up by Melvin Hooper—burgers, cheese fries, Italian sausage. That afternoon, Boggs Beckford, who by then was nearly fully recovered, was sharing a joke with Hooper, whose laugh could be heard all the way across the ball field.

Melvin had been able to reopen his café—at a new location. When Blackjack Morgan died, the *Joppa's Folly* tavern went into foreclosure. Hooper bought it from the bank for a song, spruced it up, and turned it into a family restaurant, renaming it *Melvin's Revenge*.

Not all of the mysteries were solved after that night when the *Blackjack* sunk to the bottom of the Atlantic. Carlton Robideau's remains were never discovered—but he was presumed murdered at the hand of Blackjack Morgan. And Morgan, everyone agreed, was gone forever.

But no sign of Orville Putrie, the twisted technological genius, or his inflatable raft was ever found.

And every lawyer who heard about the case would ask whether, in the trial at the Old Bailey, Isaac Joppa had been found innocent or guilty. There was simply no clear answer to that. But Will had his opinions, of course, and no one could convince him otherwise.

As Will and Fiona were motoring back to Virginia very late that night in Fiona's Saab, they joked quietly how Will's '57 Corvette was just too small for their growing family now. But Will said he could never part with it. They would simply have to use Fiona's car when the three of them traveled together.

Fiona turned and looked into the backseat. As the freeway lights intermittently washed the car with iridescent light, she caught little glimpses of Andrew, his fuzzy head bowed in peaceful slumber in the car seat, his tiny mouth half-open, a little trail of baby drool on his chin.

Then she turned back and snuggled closer to Will.

"I overheard Boggs Beckford telling someone today all about why you won the Joppa case,"

"Oh? What did he say?"

"That because Isaac Joppa was your missing witness...and when you finally had his testimony from the Old Bailey trial, that's what convinced the jury."

Will was silent.

"So...is that what you think, too?" Fiona asked.

Will was still quiet. Then he replied.

"Sure, Joppa's testimony from the London trial was important—but he really wasn't the key, I don't think."

"Oh?"

"No. Not really."

"Well...then why did your jury decide that Isaac was innocent?"

"There was another bit of missing evidence that—when we found it and presented it—well, I think that's what convinced the jury. Not just intellectually...but made them certain in their hearts..."

Fiona waited. After a few seconds, she nudged Will.

"Well? What was it?"

Will smiled, and admired the graceful beauty of his wife's face out of the corner of his eye.

"You know something, darling?" he said. "I would cross a thousand oceans if I had to—just to get back to your lovely face, and your loving arms. I'd be a fool not to…"

Fiona blushed and smiled, her dimples showing. But after a few more seconds she asked Will why he had not answered her question.

As they drove on, Will started to explain the meaning behind his comment to her.

And Fiona learned why her question actually had just been answered. And answered more truly, in fact, than either she or Will could possibly have imagined.

78

1719

London, England
After the verdict in the Isaac Joppa case

OLIVER NEWHOUSE, ESQUIRE, WAS STRIDING QUICKLY through the Sessions House Yard, which fronted the Old Bailey court building in London. Now that the jury had reached their verdict in Isaac Joppa's capital case, Newhouse was striding toward the street, his black barrister's robes flowing. That was where he expected to meet Abigail Merriwether.

They had to talk immediately, in light of the profound consequences attendant on the jury's decision.

But first Newhouse had to make his way past a few of His Majesty's officers, and the large number of witnesses milling about in the courtyard waiting for their cases to be called.

As the gatekeeper swung the gate open for Newhouse, the barrister turned and looked at the Old Bailey building, with the massive symbol of the English Crown that encircled the double doors at its front. It was a place he frequented often in his lawyer's work. Yet he never got used to the dread—the awful power that was exercised within its massive walls over matters of human freedom and captivity—over life and death.

As his gaze rested on the court building, he pondered the verdict in Isaac Joppa's case.

Then he turned, slipped through the gate, and searched the street for Abigail Merriwether's bright yellow dress.

Between the horses and carriages passing by at the mid-afternoon rush, he caught sight of her and dashed across the street.

She was waiting. She had been there in the great Justice Hall when the verdict was announced. And now she had to talk to her fiancé's lawyer.

Newhouse approached her, bowed quickly, and extended his hand in sympathy for all she had been through

The young woman had kept her composure up to now. But as Newhouse held out his hand, she began to sob. She fell into the barrister's arms, her shoulders heaving with emotion.

"Now, now, Miss Merriwether," he said, "let's remember what is important ..."

"Yes," she replied, pulling away slightly, and accepting a starched handkerchief to dab her eyes. "Thank you."

"After all, what is important to remember—"

But he stopped. Abigail's eyes were somewhere else.

Newhouse turned and smiled broadly.

Isaac Joppa, just released by the jailers, was running across the street with a burlap bag of his belongings in his hand.

The betrothed couple embraced wildly, passionately. They were entwined and inseparable.

Isaac Joppa had been found not guilty, and had been released. The two lovers held onto each other—weeping, and laughing, and expressing all those things that could, at last, be shared.

Oliver Newhouse glanced down discreetly at the cobblestones and smiled. As he then looked out over the busy street, out beyond Warwick Lane, and over the blackened buildings of the West End of London, he was convinced—and no one could convince him otherwise—that these two could now, finally, find happiness together.

Newhouse would keep track of the two, from time to time, after the trial. Shortly after the verdict they set sail for the West Indies. They were married aboard ship. They were to help in a church established there. After all, Abigail had gained experience in organizing women's groups to support the evangelistic ministry of Reverend Thomas Boston of Ettrick during the long year of Isaac's unexplained disappearance.

Isaac, with a rekindled faith of his own, one tested by the fires of adversity, had suggested to Abigail they should consider ministering on foreign soil.

They would occasionally write to Oliver Newhouse, sharing the news of their transplanted lives. How they later had a baby boy and named him Jacob. And years later they would write of the typhoid fever that was sweeping the islands. Fearing for Jacob's life—he was by then seventeen—they shipped him out from the West Indies to the American colonies. His ship would land in Charleston. They would never know that he would disavow Isaac as his father.

That was in 1736. Later that year, Isaac and Abigail sailed to England to try to raise support and medical assistance for their work. They met with only moderate success. But they did meet a popular minister by the name of George Whitefield, who was speaking publicly about his intentions of leading an evangelistic campaign in the American colonies.

"Where did you say you were raised?" Whitefield asked Isaac in their brief encounter.

Isaac studied the minister, with his prematurely white hair, tidy black coat, and white starched cleric's tie.

"A town called Bath, Reverend Whitefield," Isaac said. "It is just inland from the coast of North Carolina. Unfortunately, it is a place known mostly for piracy, rough living, and heathenism. Perhaps you would consider bringing the light of the gospel there. They certainly could benefit from it."

Whitefield smiled politely. But he suggested that he would, indeed, pray on the idea.

Isaac and Abigail also visited with Oliver Newhouse that same trip. It was a warm and delightful reunion over dinner. The lawyer could see that the two were still very much in love, though almost eighteen years had passed. The couple was to set sail for the West Indies the next day. That was the last that Newhouse would see of them.

The barrister would later learn that the two had been killed, shortly after their return, in an uprising among the locals.

But now, outside the Old Bailey court building, watching the two lovers embrace, Oliver Newhouse could only feel that, if any couple deserved the best, it was these two, as they had suffered from some of life's worst. Yet even then he knew it would probably not be so. That life would likely bring a yet greater share of rain on the heads of even such as these, who seemed to be so pure at heart.

Isaac and Abigail thanked him profusely for the victory in court, but the barrister modestly turned aside their praises.

"In truth," he said, "I could only wish that I could lay claim to your victory, Isaac. But I cannot."

"But why not, Mr. Newhouse?" Abigail asked.

"Because," Newhouse replied, "I truly feared for you, Master Joppa... that the jury would find you guilty and turn you over to the hangman's rope at Newgate. I feared your execution—that is, until the absent piece of evidence, the one missing part of the Crown's case against you was finally produced, albeit in our cause..."

"And what was that?" Isaac asked, a little bewildered.

Newhouse glanced over to Abigail.

"Why your bride-to-be, of course," he said. "I am convinced that the jury decided on your innocence when you, Miss Merriwether, testified for your betrothed."

"I am flattered," Abigail said with embarrassment, "but how could that possibly be true?"

"Because the jury no doubt decided," Newhouse said with assurance, "that only an utter fool would have willingly run away from such an unshakable love and unswerving devotion as you displayed, Miss Merriwether."

And then he smiled. "And you, sir," he said to Isaac, "are no such fool."

Isaac shook his lawyer's hand vigorously, and Abigail kissed him lightly on the cheek.

As the two walked off together, Oliver Newhouse, barrister, headed back to his offices down along Fleet Street, among the Inns of Court. And as he walked, he mused that such a sensational case as the Crown of England versus Isaac Joppa was never attended, much less reported, by the newspapers. But then again, the men from the papers were all down the hall, attending the celebrated trial of the chief assistant to the Lord Mayor of London, on trial for the theft of a silk handkerchief, allegedly later sold to cover gambling debts.

The barrister chuckled at that irony. As he entered his offices, retreating from the sounds of carriage wheels and horses' hooves clopping on the cobbled streets, one thought lingered.

That perhaps one day, years hence, some other lawyer might read of the Old Bailey case of Isaac Joppa, and what had taken place there, and would learn its lessons.

Love may not keep any record of wrongs, Oliver Newhouse mused, thinking back to Abigail Merriwether's testimony. *Yet perhaps it will keep the record, and perchance some day it will tell the tale, of those things done right.*

The barrister smiled a little at that. For he had no doubt whatsoever, that if the story were ever to be told some day, it would have to be a lawyer who would tell it.

About the Author

Craig Parshall is a highly successful lawyer from the Washington, DC, area who specializes in cases involving civil liberties and religious freedom. He is also the frequent spokesperson for conservative values in mainstream and Christian media. *Missing Witness* follows three other novels in the Chambers of Justice Series—the powerful *Resurrection File*, the harrowing *Custody of the State*, and the gripping *The Accused*.

A Note from the Author

Though this novel is part of the continuing saga of lawyer Will Chambers, it is a wholly different one in style and story structure. In a sense, it is current legal thriller wrapped inside an eighteenth-century crime mystery. And because it required a breadth of research—everything from the life and times of pirates like Edward "Blackbeard" Teach, who haunted the 1700s, to modern techniques of ocean archaeology—I depended on the help of many others.

Many thanks go to Marilyn Clifton, who helped with research on such arcane topics as North Carolina probate law and federal maritime regulations, and who typed up my final edits. Also, her son Chris was a great help by retrieving for me the "pirate's song" from *Treasure Island*. My secretary, Sharon Donehey, did a masterful job on the manuscript work, and editor Paul Gossard was insightful, as always.

Because a subplot in this story involves a near-fatal accident in one car and some engine difficulties in another, I greatly appreciated my son Joseph taking time from his university studies to give me the benefit of his certified auto mechanic's knowledge. My good friend Jim Gwinn, president of CRISTA Ministries—and a true Corvette aficionado—helped to ensure accuracy about the "care and feeding" of Will Chamber's classic 1957 Corvette—a vehicle that may have proved to be the unsung hero of this story. And, as always, Jim's personal encouragement is truly appreciated.

Much of what is contained in this fictionalized story is based, loosely, on historical fact. I relied on the painstaking research of many authors of pirate history along the North Carolina coast—too many to mention here. But a few remarks need to be made here about the line between fact and fancy.

The life of Blackbeard, the details in this novel about his chilling crimes, and the battle off Ocracoke Island where he met his just end, are true events. But visitors to the Outer Banks will search in vain for Stony Island...it is entirely a figment of the author's imagination. Many of the sailing ships mentioned in this novel—*Adventure, Good Intent,* and *Queen Anne's Revenge*—really did cruise the oceans...but others, like *Bold Venture,* the vessel so central to Will's pursuit of justice in this story, did not. I tried to make the general history of the Tuscarora Indians as accurate as possible—but the person of Indian chief King Jim Blount and his family is pure fiction.

The references to the transcript of the trial of Captain William Kidd are based, with only minor adaptations, on those found in a book titled *The Tryal of Capt. William Kidd (for murther & piracy)*, Don C. Seitz, editor—first printed in 1936 by Rufus Rockwell Wilson, Inc., New York, New York, and later reprinted in 2001 by Dover Publications, Inc., of Mineola, New York, in an unabridged version.

And, though present-day character Blackjack Morgan is the product of creative imagination, he reflects, I believe, the reality that the so-called "golden age of piracy" is really not dead…rather, the untamed sea still harbors, to this day, terrorists and criminals of all kinds.

Lastly, my wife, Janet, prominently inspired much of what is between the lines of this book—both in the Will–Fiona relationship and its counterpart, the eighteenth-century tale of Isaac Joppa and his beloved Abigail Merriwether. What lies behind the words here may be the most important story of all.

FORGIVING SOLOMON LONG
by Chris Well

Kansas City—home of the *Star*, the Chiefs, and the blues. Visit. Have the time of your life. Just don't lose it if you meet one of these players at the wrong end of his piece...

Crime boss Frank "Fat Cat" Catalano— a man with a vision. With dreams of building a legacy, Fat Cat has his fingers into nearly every business sector, legal or otherwise. But a coalition of local store owners and clergy has gotten it into their heads to band together and try to break Catalano's stranglehold.

Detective Tom Griggs—a man with a mission. He and his small task force have been shadowing Fat Cat's operations, looking for cracks in the wall. Griggs will give it all he has until the whole house comes down. No matter the cost. Even if that cost is neglecting—and losing—his own wife.

Hit man Solomon "Solo" Long—a man with a job. Fat Cat's about to make important changes in the family business...and doesn't need troublemakers rocking the boat. Solo is a "cleaner" flown in from the coast to make sure the locals get the message.

It all adds up to a thriller that crackles with wit and unexpected heart—that smokes you with machine-gun action and hits you in the gut with a powerful message of forgiveness.

THE CHAMBERS OF JUSTICE SERIES
by Craig Parshall

The Resurrection File

When Reverend Angus MacCameron asks attorney Will Chambers to defend him against accusations that could discredit the Gospels, Will's unbelieving heart says "run." But conspiracy and intrigue—and the presence of MacCameron's lovely and successful daughter, Fiona—draw him deep into the case...toward a destination he could never have imagined.

Custody of the State

Attorney Will Chambers reluctantly agrees to defend a young mother from Georgia and her farmer husband, suspected of committing the unthinkable against their own child. Encountering small-town secrets, big-time corruption, and a government system that's destroying the little family, Chambers himself is thrown into the custody of the state.

The Accused

Enjoying a Cancún honeymoon with his wife, Fiona, attorney Will Chambers is ambushed by two unexpected events: a terrorist kidnapping of a U.S. official...and the news that a link has been found to the previously unidentified murderer of Will's first wife. The kidnapping pulls him into the case of Marine colonel Caleb Marlowe. When treachery drags both Will and his client toward vengeance, they must ask—*Is forgiveness real?*

Missing Witness

A relaxing North Carolina vacation for attorney Will Chambers? Not likely. When Will investigates a local inheritance case, the long arm of the law reaches out of the distant past to cast a shadow over his client's life...and the life of his own family. As the attorney's legal battle uncovers corruption, piracy, the deadly grip of greed, and the haunting sins of a man's past, the true question must be faced—*Can a person ever really run away from God?*

The Last Judgment

A mysterious religious cult plans to spark an "Armageddon" in the Middle East. Suddenly, a huge explosion blasts the top of the Jerusalem Temple Mount into rubble, with hundreds of Muslim casualities. And attorney Will Chambers' client, Gilead Amahn, a convert to Christianity from Islam, becomes the prime suspect. In his harrowing pursuit of the truth, Will must face the greatest threat yet to his marriage, his family, and his faith, while cataclysmic events plunge the world closer to the Last Judgment.

THE MILLION DOLLAR MYSTERIES
Mindy Starns Clark

Attorney Callie Webber investigates nonprofit organizations for the J.O.S.H.U.A. Foundation, giving the best of them grants ranging up to a million dollars. In each book, Callie comes across a mystery she must solve using her skills as a former private investigator. A young widow, Callie finds strength in her faith in God and joy in her relationship with her employer, Tom.

A Penny for Your Thoughts

Just like that, Callie finds herself looking into the sudden death of an old family friend of her employer. But it seems the family has some secrets they would rather not have uncovered. Almost immediately Callie realizes she has put herself in serious danger. Her only hope is that God will use her investigative skills to discover the identity of the killer before she becomes the next victim.

Don't Take Any Wooden Nickels

Just like that, Callie finds herself helping a young woman coming out of drug rehab and into the workforce who's suddenly charged with murder. What appears to be routine, though, explodes into international intrigue and deadly deception. A series of heart-pounding evens lands her disastrously in the hands of the killer, where Callie finds she has less than a moment for a whispered prayer. Will help arrive in time to save her?